Rafael Sabatini, creator o: ,
was born in Italy in 187 d
Switzerland. He eventually settled in England in 1892, by which
time he was fluent in a total of five languages. He chose to write in
English, claiming that 'all the best stories are written in English'.

His writing career was launched in the 1890s with a collection of
short stories, and it was not until 1902 that his first novel was
published. His fame, however, came with *Scaramouche*, the much-
loved story of the French Revolution, which became an international
bestseller. *Captain Blood* followed soon after, which resulted in a
renewed enthusiasm for his earlier work.

For many years a prolific writer, he was forced to abandon writing
in the 1940s through illness and he eventually died in 1950.

Sabatini is best-remembered for his heroic characters and high-
spirited novels, many of which have been adapted into classic films,
including *Scaramouche, Captain Blood* and *The Sea Hawk* starring
Errol Flynn.

TITLES BY THE SAME AUTHOR
ALL PUBLISHED BY HOUSE OF STRATUS

The Gamester

Rafael Sabatini

HOUSE OF
STRATUS

This edition published in 2001 by House of Stratus, an imprint of
Stratus Books Ltd., 21 Beeching Park, Kelly Bray,
Cornwall, PL17 8QS, UK.

www.houseofstratus.com

Typeset, printed and bound by House of Stratus.

A catalogue record for this book is available from the British Library
and the Library of Congress.

ISBN 07551-153-5X

LA SEMAINE DE LAW

Lundi je pris des actions,
Mardi je gagnai des millions,
Mercredi je pris équipage,
Jeudi j'arrangeai mon ménage,
Vendredi je fus au bal,
Samedi a l'hôspital.

Contents

Contents (contd)

Chapter 1

DEATH OF A KING

Mr Law applied his uncanny gifts of calculation to a stocktaking of the events.

The great king by whose orders he had once been turned out of France lay dead. In this there was no matter for wonder; for His Majesty was old, and kings, be they never so great, are mortal. Yet natural though the fact might be, not merely France but the whole civilized world held its breath in contemplating it. This king, at whose frown, according to Madame de Sévigné, the very earth trembled, had reigned so long, so imposingly and so absolutely that he had assumed in men's minds a quality of immortality.

Nor was it only his body that had perished. His glory had perished with it. The veneration in which he had been held was transmuted abruptly into execration and contempt. His subjects, no longer awed by the majesty of his existence, remembered only the hardships and sacrifices his splendours had imposed upon them, considered only the hardships and sacrifices they inherited from his rule in a nation that his magnificence left bankrupt and exhausted.

His very obsequies had been marked by an indecency of jubilation. His body's last journey to the vaults of St Denis had been taken through a countryside where booths and tents had been set up for the junketings and rigadoons in which it was accounted fitting to celebrate his passing. He was scarcely cold before his will, which in life none had dared to thwart, was set at nought, and his testament, his last dispositions for the governing of France during the minority of the great-grandchild who was to succeed him, was torn up before the assembled Parliament.

His nephew, Philippe of Orléans, assumed alone the office of Regent, which by dead Majesty's bequest should have been shared with the Duke of Maine, one of the dead Majesty's many bastards.

Later, when Philippe of Orléans came to view at closer quarters the burden ambition had urged him to assume, it is possible that he may have wondered had he not been guilty of a rashness. In the moment of its assumption, however, he knew only satisfaction in his triumph.

This death of Louis XIV was to govern, as death will, the course of many lives besides his nephew's; but none perhaps more signally than that of John Law, the Laird of Lauriston, with which it had no apparent connection. The news of that death and of the circumstances attending it reached Mr Law in Turin, where in the autumn of 1715 he was paying court to Victor Amadeus of Savoy. His passport to the Savoyard's favour had been a letter from His Majesty's brother-in-law, Philippe of Orléans. The warmth of that letter's commendation by so exalted a personage provided mystification for King Victor Amadeus when contrasted with what was known of Mr Law. For, be it said at once, the Laird of Lauriston's was a disturbing history. A fugitive from England, where he had sensationally broken prison a dozen or more years ago, after having been sentenced to death for a duel in which he had killed his man, he had since been a wanderer in Europe, with no means of livelihood other than gaming, by which it was notorious that he had amassed a fortune. Report computed this at four or five million livres, and whilst the figure was certainly exaggerated, it was no more to be doubted that he was rich than that he could add to his wealth whenever he chose to approach the tables.

In France it had been his mysterious skill with cards and dice, and the vast sums he had won by holding a bank at faro at the house of that famous courtesan, La Duclos, which had led to his being requested by Monsieur d'Argenson, the King's Lieutenant-General of Police, to leave the country. There was no suggestion that he loaded his dice or marked his cards. It was universally recognized that his play was scrupulously correct, and that his good fortune was to be attributed solely to a mathematical genius and an incredible ability and speed in estimating odds. He played by a martingale of his own invention, a system for which he claimed ultimate infallibility when practised by himself, however, it might fail at the hands of less gifted calculators, and to facilitate his reckoning he employed gold counters of the value of eighty livres, especially minted for him.

Upon his expulsion from France, and perhaps because of it, had followed a similar lack of appreciation of his activities in the states of Venice, Florence and Genoa; and so notorious was he become that it is unlikely that without the credentials supplied him by the Duke of Orléans he would have been allowed to linger in the dominions of King Victor Amadeus as a more or less honoured guest. Something may certainly have been due to the singular charm of a personality which commanded the favour of His Savoyard Majesty as it had earlier commanded that of his brother-in-law.

Very tall and spare and of an excellent shape, he moved with the easy grace of a man proficient in every bodily exercise. His countenance was of a patrician cast, which, after all, did not belie his origin, for if his father – from whom no doubt he inherited his mathematical skill – was no better than an Edinburgh goldsmith and banker, his mother, whom his looks favoured, issued from the noble house of Argyle. An early attack of the smallpox had, as sometimes happens, left his face of a pallor that added curiously to its attractiveness and deepened the air of mystery that seemed to cloak him. *Il était trop beau*, said of him a French contemporary, and so the women seemed to have found him, largely to his undoing in his early years, when, after his father's death, he took his share of the family fortune to London, and dissipated it there in three or four years of reckless living.

3

Brought face to face with destitution, he sought salvation in that mathematical genius of which quite early in his father's counting-house he had given startling proof. He was to apply it further and ever more masterfully in a measure as he was matured by study, experience and observation in the course of his wanderings through Europe. As a result he gave the world a treatise on finance, *Money and Trade Considered*, which had gone far to win him the regard of that gifted dilettante, the Duke of Orléans, and at present procured him at least the tolerance of King Victor Amadeus.

He had sought more than this at the hands of His Majesty, and seeking it he had been careful to abstain in Turin from cards and dice. He flew at higher game than either could provide. The finances of Savoy were in a sad disorder. The incessant wars of Louis XIV had ruined not only France but all her neighbours. In the repairing of those fortunes Mr Law perceived a game on a more engrossing and exhilarating scale than any that the tables could provide. Unfortunately, he failed to persuade His Majesty to let him play it. After some timid flirting with Mr Law's ideas, King Victor Amadeus had declared himself with finality.

"My friend, I fully agree with Monseigneur d'Orléans. Your system appears to be everything that is shrewd and excellent. But appearances, we know, may prove deceptive. It is my duty to mistrust my judgment in a matter so profound and complex. If the system should, after all, be wrong, then ruin must follow, and I am not powerful enough to ruin myself.

"I trust that you will see in my decision no reason to terminate your sojourn in Turin. Though I shall understand if, accounting now that you waste your time here, you should wish to take your leave of us."

It was whilst he was still asking himself whether this was no more than a courteous dismissal that word came to him of those events in France. It was brought by William Law, who arrived in Turin in response to a summons from his elder brother whilst still in the optimistic persuasion that he would be given the direction of the finances of Savoy. Fortuitously William Law was accompanied by a

Spanish financier named Pablo Alvarez, a man with whom the Laird of Lauriston had been intimate during his days in Amsterdam, when he was sounding the mysteries of Dutch banking.

Don Pablo had been in Genoa, soliciting for himself the representation of the Bank of St George in England, whither he was going. In this he had failed, as he might have known he would, for the Genoese were of all people the most mistrustful. He professed himself compensated, however, by meeting there his old friend William Law, who had come by sea, on his way to Turin, and he had seized the chance to accompany him so as to offer his duty and service to the Laird of Lauriston.

"After all," as he explained, "I have travelled scarcely a league out of my way; for with or without the sponsorship of the Bank of St George, I am still for England, and Turin lies on my road. I journey overland. Tediously slow, perhaps; but then my entrails revolt at the very smell of a ship."

A short, paunchy, hairy man, his yellow face of a Semitic cast, his heavy jowl blue from the razor, the financier expressed himself in a rapidly flowing French that was slurred and sibilant and eked out by a profusion of Spanish gesture that at moments made him grotesque. If he could serve Don Juan in England, let Don Juan give him his commands. England, through the activities of the South Sea Company, offered great opportunities to men who knew their way through the labyrinth of finance. Apart from that, England was rendered by its wealth a banker's paradise; it was not, Don Pablo thanked God, a country like France, reduced to beggary by the warring follies of a king who was now in hell.

They sat in a salon of splendours on the mezzanine of the Palace of Carignano. Eastern rugs glowed on the elaborate wood mosaics of the polished floor; arresting portraits adorned the walls, an Infanta of Spain, a prince of the House of Savoy, the children of King Charles I of England, all three by Van Dyck, besides some choice pieces by lesser masters. Heavy gilded furniture, precious porcelains and sparkling lustres completed a background of the magnificence that Mr Law accounted proper to his own subdued elegance.

The talk swung back the Spaniard's strictures to French affairs, and now it was that Mr Law learnt in detail how black was France's inheritance from the glorious sun-king whose effulgence had dazzled the world.

"Faith," he said when all was told him, "the only thing that surprises me is that you should still think of England when France must offer so rich a field to a man of your gifts." His French was as harsh as Don Pablo's was liquid, but it was no less fluent.

"France!" Don Pablo was explosively scornful. "You have not been listening to me. Can penury offer a field to a financier? And then its government! In order to tear up the testament of King Louis and secure the regency for himself exclusively, the Duke of Orléans has been driven to make strange concessions. So as to purchase the suffrages of the dukes and peers, he has restored to them privileges which it was the work of Richelieu and Louis XIV to suppress. Instead of governing by secretaries of state, he has set up a council of regency for each department; unwieldy bodies to which he has appointed those whose support he required so as to exclude the Duke of Maine from the share in the regency ordained by the late king. Having accomplished this, Monsieur d'Orléans lets the rest go to the devil. So long as he is left in peace to his orgies, his supper-parties and his women, whoever chooses may govern France.

"You conceive the conflicts that follow and the ensuing confusion in a country already crippled by the lack of money. Yet you suggest that fortune is to be sought there! My friend, you want to laugh."

The opening of one of the wings of the tall double doors constrained Mr Law to postpone his answer.

A woman in blue and gold of a richness almost excessive displayed herself upon the threshold. Moderately tall, her slim firm waist surged from the ballooning hoop to the swell of a breast in the display of whose white curves there was no reticence. Her dark, chestnut hair was partly confined by a lace cap, the last adaptation of the expiring fontange. Beneath this the face, very fair of skin, conveyed an impression of gentle purity, corrected only for the discerning by cheek-bones that were a shade too high and lips that were a shade too full.

A moment she remained at gaze; then, smiling without effusiveness, smiling perhaps because she knew that smiling became her, she drifted forward on invisible feet. In English, her voice rich and musical, she gave her brother-in-law welcome without excessive cordiality. "Laguyon has only just told me that you had arrived, Will."

"My dear Catherine!" William Law almost as tall as his brother and no less shapely, advanced to meet her, took her hands and bent to kiss them.

"I wish that I could be more glad to see you. But I fear that we have only disappointment for you. John will have told you that his swans are, as usual, less than geese. Less even than farm-yard ducks." Over her brother-in-law's shoulder her eyes seemed to discover at last the Spaniard, and her brows were arched. "But is it possible? Don Pablo Alvarez, is it not?"

Don Pablo bowed himself as nearly double as his paunch permitted. "Honoured in your recollection, madame. My humble homages." His English was even more execrable than his French.

"I am to suppose," she said as she surrendered a hand to his lips, "that John's folly is to answer for your presence, too."

"John's folly! Ho, ho, madame, do you, then, discover folly in him? Might it please God I be as foolish!"

This she construed as contradiction, and did not care for it.

"Give thanks that you are not. But I keep you standing." She found herself a chair, draped her hooped skirts about her, and talked petulantly on. "Has John told you that we are packing? It's an occupation at which I seem to spend my wretched life. We are to go on our travels again. You shall tell me, Don Pablo, that I am married to the Wandering Jew."

"Never shall I tell you that. Never! The Wandering Jew he travelled for punishment, and that could not be for any man who has your ladyship for travelling companion."

Her shrug implied repudiation of the laboured compliment. "It will need more than gallantry to teach me resignation. I was not reared to be dragged with my children across the world. Nor is it as if we were willing travellers. We go because we are shown the door. My pride will not accommodate itself – what woman's would? – to being expelled from one country after another. You will agree that it is too much to ask of a poor lady."

To his discomfort Don Pablo suspected too much earnest in what he had supposed a jest. He glanced uneasily at Mr Law, to behold him standing in the cold indifference of one who does not choose to hear. It was left for William, conciliatorily, to furnish a reply.

"You'll not be forgetting, dear Catherine, that John has been hardly used by fate. Exile has been forced upon him; and the life of an exile is seldom other than restless."

"Pray, Will," said Mr Law's level voice, "do not be at the trouble of making yourself my apologist. Catherine, unfortunately, has abundant grounds for complaint, as she has long since persuaded herself and me. I am not to deny it."

"You could not," said madam, flushing.

"Meanwhile," Mr Law continued evenly, "we are to take thought for our guests."

"I do not need to be told. Will's room has been waiting for him. As for Don Pablo…"

The Spaniard broke in. "Do not give me a thought, dear madame. Alas, my plans shall not permit that I spend more than this night in Turin, and my baggage is at the Albergo Biancamano. I sleep there. For one night, you will see, it would be unpardonable to discompose you."

She remained ungraciously silent, wherefore, "It shall be as you please," said her husband. "But at least you'll dine with us."

"That, at least," she was quick to confirm, perhaps because of the opening it afforded for lamentation. "We have seen little enough company during these dreary months in Turin."

Don Pablo never heeded the plaint. "I ask myself who would refuse the invitation. I am too well acquaint' with the delights of your table."

She rose. "I will give orders. By your leave, Don Pablo, and yours, Will."

Mr Law, with formal courtesy, held the door for her, and she passed out, leaving them to resume the discussion her coming had interrupted. But it was not until later, after they had supped, that this gave indication of the fruit it was to bear.

As Don Pablo expected, he found Mr Law's table in harmony with the subdued magnificence of his environment. His cook was a Bolognese, and there are no greater masters of the gastronomic art, as the Spaniard, whose appetite was gluttonous, protested in order to excuse his excesses. They drank Falernian with the crayfish, a well-sunned red Tuscan with the stuffed ortolans, and with the sweets there was champagne.

Served in mellow candlelight by footmen who moved noiselessly under the direction of Laguyon, the incomparable steward, the course of the repast assumed a character almost ritualistic.

When at last the cloth was raised and madam had retired, Don Pablo sat back with buttons eased, to voice his wonder.

"Enviable man. Most enviable of men, there is much you might have taught Lucullus. A so noble board, and a so noble and beautiful lady to grace it!" Enthusiasm drove him into Spanish. "*Dios mio!* What are you but the pampered child of Madame Fortune?"

"Sometimes her fool," said Mr Law, and to turn the conversation spoke once more of France, and thus renewed the Spaniard's scorn.

"I've said what I think of that bankrupt country, where for every one who dies of indigestion nine die of starvation. To speak of seeking fortune there is a poor jest. Does one extract something from nothing?"

"From the illusion of nothing I have known much to be extracted by a little skill."

"Oh, agreed, where there are illusions. But here are none. Here is reality; naked reality; naked is, indeed, the word. You smile. You don't believe. In that case, my friend, why do you not explore that hunting-ground for yourself?"

"You forget that France is closed to me."

"It may have been. But you'll hardly find it closed now, ruled by a profligate who has all the vices and wears them proudly. Do you suppose he will care that you were turned out by the police when you offered your services to King Louis?"

"No, no. I was turned out because I won too much at faro. But before that the king had rejected my system when the Duke of Orléans brought it to his notice. The bigoted lecher, who was in a perpetual state of deadly sin, declined my services because I am not a Catholic."

"Mother of God! If that was all, could you not have gone to Mass, like Henri Quatre. Or are you by chance religious?"

"Not even superstitious."

"Do not let us exaggerate. There was never yet a gamester without superstition. You all make votive offerings to Madame Fortune upon whom you all depend."

"Make an exception in my favour. I prefer to depend upon my methods. And these depend upon a study of the laws of chance."

"So I've heard you boast. A contradiction in terms. Chance knows no laws. Chance is the negation of law. That is elementary."

"In logic, perhaps. But not in fact."

"*Vamos, hombre*! If a thing is demonstrable in logic, must it not occur in fact?"

"Have you always found it so? Have you never speculated upon probabilities?"

"But probability is estimated by intelligent inference from given facts."

"So is the turn of a card or the fall of the dice. If it were not, you would not have dined so well tonight. For a dozen years and more I have lived, and lived *en prince*, by cards and dice. Fortune may be blind, but it is possible to take her by the hand and guide her. The art of winning lies in the study of why men lose. Indeed," he ended on a more pensive note, "that may be the whole art of life. I do not know." His long countenance darkened. He took up a decanter. "Let me fill your glass, Don Pablo. This Tokay is from the cellars of an emperor."

"And worthy of them, or I'm no judge." The Spaniard raised the full glass in a hairy paw, and fondly observed the wine glowing like a topaz in the candlelight. "However fortune comes to you, Don Juan, I pledge you its continuance."

Mr Law raised his glass in his turn. "May you find in England all that you seek there."

William Law, watching him, observed the shadow that had crossed his face, and added it to other trifles he had noticed. But it was not until Don Pablo departed, and the brothers were alone together, that he came to utter his concern.

Mr Law had reverted to the subject of France and to what that day he had learnt of her affairs. "The news may be timely. Philippe of Orléans' old interest in my system may not be dead. Nor is Orléans merely the debauched prince of Don Pablo's account. A voluptuary certainly, yet a man of unusual vision and of many talents. I certainly might find my profit in the French distress. With no other aim in view it is worth a thought. It may even permit me to make amends to you for having brought you to Turin on a fool's errand."

"That need give you no concern. I was weary of Amsterdam, and I am quite ready to take a chance with you in Paris."

"It will perhaps be best that I first test the ground there alone. There is much to consider. Catherine, for instance. She will make me scenes, of course. But that she will do in any event. So as well may she rage at my going there as elsewhere. All's one to her so that she may glory in martyrdom and flaunt her agonies to reproach me." He laughed without mirth.

His brother's light, shrewd eyes were grave. "Then it is...it is always the same?"

"How else should it be? Human beings do not change save by deterioration."

William Law came slowly to stand beside his seated brother. He had the same dark complexion as the Laird of Lauriston, and the same long if less aquiline cast of countenance. Of the two you would judge him the gentler and kindlier, and therefore the less resolute.

He spoke on impulse, a hand affectionately on his brother's shoulder. "I am sorry, John. I'd like fine to see you happy."

"Happy? What is happiness? I have often wondered. Once, indeed, I thought to grasp it; but it went like water through my hands."

"Which means that you still rate the shadow above the substance."

Frowning, Mr Law looked up into his brother's troubled eyes. "Substance?" he asked.

"Catherine," Will answered, to add almost impatiently: "Is not she the true substance, the woman who came to comfort you in your hour of bitterest need, when you were a fugitive, exiled, outcast and discredited, the woman who threw away all for love of you, just as you had thrown away all out of infatuation for a worthless shadow? And do you still suffer that shadow to stand between you, to darken your life with Catherine? Do you…"

Peremptorily, Mr Law raised a checking hand – a long, beautiful hand in its froth of lace. His tone, however, was dispassionate. "No, no, no, Will. All that is over and done with. I put it behind me when Margaret Ogilvy took up the succession to the Countess of Orkney and became King William's mistress; when I understood how vainly I had killed Beau Wilson and thrust my neck into a noose. How else could it have been?" He laughed with reflective bitterness. "Could I have married Catherine else?"

"That is where you deceive yourself. Bear with me, John, if I speak my mind even to your hurt. It makes me angry to see you wasting yourself on needless suffering."

"Suffering? For my sins you would say." Mr Law was ironical.

"No less. You took Catherine to wife in the bitter hour of your disillusion, took her and the love she brought you as an antidote to the poison in your soul…"

"I did not know her then."

THE GAMESTER

"I am thinking that you did not know yourself. You'd be grateful for the devotion she brought you, touched by it, and maybe realizing how she had cast all away in coming to you, you'd be accounting it no less than a duty to marry her. But it was not gratitude Catherine craved of you."

Mr Law spoke on a sigh, quietly, almost humbly. "Perhaps it was all I had to give. And God knows I gave it unstintingly until…"

"Until?"

"Until Catherine herself rejected it, revealed herself exacting, shrewish, cross-grained, intractable – as you've seen for yourself. She became – or maybe she was born – mistrustful and suspicious. These are qualities that grow by what they feed on. Resentful, all things to her are fuel for grievances…"

"Has she no grounds for resentment?" Will interjected. "Do you conceive that she has no intuitions, no sense of the ghost that walks beside you, the memory of the woman who was Beau Wilson's wife until you made her a widow and King William made her Countess of Harpington in her own right?"

Mr Law looked up, still without sign of impatience. His smile was at once sad and quizzical. "You had ever a weakness for Catherine, Will. In you she possesses a stout advocate."

"I'm thinking she needs one, as you do, as you both do, if this state of unhappiness is not to be perpetuated. I tell you, John, that woman loves you. She'll be labouring under a sense of defeat and frustration that sours her nature, whilst you feed it by resenting in your turn a state of things you have created. You'll say it is no affair of mine…"

"I haven't said so."

"You should know I am speaking from the love I bear you, John. I can't remain indifferent when you are suffering."

"I understand. That is why I let you talk. It may well be, as you say, that I have no more than I have earned, and that I have no right to repine. I do not know. But suffering is too big a word. It is only the weak who linger in unhappiness. Life holds many interests for a man apart from love."

13

"But not for a woman. Have you ever thought of that?"

It was a moment before Mr Law answered. Then, without raising his voice, but on a note that made of the question a command, "Shall we drop the subject, Will?" he said. "There are other matters to engage us. This question of France which you interrupted to make philosophy on marital relations. Give me your views on that instead. It will be more profitable."

Thus enjoined, conquering reluctance, William Law abandoned his forlorn hope of arguing harmony into his brother's household. Coming, however, to the matter of his brother's financial schemes, he displayed himself less competent to give advice. If John were satisfied that he could command the Regent's ear to the extent of persuading His Highness to give him in France the scope he sought, William was as ready and willing as ever to abandon every other interest in order to place himself at his brother's disposal.

They talked late into the night, or, rather, Mr Law talked, expounding at length those banking notions which he had carefully elaborated whilst hoping to conquer the hesitations of King Victor Amadeus. When at last he stood up and spoke of bed his decision was taken.

"I'll pack no later than tomorrow and set out within the week. But I'll first test the ground before I summon you to join me. If the Regent should look upon my system with as much favour as when last I saw him, why then a golden prospect should lie before us."

Chapter 2

THE REGENT IN COUNCIL

On a dull morning of late October of that year 1715 a gathering of nobles and some others awaited the Regent in a spacious tapestried chamber of the Palais Royal, that palace built by a cardinal to express his grandeur and ceded by him to his king, as had happened once in England to another great palace built by a prelate.

Dominant in this assembly, as was proper considering its purpose, were the members of the Council of Finance, all of whom were noble, and four of whom were dukes: the ascetically handsome, haughty Noailles, who was President of the Council and conceived himself, not without some reason, of great authority in financial matters; the rather epicene La Vrillière, who discharged the functions of secretary; the dapper little Duc de Saint-Simon, who was perhaps closest in the intimacy of the Regent, and who accounted an understanding of finance beneath the dignity of a gentleman; and the still foppish old Maréchal Duc de Villeroy, lean of shanks and with red-raddled cheeks, who was governor of the infant King and who shared some of Saint-Simon's scorn of too close an acquaintance with affairs. Of the remaining eight, the most notable, on the score of his self-assertiveness and entire devotion to Noailles, was Rouillé du

Coudray, a gross untidy fellow with the flushed, veined countenance of the heavy drinker.

With these members of the Council of Finance there were this morning eight Councillors of State, including the Marquis d'Argenson, the King's Lieutenant-General of Police, who from his sinister looks was known in Paris as the Damned, and the well-favoured, portly Chancellor d'Aguesseau, a jurist of talent and of an integrity that had become proverbial and was now imperilled only by too great a loyalty to Noailles.

Whilst some of these gentlemen of quality lounged about the oval council-table and others formed groups in the embrasures of the tall windows that overlooked the vast courtyard, some thirteen other men, who had been especially summoned, held themselves modestly apart in the background, as became persons conscious of their commoner clay. They were France's leading bankers and merchants, sober in dress and demeanour if we except that financial giant Samuel Bernard, whose long, lean person was gaudily ostentatious in purple coat, gold waistcoat and elaborate periwig. He, it is true, could claim nobility; for he had been knighted by Louis XIV for valuable pecuniary services. But because there was in France a sharp discrimination between the noble and the merely ennobled, he had wisely decided that his place was among his fellow-bankers.

To the councillors this invasion of their debates by these enriched plebeians was an abominable desecration. Only the parlous state of the finances could bring them resentfully to submit to it. It was intolerable that gentlemen of birth should be constrained to debate in the presence of vulgarians, particularly remembering the acrimony in which their contentions commonly developed. It was an acrimony springing inevitably from the divergence of their views on the remedies to be applied and from the sharp rivalries by which their political ambitions moved them. Wrangle as they might, however, they had made no progress towards the solution of the problem of a national debt amounting to two and a half milliards; for when out of a revenue of one hundred and forty-five million livres they had discharged the annual expenses of government amounting to one hundred and forty-two millions, they were left with a bare three millions out of which to find the interest for that monstrous balance.

From the outset the Duke of Saint-Simon had ingenuously urged the convocation of the States-General and the declaration of a national bankruptcy, as the only way to save the country from a revolution. He took the view that a prince should not be bound by the liabilities of his predecessor, and that the edicts of a king who had been lodged in the vaults of St Denis were, like himself, so much dust. He pointed out what everybody knew, which was that commerce was languishing, industry paralysed, unemployment swelling daily, the land devastated by war, agriculture ruined and famine already stalking the countryside; and he concluded that there could be no improvement until the finances were set in order, which could be attained only by making a fresh and unencumbered start.

The old Duke of Villeroy's prescription had been a capital levy. But d'Aguesseau, the Chancellor, called in to give upon this the benefit of his renowned wisdom and experience, had demonstrated that even if they set the levy as high as one-tenth they must find the result far from commensurate with its inevitable aggravation of the miseries and injustices under which the country was already groaning. He submitted, however, an alternative. For years there had been no surveillance of the farmers of the taxes, and it was known that they had taken advantage of this immunity so as to grind the very bones of the King's subjects. Let their affairs be investigated by a special Chamber of Justice, as had been done under Sully, a hundred years ago, and let them be made to disgorge their illicit plunder. The yield should be rich.

This was a matter still under consideration together with that of an arbitrary and not very honest reduction in the interest on the State Bonds and a still less honest devaluation of the currency. This last was an old expedient. The louis d'or had changed its value a score of times in almost as many years. The latest depreciation, of one-fifth, had enriched the Treasury by no more than seventy millions, too paltry a proportion of the vast indebtedness to compensate for the further depression and disorganization of trade which had followed.

There matters stood on that October morning when a disgruntled Council of Finance was saddled with the unwelcome collaboration of a band of *roturiers*. And there was worse. As if it were not enough to constrain these proud fastidious gentlemen to display the sores of the body politic to that plebeian audience, their lordships knew that they were summoned for the further derogation of listening to the opinions of a foreigner of no account, a man of whom no good was known, an adventurer who once already had been expelled from France. They mistrusted mysterious men, and mysterious they regarded this fellow who for years had lived entirely by gaming, a man of obscure origin, known for a dissipated past, a tragic duel and a romantic evasion from prison.

It certainly did not mitigate his offence in their eyes that he should in the past few weeks have brought the Duke of Orléans so completely under the yoke of his spurious charms as actually to have been a guest at one of those supper-parties of the Regent's which were the scandal of Paris and to which only the most intimate were bidden.

For the rest, his very personality, his good looks and a bearing that so admirably blended pride and urbanity, were regarded as fraudulent by men who without actually possessing these attributes, regarded them as the exclusive right of persons of their station.

They were brought from their lounging attitudes and ill-humoured mutterings by the sudden opening of the tall double doors and the loud voice of an usher, announcing:

"His Royal Highness!"

The Duke of Orléans, in grey velvet, a star of diamonds on his breast, short of stature, despite his high heels, and of a plumpness that was increasing as he approached his fortieth year, came in briskly, florid and smiling, rolling a little in his gait, and smelling faintly of musk.

He was followed closely by a man who, by contrast, was of more than common height and of a singular ease of carriage.

There was a scraping of chairs and shuffle of feet as the assembly stood respectfully to receive the Prince.

The late King, who loved to savour his power, would have come in with leisured majesty, measuring his steps, hat on head; he would have considered them with the cold contemptuous eyes of a god; he would have taken his seat, leaving them standing until he had delivered himself of an address amounting to no more than a statement of his will, which none would dare to gainsay.

But the Regent had changed all this. Easy-going, affable, careless of etiquette and impatient of ceremony, he came to the head of the table, with that friendly smile on his pleasant countenance to set them at their ease, a friendly plump white hand to wave them to their chairs.

"Be seated, messieurs. Be seated."

He was bare-headed, and framed in the black periwig, to correspond with his own black hair and eyebrows, his full countenance with its shapely nose and generous, indolent mouth, was still uncommonly attractive, despite the high congested colour with which persistent excesses were stamping it.

When this congestion, combined with the shortness of his neck, had led Chirac, his physician to warn him that his hard-living might end in an apoplexy, all that he had found to answer with his careless laugh was: "And then? Do you know of a pleasanter death?"

His expression, singularly winning, gathered an increase of gentleness from the short-sightedness of his blue eyes, one of which was perceptibly larger than the other.

However much his exterior might announce the careless voluptuary, Mr Law was right in accounting exceptional his mental endowments, and if nature had but accorded him the energy to match them and the strength of will to keep his self-indulgence within reasonable bounds, his fame must have stood high. His Bavarian mother spoke truly enough when she said that the fairy godmother who attended his birth had bestowed upon him all the talents save only the talent of making use of them.

Under his insistent gesture the nobles rustled into their places, whereupon His Highness indicated the stranger on his left.

"Messieurs, I bring you my friend, Monsieur le Baron Lass."

Thus he translated the Scottish title of Laird, possibly with intent to command from these stiff-necked gentlemen the consideration due to birth, whilst "Lass" – to rhyme with "*Hélas*" – was the pronunciation the Scot's name obtained in France.

"I have brought him," the Regent pursued," in the belief that the great mathematical talents which have made him famous in all Europe, and his exceptional understanding of finance may prove of assistance to us in our difficult deliberations."

Then, looking beyond the councillors, who, cold-eyed and some with curling lip, remained glumly silent, he addressed the group of professional financiers, modestly huddled in the background. 'With the same object I have required the presence of you other gentlemen, who are foreign to our Council so that we may have the advantage of your expert views upon the expositions with which the Baron has consented to favour us."

He sat down, leaving Mr Law to bow stiffly to the company before taking his own seat on the Regent's immediate left, imperturbable under the scrutiny of which he was the object. These gentlemen loved him no better for his indefinable air of grandeur in harmony with the flawless elegance of all his appointments.

His full-skirted coat of heavy ribbed silk of the colour of cinnamon was fastened only at the waist by three of the small gold buttons that ran in a close-set line from neck to hem. His bulging ruffles were of the finest Malines, and an emerald of great price glowed on his Steenkirk of black satin. The lean patrician countenance between the heavy wings of his black periwig was sternly placid.

As d'Argenson was to express it later, to the deep mortification of Saint-Simon: "Our nobility is proclaimed by our clothes – this rascal's is imprinted on his skin."

The amiable Regent continued the commendatory introduction. Monsieur Lass, who had his full confidence, and who had now closely studied the details furnished him of the state of France's unhappy affairs, came to them to propound a definite system. His Highness would say no more than that he should not have troubled Monsieur Lass to appear before them if he did not regard this system as worthy of their earnest consideration.

"Monsieur Lass, the word is with you."

Mr Law, still cool under those hostile eyes, perhaps, indeed, stimulated by them, came to his feet again, and very quietly, his tone conversational, his delivery so easy and fluent that his harsh foreign inflexions were scarcely remarked, began to address them.

"His Royal Highness has done me the honour to acquaint me not only, as he has told you, with the financial difficulties of the kingdom, but also with the various proposals which have been urged by this Council for their solution. Of these proposals some, I understand, have already been put into practice and have proved sterile, or very nearly so. Before two proposals vastly more far-reaching in their effects I am informed that you hesitate, and in my view this hesitation does credit to your judgment."

The old Duke of Villeroy sniffed audibly in resentment of a commendation which he accounted an impertinence. It earned him a repressive frown from His Highness, and the utter indifference of Mr Law.

"One of these proposals is the declaration of a national bankruptcy, the other is the establishment of a Chamber of Justice by which it is hoped to bleed the tax-farmers of their illicit gains in recent years.

"The first – the repudiation of the debts of His late Majesty – must provoke the bitter resentment that ever waits upon dishonest practices in those who govern."

"Dishonest!" It was an angry interjection from Saint-Simon, who had fathered the proposal. He glared at the Scot out of a swarthy countenance suddenly congested. His black brows, naturally arched, flanking his beak of a nose, lent him the expression of an angry owl.

"That is what I said. If I am to be understood, if I am to be of service, I must call things by their proper names. Euphemisms may serve to gloze a fact; they do not alter it. I describe repudiation as dishonest because since the King never dies, the King's debts remain the King's debts. They are the debts not of the individual, but of the office."

Before Saint-Simon could utter the rejoinder his fretful air announced, the Regent had forestalled him. "Parbleu! that is the phrase that I have sought but failed to find. It gives you, messieurs, in a dozen words the complete and final argument." He waved his plump white hand. "But I interrupt you, Monsieur Lass."

"Nor," said Mr Law, 'is dishonesty all that can be urged against it. Repudiation must create such confusion as to bring the affairs of the Kingdom to a chaos from which it is difficult to discern the issue. You will have witnessed the bankruptcy of an individual, and you will have seen the utter ruin and destitution – almost the obliteration – of that individual's family. But can you picture the national ruin, the terrible disruption that must attend the bankruptcy of the State. It needs imagination to perceive the full horror of the spectacle. But I will endeavour to help you to perceive it if you wish it."

"It is not necessary," said the Duke of Noailles, who had never favoured the course, whilst Saint-Simon with an ill-humoured shrug sat back in his chair.

Having received that assurance, Mr Law passed on to deal with the question of the Chamber of Justice. In equity, he admitted, there could be no objection to it, nor yet in expedience. Because of the odium in which tax-gatherers are ever held the measure would certainly be received with public jubilation.

If, however, they would look closely into what happened under King Henri IV, when Sully set up such a tribunal, they would discover that so heavy were the expenses it entailed, so considerable the army of administrators to be salaried, and so vast the corruption almost inevitable in their ranks, that most of the plunder merely passed from one set of robbers to another.

The profit to the State, he concluded, was negligible and certainly far from compensating for all the labour involved.

"By Your Highness' leave!" The interruption came from the Marquis d'Argenson. Big, swarthy, and masterful in his startling ugliness, some part of his sixty-three years dissembled by his heavy black periwig, the Marquis had developed during twenty years as Lieutenant-General of Police all the attributes of the bloodhound and in his heavy-jowled countenance something of a bloodhound's traits.

It dismayed him to hear this adventurer whom once he had turned out of France, calmly and authoritatively sweeping away the notion of prosecutions which as Lieutenant-General he instinctively cherished.

The Regent's nod, giving him leave to speak, brought him to his feet. He delivered himself shortly, in a deep booming voice that well became the forceful eloquence he could at need command, so that as an advocate he was without a rival.

"To what Monsieur le Baron says of the operations of the *Chambre Ardente* under King Henri IV I am prepared to testify. But his *a priori* contention – nay, his gratuitous assumption – that what happened then must happen now is inadmissible. His only evidence is his opinion." He sat down, conceiving that on this point at least he had checked his man.

A gentle smile quivered on Mr Law's thin lips. "Monsieur le Marquis will be acquainted with the saying that history repeats itself. His great experience of mankind will inform him, I am sure, that men do not change however circumstances may vary." The tone of his insistence was so courteous as to be innocent of offence. Without waiting for the Lieutenant-General to reply, he went straight on: "However, this, too, is an opinion of my own, to which each of you will attach the importance that seems good to him.

"Let me return for my purposes to the question of bankruptcy. The notion of its necessity held, gentlemen, by some of you, is – I do not hesitate to make the assertion – based upon a fundamental error: the belief that the nation is, in fact, in a bankrupt state."

Saint-Simon expressed his astonishment in a sour laugh. "And can you say that it is not?"

"With all the emphasis at my command," he announced, and went on to do so. They might say of a nation possessing the almost inexhaustible resources of France that it was bankrupt only by the utter misconception of what constitutes wealth. The Treasury might be empty, and the State without money to meet its needs. But money was not wealth; it was merely the vehicle for its circulation; like blood, which without being life, nevertheless, carries life and warmth to every part of the body.

The wealth of a nation lay, he asserted, in the industry and productivity of her people, in the fertility of her soil, in the freedom and volume of her trade, in the genius, inventiveness and application of those who develop her arts and crafts or direct her commerce. "When you come to agree with this, as agree you surely must, you will perceive as I do that France is rich beyond all need for concern."

He paused there as if for a reply, and the Duke of Noailles, sauve and courtly, took advantage of it to address the Regent.

"What Monsieur Lass has said is too evident for any here to wish to quarrel with it. But what he describes is potential wealth, whilst our need – our urgent need – is for actual, immediate wealth; in short, for ready money with which to meet our pressing engagements."

The Regent inclined his head in acknowledgment, and his smile invited Mr Law to answer.

"If it were not my purpose," said the Scot, "to show how wealth that is potential may be rendered actual, my presence here would be an idle impertinence. Give me your patience, messieurs."

With a seductive fluency of speech and a lucidity of phrase that cast full light into the dark corners of his theme, Mr Law expounded.

He began with the admission, which here seemed supererogative, that where currency is in short supply for purposes of trade and the hire of labour, productivity, which was the creation of wealth, must of necessity be retarded. It followed, therefore, that for a nation's prosperity, its supply of currency must always be equal to its needs.

Impatient shrugs and one or two short laughs scorned the notion of bringing an obscure foreigner to weary them with such a disclosure of the obvious. Monsieur de Noailles, as if losing interest, drew a sheet of paper forward, dipped a quill and began to sketch.

But soon came matter that was to startle him and the others out of their scornful impatience.

Mr Law invited them to cast a glance at the banking methods of Holland, methods which had built up her great prosperity. "Methods which will be familiar to you gentlemen of this Council," he unwarrantably assumed, "and even more familiar perhaps to you other gentlemen who are professedly merchants and bankers. It is in those methods that I discover authority for my own theories."

This brought him to the contention that if it was correct to hold that the present crisis in the affairs of France resulted from the lack of currency, then the first measure in order to mobilize the nation's resources was to increase it. If they regarded this as impossible, it was only because, wedded as they were to the notion of a metal currency, they did not at all perceive that gold and silver were not necessities. Paper could not only take their place, but it could do so with manifest advantages to trade, since paper is conveniently portable, easily circulated and readily replaced.

At this Villeroy exploded. "Paper the equivalent of gold and silver! God save us! That absurdity is too easily exposed. A louis d'or from which you have effaced all imprints still retains its value as a piece of gold. Can that be pretended of paper?"

"No. But if the paper is known to be convertible into gold on demand its value will be the same."

He elaborated this by the contention that in order to render paper acceptable all that was necessary was to establish credit, and so came to his proposal for the accomplishment of this. It lay in the foundation of a State Bank on the model of the famous Bank of Holland, but more perfected and of wider scope. Such a bank would possess the privilege of issuing paper money, which he would term banknotes; it would discount commercial bills, open accounts for traders, make transfers of funds from one centre to another, support trade and agriculture by loans, collect the taxes and thereby abolish the bad and wasteful system of tax-farming, provide the royal revenues, and become the depository of gold and silver specie as funds of guarantee for its paper issues.

"Thus," Mr Law ended, "a general credit may be established that will offer advantages to every party in the State."

Pausing there, he observed on almost every countenance scepticism, and on some even consternation. The proposal was too empirical, too revolutionary, as it seemed, for the stomachs of these gentlemen.

Noailles had suspended his sketching, and was favouring Mr Law with a stare of undisguised contempt. But it was left for the coarse-mouthed Rouillé du Coudray, who as Director of Finance was Noailles' chief coadjutor, to voice the general thought, and voice it brutally in a sneer.

"You have used the word *credit* very freely. I wonder what exactly it means to you. It should be interesting to hear."

"Credit is essentially faith," was the simple answer.

"Ah! Faith." Coudray laughed noisily. "That is the art of believing things for which there is no evidence. Do you expect French merchants to be moved by it?"

"Not if it were confined to your definition. Confidence is yet another term for faith, and I should certainly expect merchants to be moved by that. Just as we freely lend money to a person when we are confident of repayment, so we may lend money to an enterprize from faith in its future profits.

"It may be within your knowledge – it is certainly within that of those gentlemen engaged in commerce – that the capital of bankers and merchants is decupled by the trust they enjoy, which removes the need for immediate payments. What is possible to every trader would certainly be possible to the State. If the State becomes the universal banker, and centralizes all values, the public fortune will similarly be decupled, and your difficulties are solved.

"But let me widen the definition of credit still further. It is an anticipation of the future, which it sets in circulation as a value; or, in other words, it is the simple perception of a value which has not yet been evoked into activity, not yet been mobilized, but which, nevertheless, exists and in which we believe. And this belief is one that may be aroused and stimulated; for it is a fact that credit possesses this advantage over specie, that whilst specie cannot be augmented by the mere perception of value, credit may be so increased almost without measure."

Du Coudray's harsh sneering voice was uncompromising in its censure. "A gamester's reasoning."

"Just that, pardieu!" old Villeroy agreed, a grin of disgust on his faded face. "It's the least that can be said of it." And the snap of the lid of his snuff-box seemed to add viciousness to the assertion.

The Chancellor d'Aguesseau intervened, to ask a question. "Give me leave, Highness." His mellow voice was quietly deliberate. "Setting aside for the moment the question of currency, we have not yet heard to what extent and by what means it would be applied to the mobilization – as Monsieur le Baron expresses it – of those resources which he rightly discovers in the State."

"Will you tell them, Monsieur Lass?" the Regent invited.

"Without difficulty. The aim would be to form a central board to direct and control all great commercial undertakings, to provide occupation for the poor – that is to say, the workers – by the encouragement of mining, fishing, manufacture and the rest, and to effect a sensible reduction in the rates of interest."

In a voice that crackled with indignation the old Maréchal flung in the question: "Is it, then, proposed that the King should turn banker and trader? Such a thing may be possible in the country of Monsieur Lass; but in France…" A gesture concluded the sentence, words failing him in which to express his disgust.

It stung the Regent into sharpness. "Not the King, Monsieur le Maréchal. The State. Pray perceive the difference."

"His late Majesty," grumbled Villeroy, "did not perceive it. We have it upon his authority that the State is the King."

Ignoring the retort, the Regent nodded to the Chancellor, whose glance again begged leave to speak.

"The opinion, monseigneur, which I feel it my duty to express," said d'Aguesseau, "is that to found a system of finance upon the basis proposed would be to plunge the State, and consequently the entire nation, into all the risks of commercial speculation without the guarantees of that enterprise, zeal and prompt resolution which able and experienced men of affairs – and others do not survive to count – are alone able to bring to their undertakings. Shopkeeping and government are activities that call for very different qualities and very different knowledge. To combine the two is to succeed in neither."

Considering the Chancellor's great reputation for clear-sightedness and his renowned integrity, and hearing the general murmur of agreement with him, Mr Law already perceived here his defeat. Yet with unimpaired placidity he was waiting for that murmur to exhaust itself when support came from the last quarter in which he would have sought it. D'Argenson had reared his great black head, heavy eyebrows knit above bold eyes, to apply a check to the hasty scorn that was threatening to bring the meeting to an end. He drawled in sarcasm.

"Are we not in danger, monseigneur, in yielding to emotions, no doubt lofty in themselves, to overlook that we are no longer in a position to afford them?"

"I should have thought so," His Highness answered on a sigh. "Another consideration which I would have you bear in mind, whatever may be decided, is that Monsieur Lass leaves us in his debt by his readiness to come before the Council. You will remember this, if you please, gentleman. You will remember also that his views are the fruit of studies probably deeper than those of any man of our day, pursued by a mind of singular and well-known mathematical acuteness." He looked round, and d'Argenson purposefully caught his eye.

"You have something to add, Marquis?"

"The Chancellor, no doubt rightly, in his wisdom, has confined his censure to that part of the Baron's system which is concerned with commercial enterprise. And to that extent I am in agreement with him. But since he has not touched upon the banking methods expounded by Monsieur Lass, it will be that he has nothing to oppose to it. It remains, however, that to carry out that part of the system time will be needed, much time, the time between sowing and reaping, and it would still remain to discover what provision there can be for our immediate needs, which are of a distracting urgency."

"Monsieur le Marquis," said Mr Law, "has overlooked that which I imagined to be implicit in my exposition.

"All royal revenues would be paid into the State Bank by the tax-farmers, and to the extent of those payments the bank would issue to the Treasury its notes in the values most convenient for circulation. All those to whom the State is indebted would receive from the Treasury payment only in these notes, which they may at their pleasure exchange for specie at the bank, none, however, being compelled to retain them or even to accept them in the course of trade."

And now, at last, the Duc de Noailles, the President of the Council, its oracle in money matters, tossed aside his pen, and expressed himself. "In that case, Highness, I perceive no purpose in these banknotes."

"And yet," he was answered by Mr Law, "I do not hesitate to assert that once their utility is realized, with assurance that specie may be had for the paper whenever desired, men will eagerly prefer it to coin. The incomparably greater facility of handling currency in this form alone will make it preferable. And once confidence in the paper is established you will perceive that the bank, by an issue of notes equivalent to the amount of specie it holds, will double at once the capital which it may apply to financial operations. For every million in gold, which it will retain as a fund of guarantee, it may confidently, and safely issue a million in paper currency." He paused for a moment before adding: "That, I think, is all that I can profitably tell you."

With a glance that begged the Regent's leave, he resumed his seat, dabbing his lips with a fine handkerchief.

The Regent cleared his throat. His expression was not happy. "You have heard Monsieur Lass, and whatever views you may hold on his system for the alleviation of our difficulties, you will wish to felicitate him upon the clarity with which he has explained it. Before the Council pronounces upon it, I should be glad to hear the opinions of you others, of the world of trade and finance who have been good enough to attend. If you please, messieurs."

A merchant named Lenormand and one other after him pronounced at once in favour of the establishment of the proposed bank. A third, less downright, opined that it might be useful at some time other than the present. And then the opulent contractor, Samuel Bernard, perhaps because annoyed at not having been allowed to speak first, as he accounted due to his rank amongst them, and so as to put down those who had usurped that privilege, condemned the system in uncompromising terms. Using arguments similar to those of the Chancellor, he stigmatized it as dangerously speculative, and because of his renowned financial ability, he swept with him every remaining member of his class.

After the last of them had spoken, the Regent thanked them for their attendance, and gave them leave to depart.

They went out backwards, bent double and clustered ludicrously together as if for mutual support under the haughty eyes of the nobles.

When the doors had closed upon them, His Highness required the votes of the members of the Council and invited the Duke of Noailles, as its president, to lead the way.

Mr Law leaned back in his armchair, and dabbed his lips again. It was the only sign he gave of any feeling, and this was not readily to be interpreted. In his shrewdness he could have no doubt that already the dice had fallen against him. The deadly cast made by d'Aguesseau had been confirmed by Bernard, who was destined before long bitterly to regret that presumptuous condemnation. Yet one desperate attempt Mr Law made, with the Regent's leave, to amend the throw before it was too late.

"It is no more than a word of warning against permitting the views of Samuel Bernard and his kind to impress you unduly. You will not overlook, gentlemen, that a system such as mine would make an end of the enrichment of all Samuel Bernards. Their monopolies would be wrested from them to be vested in the State. His hostility to my system is the measure of his fear of its success. Do me the justice, gentlemen, to bear that in your minds. Then you will be doing yourselves justice also."

He had done, and he sat back again, to hear Monsieur de Noailles.

His Grace courteously confessed himself persuaded of the utility of the proposed bank, but he could not find that the time was suitable for its establishment, particularly in view of the opposition of the merchants, whose support must be considered essential to its success.

He urged that, instead, the Council should devote itself to economies and the suppression of all useless or avoidable expenditure. This and the perception of the attention devoted to affairs by His Highness should suffice gradually to restore the nation's confidence in the government.

The Chancellor followed with the simple assertion that he was completely in agreement with Monsieur de Noailles, and that nothing that he had heard could cause him to change the opinion he had already expressed.

Rouillé du Coudray was another who could add nothing to what he had said already, and he repeated it: "Which is that what we have heard is a gamester's proposal, as might be expected, considering the source of it. The views of Monsieur Lass are perhaps natural in a man of his nationality."

Whilst His Highness was frowning his disapproval of this offensiveness, the others who followed to damn the system, damned it at least in the more courteous terms employed by Noailles.

Monsieur de Saint-Simon was even generous in his opposition. "I account it excellent in itself and likely enough to succeed in a republic or in a strange kingdom such as the English, where the sovereign cannot levy a tax without the vote of Parliament; a country where letters of *cachet* are unknown, and where a certain Mr Locke is permitted impudently to set up a natural right in opposition to divine dynastic right; a country in which the finances are governed solely by those who furnish them and who furnish them to the extent and in the manner which they think proper. But I can see no success for a system of that kind in an absolute monarchy such as France."

Only the voice of d'Argenson, in all that Council, was raised in Mr Law's favour. Unintimidated by the unanimous body of contrary opinion, and at no pains to dissemble his contempt for it, the Lieutenant-General forcefully opined that the bank of Monsieur Lass' happy conception, properly regarded, would be, in fact, His Majesty's cash-box, and would permit them to sweep away the tax-farmers with immense profit to the State.

It was a conception certainly worth a trial, and, if properly conducted, the Lieutenant-General could not doubt that it would have the effect of easing their difficulties.

It was a stout defence delivered by d'Argenson with jaw out-thrust and that defiance of contradiction which made him so formidable an advocate. But his single voice, however, sonorous and forcible, could not stifle that of the main body of the Council.

The Regent sighed once more in reluctant resignation, and looked ruefully at Mr Law. It no longer needed the apologetic expression of that full, pink face to tell the Scot that his cause was lost. He could not conceive it to lie in the nature of this amiable, easy-going prince, whatever his personal convictions, to exert himself to the extent of successfully opposing the hostility confronting them.

Once only in his short career since the late King's death had His Highness roused himself from his moral indolence to do battle. That was when he had demanded of the Parliament the destruction of the will of Louis XIV with its provision that Madame de Montespan's legitimized bastard, the Duke of Maine, should share with the Duke of Orléans the Regency of France and the guardianship of the young King.

With the vigour and something of the majesty of his departed uncle he had then constrained the Parliament to exclude the Duke of

Maine from those offices, leaving himself in the sole possession of the Regency.

All that, however, as Mr Law reflected, was a battle fought and a victory won for his own prerogatives, and nothing less was ever likely to rouse him again to a similar display of energy.

He sat in silence for some moments after the last member of his Council had spoken, his chin in the laces at his throat, his brow rumpled in thought.

It may be that this was one of those moments in which he cursed the political expediency which had led him to set up the various councils, of which the Council of Finance was one, instead of governing by ministers who could more easily be governed in their turn. At last he expressed himself in a weary tone.

"The Marquis d'Argenson, messieurs, has perfectly uttered my own opinion. It is an opinion, let me say, to which I have been guided by that masterly essay *Money and Trade*, of which Monsieur Lass is the author, and of which each of you has had the advantage of being furnished with extracts. Had it been otherwise, had I taken a less confident view of the advantages offered by his system, I should not have put Monsieur Lass to the trouble of coming before you to explain it.

"Still believing in it, as I do, it follows that I must deplore that with the single exception of Monsieur d'Argenson, you should pronounce against it. However, your unanimity leaves me no choice, profoundly though I regret it. It remains for me only to declare the project abandoned and that we must look elsewhere for the solution of our difficulties."

Abruptly, with a hint of weary ill-humour, he ended: "There is no reason why I should detain you longer today, messieurs. You have my leave to withdraw."

Chapter 3

THE EARL OF STAIR

There is no gamester worthy of the name who cannot lose without change of countenance. And although John Law had played for a stake not of mere thousands, but of millions, his placidity did not desert him.

His Highness had detained him after dismissing the Council, and it was as if to express an undiminished sense of esteem that he leaned upon the Scot's arm as they passed along the noble gallery leading to the main staircase, whilst graciously expressing his personal chagrin at the issue of the affair.

Nothing could have been more unexpected than Mr Law's reply. "If I share to the full your regret, monseigneur, it is only because I see you deprived of services by which I had counted upon resolving your grievous difficulties."

For a moment the Regent was taken aback by what he accounted an arrogant fatuity, and Mr Law was made aware of it by a lessening of the ducal weight upon his arm.

"Ah!" His Highness drew breath audibly, and there was a pause before he added in a cooler voice: "at least you relieve me of the fear that you have suffered a disappointment. But let us not yet despair. It may well be that with the increasing embarrassment in our affairs which seems inevitable, these gentlemen may be brought to reconsider today's unfortunate decision."

They were within a dozen paces of the head of the great staircase. The Duke checked. "Meanwhile, do you ask for nothing?"

"I thank Your Highness." Mr Law bowed under those friendly eyes. "I am in need of nothing."

"*Corbleu!*" The Regent's smile broadened. "To hear a man say that, is to renew my faith in human nature. I trust that you do not yet think of leaving us."

"Not until Your Highness tells me that I can be of no service."

"Faith, I hope that I shall never tell you that." He moved on again towards the wide marble stairs, where an officer was in attendance. "Here is Major de Contades. He will accompany you. You shall hear from me soon again. Meanwhile, my dear Baron, in any need remember that I am here with an undischarged obligation."

Thus dismissed, Mr Law departed, not without hope.

He was becomingly, if only temporarily, installed in a handsome house in the Rue de Grenelle, which his steward Laguyon had found and rented for him. He came home that day to learn from his wife that in his absence they had been visited by the Earl of Stair.

Mr Law's brows were raised. "Johnny Dalrymple? What a plague should he want with me?"

"To bid you welcome to Paris."

"Since when has he owned it?"

"Well, then, to pay his respects to you. What's to frown at? He was very civil. He is to bring Lady Stair and Lady Sandwich to visit me and some other of his English friends here."

Mr Law shrugged, and found himself a chair. "*Timeo Danaos et dona ferentes.*"

"Is that Spanish?"

"No. Virgil. It means, 'I fear the Greeks when they are bearers of gifts'."

"Do you mean that for Lord Stair?" She spoke with the indignation to which nowadays she was quickly moved when he expressed opinions in conflict with her own. "I can't think why you should. A very proper man."

"I have known few more improper."

"We do not judge by the same standards."

"I have long suspected it."

"He will not be of the quality among which you usually seek your friends."

"God be thanked."

She looked at him disdainfully, and he observed with an odd detachment how very attractive she was in a gown of peacock blue, her body springing shapely and slender from the billowing petticoat. He wondered impersonally whether Dalrymple had found her to his taste and made her aware of it. For a grievance which he had not mentioned to his brother was that she was too responsive to gallantry. Had he done so, William, as her advocate might have answered that it was natural she should desire him to remark that other men were eager to pay her the court which he denied her.

"I suppose you'll know," she said, "that Lord Stair is in Paris as the English ambassador."

"It would surprise me less if he were an English spy. The best I know of him is that he's a damned whig. There's little good in an English whig. In a Scottish one there is none. And that, I repeat, is the best I know of him. The worst isn't fit for your ears, although, God knows, you're no prude. Besides, he'll supply it you, himself, if you afford him the occasion. Ah well! If all he told you of his purpose in visiting us was a desire to be civil, we shall have to wait until he comes again in order to discover the true reason."

She shrugged and moved away in annoyance. "I vow you delight in being provoking. It is fortunate that I know how to keep my temper. I suppose things have not gone well for you at the Palais Royal this morning."

"A good guess," he admitted smoothly.

"No guess at all. You advertise it by your bad manners. So you've failed again? It was to have been foreseen, of course."

"Spare me your sympathy."

"La! Did you expect it? At least I can congratulate you upon taking my advice not to bring Will to France. You are saved the humiliation you suffered in Turin. A pity you don't heed me more often. But, to be sure, I know that you despise my intelligence. Not the least of your errors that. Heigho! And what now? Do we go on our travels again?"

Of all her tirade this was the only question that he answered, speaking quietly. "Not yet awhile. His Highness offers me the hospitality of France for the present."

"Until you forfeit it, I suppose, in the usual way."

"Until then, of course. Meanwhile," he added with scarcely perceptible sarcasm, "we may be vouchsafed the occasion to improve our acquaintance with Lord Stair."

They had not long to wait for this. His lordship came again no later than the morrow: a short, spare man, still young, of Mr Law's own age, with a handsome, if crafty, face and an assurance of manner that bordered normally upon arrogance and procured him few friends. This, however, was subdued on the present occasion. His low-lidded eyes, set on the very surface of his face, under arching brows, glowed flattering homage of Madame's beauty as he bowed over her hand.

"I vow your graciousness renders me importunate," he murmured.

Mr Law, under his wife's anxious glance, was formally polite. "Your lordship honours us."

"That is too civil, my dear Baron."

Suspecting raillery behind the smile, Mr Law was quick to curb it.

"I am a baron only in French. That is how His Highness chooses to translate a Scottish title for which there is no precise equivalent in France."

"A translation that does credit to His Highness' good sense. I am proud to know, sir, that he honours you with his friendship."

"Do not let us exaggerate."

"It were an affectation of modesty in you to disclaim so notorious a fact. As the representative here of King George I must rejoice in it."

"You'll have a great faculty for rejoicing, sir, to rejoice over so little."

"So little? You don't know what you are saying. Wait until you learn how much it is."

Laguyon appeared, ushering two footmen in claret and silver who bore between them the elements of a chocolate service. It was, Mrs Law announced, the hour of their collation. My lord would do them the honour to drink a cup of chocolate.

"Ma'am, it is to overwhelm me," Stair protested. "I feel more than ever that I come untimely."

She simpered. "Most timely, my lord, and very welcome."

Sipping his chocolate at the goat-legged table over which Mrs Law was now presiding, his lordship came at last to the reason for his presence.

"If I am here to ask a service of you, Mr Law, I am in the fortunate position of being able to give service in return."

Upon this Mr Law offered no comment; but looking up from his cup his cool glance plainly invited my lord to continue.

"I have had the misfortune to incur the displeasure of the Regent, who, to our great regret, continues to give shelter in France to the Pretender. There was an unfortunate incident some months ago, at the time of the late Jacobite rising in Scotland, brought about..." He paused. "We are private here, and if I speak freely it is entirely in confidence." He resumed. "Brought about, I was saying, by the Regent's having broken faith with us. He had given me his word that should James Stuart attempt to cross France so as to embark to put himself at the head of the rebels, he would be detained. His Highness was, as the French say, swimming between two waters. On the one hand he did not wish to provoke King George; on the other, he did not wish to hinder the Pretender, lest a successful rebellion should place him on the throne. Because I had reason to suspect this, we were not content to rely upon His Highness' word, but kept watch for ourselves. Perhaps you know the rest."

"I have heard of an attempt by a Colonel Douglas to intercept and assassinate the Pretender as he was making for Brittany."

"Assassinate!" Lord Stair was shocked. "Oh, no, no. That is just the vulgar calumny."

"Your lordship should know, since it is understood that Colonel Douglas was acting upon your orders. But if you had caught your man, I don't see what else you could have done with him."

My lord smiled ruefully. "That, of course, was the popular view, just as it was, as you've said, that Douglas acted upon my orders."

"Monstrous," murmured Catherine. "But so natural to vulgar rashness."

"I thank you, ma'am. Your intuitions are as I should expect in you. However, Colonel Douglas, who was well viewed in Paris and in favour at court, has left France in disgrace, and some part of that disgrace attaches, I grieve to say, to me, with hampering consequences."

Again Mrs Law afforded him her sympathy. "That is shameful!"

"You give me heart, ma'am." Gratitude gleamed from his hooded eyes. "Formerly I was growing in favour with His Highness, but since he has lent an ear to slander he refuses to receive me in private and turns his back upon me in public." He became proudly disdainful as he added: "For myself this is no matter. But it happens that I have a duty here, a conciliatory duty, which I am finding it impossible to discharge. It is in this that I solicit your aid."

"My aid?" Mr Law looked blank, whilst Catherine was protesting effusively: "Of course he'll be proud to lend it."

My lord set down his cup, wiped his lips with a napkin, and explained himself. If now that Mr Law's credit with the Regent stood high he would employ it in the British interest, his lordship might be able to do something for Mr Law no less valuable in return.

"I am dull," said Mr Law. "I do not perceive exactly what my voice could plead even if my favour with the Regent were as high as you suppose."

"Will you suffer me to instruct you?"

"I am sure that it is all that he needs," the lady assured him, to earn again his lordship's warmest smile.

"Brutally stated, the argument to be employed, is that one usurper should support the other."

"Brutal, as you say. One usurper will be King George, though that your lordship should say so robs me of breath. But the other? I don't discern him."

"The other, a usurper at present *in posse*, may well become a usurper *in esse* if the young Louis XV should die; for Philip of Spain, as the son of the Grand Dauphin, can show a stronger claim to the throne of France than Philippe of Orléans, and Philip of Spain is not without a party here, a party which is likely to grow under the fostering of the Duchess of Maine. That hot-tempered little grandchild of the great Condé makes no secret of her designs."

He went on to divulge that lately a guest at the magnificent country seat of the Duke of Maine at Sceaux, and whilst appearing absorbed in the extravagant junketings, the literary tournaments, the Venetian water parties, the masques and the play-acting conducted by the Duchess, he had used his eyes, his ears and his wits.

After all, the folk at Sceaux, histrionic in all things, were of a monstrous indiscretion. Her grace did not hesitate to avow that she was on fire to avenge not only her husband's exclusion from the regency, but even more fiercely the project to deprive the bastards of the rights of Princess of the Blood conferred upon them by Louis XIV when he legitimized them.

The Duchess of Maine had dreamed of being one day Queen of France. That dream Philippe of Orléans had shattered. She was saying openly and on every occasion that when one has once acquired the ability to succeed to the crown, rather than suffer the robbery of it, one should set fire to the four corners of the kingdom.

"And this is not mere talk," Lord Stair went on. "From what I have seen I have reason to believe that she is actively corresponding with Philip of Spain. The Prince of Cellamare, the Spanish ambassador, is nowadays a frequent visitor at Sceaux. If you were to acquaint the Duke of Orléans with that, in proof of your devotion to him, he would believe you moved to serve his interests and would be the more ready to listen when you dissuade him from supporting the Pretender, so that in his own possible need he may, in return, count upon King George to give no support to the King of Spain. You will not be the only one to urge this upon the Regent, but the more of those whose wits he trusts become the advocates of this course, the more likely will he be to follow it."

Mr Law was left in no doubt that Stair must be under instructions to bring about an offensive and defensive alliance between England and France, and that he perceived a way of furthering this object by flaunting before the Regent the menace of Spain. He smiled thoughtfully as he shook his head.

"You put too high an estimate on the confidence I enjoy. It has been exaggerated to you. In fact, such as it may be, it has just suffered a setback. And, anyway, the Regent may believe in me financially, but not politically. So I am spared the trouble of adding that I am without eagerness to serve England or her King."

Stair's eyebrows became still more arched. "You're not telling me that you're a Jacobite."

"No, my lord. I am an exile on quite other grounds."

"That was in King William's day."

"But the ban has never been lifted. Actually, I am less an exile than a fugitive. A fugitive from what passes for justice in England."

"After all, Mr Law, you killed a man," my lord protested.

"In a duel."

"But an irregular duel, without the proper complement of witnesses. No matter. I spoke of advantages to yourself in serving us. What if I could promise you a pardon and freedom to return to England as the price of your service?"

"I should answer that I have lived so long out of England that I feel more at home abroad."

"In short, you refuse?" His lordship's face had darkened. It was plain that he strove with a temper which opposition was never slow to stir.

"If I am to be entirely frank, let me say that I have hopes of my own to gratify, and that I will not jeopardize them by advocating those in which I have no interest."

His lordship breathed hard. "I may thank you at least for your candour." Then he laughed. "I could show you, I think, that your hopes might best be served by serving mine. It is not only the Regent's affairs which will prosper from an understanding with King George, but those of all whose interest it is that His Highness should continue in the regency. And you, Mr Law, I take it, are of these. Give it thought, sir. Take your own time. You may perceive your profit in it."

Without waiting for an answer, he swung to Catherine, whose darkened countenance gave him added hope. "I'll never believe, ma'am, that you share your husband's indifference to life at home in England, where so many would be proud to welcome you."

"You are too kind, my lord. And, indeed, having lived a vagabond, nothing could please me better."

Lord Stair displayed enchantment. "Let us then make an alliance to conquer this curmudgeon. I dare swear that he will thank us in the end."

"You hear his lordship, John."

Mr Law roused himself from the thoughts sown by Stair's last words. "I hear," he said, and laughed carelessly.

My lord was content to leave the matter there. Deftly he swung the talk into channels concerned with the delights of English fashionable life, of the attractions and gaieties of which its great wealth made it prodigal. By contrast existence, he vowed, was almost colourless in poverty-stricken France. He bewailed that duty constrained him to continue abroad, and eagerly looked forward to the day when, that duty accomplished, he might return to the pleasures of London.

He so visibly inflamed the lady by the pictures he painted, by the triumphs he promised her at home, that when at last he departed it was in the conviction that he left a zealous advocate to plead for him.

"Think over what I have told you," he said, as he took his leave of Law, "and especially your own profit in it. Upon reflection I am sure that you will perceive it."

He had not left the house before Catherine was bringing her guns to bear upon her husband. Was he quite mad, she wondered, that he could hesitate before this chance of rehabilitation.

"I do not hesitate," was the cold comment that drove her to fury.

"You mean that your mind is made up; that nothing will shake it?'

When he admitted that this was the case so far as concerned a return to England, the storm of her anger crackled in unmeasured terms about his head. What perversity was it that governed him? His plans for France had failed, as she knew they would. What, then, retained him? Was there some woman here who had cast a spell upon him? He had always, she vowed, been the willing prey of women. Always *un homme à femmes*.

Was that the reason for his present obstinacy? If it was not, then to what was he sacrificing her? Was he resolved that her entire life should be a martyrdom? And what of their two children, born abroad? Were they never to know the homeland, never to enjoy the advantages of an English rearing?

Well might she curse the day she had wed a gamester, to whom her happiness, her peace of mind, her very life were as mere stakes upon a board.

He heard her out in an impassivity that fed her fury. The lovely face grew pinched and shrewish, the voice that could be so musical and caressing became strident, and at moments coarse insults gave an added venom to her plaint. Thus until at long last she grew conscious of making no impression upon the panoply of his indifference, whereupon she sat down to weep.

Time had been when her tears had melted him; but that was in the days when he had stormed in answer to her storming; that was before contempt for her licences of temper, for the lack of restraint in her invective, had killed his feeling where she was concerned.

He had learnt that to dispute with her was merely to furnish unworthy fuel to her tantrums. He had learnt, too, that if nowadays she was seldom really amiable, her outbursts were as brief as they were wild. Within an hour or so of utterances that would seem to open an unbridgeable chasm between them, she would meet him as normally as if the surface of their peace had never known a ripple.

He spoke quietly now, as he turned to go. "Some day, Catherine, I may find you more tiresome than I can endure. Until then I will do as I can."

Chapter 4

MR LAW'S BANK

In the months that followed, months of waiting in the hope of being yet served by opportunity, Mr Law did little more than cultivate relations that might, if he were fortunate, be of ultimate service.

Knowledge of his great favour with the Regent opened wide the doors of that fastidious *beau monde* for himself and Catherine. She, taking full advantage of this, was soon launched upon amiable distractions. In addition to her husband's fame she enjoyed the patronage of the British ambassador and his lady, and in herself she commanded attention by a beauty and vivacity typically and delicately English that still seemed to preserve the freshness of girlhood. All this came timely to reconcile her to her Parisian sojourn.

As for her husband, his closest associates in those days were the Marquis d'Argenson, who had stood his friend before the Council; the Duke of Antin, who enjoyed the distinction of being Madame de Montespan's only legitimate child; the Count of Horn, that engaging libertine who was a member of one of the noblest houses in Europe; and the Abbé Dubois, between whom and himself the link was purely one of mutual ambition.

Dubois, of whom the Duke of Saint-Simon has left us in his encyclopaedic mémoirs a repulsive portrait, was of a very different stamp from the other three. Of the lowest extraction – the son of a poor apothecary of Brive la Gaillarde – but of great talent, exceptional parasitical instincts, and an unparalleled audacity, he had known how to profit by a succession of happy chances.

Appointed reader to the Duke of Orléans whilst his Grace was still Duke of Chartres, he had found his foot on the first rung of a ladder from which nothing could thereafter shake him. It was said that he had won the good graces of the young duke by a servility so base as not even to have scrupled to become his pander, guiding his first essays in those arts of debauchery which in the public eye had obscured the great and varied ability of his pupil.

Be that as it may, now that Philippe of Orléans was Regent of France and – having flung the bastards from the right of succession – heir presumptive to the throne, Dubois was become, under the Duke, the greatest man in the State.

His clerical title was a mere usurpation. For any man who could boast no birth, the title of Abbé served in some small degree to supply the lack, conferring a vague social distinction which had been of advantage to Dubois in his early days. His claim to it rested upon no more than that like many a seminarist who never ripened into priesthood, he had taken minor orders at a time when he was still destined for the Church. That he was no priest did not deter him from seeking further ecclesiastical honours.

Hoping to become a second Mazarin – who also was no priest – he aspired to wear like Mazarin the red hat of a cardinal. For the ultimate gratification of this ambition two things were necessary; political eminence and wealth.

The first he had acquired and was rapidly increasing; for the second, with the vision that made him what he was, he recognized in John Law a manipulator of the philosopher's stone, whom it might repay him to support.

It was to him that Mr Law, whose vision was no less acute, turned at last for assistance in creating opportunity when weary of waiting for opportunity to manifest itself.

The Abbé was lodged in the Palais Royal, in the very quarters which he had tenanted as a modest tutor to the young Duke. But he had very materially embellished them, and he was known to keep an excellent table. A wizened little man in black cassock and skull-cap, his lean sharp face was deeply lined and sunken of cheeks as if most of his molars were missing. His hair was red and his pink-rimmed eyes were uncannily piercing. He was accounted by many to resemble the satirist Arouet, whom the Duchess of Maine was patronizing and who later was to call himself Monsieur de Voltaire.

He received Mr Law with effusive purrings, gave him the best chair and called for wine to refresh him, and then anticipated his purpose by an admonition.

"It is not by sitting patiently at home, my dear Monsieur Lass, that one conquers the world. The world does not offer itself like a slut to be possessed. It is necessary to go forth and subdue it."

"I perceive it," said Mr Law. "That is why I come to ask you if you can find me a pretext for reawakening the Regent's slumbering interest in me."

"A pretext! One doesn't find pretexts. One invents them. *Inveniam viam aut faciam.*" He glanced at the ormolu timepiece on the mantelshelf. "I will accord you ten minutes in which to invent one now. Then I shall take you to His Highness, and I shall expect a man of your wit plausibly to justify the intrusion."

Casting about him for this justification, Mr Law opportunely recalled not so much the Earl of Stair's neglected request for political assistance, as the information gleaned from his lordship on the events at Sceaux; and by the time the Abbé had introduced him to the Regent's presence he had cynically discovered that in this lay all the pretext he required.

A prince who was glad to dispense with etiquette on every occasion received him without ceremony in his laboratory, perhaps the oddest of the many settings with which the Regent of France provided himself. It was a chamber plainly furnished, with bench and furnace, fantastic retorts, cabinets of phials, and mysterious utensils.

His Highness, in a coarse smock, to protect his finery, was amusing himself with the chemical research which added an addiction to occult practices and even to the distillation of poisons to the scandalous reputation he enjoyed.

"My dear baron, I have to reproach you with neglecting me."

This was encouraging. "I have been hoping for monseigneur's commands. If I intrude without them now, it is because that has come to my knowledge with which I account it my duty to acquaint Your Highness."

"Why speak of intrusion? You find me at work upon a mere decoction of herbs. If I am not," he laughed, "at the alchemist's more serious business of making gold, it is because for that I prefer to put my faith in such arts as yours. But sit, baron. Sit." He indicated a three-legged stool, and found a perch for himself on the edge of a table. "So you bring me news, do you?"

Mr Law, in some inward shame of his own disingenuousness, disclosed what he had learnt of the plotting at Sceaux, without, however, revealing the source of his information.

To Mr Law's surprise, and perhaps to his relief, the Regent was content to laugh. "Is that all? My faith, let them conspire by all means if it amuses them. I am aware of it, and I prefer that the cripple and his dwarf should plot rather than employ their poetasters to write scandalous doggerel about me. There's one of them, a disgustingly witty fellow named Arouet – an ordure – thinking things over in the Bastille at this moment. It is sad to punish men for the offences of that little *cabotine* of a duchess. But what would you?"

Thus, in amused contempt, he would dismiss the matter, alluding to the Duke and Duchess of Maine in the terms commonly applied to them by His Highness' outspoken Bavarian mother – as the cripple and the dwarf – because the duke was lame and the duchess had never outgrown the inches of a child.

Even when Mr Law found it expedient to add that the Spanish ambassador was taking a hand in the present activities, the Regent was merely moved to further scornful amusement. "Cellamare! Bah! The old rake is probably an aspirant for her grace's favours, exiguous though they be and he plays comedy to humour her. I esteem your solicitude, my dear Baron; but it's all not worth a thought. You disappoint me. The sight of you brought the hope that you might be seeking me with some irresistible argument for the Council. And speaking of money, I hear that a few nights ago you eased the Count of Horn of five thousand louis. A handsome, round sum. Has he paid you?"

"I have his note of hand."

The Regent laughed. "To be sure you believe in paper. I wish you could persuade my Council to do the same."

This, thought Mr Law, was his cue. He might wait in vain for a better.

"Persuasion is vain against obstinacy. But I might possibly prevail by demonstration."

"Demonstration?" The Regent looked at him with keener interest. "Have you a demonstration in mind?"

Mr Law had. "Grant me a charter, monseigneur, to found a private bank at my own risk, and by it I will undertake to prove my case."

"A private bank, eh?" The Regent, chin in hand, took thought. "It will need money, my friend."

"Six millions should suffice as a beginning."

"Do you possess six millions?"

"I possess two. I can create another two by an issue of banknotes for that amount, to which the original two in gold would serve as a fund of guarantee. This would give me four millions. The remainder I could coax into existence."

"In God's name tell me how."

"By an issue of shares – of, say, five thousand livres each."

"And who will buy them?"

"Those who are wise enough to have faith in me."

"It is possible that there may not be much wisdom in France."

Mr Law revealed that he had an inducement to offer. He would make his shares payable in four instalments, one quarter in gold and three quarters in State Bonds, which he would accept at their face value although at the moment they were worth not more than one half of it. He would count upon this to render his shares attractive at least to the bondholders, whilst to render his plan attractive to the Regent there was the prospect of absorbing some of the bonds and to that extent relieving the State of some part of the burden it carried. Nor was that all: in order to create an actual demand for his banknotes he would make them payable in specie of the weight and value which it enjoyed at the time of its issue. Thus, being guaranteed against any fresh debasement of the coinage, this novel paper currency would possess the allurement of a stability with which gold was no longer credited.

The Regent was impressed. He consented to discuss it further and at great length, until filled with increasing wonder of this wizardry, as he accounted it, he ended by promising Mr Law his charter for a private establishment in which, after all, the State would be nowise compromised.

Mr Law departed well content, summoned his brother to Paris, and without waiting for his arrival set about seeking a house for his purposes.

He found it in the Rue Quincampoix, a moderately wide street, some four hundred yards long, situated between the Rue Saint-Martin and the Rue Saint-Denis. It did not enjoy the best of reputations, being tenanted chiefly by money-changers, usurers, and men describing themselves as bankers, who were no better than pawnbrokers. The house he found, however, was large and roomy, and there in early May of that year 1716, when he received his charter, he set up his establishment, under the designation of the Banque Générale and the patronage of the Regent.

It became at once the object of the hostility of Noailles and his following, who feared that this *Banque Générale* might be no more than a stepping stone to that financial ascendancy which Mr Law's exposition to the Council of Finance and his favour with the Regent seemed to foreshadow. Under the Duke's inspiration, the pamphleteers went to work to shape public opinion. They poured scorn upon the undertaking. The *Gazette de la Régence* in terms of raillery invited the world to laugh at a folly doomed to failure.

Nevertheless the Bank made headway. Mr Law knew what he was doing. His money-changing and his discounting of bills offered rates so advantageous that very soon the usurers of the Rue Quincampoix were in danger of being put out of business. Easy too were the rates at which he advanced money on reasonable security, whilst his paper issue, mistrusted at first, came gradually to commend itself to traders, as he had reckoned, on the score of its convenience, particularly as a means of making remittances.

In establishing the credit of this paper the government itself took a hand. It made use of the banknotes for its payments, and once the public discovered with what promptitude these were cashed confidence awoke. Lastly, when it came to be fully appreciated that the notes were immune from any of those devaluations of specie which had been so disorganizing to commerce, Mr Law's paper was so far preferred that men actually brought gold to the bank to be exchanged for it. Soon it was being sought so eagerly that by the end of the year it actually stood at a premium of one-tenth above specie.

The pamphleteers were at last silenced, and the *Gazette*, no longer pointing the finger of derision, ate its words and confessed that the bank was growing in favour.

Commerce, which had been languishing, began to derive a stimulus from the liberal assistance which Mr Law supplied. Merchants were encouraged to increase their productivity by advances enabling them to extend their acquisition of raw materials and to increase the number of hands employed. This was the triumph of the gamester who, depending upon the astuteness of his calculations and his ready estimation of a merchant's prospects, was ready to balance the risk of loss in one quarter with the certainty of gain in another.

When at the end of the year he announced a dividend of eight per centum, confidence rose to enthusiasm. The premium on the Bank's paper went higher still, and with a capital of six millions now in gold, Mr Law discovered no inconvenience in increasing to sixty millions his issue of banknotes. With this capital he spread the financing of traders in an ever-widening circle, extending his operations into the provinces, where he set up branches of the bank.

The demonstration of the value of his revolutionary banking system was complete, and he could now laugh at the financiers of the school of Samuel Bernard, who had denounced it as an application of the methods of the gaming table, which if lucky today might well crash tomorrow.

Because the Regent was displaying in the success of the Banque Générale something akin to the pride of a parent, Noailles perceived in it an ever increasing menace to his ambitions. He regarded his presidency of the Council of Finance merely as a stage towards the coveted office of first minister, and if he should be deposed from the former, his chances of the latter would be gravely diminished. So he seized upon the argument of the financiers and used it secretly but diligently to sap the foundations of the bank. He persuaded Rouillé de Coudray and even d'Aguesseau to work with him to the same end.

"Duty and honour alike," was his text, "demand that we put down this foreign adventurer, this gamester who has the effrontery to bring the morals of faro into French banking."

With that same specious argument he was able also to stir the Parliament into hostility of the foreigner.

In the matter of intrigue, however, Mr Law, on his side, did not stand idle. Well aware of how Noailles was working against him, he gave attention to a little countermining.

He began with Dubois, whom he had already bribed with a substantial present of shares in the Bank, and who, in order to frustrate the aims of Noailles which were a menace to his own, was concerned to promote the banker's interests.

The wide mouth of this Richelieu in embryo was stretched in a grin. "Count on me, my dear Baron. With a little patience we shall dispose of Monsieur de Noailles. Meanwhile there are two men who would be glad to lend a hand. The first is d'Argenson, with whom I know that you stand well. To him let your complaint be chiefly of d'Aguesseau, who is Noailles' chief collaborator. Destroy d'Aguesseau and you leave Noailles drained of half his blood; and to destroy d'Aguesseau I know of no one more eager than d'Argenson. The Marquis covets the Chancellorship. So enlist him. Then there is Saint-Simon. He bears Noailles a Satanic malice, and will be glad to lend a hand. We'll think of others. Meanwhile, go to work upon those two."

Mr Law saw d'Argenson that very day and complained of the Chancellor's hostility.

"Ah! d'Aguesseau!" There was scornful laughter in the great voice. "An able man, but he goes in awe of dukes. That is the heel of this Achilles. Noailles does as he pleases with him. Decidedly, my dear Lass, the Regent must be put on his guard against their slanders. That comes within my province as Lieutenant-General."

To make a friend of Saint-Simon, the sometime apostle of bankruptcy, it sufficed to announce that Noailles was proving himself an enemy.

"I confess to you frankly, Monsieur Lass, that I am ignorant of all that concerns finance. After all, it is a confession which a French noble need not blush to make. But I am assured by those who understand these matters that you give proof of uncommon ability with your Bank, and I am sure that you need not allow the jealous hostility of Monsieur de Noailles to trouble you. I shall certainly say so to His Highness."

"Honoured by your support, Monsieur le Duc," Mr Law flattered him, "I may certainly dismiss all uneasiness."

And so when, presently, the Regent issued an edict authorizing the collectors of taxes to receive payment in notes of the Banque Générale, and the Parliament, suddenly mutinous, refused to register it, Dubois, the secret Mentor and confidential agent of the Regent, accounted it his duty to inform his indignant master that Noailles had been the chief promoter of the Parliament's presumption. At the same time it was no less the duty of the Marquis d'Argenson, as the King's Lieutenant-General, regretfully to make known to His Highness that the Chancellor, in rendering himself the catspaw of Monsieur de Noailles in the attempted resistance of the Royal Edict had been guilty of nothing less than a betrayal of his trust. Finally Monsieur de Saint-Simon, his dark face primly set, offered His Highness the opinion that if the Duke of Noailles took a greater interest in finance than became a gentleman, it was clear, at least, that he knew no more about it than a gentleman should.

Each was gratified, and perhaps surprised, that his comments should be received by His Highness without levity. Confirmed in his intentions by the advice of men so trustworthy as these three, the Regent peremptorily ordered the Parliament in the King's name to register the edict without further discussion or delay. Against this haughty insistence it was idle for Noailles and his friends to argue that in such a matter the Parliament should bow only to an order from the Council. The Parliament intimidated by the Regent's firm tone, indeed, shocked now by its own temerity, but deeply resentful of Law, whom it held responsible for the rebuke, supinely yielded.

Well pleased, Mr Law bore the news to his brother, who was now at work in that busy hive of the Rue Quincampoix, and presiding over its activities.

William Law glowed with satisfaction. "I am thinking that is fine. It'll make your work complete."

"Complete?" Mr Law tossed his head in derision. "We've no more than cleared the table for the game I hope to play when I am dealt the cards."

His brother's enthusiasm diminished. He was by nature cautious. "Will we not rest content with what we have? So far all is soundly planned. We've a superb system of credit, so strong that you command a capital of over sixty millions, which cannot but increase. Man, is not that enough for you?"

"God save us, Will, am I just a peddling merchant, scheming to earn a living? Faith, it seems you don't know me yet. What do I care for the money? It's the game that counts. And there was never a game for such stakes as the one you shall see me play."

Will, who had none of the gamester's temperament, considered him soberly. "I think, John, that I should love you even if you were not my brother. Yet I'll not be concealing from you that there are times when I think you're very near detestable."

Chapter 5

EXTREME-UNCTION

The cards for which Mr Law waited were not dealt him until a few months later. But dealt him they were at last, and the deal supplied a climax to the exasperation of Monsieur de Noailles and his friends.

Ever since the days of Richelieu and Colbert, the monopoly of maritime commerce and colonial exploitation had been granted for a term of years to such companies among others as the Compagnie de Chine, the Compagnie du Sénégal, the Compagnie du Canada.

In the autumn of this year 1717 Crozat, who had controlled a company for the exploitation of Louisiana and the Valley of the Mississippi, finding it unprofitable, surrendered the concession.

At once Mr Law perceived the chance to begin to realize his dream. This comprised no less than the ultimate gathering into one establishment under his hand the banking, the administration of the public revenues and the direction of all monopolies, so that the State should become one vast commercial undertaking over which he would preside. It had all been foreshadowed in that system of his which the Council of Finance had rejected.

Already something of a power in the State by virtue of the rapid and phenomenal success of his Bank, accounted a magician in finance and reputed of inexhaustible wealth, he could now afford to ask, without circumlocution, to be accorded the concession relinquished by Crozat.

The Regent began by demurring. "You will not be aware of the sad account of the colony which Crozat renders. He reports it in a state of misery, the colonists idle and incompetent, the troops mere brigands without discipline, and all a prey not only to endemic fevers but to actual famine."

Mr Law had been aware of it all and was not dismayed. "I did not suppose that Monsieur Crozat would abandon a colony that is thriving. If it is not, that merely casts discredit upon his methods. Men should not set their hands to undertakings beyond their strength. I have been at pains to inform myself, and I find the land of Louisiana of an unparalleled fertility, its products of an abundance unknown in the old world, its minerals, including gold and silver, of a richness beyond those of Mexico or Peru.

"Give me the control of this colony, monseigneur, and I will undertake to rid France of all her debts in a very little time. If I promise confidently I may boast that Your Highness has not found me given to vain promises."

He went on to reveal the extent to which the enterprise was already plotted in his mind. The bait he dangled before the eyes of the Regent was again, as when he had won the Regent's sanction for his bank, the prospect of a further amortization of State Bonds; but he employed it now in far bolder measure. To finance the scheme he would require, he announced, a hundred million livres.

"God save us!" ejaculated the Regent.

Composedly, Mr Law explained. He would found a company, issuing two hundred thousand shares of five hundred livres, a price that would bring them within the reach of all. To initiate operations, however, twenty-five millions in cash was all that he would require. For the balance he would accept payment for the shares in State Bonds at their face value, which was practically twice their current worth.

The temptation to transfer depreciated capital at par into so golden an investment should, in itself, ensure the subscription of the shares, and so provide the necessary initial fund of twenty-five millions in cash. It would be for the earnings of the company, in a measure as it expanded under proper management, to produce the balance of the hundred millions represented by the issue.

In the meanwhile the public debt would thus be reduced by one hundred and twenty-five millions. In return for what, by this manipulation, amounted to an advance from the company to the State, the Treasury should pay the company an annual interest of three millions, which would be added to the company's profits for division among the shareholders.

"In short," Mr Law summed up, "the State will be surrendering to its creditors the property and trade of Louisiana in exchange for an additional twenty-five millions from them in cash for the establishment of the colony."

His Highness began by confessing that his senses reeled in their endeavour to comprehend a scheme of such complex and unparalleled audacity. But by the time his keen mind had fitted each of its component pieces into the design he was filled with wonder by its ingenuity and dazzled by its promise.

It was impossible to hesitate. Eager to see the plan at work, eager to gather its rich fruits, and more than ever confirmed in his belief in the genius of Law, the Regent, without even troubling to lay the matter before the Council, granted the concession by an edict in which the company was named the *Compagnie des Indes Occidentales*.

The astuteness of a gesture which had the appearance of an altruistic endeavour to liquidate a part of the public debt was soon revealed in the enthusiastic response from the holders of State Bonds. These, as he had calculated, were ready enough to avail themselves of the heaven-sent chance he offered, and to provide the initial capital that he required.

In the rest of the public, however, the tales of fabulous riches, of inexhaustible mines of gold and silver, of precious stones of enormous size, even of a great rock of emerald, aroused little ardour.

The shares once issued were changing hands at less than half their face value, which was but natural, considering that by the terms on which they had been acquired, this was their actual cost.

Mr Law, however, did not intend this state of things to endure. With a clear perception of those arts, not yet understood, of manipulating markets, he worked diligently through his agents to create those fluctuations in value which are a lure to speculators. By this stimulation of interest, and by the timely invention of options and of that extension of credit known as a carry-over, he was contriving, if but slowly, to improve the value of the stock.

In the meantime he was active in other directions. He had taken over from Crozat the ships employed in the traffic with Louisiana, and he was adding to them so as to possess a fleet equal to the trade which he expected.

Simultaneously the end of that year 1717 provided abundant other matter to engage his energies.

The expansion of his financial position from the ever-increasing prosperity of his Bank and the launching of his company, now popularly known as the Company of the Mississippi, brought with it, as was to be expected, an extension of the jealous hostility of Noailles and his associates.

These included most of the members of the Council of Finance, all of whom felt that the growth of Mr Law's influence and power was diminishing their own.

They had further grounds for this in the lessening of the Regent's former easy-going amenability to their views, as a result of his increased esteem for Mr Law, who had relieved him of so many cares and was always ready now to provide supplies for his outrageous extravagances.

Drastic measures became necessary in the view of Monsieur de Noailles if this insolent foreigner were not to extinguish them completely.

Antagonism at last boiled over when Mr Law, by exposing the iniquity and sheer fruitlessness of the salt tax, known as the *gabelle*, urged its abolition so convincingly that the Regent was persuaded to carry this proposal to the Council.

Respect for the Regent's royal blood scarcely sufficed to prevent the indignation from exploding into uproar, and even if subdued, it was, nevertheless, so bitter that His Highness, shirking strife, did not insist. Instead, he retained the Duke of Noailles when the Council broke up.

"My dear Duke, I did not press the matter further today," he said, "because, to be frank, I do not feel myself able to do justice to the arguments in favour of this abolition."

"The arguments of Monsieur Lass, I presume."

His Highness refused to perceive the sneer. "I was about to say so, and to add that it is my wish that you should hear them from Monsieur Lass himself."

Noailles was all frosty dignity. "If you bring an advocate, monseigneur, permit me also to bring one, a man who will be equal to meeting the arguments of Monsieur Lass."

His Highness was more than usually gracious. If Monsieur de Noailles would offer him supper tomorrow night at La Roquette, he would bring Monsieur Lass, and they could discuss this matter amiably at table.

To that supper party at the Duke of Noailles' mansion of La Roquette his Grace invited not only the Chancellor, which was what the Regent had expected, but also Rouillé du Coudray.

It was not until the end of supper, of a quality to satisfy even the fastidious Regent, with a wine of Cyprus to mellow their moods, that His Highness begged them to hear the reasons of Monsieur Lass for the abolition of the *gabelle*.

The Scot was taking a moment to choose his words when, at an imperious glance from Noailles, the Chancellor smoothly interposed.

"They must be weighty reasons, indeed, that would induce the King to forgo so profitable a source of revenue."

Mr Law's reply was prompt. "If the tax were that, I should not advocate its abolition." He turned to the Duke. "As head of the Council of Finance, your Grace will know what was the yield of the tax in the last year."

"*Mon Dieu*, Monsieur Lass, can you suppose that I carry such figures in my memory?"

Mr Law met this contempt with a polite smile. "In that case I have the advantage of you, Monsieur le Duc; perhaps an unfair advantage; for I carry them in mine. In the last year the *gabelle* yielded to the Treasury the paltry sum of twenty thousand livres."

"That is absurd," shouted du Coudray.

"Worse," said Mr Law. "It is ludicrous. Not even a thousand louis."

"You misunderstand me intentionally," Coudray resented.

"Of course," Noailles agreed. His handsome dark face was suddenly flushed. "You are not to suppose, Monsieur Lass, that we can accept your figures."

The Regent languidly interposed. He had thrust back his chair, and sat with an elbow on one of its arms, a hand held before his face as a screen to the glare of candlelight reflected on the polished table as in a brown pool.

One of his eyes had recently been damaged, by a blow, according to some, from a tennis racquet, according to others from the fan of Madame de la Rochefoucault, with whom he had made too free. Despite his doctors' efforts – or perhaps because of them – it continued inflamed, and his sight was impaired.

"If you say, my dear Noailles, that you do not carry the figures in your mind it does not seem to me that you are in case to reject those of Monsieur Lass. Actually I have, myself, examined them, and I am able to tell you that they are entirely correct."

Noailles sat back, biting his lip, momentarily baffled. D'Aguesseau, smooth and ready, came to his aid. "That sum, as Monsieur Lass has said, is ludicrous. But far from being an argument for abolishing the tax, it seems to me to be a reason for prosecuting its collection more vigorously, so that it becomes again the profitable source of revenue which it certainly should be."

"Of course," Noailles impatiently supported him.

"It is the only answer," said Coudray.

Mr Law looked from one to another of them. Slowly he shook his head. "A labour of Sisyphus. It is beyond accomplishment."

D'Aguesseau and Noailles spoke together, in a burst of indignation. "Beyond accomplishment!" to which du Coudray added his jarring laugh.

"Give me leave, sirs," said Mr Law. "I have still some figures for you. There are – the number almost defies belief, being the equivalent of a couple of armies – no fewer than eighty thousand men employed by the State in the collection of the *gabelle*." He gave them time to gasp their amazement and then went on: "These *gabeleurs*, these wretched Jacks-in-Office, are proving ruthless in the execution of their odious tasks; they do not hesitate, I am informed, at any horror when through the penury of the people they encounter difficulties in collecting moneys which have little purpose beyond providing their own emoluments."

"Monsieur Lass," cried Noailles, "you are permitting yourself to defame officials of the French Government."

The Regent interposed with a laugh so as to dispel what might be the elements of a storm. "Let me protect my good Monsieur Lass before you disembowel him with your irrelevancies. For myself, I hope I shall never regard honest criticism as ill-mannered."

"Your Highness' indulgence is notorious." Noailles' sarcasm was so manifest that it had a sobering effect upon the Regent.

"You should be thankful, Monsieur le Duc," he said, with a sudden hardening of his tone which served to recall Noailles to his duty.

It was left for Mr Law to attempt to soothe these ruffled spirits. "Let me confess to having said perhaps more than is becoming. It is the more unpardonable because unnecessary. It is only a bad case that needs to be urged intemperately. To return to it, we should remember that whilst the *gabelle* exists in most of the French provinces, it does not exist in all. This serves to aggravate the grievance felt by those who are the subjects of it."

Noailles was again impatient. "That is merely frivolous. To be aggrieved is the normal state of the taxpayer."

"That," said Law composedly, "is a reason for avoiding a tax that is not only unjust, but so futile that the tax-gatherers are the only ones to profit by it. You have, as I have said, eighty thousand of these. Eighty thousand, living by extortion upon their fellow-countrymen. Eighty thousand unproductive souls, who if driven, instead, to become productive by honest work, as artisans, craftsmen, mariners, agriculturists and the like, must contribute to the wealth of the State instead of merely preying upon it."

It was a long moment before any of his three opponents, taken aback as they were by so novel a point of view, could find an answer.

Then, at last, d'Aguesseau addressed himself to the Regent. "Admitting, Highness, that there may be some force in what Monsieur Lass has said, the remedy would seem to lie, as I have already pointed out, in more vigorous measures to collect the tax."

The Regent's sidelong glance invited Mr Law to answer.

"My remedy is simpler and more remunerative. Of all commodities there is none in such universal use as salt. Since it is something that every man must have, it should be one of the most productive sources of revenue instead of a mere waste as at present. Let the King buy up the salt pans, equitably compensating the owners, and render salt a free, taxless commodity of which each may purchase what he will. These purchases would very soon produce the cost of the salt pans, after which there should be a substantial revenue. That is the remedy I suggest."

The Regent, pink-faced, benign, sat back, still shielding his eyes with his hand, and watched them with amused interest.

Slowly the Chancellor shook his head, his face grave, his tone quietly courteous. "Such a proposal could come only from one who is a stranger to our country. There is in France no law under which we can expropriate a man's possessions."

"It would not be impossible to make one," ventured His Highness blandly.

"Not impossible," d'Aguesseau agreed. "But, with submission, Highness, not easy. Too many principles would have to be jettisoned. The Parliament would be in its duty in resisting the registration of such a law."

"But if it is to benefit the State?"

"The Parliament may well hold that such benefit is outweighed by the dangerous precedent that would be established."

Noailles, still flushed, his voice shaking with annoyance, impatiently broke in. "So much for the legal aspect of the matter. But there is a graver side. The proposal amounts to this, that the King is to deal in salt. He is to become a tradesman. Is that the Baron's conception of royal dignity in France?"

Du Coudray was no less uncompromising.

"It is evident that whatever may be possible in England or in Scotland, Monsieur Lass is not aware that in France a simple nobleman may not, without derogating, do that which he proposes that the King should do."

Noailles came back to turn the knife in the wound. "As you say, Coudray, he does not understand. So we may at least acquit him of intentional offensiveness."

"Messieurs, messieurs!" The Regent removed his hand from his eyes to wave it in protest. "Here are too many words. Far too many. I think you forget, Noailles, that Monsieur Lass is your guest."

"I fear," said the Duke with an instant assumption of contrition, "that I have again been guilty of allowing my respect for the crown to carry me too far."

Mr Law, quite at his ease, permitted himself a laugh. "If that is an apology, Monsieur le Duc, I accept it freely." And whilst Noailles was inwardly writhing at the covert mockery, he went on: "You have no cause, Monsieur le Duc, nor you, Monsieur du Coudray, to visit your heat upon me. The profitable solution which I perceive to this matter of the *gabelle* had so far commended itself to His Highness that it is by his wish that I have explained it to you."

"Just so," said the Regent. "Just so. And the strictures you have passed become my affair, since mine is the responsibility. In the interpretation that it is proposed to make a tradesman of the King, I perceive some ingenuity, but nothing else. A displaced ingenuity. Almost, I might say, a disingenuous ingenuity."

His pleasant laugh took some of the sting out of his words. But enough remained to place Monsieur de Noailles under the necessity of defending himself. "Yet to me, monseigneur, it remains a fact and a matter for indignation."

"Let it so remain then. I am not to instruct you. Perhaps because my blood is royal it does not feel the need to boil so readily. What troubles me is the Chancellor's view of the legal aspect of the measure. I suppose, Monsieur d'Aguesseau, that you would account it the duty of your office to put that view to the Parliament."

"I fear so, monseigneur."

"At need, in fact, you would have to insist that the Parliament adopt it."

"Honestly holding it, myself, monseigneur, that would be my painful duty."

The Regent sighed, and rose from the table. "*Eh bien!* We must endeavour to avoid placing you under the necessity of performing a duty you find so painful." The Chancellor, suspecting ambiguity, looked up quickly, to meet only a bland smile. "I think we perfectly understand each other."

In the coach, as he drove away from La Roquette, with Mr Law, His Highness laughed softly. "I certainly think we perfectly understand each other, Monsieur d'Aguesseau and I. It is the bad faith of their arguments that has decided me, and I should think that they will be perceiving for themselves that what they have received from me is their extreme unction."

Chapter 6

THE COUNT OF HORN

If Mr Law had any doubt of what the Regent meant by extreme unction, that doubt was resolved before the week was out.

To the Chancellor His Highness sent on the morrow the Duke of La Vrillière, to demand of him his seals. D'Aguesseau, startled by this abrupt dismissal from office, begged to be allowed to see the Regent. But La Vrillière had his instructions.

"I am required to assure you that it could serve no purpose. His Highness relieves you of an office the duties of which, you have indicated, might in certain circumstances become painful. It is important that the seals be held by one who in any conflict with the Parliament will account himself the representative of His Highness. He also suggests to you that you withdraw from Paris to your estate at Fresnes."

Perceiving in this exile time extent of his disgrace, d'Aguesseau attempted no further argument.

All that it remained for him to do before departing was to send word to Noailles of what was happening as a result of the intrigues of the abominable Monsieur Lass, thus putting the Duke in the way of receiving also his *viaticum*.

Noailles not unnaturally went off at once to the Palais Royal.

However his Grace might have intended to broach the matter, he found his cue when he beheld the Chancellor's seals on the Regent's writing table.

He affected surprise. "Will Your Highness permit me to ask if this means that d'Aguesseau has resigned his office?"

"At my request," was the gentle answer. "It grieved me, but it would grieve me still more to have him troubled, as he told us that he must be, by his conception of duty. So as to spare the poor gentleman I have required his seals."

"Your Highness, no doubt, will already have chosen his successor."

"Monsieur Lass has suggested that d'Argenson would be an excellent Chancellor; indeed, just the man to handle the Parliament if it should again show itself mutinous. Don't you agree, Noailles?"

It was beyond the Duke's histrionics to dissemble his annoyance. By that question in an artless tone, it seemed to him that he was mocked. He flushed as he answered: "I am so far from agreeing, and so aware of what is taking place, that I beg your Highness' leave to resign my commission of the Finances."

The Regent thrust out a lip in polite regret, smiling at the same time, so as to mark its insincerity. "As you please, my dear Duke."

From red that he had been, Noailles turned white in mortified astonishment. He stood a moment undecided. Then, not trusting himself to make any answer, he abruptly bowed. "I take my leave, monseigneur."

"Do you ask for nothing?"

"For nothing, monseigneur."

"Ah!" The Regent sighed. "I have reserved a place for you on the Council of Regency."

"I shall make little use of it."

The Regent, however, refused to be offended by this insolence. "As you please," he said. "You have my leave."

Noailles went off to pour his rage into the ears of all who esteemed him or who would listen. The sum of his grievance was that France, governed by a cabal, was permitting her finances to fall more and more under the control of a foreign adventurer, a gamester who had been turned out of every country in Europe. Under the indolent regency of Philippe of Orléans, France was heading for irreparable disaster.

All this coming from a man hitherto regarded as one of the chief supporters of the Regent, could not fail to make its impression. The Parliament was peculiarly stirred to resentment by the manner in which the case was presented to it by Noailles, by some of his friends, and by the vindictive Duchess of Maine, acting through Pompadour, Malézieu and other of her devoted agents.

But whilst a powerful party of nobles and place-seekers hostile to Law was coming into existence, Mr Law, warned by Dubois, who kept his ear to the ground, was creating a party of supporters just as high-placed. Admitted freely now to Court, and moving there with the ease of one in the exercise of an imprescriptible right, his handsome person, and courtly manners won him friends on every hand.

In addition, his friendship was already proving profitable. For the singular foresight of his calculating mind had obtained a decree by which members of the nobility, debarred by their ranks from sullying themselves by participation in trading concerns, were permitted without derogation to acquire stock in the Mississippi Company. And his manipulations of that stock, with a view to bringing its value steadily upwards until it should arrive at par, gave many opportunities for quick profits, in the indication of which he was extremely generous.

Then there were such other monopolies in existence as the China Company, the East India Company, the Company of Sénégal, none of which was prospering, and upon all of which Mr Law had an eye, counting upon being able presently to bring them under his control. So he, too, rallied his friends and supporters among whom were the Duc d'Antin, the Prince de Conti, the Duc de Bourbon, the Duc de la Force, and, oddly enough, considering the man's intimate relations with Noailles, the Count of Horn.

Horn, as it chanced, was at the moment deeply indebted to Mr Law. He had lately sought his advice, which was but a way of seeking his assistance. He had, he said, unexpectedly received an important sum of money which he desired to place, and he would be grateful for the guidance of Monsieur Lass in such a matter.

Mr Law was moved by no particular affection for this handsome, dissipated idler, a younger brother of the Prince of Horn, and related to half the princely houses of Europe, which had not prevented his dismissal in disgrace from the Austrian Army. It was reported that recently, whilst in England, he had married a lady of great wealth, who, however, had not accompanied him to France, and Mr Law assumed that this might account for the possession of that sum of money which Horn described as considerable.

It did not favourably impress him that despite this sudden affluence, there should be no mention by the Count of that old debt of five thousand louis which long ago he had lost at faro to Mr Law and for which the Scot still held his note of hand.

Nevertheless, pursuing his policy of making friends in high places and considering the great connections of this young libertine, Mr Law was prepared to guide him. He had lately been looking into the affairs of the Compagnie de Gambie, another of the colonial monopolies, and he had found them in such desperate case that the owners of the stock would be glad to dispose of it for a tenth of its face value. He had decided that eventually he would assume control of it and add it to his other undertakings.

He advised a purchase of this stock to Horn. "Buy all you can of it, proceeding discreetly. It should make you a fortune."

The Count accepted the advice, and as if his regard for Law were increased by gratitude, he became more assiduous than ever as a visitor in the Rue de Grenelle.

Catherine Law, sharing, as was natural, the social eminence to which her husband was attaining, had become in those days less querulous, mellowing under the flattering attentions of the distinguished company that came to pay its court to the financial wizard whom the Regent delighted to honour.

Not that she chose to acknowledge in this anything for which to thank a husband who gave her no other cause for gratitude. She had ways – and they were none too subtle – of conveying to him that she had merely come to occupy the position that was rightly her due and to which ultimately she must inevitably have arrived by the right of her own qualities.

It was a point of view which he, wrapped in his cold aloofness, never attempted to dispel. Holding it, she accounted it her duty to entertain with splendour, and set herself to convert the mansion in the Rue de Grenelle into a Mecca of the *beau monde*.

One of the many parties that she gave, and this at her husband's own suggestion, was to celebrate the Marquis d'Argenson's appointment to the Chancellorship, an elevation for which the Marquis did not conceal that he was indebted to the arts exercised by Mr Law in connection with the salt tax.

The guests – a score or so – were brought together from different quarters of life's higher levels. Diplomacy was represented by Lord and Lady Stair; the Regent's circle by the Marquis of Canillac and the Count of Horn; the blood-royal by that malicious young hunchback the Prince de Conti, and the robe by d'Argenson himself.

Then there were such prominent men as the gay Duc d'Antin, who as Madame de Montespan's one legitimate child, accounted himself superior to his adulterine half-brothers who had the King for father, and there was Hector de La Grange, the banker, a man of fine presence, engaging manner and great wealth, who was everywhere received.

Over a princely entertainment Mr Law presided with that suave charm of which he was master. It may be doubted if his table could be matched in any house in Paris. Its plate of gold and silver and choice ceramics, like the exquisite Murano glass, were appointments which had come with him from Savoy, together with his Bolognese cook, his cellarer, and his impeccable maître d'hôtel.

Darkly handsome and unostentatiously elegant from the curls of his brown wig to the red heels of his shoes, he was seated at that gleaming board between the angular haughtiness of the Countess of

Stair and the warm loveliness of Madame de Sabran, neither of whom, as it happened, was paying much heed to him.

Lady Stair was concerned with the observation of her husband, who placed between Catherine Law and the beautiful Madame Raymond, was neglecting his hostess in his over-assiduous attention to his other neighbour. Madame Raymond might contrive to preserve the diffident airs of a vestal; but Lady Stair was more impressed by her too-revealing décolletage, which also appeared to hold the hooded eyes of the ambassador. Her ladyship's lips grew pinched as she watched.

Catherine Law might have resented the neglect of his lordship, usually so effusive to her, had she been less deeply engaged on her other side by Horn. Under his provocation, laughter rippled from her in a continuous, if subdued, stream, and so engrossed were they in their own mirth that they had no ear for d'Argenson, who was being cruelly witty on the score of the misfortunes that were overtaking the financier Simon Bernard.

It was d'Argenson's way to discover amusement in most things, since rare in his view were the things that escaped the imprint of human folly. In Simon Bernard he now perceived that most diverting of spectacles, a man hoist with his own petard. Because the financier had feared for his interests, he had led the opposition of his compeers to Law's system when it was before the Council. As a result the Council had been thrown back on its other expedients for raising money, and of these the chief was the squeezing of the tax farmers.

D'Argenson likened them to grapes in the press, left with only their skins. Bernard, a master of corruption, had run round in panic from one to another of the Regent's intimates, offering millions to any who would employ his influence to the end that proceedings against him should be abandoned.

"Evidently," said d'Argenson with relish, "the Hebrew knight failed to find a friend at Court. For he's a ruined man today, and actually in fear for his life."

"If he did not find a friend at Court," said La Grange, "he certainly found an *escroc*, to pose as a friend and accept a million for services that were never rendered."

This riveted attention upon the banker; for in what he said there was the hint of a story spiced with scandal. Even Horn ceased to be merry for Catherine's delight.

"How do you come to know that?" asked d'Argenson.

"From Bernard himself. The unhappy man came to solicit my assistance and had the impudence to offer me a bribe. He complained bitterly that a nobleman, one of the Regent's roués had accepted a million from him and had not lifted a finger to help him."

"A nobleman, did you say?" croaked the Prince de Conti.

"So Bernard described him."

"An ignoble man," said Mr Law, "would describe him better."

"One of the Regent's roués, you said," cried Canillac, who was himself a member of that happy band. "I hope he named him."

"The odd thing is that he did not. Nor did I press him. But he did let fall that the scoundrel is a count."

"A count!" cried de Conti. "Faith, Horn, there are not so many of you that you should let it lie there. It brings you all under suspicion."

"Under suspicion of what?" Horn was contemptuous. "If what this Jew says is true, he was well served for his impudence in attempting to bribe a gentleman. But probably it is all a lie."

"Bernard may be a thief, but he's not a liar," said d'Argenson. "Nor can I agree with you, Monsieur de Horn, that his impudence in offering a bribe would excuse a gentleman for robbing him."

"Let us be content to disagree then, Marquis," was the easy answer, which put an end to the topic and left the flow of conversation to become general again.

Mr Law was remembering the tale of a considerable sum of money for the placing of which the Count of Horn had sought his advice, and all things considered he was wondering might he not have been mistaken in assuming that the money came from England and the wealthy Countess, and whether Horn, who had never troubled to discharge to him a debt of honour of five thousand louis, might not be the Count accused by Bernard of having practised this swindle.

He was haled out of his thoughts by Lady Stair's voice, charged with acid, murmuring in his ear: "Your wife and my husband, Mr Law, are manifestly in the mode which makes the wives of other men and the husbands of other women more attractive."

"Has it still the power to surprise your ladyship?"

"And to disgust me. But perhaps I am plebeian in my views."

"If it is plebeian to be virtuous. I do not know."

She turned her head so as to look him fully in the face, and he found himself pitying her for her unattractiveness. Close-set eyes in which there was no sparkle flanked a lean high-bridged nose; patches on chin and cheekbone dissembled in each case a wart; her mouth was coarsely shaped and her chin receded. She resembled he thought, nothing so much as a hen. But she was dressed with care and taste. Diamonds gleamed on the dull flesh of her bosom.

"You do not know?" she echoed. "Does that mean that you do not care? If so, you are oddly changed since you left England."

"It means, my lady, that I discover no reason for caring."

"Do you not?" She turned her head again, and looked straight down the table at Catherine and Horn, who again were engrossed in their mirth, their heads almost touching. "Do you not?" she repeated. "You amaze me."

What she suggested was as clear to him as her own meanly, malicious nature, embittered by her husband's promiscuous gallantries, and taking satisfaction in uncovering the weaknesses of others. And yet it was impossible to deny that there was some justification for her hints. That the relations between Catherine and Horn were innocent enough he could not doubt, just as he could not suppose that they would remain so if Horn pursued his usual courses. He recalled how, at one of the Regent's supper parties, when first he had met Horn, and when oral licence knew no bounds, the young Count had boasted in nauseating detail of his *bonnes fortunes*.

Lady Stair was again commanding his attention. "For myself I could dare to give a name to the count who accepted Bernard's bribe. I know of only one man of that rank capable of such a meanness."

"You leave me to guess why you should be so sure."

Her lips tightened in a sour smile. "All the world knows that he is hard-driven by necessity. A gamester, and an unlucky gamester, he is crushed by debt. Such men are always ripe for bribery."

As it was the Stairs who had first brought the Count of Horn to his house, Mr Law found this peculiarly distasteful.

"Your ladyship is singularly well-informed."

"Not singularly. It happens that the gentleman in his fortune-hunting has married into my family – oh, a distant kinswoman of whom I have no cause to be proud, yet whom I can pity, poor deluded soul. He dazzled her, I suppose, with his good looks and high connections. Anyway, she married him a year ago in England." Her tinkling laugh was charged with malice. "He conceived her a wealthy woman, as, indeed, she is; but her wealth is so cunningly tied up by entails and the like that he cannot come by a shilling of it save by her consent. So that of those two she is not by now the only disillusioned one." Again there was that faint ripple of cruel laughter.

"Poetic justice," said Mr Law. "And she remains in England?"

"She has certainly shown no eagerness to join him. But she is in Paris now. She arrived some days ago. But I doubt if she will pay his debts for him. And I am told that he owes money everywhere. I believe that you, too, are one of his victims, Mr Law."

"Oh, an insignificance."

She raised her brows and stared at him. "I heard it put at five thousand louis. A hundred and fifty thousand livres. Do you call that an insignificance, Mr Law? La! I wonder by what yardstick you measure wealth."

Mr Law laughed. "I do not trouble to measure it. My business is to create it."

"Like the alchemists."

"More successfully, I dare assert."

"You'll need the success if you allow such men to owe you such sums. In your place I should compel him to disgorge whilst he still has something left of Bernard's million. Perhaps you find me vindictive. I am when I think of my kinswoman. My hope for her is that she may leave him and return to England since he no longer possesses a roof under which to shelter her. He has been living near St Philippe du Roule in the lodgings of a certain Colonel de Mille, a soldier of fortune, a man of his own kind, who was with him in the Austrian service, and turned out of it at the same time."

Mr Law was growing weary of her scandal-mongering. "Ah, well, he should be able to find a roof of his own now. I have advised him a purchase which should yield him a fortune before the year is out."

But the lady's venom was not yet exhausted. "And he repays you by making love to your wife. It is what I should expect of him."

"Let me assure your ladyship that he wastes his time."

"It is for you to make sure of that," she said, and at last gave attention to her other neighbour, leaving him free to devote himself to Madame de Sabran, who was warmly genial to all men.

Later, when they had risen from table and passed into the salon, the Count of Horn came urging Mr Law to make a faro bank. Considering what Mr Law had just learnt the moment was ill-chosen. He shook his head. They were standing apart from the others.

"There are," he said, "two excellent reasons why I should not: I do not care to make a bank in my own house, and it is my practice never to play with a debtor."

Horn, taken aback, flushed before he answered with a laugh: "That is to deny a man his revenge."

"Oh, no. From me any loser may have all the revenge he pleases. But not until he has paid his last losses. There is a bagatelle of five thousand louis for which I hold your paper, Count."

"And you are pressing me for payment?"

Law suspected the impertinence of a sneer.

"By no means. Take all the time you need."

"You should know that every louis I possess is in the Compagnie de Gambie."

"How much have you contrived to buy?"

"All that I could pay for. Some seven thousand shares at about one hundred livres."

"Take them to my bank, hypothecate them for half their cost, and with the proceeds make a further purchase."

"If one could be quite sure…"

"I think you may be. But be discreet, or we shall have the price rising prematurely."

"Depend upon me. And now, this faro bank?" D'Argenson and La Grange were approaching. He appealed to them. "Come and persuade the Baron to give us a deal at faro."

"You would waste your breath," Mr Law assured them. "It is too distasteful to me to win money from my guests."

"Must it be forgone?" La Grange asked him.

"Not forgone. But it might happen, and I dare not have it happen under the eyes of Monsieur d'Argenson."

"Will you always rally me for what is past?" grumbled d'Argenson. "The fact is that I actually acted as your advocate with the King. I protested to him that having had you watched I was convinced that your play was as scrupulously fair as your luck was uncanny."

"Your agents did not watch me closely enough."

"Eh?" D'Argenson was startled.

"Otherwise they would not have attributed all to luck. They would have perceived that mere luck could never be so consistent. No, no. I am never tired of announcing that I win by avoiding the errors by which men lose."

"Do you never suspect, Baron," asked La Grange, "that that is something which your good fortune has deceived you into believing."

"Let me show you a thing," said Mr Law. "It is a crude, simple, elementary thing, perhaps, but it will serve to demonstrate calculation's part in gaming. In all your experience as Lieutenant-General, Marquis, have you ever known a punter win at lottery dice?"

"I'll not pretend to have taken much interest in the game. So that I can't answer you."

"Then you'll never have observed that the high prizes that tempt the punters are on numbers so improbable as to be almost impossible, whilst on the probable ones the prizes amount to a mere return of the stakes."

"I don't understand," said d'Argenson, "how it can be said of any numbers that they are probable."

"If the casts are honest," added La Grange, "one number is as likely to be thrown as another."

"So they say who lose their money."

From the drawer of a lacquered cabinet he took a dice box, and moved to a card table, about which his guests came clustering.

"Here are seven dice: the number used in these lotteries. With these any number may be thrown from seven to forty-two. Let me make a cast with them."

He rolled them from the box, and when they had come to a standstill the dots added up to a total of twenty-three. "Imagine that to be the main, and accept it, or any of the three numbers immediately following, as constituting a nick. My wager is that I will throw one of those four numbers out of the forty-two that may be thrown."

"If you are really serious," said Horn, "I will lay you a thousand louis to a hundred against it."

Mr Law shook his head. "Afterwards I should be accused of robbing you."

Lord Stair interposed. "Let others share the risk with the Count. I'll gladly bear a part of the wager."

"As I will," said d'Antin.

Still Mr Law refused. "Afterwards, if you still wish it. But for this first cast I'll accept no more than a wager of ten louis to a louis from the Count of Horn."

On the word he rolled the dice from the box. When they had settled it was d'Argenson who called the score in a voice of stupefaction. It was again twenty-three.

"Twenty-three !" echoed Horn. "*Mordieu*, that was a near escape."
His laugh was strained as he lugged out his purse. "Faith, it was
worth ten louis to see you do it."

"If the dice are honest," said d'Argenson, "you deal in magic. How
else could you make them roll as you bid them?"

"Only the magic that lies in numbers for those that understand
them. With seven dice the number of possible combinations is in the
region of no less than forty thousand. But there are only seven
chances of throwing seven and the same number of chances of
throwing forty-two; that is to say, there are only seven combinations
out of forty thousand that will give either of those numbers. But
there are some twenty thousand combinations that will add up to
any of the four numbers I have chosen. In that simple fact lies the
deception. The odds, low at the extreme numbers, increase steadily
in favour of the caster in a measure as you approach the mean
ones."

He took up Horn's ten louis. "If now you care to wager your
thousand louis against my hundred, I shall be happy to oblige
you."

The Count shook his head, and laughed. "Faith, I should thank
you for having made the lesson so cheap."

"I wonder have you really learnt it. If so you will realize that the
principle is always the same, no matter what the number of dice
employed. If remembered at hazard, a quick calculation of the odds
of any throw will make fortune your servant in the long run,
however, at moments she may fail you."

D'Argenson wagged his big head. "I begin to think that the old
King was right. You know too much about these things."

Chapter 7

WARNINGS

Throughout that spring, the affairs of his Bank were expanding in every direction and the Mississippi Company gradually increasing in credit. If the shares were still well below their face value of five hundred livres, this was no more than natural, considering the temptingly reduced terms on which they had been issued.

Mr Law moved without haste now that he felt assured of ultimately prevailing, and he devoted a deal of attention to tightening relations with the Regent. In this he encountered no difficulty. He was encouraged more cordially than ever to frequent the Palais Royal, and was always received there by His Highness with easy affability.

Sometimes he renewed acquaintance with the Regent's laboratory, and discovered how wide was that versatile prince's knowledge of chemistry and medicine. Sometimes he was entertained in the tennis court. His prowess there was such that the Regent, who delighted in the game but was an indifferent performer, would match him against Biron or Canillac or another of his best players and watch with interest the Scot's display of mastery. At another time it would be in the *salle d'armes* that Mr Law would be required to exhibit a skill in swordsmanship that took full advantage of his height and uncommon reach.

On one occasion he was again admitted to that inner circle of intimates with whom the Regent made up those supper parties of which the fame, distorted by calumny into infamy, was being bruited through the land. Here His Highness set aside the last remnant of his royalty, to become the boon companion of guests whose motley quality was a surprise to Mr Law and diminished his pride in being among them.

Biron and Canillac were of these, as well as the Duke of Brancas and three or four others of those whom the Regent described as his *roués*, and who gloried in the description, besides less regular guests such as the Count of Horn and the actor Bouldac.

To the ladies of the great world, including Madame de Parabère, the Regent's present *maîtresse-en-titre*, appropriately named, it was said, Marie-Magdalène, Madame de Sabran, who had formerly held that exalted office, Madame de Phalaris, who was presently to succeed to it, and – amazingly to Mr Law – the Regent's own daughter, the Duchess of Berri, were added a couple of opera-girls, whose conduct, scandalously loose, was almost a pattern of decorum to their nobler sisters.

Servants were excluded, so as to abolish all restraint. If in one sense this was desirable enough, in another it left speculation of what occurred behind those closed doors to paint a picture far more scabrous than any that reality could have presented. Yet the reality in the eyes of Mr Law, who was not squeamish, was scabrous enough.

The abundant, rich and varied cold buffet, which the servants spread before departing, was supplemented by hot dishes cooked upon the spot by means of spirit stoves and kitchen batteries entirely of silver. Here, whilst Madame de Sabran fried exquisite little Italian sausages in one pan, Madame de Parabère made an *omelette royale* in another, with cocks' combs and carps' roes, and explained to the astonished Mr Law that the secret of its excellence lay in an extravagance of butter.

At table all ate to excess, following the example of the Regent, whose peculiar notion of gastronomic hygiene was to make this his only square meal of the day, his dinner consisting of no more than a cup of chocolate.

They drank to an excess even greater, and in a measure as the wine flowed, the talk loosened. Witty at first and ranging indifferently over a variety of topics, it would quickly become ribald, and then, more limited in subject, licentious and even *grivois*. And in a measure as the wit faltered the laughter grew, and in lack of restraint the pretty young Duchess of Berri was without a rival in that abandoned company.

By four o'clock in the morning, the Regent in his armchair amiably somnolent, leered upon a drunken company and at last announced that it was time for bed.

Mr Law, almost the only one to walk without a stagger, and thereby increasing the Regent's regard for him, courteously declined the further proffered hospitality coyly pressed upon him by one of the opera-girls, and came out into the chilly dawn by the little side door that opened upon the Rue de Richelieu. He awoke his chairmen who waited there, and had himself carried home, reflecting that a wise man should sup as rarely as possible with princes.

It resulted from his having been presented to the gay Duchess of Berri in such intimate surroundings that he received a few days later an invitation for himself and Catherine to a ball at her Grace's Palace of the Luxembourg, where she assembled the very flower of the Court.

There, at some time after midnight, the Regent with the imposingly lovely Madame de Parabère on his arm, sauntering through the succession of splendid scented antechambers, all gaily lighted and gaily peopled, came upon his daughter punting at a faro table under the guidance of Mr Law. The tall, dark Scot, resplendent in gold brocade, white stockings and red-heeled shoes with glittering buckles, leaned over her Grace's chair, directing her play.

The dealer was the elderly Marquis de Dangeau, a player of skill, who had the repute of enjoying the favour of Fortune. Tonight, however, it appeared that neither skill nor luck availed him against the Duchess and the famous martingale of Mr Law, by which her punting was governed. Gold and notes flowed in a steady stream across the table, to swell the pile that rose before her Grace.

The Regent paused, a hand familiarly on Law's shoulder. "In the intervals of mending my fortune I find you engaged in making my daughter's. I would I had more friends as devoted to my family."

"Your Highness suffers from no lack of friends," said Mr Law.

"But they – alas! – suffer from a lack of your Midas' touch."

"Is that so enviable? King Midas found it a curse."

"He lived in other times. Today, though I hate to confess it, there is nothing that gold will not do for you."

"I cannot boast that I have found it so," said Mr Law.

"He is lugubrious," said the Duchess. "Like a victim of unrequited love."

The Regent pinched her cheek. "You assume too much, Jouflotte. But I interrupt. Continue to strip the Marquis naked."

"Fie! He is no longer of an age to bear the exposure."

The Regent laughed, and sauntered on with Madame de Parabère, and very soon thereafter Dangeau got up to announce that he had had enough, and that whoever cared for it might take his place.

The Duchess waited for no more. She rose, ordered an elegant stripling who attended her, discharging the functions of an equerry, to collect her winnings, and commanded Mr Law's escort to the ballroom.

Side by side the tall Scot and the gay, plump little Duchess, who was a blaze of diamonds upon shimmering white, passed from room to room through the dense courtier throng, and so came to the threshold of the ballroom, whence fiddles, flutes and hautbois were giving forth the strains of a minuet. Here, in a space which deference for him had made, stood the Regent with Madame de Parabère, observing the scene.

In the middle of the great ballroom a square had been cleared and was maintained by four lackeys, one at each corner, serving as posts for a heavy rope of scarlet silk which offered a barrier to the glittering throng. Within that square a half-score of couples were treading the measure.

"We are too late," said the Duchess. "It was my hope, Baron, to step it with you, in token of my gratitude."

"And in defiance of your rank?"

"Oh, as to that, I can sometimes be my father's daughter."

The Regent spoke over his shoulder. "Too often, alas! For I am hardly the model father. But is it possible that you have denied Dangeau his revenge?"

"He owned defeat, and fled the field. As for me, as a gambler I am ruined; for I vow that I shall never again dare to sit down to faro unless Monsieur Lass is beside me."

But the Regent was no longer listening. Madame de Parabère had claimed his attention for an approaching couple. The man richly dressed in black was short, elderly and wizened, his sallow face deeply lined. Short as he was, yet he was under the necessity of stooping so as to catch the words of his companion whom from her stature you might suppose a child had not her face corrected the impression, a sharp, petulant face with a pointed chin and dark, staring eyes. They were the Prince of Cellamare, the Spanish ambassador, and the Duchess of Maine; and the sight of them in such intimate conversation awakened memories in Mr Law of what the Earl of Stair had told him. It appeared to have a similar effect upon Madame de Parabère, for she was murmuring to the Regent: "You see?" adding almost indignantly the question, "How does she dare to be here?"

The couple in their passage had come close, and the little golden-haired woman's fierce expression changed abruptly, as she caught sight of them and found herself observed. She broke off in her speech to Cellamare, and paused to drop a curtsy to the Regent, who, smiling, acknowledged it by an inclination of the head and a lift of the hand. As she passed on with her escort, he answered Madame de Parabère's question.

"Faith, is my daughter to close her doors to my brother-in-law's wife?"

"When she permits herself to threaten you."

"Shall I take account of the outbursts of a lady in a temper?" He spoke with his easy tolerance. "If I were to deal vindictively with all those who inveigh against me, I could fill the Bastille from the attendance here tonight."

"I thank you, sir, for your opinion of my guests," said his daughter.

"It is that he must make light of everything," Madame de Parabère complained. "Will you tell me, Philippe, what that little dwarf has to do with the ambassador of Spain that she should be so close and intimate with him?"

"Fie, madame! What are you suggesting? Monsieur de Cellamare may no longer be as young as Madame du Maine's friends might wish. Still, if she displays a taste for the antique, who are we to sit in judgment."

Madame de Parabère became prim. "That is not amusing. If that woman had her way, you would be at war with Spain by now."

"Likely enough," he agreed. "So we may laugh when we reflect how much there is to frustrate such wickedness. There is no lack of those who wave this bogey before my eyes. Even Monsieur Lass, here, has been guilty of it, and now behold milord Stair, another of the same fraternity."

His lordship, all in white, with the star of the Thistle on his breast and Madame Raymond on his arm was drawn by the Regent into his group. He was all compliments and felicitations for the Duchess on the splendour of her ball, full of glib adulation for the Regent, and then permitted himself a flattering allusion to Mrs Law which was calculated to sting.

"I do not remember to have seen the Baroness in such beauty as tonight. Monsieur de Horn is likely to have a dozen challenges on his hands before morning from the gallants whose eagerness he is frustrating."

"You should beware of the Comte de Horn, Monsieur Lass," tittered Madame Raymond. "A very dangerous man."

Mr Law smiled. "But we'll hope not rash."

"Hope!" She tittered again. "Hope is the dream of those that wake. So says Lord Stair."

"He reads too much poetry," said Mr Law .

"Horn writes it," the Regent warned him. "For a gentleman, a rather gifted rhymster. It ensures him a welcome at Madame du Maine's poetical court at Sceaux."

"Take heed, Baron," the Duchess rallied. "He looks as if he might be making verses now."

Following the direction of her glance across the thronged ballroom, to a semi-circular alcove, his eyes had found his wife. She occupied a little rounded settle placed under a white statue of Diana, and the lower half of her face was screened by her fan.

Her petticoat of lace frills and rosebuds on a ground of ivory satin filled the settle on either side of her, so that there was room for no one else. But over the back of it, his youthful head almost touching hers at moments, leaned the Count of Horn, in an attitude infinitely more intimate than any in which he might have sat beside her.

Mr Law was at his ease. "If that be so, I can trust Madame Law to supply him with all the rhymes for impudence that he may need."

"Sublime faith!" Stair mocked him.

"And fortunate for Monsieur de Horn," laughed the Duchess. "Monsieur Lass, if what we have heard is true, has not always been quite so trusting."

"I have not always had the same grounds for trust," said he. "But give me leave. It is possible that this good Monsieur de Horn is waiting to be relieved." Bowing, he detached himself from the group, leaving the Duchess in the care of the Marquis de Canillac, and was gone.

Stair's eyes followed him balefully. He found himself suddenly alone with Madame Raymond. The Regent and his ladies had moved off into the ballroom, where the minuet was now coming to its end.

"Insolent upstart," he muttered under his breath.

Tinkling laughter answered him from his companion. "Horn will lower his crest for him. It's but a question of time with that *homme à femmes*, once he's committed to the chase."

"I wish him luck, and, faith, he'll need it. The Laird of Lauriston can be dangerous.'

She was scornful. "So I've heard. But he does not look dangerous now. At least he seems to know his place."

Mr Law had joined his wife and Horn, and could be seen addressing the Count with every sign of courteous affability before offering his arm to Catherine.

"You must beware, my dear, of abusing the graciousness of Monsieur le Comte by too long an encroachment upon his attention."

Horn wondered, was he mocked, but deemed it best to take the speech at its face value. "Sir," he protested, "you state the opposite of the fact. The encroachment was mine; the graciousness madame's."

"That is to smother all in condescension. We take our leave, monsieur."

He bowed. Catherine sank in a curtsy, extending a languid hand. Horn, raising her by it, bore her fingers to his lips, with a murmured "Serviteur!"

Not until they were home, and the sleek Laguyon had ministered to their needs and been dismissed, whilst Catherine, herself, was on the point of withdrawing, did Mr Law offer any comment.

"A moment, Catherine, if you please. I have a word to say."

On her way to the door she paused and half turned. The ungraciousness of her tone was normal and calculated. "Will it not keep until morning? My woman is waiting to undress me."

"I will make it brief," he assured her, coldly courteous. "Indeed, no more than a word. A word of warning."

"Of warning?" Her brows were puckered.

"Against abusing this graciousness of Monsieur de Horn. That was how I described it to him. But I doubt he has no sense of irony. Probably little sense of any kind. A mere animal."

She had swung completely round and was staring at him. A sudden pallor overspread her face. There was a queer light in her eyes, a queer smile parting her full lips, almost an eagerness in her voice. "My God! Is it possible that you are jealous?"

"No, ma'am. It is not possible. But I do not care to be the butt of ribaldries. I do not care to be told, as I was told by Lord Stair's Madame Raymond, that Monsieur de Horn is a dangerous man. You will oblige me, Catherine, by remembering it."

The abrupt change in her expression might have been revealing had he been properly attentive. The queer, almost eager little smile perished on lips that were suddenly distorted. From pale that they had been, her face and neck were scarlet now. Her eyes blazed. From the depths of her indignation she seemed unable to draw words.

But he was not looking at her. "It may profit you also," he was adding, "to remember another man who was reputed dangerous."

"Is that a threat?"

"To Monsieur le Comte, perhaps."

Her anger boiled over at last. She struck to wound, blindly. "You fool! Do you think a man of his blood would cross swords with a...a...professional gambler?"

He smiled and sighed as he answered. "So that already you compare me to my disadvantage with your *cicisbeo*. No matter. You are warned. I'll not detain you. I have no more to say."

"But I have," she cried, which need not have surprised him; and thereafter she said it, pouring over him a torrent of words that held little sense. "I am warned, am I? Of what am I warned? What is there, do you suppose, that I can fear? Nothing that you could do. Embroil yourself if you choose with the Count of Horn. He will break you for your pains; break you like the rotten make-believe you are. Who are you, what are you, to match yourself with a man of his quality, to vent your evil spleen for no better reason than because he chooses to be my friend?"

Her anger mounting ever, fanned perhaps by the cold impassivity in which he stood before her, she raged on: "Am I to deny myself all friends because I have the misfortune to be your wife? Your wife! When I am not even that. Your victim; your prisoner. You are a fool to suppose a woman would submit to it. And, anyway, you had better understand that I am not that woman. And what manner of husband are you that you dare to reproach me with encouraging gallantries? Why should I not, if it suits my inclination? What fidelity do I owe you? How many infidelities of yours have I not endured and condoned in these miserable years? You warn me, do you? Let me warn you in my turn that I am no man's slave and no man's chattel. I belong to myself. Understand that. I'll have the bestowal of myself as to me seems best."

She paused there a moment, staring at him; as if waiting for his reply. But as he offered none, either in defence or in remonstrance, she finally exploded, sobbing: "So now you, too, are warned."

On that she swung round again, and swept weeping in fury from the room.

Chapter 8

INVITATIONS

Those summer days were busy days for Mr Law, perfecting his measures for the entire control of all French colonial possessions, of America, Asia and Africa.

Meanwhile, the news from Louisiana was far from good. Of the precious metals in which the land had been described as rich, little or nothing was yet being extracted; no more was heard of the fabulous ubiquity of precious stones, the reports of which had served to build up the credit of the Mississippi Company and attract buyers for the shares.

None of this perturbed Mr Law. The gold and silver and the gems might or might not exist; but the fertility and productivity of the land were facts upon which he could confidently count to yield the riches he promised to his shareholders. Meanwhile he was careful to suppress the unfavourable reports he had received, lest their publication should have an unnecessarily discouraging effect not only upon the stock of the Mississippi Company but upon that of those other companies which it was already rumoured that Mr Law would shortly be controlling.

His social consequence standing already so high under the Regent's patronage, earned him in those summer days an invitation to spend a week at Sceaux.

It came as a surprise, for whilst he had enjoyed the honour of presentation to the Duke and Duchess of Maine, he could hardly conceive that the pursuits to which he owed his fame would commend him to a lady who, outside of the noblesse, sought only wits and men of letters, both to promote and to share in the delights of her court at Sceaux.

"*Semper sursum*," was his comment to Catherine, with whom, as was usual, relations had resumed their coldly courteous normal after the explosion on the night of the Duchess of Berri's ball. "*Semper sursum*. Ever upwards. I may be the ignoble adventurer you like to account me, but it remains that I carry you from height to height. Our company is desired by her Grace of Maine, no less, the lady with secret aspirations to be Queen of France."

He thrust before her the scented note from the Duchess' secretary Malézieux. It was charged with the device of a hive and a bee, emblems of the Society of the *Mouche-à-miel*, the invention and presidency of which made up the affectation under whose cover her Grace pursued the more dangerous affectation of conspiring.

Catherine looked it over coolly. "Ah, yes," she said. "The Count of Horn had told me to expect it."

She made the statement with such calm that her husband not unreasonably suspected defiance. Despite his warning she had continued to encourage the Count's frequent visits in the Rue de Grenelle and his regular attendance upon her on every occasion of their frequent meetings elsewhere.

Latterly Mr Law's brother had mentioned to him that there was talk of her constantly being seen with Horn among the fashionable riders who frequented that chestnut-bordered avenue along the river, the Cours la Reine. Mr Law fully aware of this, observing it, knowing himself deliberately defied, continued amiably indifferent, adding no word to the representations he had made. It was a silence that left Catherine vaguely uneasy, secretly tormented by suspense, and it was in a passionate desire to end it that she flung down the name of Horn like a gage of battle.

"The Count of Horn?" he echoed reflectively. "So that is the explanation. I was puzzled to think why our company should be desired at Sceaux, and hardly flattered."

"Not flattered? You are exigent. We could be paid no higher compliment short of a command to Versailles."

"That, of course, will be the view of Monsieur de Horn. It does not accord with mine. I owe my loyalties to His Highness, the Regent, and unlike your Monsieur de Horn, I give my loyalties where they are due."

"What do you imply against him?"

"That affecting devotion to the Regent, he would do better to hold aloof from that court of discontent, the household of the Maines, where calumny of His Highness is the least of the offences, and treason the worst. It is of a piece with all the rest I know of your Monsieur de Horn, an *escroc*, contemptible and faithless. If you felt the need to pick a gallant, it would have been more flattering to me to have picked one less disreputable."

"I was not concerned to flatter you."

"You make it evident."

"Nor does slander affect my esteem for a great gentleman."

"Slander?" He uttered a short laugh. "A rascal who was kicked out of the Austrian Army, an *escroc* who is in everybody's debt, a swindler who takes money – a million – from Bernard the Jew for corrupt services which he neglects to render. That is your great gentleman. Be proud of deserving his attention."

"Lies will not diminish that pride. And when we go to Sceaux…"

"We do not go to Sceaux."

Dismay loosened her mouth. "How? Not go to Sceaux? You would dare to refuse what amounts to a royal command?"

"I have given you my views on Sceaux and its activities. That should suffice."

"Very well. As you please." She stood tense and quivering. "But understand that whether you go or not, I certainly shall."

"Ah!" He merely sighed. "That would give rise to comment. I mean, if you went without me."

"Then perhaps you will perceive also the propriety of accompanying me."

He strove with his impatience. "I have tried to tell you that loyalty to His Highness makes it impossible that I should go."

"That is but a pretext. The Duke and Duchess of Maine were at the Duchess of Berri's ball at the Luxembourg. How, then, can you talk of disloyalty in good relations with those whom even the Regent's daughter receives? Besides, there is no reason why I should be bound by such ties of loyalty as yours."

"Or any other ties, it seems."

"Or any other ties," she agreed. "So make your decision without regard for me. For whatever you may decide, I shall certainly be the Duchess of Maine's guest." She turned to go. "You understand?"

Very quietly he answered her. "I understand that I have Monsieur de Horn to thank for this defiance, and that he becomes too troublesome. It has never been my way to prevail with you by violence, Catherine, and since I cannot prevail with you by reason, I must hope to do better with your Count."

She turned again, to face him, and she had lost some breath, "Are you mad? How do you suppose that he will receive you? Do you dream that a man of his station will tolerate your impertinences?"

"Reassure yourself. I shall be strictly pertinent."

She gave him a long, silent look of dislike. Then she shrugged. "You must rush upon your ruin if you will."

On that she left him, and it was some moments before he moved. He was roused by the clock on the overmantel striking the hour of ten, the hour at which almost invariably he paid his morning visit to the Rue Quincampoix, to cast his expert eye over the operations of the day and issue instructions for the guidance of his brother, who remained as his deputy on the spot.

Suddenly realizing that he was late, he cast off the gloomy absorption in which Catherine had left him and was moving towards the door, when it was opened by a footman. With a murmured apology, the man would have withdrawn again, but that Mr Law checked him.

"What is it, Gilles?"

"Pardon, monsieur. I am seeking Madame. It is that Monsieur le Comte de Horn is here."

"Here? Then why do you not introduce him?"

"He is below, monsieur, on horseback. I am sent to inquire if Madame will be riding with him this morning."

Mr Law glanced at the timepiece. He drew a bow at a venture.

"Monsieur le Comte is rather early."

"I think not, monsieur. This is his usual hour."

It was what Mr Law desired to know. These morning rides, then, slyly undertaken in his absence, were something of a regular practice. No wonder that tongues were wagging and that a rumour of scandal had reached the ears of his brother.

From the tranquillity of Mr Law's countenance, the footman could gather no hint of the indignation within him. "Ask Monsieur le Comte to give himself the trouble of coming up."

The footman bowed himself out, to return presently ushering the visitor. Horn, booted, spurred and handling a riding switch, came in briskly, his manner effusive. "My dear Baron! I had no thought to intrude upon you. It is Madame la Baronne whom I seek, for the honour of escorting her should she choose to ride this morning. I trust I do not disturb you."

"In fact," said Mr Law, "you begin to disturb me a good deal."

"How?" The handsome face became serious, the tall figure was drawn stiffly to its full height.

"It occurs to me that Madame may have been riding with you too often lately." He spoke with the utmost urbanity. "It is giving rise to talk. You would not know that, of course. But now that I tell you, I am sure you will agree that she should decline the honour for the future."

The young Count, at his ease, smiled with a touch of insolence. "I understand. If you assure me that it is Madame la Baronne's wish, I must regretfully bow to it."

"I can assure you that it is mine," said Mr Law. Quickly, without giving the other time to speak, he went on: "And there is another matter on which I am glad of a word with you. I understand that it is by your good offices that we are honoured with an invitation to Sceaux. It is flattering, but unhappily my affairs, as you will understand, do not permit me to be absent from Paris just at present. We shall, therefore, be reluctantly constrained to decline that honour also."

The Count's face had darkened; his manner became more distant. "That your affairs should keep you here was more or less to be expected. A money-changer – your pardon, a banker – must wait upon his clients. But, to be frank, my dear Baron, I perceive in that no reason to deny Madame la Baronne the entertainment Sceaux will offer her. The Countess of Horn, who returned a little while ago from England and who is a compatriot of the Baroness, will be accompanying me to Sceaux, and we shall be happy to have your lady with us."

"Even so, however, too much honour. I do not choose that my wife should go without me."

For all that from the outset Horn had been conscious of the hostility under the courtly phrases, the steel under the silk, he was now momentarily at a loss. He stumbled a little in his protest. "For that, in the circumstances, I think I have the right to ask a reason."

"It is the same as the reason why I do not wish that Madame la Baronne should ride with you again."

Horn flushed. His temper was beginning to slip from him. "Do you know, my dear Lass, that I begin to find you almost offensive."

"Is it possible? It is an impression that I have earnestly sought not to convey."

"Then let me tell you that you fail. I have no more to say to you, I think." He bowed perfunctorily. "I shall have the honour to wait upon Madame la Baronne, to take her wishes in the matter of Sceaux."

"A moment, Monsieur le Comte. It is foolish not to perceive that my wishes are those that count, and you are already aware of them.

I fear you compel me reluctantly to inform my servants that you are not again to be admitted."

The Count's face was suddenly white. He lost his head. Perhaps he forgot how deeply he stood in this man's debt; or perhaps, in his passion and arrogance, he did not choose to remember it. His hand tightened on his whip. "*Canaille!*" he said, through his teeth, and yielding to an impulse of passion he slashed at Mr Law's face.

Only by promptly raising his arm did the Scot save his countenance. Even as he parried, his hand closed over the whip and a swift wrench snatched it from Horn's hand. Mr Law bowed, calmly ironical.

"So much was not necessary, monsieur. But at least it has the advantage of being definite. My friends shall wait upon you today." And he cast the whip at the Count's feet.

"On me? Your friends? My God! Have you the impudence to conceive I'll meet you? Do men of my quality fight with money-changers? It may be done in England, or, perhaps, in Scotland."

Mr Law looked at him steadily without replying, whilst Horn continued.

"It does not happen in France, let me tell you, my good fellow." He shook and slobbered in rage, and all the while Mr Law, with the imperturbability of the complete gamester in the face of whatever stake may be on the board, continued steadily to stare at him. "For low rascals who forget their place a gentleman has a cane or a whip, as you've discovered."

He stooped to recover his whip, whereby he lost some dignity. Then resuming it, he turned on his heel and stalked towards the door.

"At your pleasure," said Mr Law . "After all, there are weapons more suitable than the sword for *escrocs* and cheats and such folk who forget the obligations birth imposes. I shall see that you discover it, Monsieur le Comte."

But the Count had already reached the threshold, and gave no heed.

"Well, well! You go off with the honours," Mr Law called after him. "For today."

Chapter 9

THE GAMBIE STOCK

Mr Law came on a Monday morning of July into the room above stairs, which he had made his own in the Rue Quincampoix. It was the best room in the house, spacious and furnished so as to provide a characteristic setting for its fastidious tenant. A heavy Aubusson carpet covered the floor. Two tall Venetian mirrors in rococo bronze frames rose above swag-bellied consoles in marquetry and ormolu, and between them on the sage-green panelling there was a replica from the master's hand of the triple portrait of the First Charles, which Van Dyke had painted for the purposes of Bernini.

An affection for the Stuarts was natural in a well-bred Scot even when a kinsman of Argyle's. A rustic scene by Watteau, gay with colour and sunshine, and a couple of mezzotints by Carpi decorated the opposite wall. A great writing table of rosewood, on cabriole legs with massive ormolu incrustations, stood in the middle of the floor. The windows – there were two of them, opening on to a narrow balcony – stood wide to the warmth of the morning and the sounds of the street below.

The establishment there of Law's Banque Générale had already created in the Rue Quincampoix an activity very different from that which it had formerly known. It had been increased by the foundation of the Mississippi Company and the traffic in its shares, and this increase had steadily grown and was being further swollen of late by the confident rumours that Monsieur Lass would shortly be assuming the control of other named colonial monopolies, in the depreciated stocks of which men were already dealing freely.

Mr Law seated himself at his writing table, which was quite bare, save for an inkstand in black onyx and silver, a silver pounce box and a tray of cut quills. In a moment, by the door which he had left open, his brother followed him into the room.

"Good morning, John."

"Good morning, Will. You have your notebook, I see."

"As you requested. And what of Catherine? Have you no word from Sceaux?"

"No direct word, since she went in spite of my wishes. It was not to be expected." He spoke without heat. "But I receive my reports. By these Catherine is a great success with the wits of Sceaux."

"Is that so? Yet, greatly as I esteem her, I should hardly be describing Catherine as witty."

"Would you not? My dear Will, in a woman a fair face and a white breast are a form of wit that's most esteemed by men. She does not appear to be quite such a success with the women. Her conduct with Monsieur de Horn, I hear, lacks reticence, though why that should fail to commend her to the *beau monde* is not readily to be understood. Perhaps her sisters, made censorious because suffering from neglect, are virtuous in spite of themselves."

William, something of a puritan, considered him with grave disapproval. "Will you really be as patient as you pretend?"

"I have no cause to be other."

"Whilst the Count of Horn..."

"Makes love to my wife. But so far, I am credibly informed, he suffers frustration. Madame de Horn, whose presence there made it possible that Catherine should go to Sceaux, appears to be seeing to it that her husband shall have no undue grounds for satisfaction therein."

Will's face was dark, his mouth scornful. "Do you really care so little? If that were my only warranty of my wife's virtue, I'd as lief have none."

"But then, you're not married, Will. No matter." A wave of his fine hand dismissed the subject. "Let us come to business. I asked you to bring your notebook so that you might tell me how much stock in the Compagnie de Gambie has been bought by Horn."

Will drew a chair to the other side of the writing table, sat down and opened his book. "I know that he originally purchased seven thousand shares at a cost of seven hundred thousand livres, because he hypothecated them here for half their value in order to buy another thousand at four hundred and fifty livres. His total holding today is of eight thousand shares for which he has paid rather more than a million and a quarter."

"And of this, then, he owes three hundred and fifty thousand to the bank. The balance probably represents all that he possesses in the world; indeed, rather more, for he'll have no lack of debts. Tell me, what is the value of his holding today?"

"The stock will be standing at five hundred. He could sell his shares for two millions. A braw profit." Then Will laughed unpleasantly, "You go beyond my understanding. It is not every day that a man'll be making the fortune of his wife's gallant. Will it be your notion of how to protect her?"

"You think that humorous? Maybe it is. But as a prophecy I have no opinion of it. Tell me what is the issued capital of the Compagnie de Gambie."

Will referred to his book. "It is of six millions in shares of a thousand livres."

"And of these Horn now holds two-thirds."

"Ay. Such is his faith in you."

"Where is the balance of two thousand shares?"

"We, ourselves, hold nearly half. The remainder is with the general public."

"And the present price is five hundred livres?"

"Thereabouts; that is, if you can find sellers. But they're none so easy to discover at present in view of the expectations. Before the rumour started that we are to take control, you could have bought your fill at a hundred livres."

"We must scotch that rumour," said Mr Law quietly, to Will's surprise, and went on to astonish him further. "You'll offer a hundred of our shares today at four hundred and fifty, and another hundred tomorrow at four hundred. After that, we'll see."

"But, man," protested Will, "if you want to sell our stock, there's no need to lower the price."

Mr Law smiled. "Say it's a caprice of mine. Let McWhirter attend to it."

"McWhirter!" For a moment Will was speechless. "But that's to tell the world that you're the seller. You see the inference?"

"Ay, I see it fine." Mr Law took snuff delicately, and proffered the open box to his brother. "Didn't you hear me say I am wanting to scotch that rumour. This should do it."

"But you'll be throwing away a fortune," cried Will in pain.

Mr Law snapped down the lid of his snuffbox. He dusted some fragments from the lace at his throat. "What's a fortune more or less? A few millions are of no great account."

What sharply followed does not need many words. By Wednesday morning Angus McWhirter, known to be Mr Law's man, was offering the stock of the Compagnie de Gambie at three hundred, and by Wednesday evening word ran in the Rue Quincampoix that there could be no foundation for the rumour that Mr Law was interested in that Company. Upon learning this, Mr Law's instruction were that McWhirter should offer five hundred shares at two hundred.

"But we don't possess them," his brother protested. "We've scarcely a share left."

Mr Law smiled. "Yet we may sell in the confident expectation of a further fall."

His brother's eyes were round. It was a novel notion for him that a speculation may be as profitable on a falling as on a rising market. It was something new in the art of gambling, and if it did not now succeed, that was only because the last buyer vanished when McWhirter made his offer.

By that evening the clerks of the money-changers in the Rue Quincampoix were vainly offering the stock of the Compagnie de Gamble at prices which had successively fallen to fifty livres. When the market opened on the following day there were one or two speculative buyers at ten livres. The stock had become practically worthless.

"I hope you're satisfied," said Will indignantly. "Judiciously handled this stock might have produced four or five millions for us."

"I am quite satisfied. Indeed, I would not sell my satisfaction for twice that sum."

On the Saturday of that fateful week Catherine returned to Paris, as airy and as much at her ease with her husband, as if there had been no difference between them on the subject of her absence. It may have surprised her that Mr Law accepted without comment or allusion to her defiance the act of oblivion which she passed over it. For the rest she came back a little intoxicated by her success in the rarefied atmosphere of Sceaux. She boasted of the attentions shown her by the Duke of Maine, and of the court paid her by so many of the gallants among her fellow guests. She had been made a Companion of the *Mouche-à-miel*, the order of chivalry founded by the Duchess of Maine, and she displayed with pride the gold medal of the order with the bee on one side and the head of the Duchess on the other, and with scarcely less pride she announced that the famous Malézieu had written some verses in her honour.

Upon this Mr Law's comment was bittersweet. "I rejoice that he still discovered in you sufficient honour upon which to hang his rhymes."

"Honour?"

"Say virtue, if you prefer it."

"Must you always be churlish?"

"Is it churlish to rejoice in the unlikely?"

101

"The unlikely!" Her exclamation combined indignation with alarm.

"You would give Malézieu and his ineffable kind every reason to believe it so, and no doubt Monsieur de Horn would be at pains to afford them added cause."

"You believe that!" Her eyes were black pools in the sudden whiteness of her face.

"I believe that you have something for which to thank the Countess of Horn, although you may not yet perceive it."

"I will not pretend to misunderstand you. I wonder, John, is there any insult your mind will spare me." Then abruptly, casting off all defiant mockery, she surprised him by pleading. "John! If I were to say that I am sorry for not heeding you, sorry that I went to Sceaux…"

"You would leave me wondering what was the experience that chastened you."

She drew nearer, under the strong urge of a conciliatory impulse. "I did not know when I went that he had quarrelled with you, that he had struck you and then refused to meet you in terms of further insult."

"It should not surprise you. It is what you foretold. But I see that he informed you of it. Expecting your applause."

"Can you suppose that he received it?"

"Can you assure me that he did not?"

"Does it need that I assure you?"

"Your memory is short. You'll have forgot, it seems, the terms you used with me when I desired you not to go to Sceaux."

Her face puckered. She twisted one hand in the other. "If you knew, John, how bitterly I regret it all."

Matter and manner filled him with increasing wonder by their unusualness.

After a moment she added: "At least I have signified it plainly to Monsieur de Horn, and I hope that I shall never see him again."

"Ah! It is likely, then, that you will not." He moved towards the door. With his hand upon the knob, he turned to add with a grim smile: "Do not be troubled about me as concerns Monsieur de Horn. He is paid."

"Paid?" she questioned. But he went out without explaining.

Of that payment Monsieur le Comte was made aware on the following Monday, when he, too, came back from Sceaux. He found a note awaiting him from the Banque Générale, requesting him to give himself the trouble of calling upon the director on a matter of the utmost urgency.

Considering, however, the state of his relations with Mr Law it was not his intention ever again to set foot within the Bank. Nor, he might and did congratulate himself, was there the need. His operations in the stock of the Compagnie de Gambie, for which it amused him to think that he had to thank Mr Law, were already showing him a rich profit. Already he had virtually doubled the money he had received from Bernard, that other fool of a financier.

For the moment, and in order to spare himself embarrassments, all that was necessary was that he should give a broker of his choice an order on the Banque Générale for the stock it held in his name. The man he chose was one Hoquet, a money-changer, whose counting house was actually in the Rue Quincampoix, a man with whom he had had some dealings in the past.

Before his airy announcement that he proposed to transfer to the care of the Sieur Hoquet all his effects with the Banque Générale, a matter of a million and a half, the banker abased himself and was voluble in assurances of how well the interests of so exalted a client would be served. But when he had cast an eye over the Count's order on the Banque Générale, the pursy little man's expression changed. Knowing his place, he addressed his noble client in the third person.

'Is this the total of Monsieur le Comte's effects?"

"The total." Horn was complacent. "It should represent today a good round sum. At what do you now quote the Compagnie de Gamble?"

Hoquet blew out fat lips in deprecation. "Monsieur le Comte will have been out of Paris lately, I suppose. Actually the last sales made were at thirty. That was two days ago. On Saturday."

"At thirty?" Horn's brows darkened in bewilderment. Then they cleared. "Oh! At thirty louis."

There was a hollow laugh from the banker. "Livres, monsieur. Thirty livres."

This made Horn stare in speechless amazement. Slowly the colour mounted to his face. "What the devil are you saying? Are you drunk by any chance?"

Monsieur Hoquet drew himself up as stiffly as his podgy figure permitted, whilst Horn raged on.

"When I left Paris, ten days ago, the stock stood at five hundred and was rising daily. How can it possibly be at thirty today? What ails you, my man?"

"Ah! I was right in supposing that monsieur had been out of Paris, not to know what has happened. There has been a collapse in this stock during the past week." He cast an eye over the figures on the sheet. "Faith, monsieur would be fortunate today if he could realize a thousand crowns on this."

"A thousand crowns! Six thousand livres!" Horn's face was grey.

"I doubt if monsieur could get even so much. The stock is virtually worthless."

"Worthless! My God!" However much his rank might urge a dignified impassivity, the Count found it impossible to contemplate impassively the incredible melting away in a few days of a fortune of a million and a half. "Oh, but that is impossible." He jerked himself to his feet. "Impossible, name of God! How can such a thing happen?"

"Oh, as to that, this stock has been unreasonably inflated by an assumption that Monsieur Lass would take over the monopoly of Gambie and add it to the Mississippi."

"That was no assumption," roared Horn. "I know it to have been his intention."

104

"Monsieur is no doubt right. But clearly it is his intention no longer, for he has been selling what stock he already possessed. That is what has caused this *dégringolade*."

"Give me that paper." The order upon the Banque Générale was almost snatched from Hoquet's hands. "You shall hear from me again when I have seen Monsieur Lass."

He stamped out, violently swinging his long cane, and went down the street, to storm into the Banque Générale, breathlessly clamouring for Monsieur Lass.

An elderly clerk conducted him upstairs to Mr Law's handsome room. It was not, however, Mr Law who presently came to him there, but a gentleman almost as tall and dark, of the same courtly fastidiousness in his dress and placid urbanity in his manner. Announcing himself the servant of Monsieur le Comte, he professed himself grateful for this prompt response to the note in which he had prayed for the honour of a visit.

Horn cut him short. "It is Monsieur Lass I have come to see. Be good enough to call him."

"But Monsieur le Baron is not here. Permit me to present myself. I am his brother and his deputy in the direction of the Bank."

"So there are two of you in this thieves' kitchen?"

"Monsieur says?"

Horn spoke of his stock in the Compagnie de Gamble, indignantly repeating what Hoquet had told him, and still more indignantly demanding to know if it were true, and, if so, how it came to be true that a fortune of a million and a half had vanished in a week.

William Law was grave. "I am afraid that it is rather less than the truth. For not only has your million and a half vanished, as you say, but it has swept with it a matter of three hundred and fifty thousand livres which the Bank lent you on the stock of your original purchase. That is the present extent of your debt to us, which," added William Law pleasantly, "we shall be glad to have you settle at your early convenience."

Limp, white-faced, chap-fallen, Horn stared at the smiling banker, who so urbanely announced to him his utter ruin. At last, "Have you the courage," he cried, "to add mockery to your tricks? Have you the effrontery to say that I am in your debt?"

"You would surely not have the Bank be at the loss of the advance it has made you?"

"To the devil with your Bank and its loss. What of my loss?" There was foam at the corners of his lips, his eyes had become blood-injected. "What of the swindle that has been practised on me? My God! you villains, do you imagine I will submit? I bought this stock in Gambie on your brother's recommendation, on his assurance that he would be taking control of the company and that its stock would rise, as rise it did at first."

"At best," he was answered, "that could be no more than an opinion. In such matters no man can be infallible."

"That he was to assume direction of the Compagnie de Gambie was no matter of opinion. Was it a lie?"

"I cannot tell you what was in my brother's mind. But if he told you that, he must so have intended at the time. In finance a change of intention is always possible and may result from a variety of causes."

"So that is how you explain this…this cursed swindle."

"I do not think," said William with frosty dignity, "that it can profit us to continue this discussion."

"Do you not?" The Count stared at him for a speechless moment out of a grey face from which the normal beauty had been distorted. Then, abruptly, he broke into laughter, made horrible by rage. "My dear sir, I begin to find you an amusing scoundrel. Not only am I to be at the loss of a million and a half, but I am to pay your rascally Bank a further three hundred and fifty thousand livres for the privilege of being robbed by you. I'll see you and your damned brother broken on the wheel before you have another liard of mine. And broken on the wheel I'll see you in any case. Do you dream that I'll suffer myself to be robbed in this impudent manner?"

William had risen, and was crossing the room. He opened the door.

"Your servant, Monsieur le Comte!"

From the manner in which Horn gripped his cane, the banker thought him about to strike with it. But perhaps he remembered in time what the last blow of that kind was costing him.

"You shall hear from me soon again, you scoundrels," he bellowed. "The Regent shall hear of it. He shall have the whole story. His Highness is my kinsman. Perhaps you rascals had forgotten that. But as God lives I'll make you remember it to your cost."

He flung out still raging, to find a hackney coach in which he had himself carried at once to the Palais Royal.

He arrived there, as it appeared to him, at a fortunate moment. But the appearance was to prove deceptive. The Regent, newly risen from the council table, was able and willing to see him at once, and he was ushered into the Duke's study, the light and rather gay room in which his versatile Highness sometimes painted, sometimes wrote music and sometimes gave himself to the study of the works of others in a variety of fields. The Abbé Dubois, lately promoted to be Secretary of State for foreign affairs, was with him when Horn was introduced.

"Ah, Joseph! What is there for your service?" Thus the Regent, familiarly, with a lift of the hand.

Horn's patronymics were Antoine-Joseph, and to all his intimates he was Antoine. It was characteristic of His Highness that he should find ironical amusement in the use of the second name, so much at variance were its chaste associations with Horn's proclivities.

Still quivering with an indignation which reflection had merely deepened, indifferent to the presence of Dubois, caring, indeed, nothing who might hear of Law's infamy, he poured out his tale of the shameful swindle of which he was the victim.

The Regent, seated at his ease, heard him at the outset with a gravity which diminished as the account proceeded. When it was done, to Horn's horror, His Highness actually laughed. "*Corbleu!* Do you seriously tell me, Joseph, that you disposed of a million livres?"

"I do not think that even Lass will deny that."

"I wish you would give me the secret of where you find your millions. How did you come by it?"

There was a splutter of laughter from Dubois, who permitted himself every liberty.

"You hear. Even my good Abbé finds it amusing."

"But not so amusing," chuckled Dubois, "as might be the answer."

"Ah! You seem to know something of this, Abbé. What is the mystery, my dear Joseph?"

Horn glared venomously at Dubois, whose malice put him momentarily out of countenance. "There is no mystery, monseigneur. That I have been subjected to a foul swindle is plain enough."

His Highness' arched brows were further arched. "But unless I know how you became possessed of a million, how can I believe that you were swindled of it?"

The Count took refuge in dignity. "Is not my word sufficient, monseigneur?"

Still the Regent playfully rallied him. "For a million? That's a deal with which to load your word, my friend."

"Your Highness is amused at my expense."

"But no, but no. It is your tales that are amusing: one, that you possessed a million; the other, that my friend Lass has robbed you of it. Faith, I don't know which is more unlikely."

The Count breathed hard. "I see that Your Highness refuses to take me seriously." He was quivering with anger. "I beg leave to withdraw."

"Eh?" The Regent's plump, smooth face became suddenly sober. "What the devil's this, monsieur? You do not happen to be hiding something so as to abuse my faith? To be dealing in half truths?" Surprising a sly grin on Dubois' lips, he asked him bluntly, "What do you know of this, Abbé?"

The Abbé was rubbing his hands, his back arched like a cat's; the wide, almost lipless, mouth became further extended. "Very little. Nothing of what Monsieur Lass may have done. But enough to assure Your Highness that Monsieur de Horn is not exaggerating when he says that he possessed a million. There's a whisper that he had it from Samuel Bernard."

The Count bit his lip, perhaps to stifle the curse that rose to it.

"From Bernard? From that scoundrel?" His Highness was now entirely serious. "And for what, if you please?"

With all the air of hastening to Horn's assistance, Dubois calculatedly made matters worse. "Oh, but just one of those little presents with which financiers seek to win favour at Court."

The Regent scowled. "Is it possible that you accept such presents, Comte? I refuse to believe that you are without the prejudices with which a gentleman is born."

The Count quivered as if struck. Inwardly sick with rage and no longer master of his wits, he was shamed into the blunder of a lie. "It should scarcely be necessary. It is surely inconceivable that I should accept presents from any Samuel Bernard. This was a loan, Highness."

"A loan?" His Highness' short laugh suggested incredulity. "I should have thought that even more inconceivable. But no doubt you were able to give him good security."

"Naturally, monseigneur."

"Naturally, of course." The Regent waited. "Well? You do not choose to tell me what it is?"

"I did not realize that Your Highness was demanding to know."

"Demanding? Of course I don't demand. How could I? But there is an oddness here which I thought you would be anxious to explain. Bernard is in gaol. He has been squeezed in the press of justice until he could drip no more ill-gotten gold. In the circumstances I should expect him to be eager to collect all his resources."

But Horn was not to be pinned. "I have no doubt that he is, and that is now my danger, thanks to this cold-blooded swindle by Lass."

"You mean the danger that Bernard will realize on the security he holds." As if in kindly interest, he added: "Would that be so disadvantageous to you? I cannot judge without knowing the nature of it."

"Its nature?" Horn contrived another wriggle. "If you must know, monseigneur, it is a security supplied by my wife."

"You are fortunate in your lady. Not her jewels, I hope."

"Not her jewels. No." He was recovering his self-possession, and feeling reassured. "What matters is that she should not be at the loss of it, which is why I have been so bold as to ask Your Highness for justice against this man, Lass."

"Ah, yes. Against my friend Lass," the Duke corrected. "He told you, you say, that the Compagnie de Gambie would be passing into his control?"

"It was on this assurance that I bought the stock."

"Borrowing for the purpose from Samuel Bernard?"

"Precisely, monseigneur."

"And, of course, you possess the stock?"

Horn laughed unpleasantly. "I hypothecated it to the Banque Générale for a loan to lay out on further stock, and repayment of this is now claimed from me. It is all part of the swindle."

There was a clucking sound from Dubois.

"What is it, Abbé?"

"The folly of some noblemen when they adventure into the kingdom of finance. They are as naked children exposed to the blasts of a cold, calculating world."

"You mean of cold, calculating swindlers," cried Horn.

"But – *mon Dieu*! – who has swindled you, monsieur? The stock is there which Monsieur Lass advised you to acquire."

"Haven't I said that it is worthless?" Horn was impatient. "For a week past Lass' own agents have been selling the stock. Does that look as if he were to acquire control of the company?"

"Neither the Abbé nor I can answer that at present," said the Regent. "So that when all is weighed I see no help that I can render you. But what I can do, my dear Horn, I will. The security which you tell me is held by Bernard actually, like all his property, now belongs to the State, and to the State Bernard shall be required to surrender it.

"The State, as you know, my dear Count, is far from affluent in these days; but it can still, in exceptional cases, afford some generosity, and I shall see to it that the State restores your property, or, rather, your lady's property. I could not suffer the Countess of Horn to be at such a loss."

The resolve was characteristic of this generous, extravagant, improvident prince, who not only had never learnt to refuse, but who could bestow with prodigality without even waiting to he asked.

Horn, however, was in no case to savour this generosity. Nothing could more profoundly embarrass him. He perceived how, blinded by anger, he had rushed into a trap.

He should have foreseen that the Regent, so fully aware of straitened circumstances which his bounty had more than once relieved, should wonder how he had come by a million, and inevitably ask him. He should have foreseen that the question was one that could not be met, save by plunging into this morass of falsehood, from which there was no escape without disgrace.

Willingly, indeed, almost gladly, would he now have abandoned his million as the price of extricating himself and effacing all his misrepresentations.

Speechless, pale and with beads of sweat along the line where wig met brow, he stood before the Regent, who smiled as he waited, and before Dubois, who also smiled, but in sheer derision.

"I hope," said His Highness, "that this will content you without the need to trouble Monsieur Lass." Over his shoulder to Dubois he added: "You will make a note, Abbé, to have Bernard questioned tomorrow in this matter."

Desperately, under the stress of fresh necessity, Horn floundered further. "Surely that will be idle. Bernard will deny it, of course."

The Abbé looked shocked. "Deny it?" he cried. "Deny that you had a million from him? How could he deny it? How do you suppose that I happened already to know it?"

A grin tightened the skin of that lean face as he paused before answering his own question. "You see, Monsieur le Comte, we have seized Bernard's papers. That is where I found the record of it. Perhaps it had not occurred to you."

"Did you find…" impulsively Horn was beginning, when he stopped. "No matter. I…"

"You were about to ask, I think, did we find a record of the consideration he received. There was a note in cipher. It did not suggest a security."

The Regent looked at the Abbé with sudden sharpness. "How can you say that, unless you can also say what it did suggest?"

Dubois was softly rubbing his hands again, a gesture that Horn found hateful. "But I am quite prepared to say so, Highness, although the notion may seem absurd, and Monsieur le Comte will no doubt deny it. It suggested – how shall I say it? – it suggested that Bernard made this payment for services rendered, or to be rendered."

"Impossible," said the Regent. "What services could be in question?" He looked from the Abbé to the Count.

"Several instances were discovered," the Abbé slyly answered him, "of large sums paid by these *maltôtiers* to persons of influence at Court for – ah – protection."

"I suppose you mean bribes," said the Regent, scandalized. "But you are not implying that Monsieur le Comte…" He broke off to look keenly at Horn. "You say nothing! Is it possible that you don't deny it?"

The Count was at the end of denials, whose ultimate futility had become all too plain, serving only to deepen his defilement. He stood with bowed shoulders, a scowl of defeat on his white face. "To what end?" he asked, with sullen defiance, and shrugged as he spoke.

It was a moment before the Regent appeared to interpret the man's attitude. At last, "My God!" he said, and emotion brought him to his feet. "Is this really possible?"

Avoiding the Regent's glance, Horn partly raised his arms, and let them fall heavily to his sides. It was a gesture of despair. "I… I was hard pressed," he growled.

"So hard pressed that you, a gentleman, took a bribe from this thieving Jew. And did you even earn it? I do not remember that you interceded for him."

"I…I had not so much effrontery."

"Not so much effrontery? Really! But you had effrontery enough to come here complaining that you had been defrauded of this million which you obtained by fraud. You had effrontery enough to stoop to falsehood…"

"Monseigneur!" It was a cry at once of pain and of anger.

But the easy-going Regent was for once implacable. "Is that too much to say? How do you suppose that men of honour will describe it?"

He went on without waiting for an answer, "I have known you guilty of irregularities in the past, monsieur. More than once for the sake of your blood I have helped you to extricate yourself from situations that imperilled your honour. But that you should lie to me like a lackey! That is something that I will not condone. I am ashamed for you. But there!"

He sighed, and let fall some of the sternness that was so foreign to him and in which his indolent nature was uncomfortable. "It is useless to say more. I will do you the justice to suppose that I could say nothing that you will not already have said to yourself. You are permitted to go."

Almost sorrowfully he added: "And, of course, you will understand that you cannot again be received here."

The Count bowed low in silence, his face twitching. He moved backwards towards the door and in silence went out.

The Regent sat down on the clavichord stool, with his back to the instrument. He took snuff to soothe himself. "Poor devil!" he sighed.

"Your Highness wastes pity," said Dubois. "A *mauvais sujet*."

"Ah! And what are you, Abbé? Have you never taken a bribe? How much does Lord Stanhope pay you to keep me well disposed towards England?"

Dubois swelled indignantly. "I have never taken a louis that was not to further your interests."

"Oh, to further our interests, of course. And, anyway, you were not born a gentleman. So it's no great matter. You may perceive that the condition has its disadvantages."

"A scoundrel," said the Abbé sententiously, "is a scoundrel however he may be born."

"That is what madame my mother says when she speaks of you. Like you, she lacks charity, which may be pardonable in a woman but is abominable in a priest – even a nominal one. That poor devil was hard driven by temptation, which is something you have never known."

"Oho! Have I not, monseigneur?"

"I do not mean that it is temptation you have never known. What you have never known, is to be hard driven by it. You have always yielded readily. But no matter. It is not you who gives me concern. It is this unfortunate fellow of whom necessity has made a rascal. I hope that he will have the good sense to leave Paris for a while."

Monsieur de Horn, however, had no such notion. If the shame in which he left the Palais Royal was deep, deeper still was the rage at having been so trapped, and the object of this rage was, of course, the Laird of Lauriston. He took the view, not only that Mr Law had cruelly defrauded him, but that it was Mr Law's credit with the Regent which had denied him redress and turned the tables upon him by uncovering his questionable transaction with Samuel Bernard. Utter disgrace must follow upon the disclosure of this as the reason for his expulsion from Court, as if there were not already enough to bear in the complete financial ruin which, in an excess of irony, had overtaken him at the very moment when financial redemption had seemed firmly within his grasp.

In his desperately vindictive mood and in casting about him for means to gratify it, he thought of his friend de Mille, and sought him out in his mean lodging opposite Saint Philippe du Roule.

A large man of a rather raffish exterior, mitigated by an air of command, acquired in the course of his military career, it was one of the Colonel's delusions, based upon a couple of easy victories over fledgelings, that he was something of a swordsman. Therefore the Count's commission flattered him. Ignorant of that sinister side of Mr Law's past history, it did not occur to de Mille that a money-changer might be an awkward opponent on the field of honour. But he wondered why Horn's deadly animosity should not fire him to act for himself, and he said so.

"Don't you understand that I am in disgrace with the Regent on this man's account?" Horn asked, by way of explanation. "If I were to defy the edicts I should not be forgiven."

"Whilst I may defy them and go hang."

"Arrange it so that the provocation comes from Lass, and since there is no prejudice against you, that will be a sufficient answer. I can contrive a hundred louis at once when it is done, and in the future, when I am in funds, you can count upon me as in the past."

De Mille's resources in those days permitted him neither to refuse a hundred louis nor to decline to oblige a man to whom he owed so much and to whom in the future he hoped to owe so much more.

He sought his opportunity, and was some days in finding it. It was provided at last by merest chance when he happened to be one of a party at the Duke of Antin's, which included also Mr Law. After supper a half-dozen of them sat down to dice for easy stakes. De Mille, himself, was not of the players, but hovering about the table as an onlooker he presently perceived his chance. Mr Law had made a cast, called the main, doubled the stakes, thrown again and won.

"Uncanny!" said the Colonel with an unpleasant laugh. "Permit me." He leaned over, picked up one of the dice, and indifferent to the stares of amazement, balanced it by its corners between finger and thumb. "In effect, it does not turn," he said in tones of surprise, and tossed it back on to the table.

On the deadly silence there was the sharp clap with which Mr Law set down the dice box. "What does that mean, Colonel de Mille?"

"A habit of mine," said the Colonel with his impudent laugh. "It's prudent to test the tools of a professional gamester."

D'Antin heaved himself up in anger. "Are you crazy, Colonel, or merely more drunk than usual?"

But Mr Law had lost none of his placidity. "He is neither, my dear Duke. He is merely provocative, the bully swordsman hired to a job."

"Do you say that of me?" roared de Mille. Nor was his anger simulated. The cold contempt of Mr Law's quiet voice had cut him to the soul.

"It's no more than you deserve," d'Antin condemned him.

The Colonel wrapped himself in dignity. "I'll venture to remind you, monseigneur, that I am your guest, and that my affair is with your foreign friend."

Mr Law smiled. "You admit to an affair, then?"

De Mille was cautious. It was for him to take and not to give offence. "Quite enough has been said."

"Too much in fact," cried d'Antin, whilst the others looked on in forbidding silence.

"As you say, Monsieur le Duc; too much. My friends shall wait on you, Mr Law, so that we resume the discussion on another plane. I take my leave, monseigneur." He bowed, first to the Duke and then to the company, and stalked out with airs of righteous indignation.

D'Antin was distressed. "My dear Lass! That this should happen in my house!" And he added: "You are under no necessity to meet that fellow."

"Could I deny myself the pleasure?" laughed Mr Law.

The meeting took place in the Bois de Boulogne two days later, with d'Antin as Mr Law's second. As a spectacle, the onlookers – most of whom had been at the Duke's party – found it disappointingly brief. At the end of not more than a half-dozen disengages, Mr Law, putting aside a high thrust, stepped inside his opponent's guard, and drove his blade through the Colonel's sword-arm.

Whilst the surgeon in attendance was bandaging the wound, Mr Law stood close to the wincing de Mille. "It would have taken me even less time to run you through the body, my Colonel. Let me advise you not to recommence; for you cannot expect me again to be at so much trouble."

That was humiliation enough for a swordsman who accounted himself a *ferrailleur* to be feared. But there was worse in store for him that evening when Horn came to see him. The Count stared in disgust at the sling in which the arm was carried.

"What the devil is the meaning of this?"

"It means," he was sourly answered, "that you were wise to employ a deputy. I suppose you knew that the fellow is a damned fencing master."

"Bah!" snapped the Count. "I thought you were a swordsman."

And that was all the comfort the Colonel had from an employer who was far too much in need of comfort for himself. In his almost despairing quest for it Horn bethought him of Noailles and of Noailles' implacable hatred of Law, who had so mortally wounded him in his vanity and his ambition. For it was, of course, to Law that his Grace attributed his dismissal from the Council of Finance, his loss of influence with the Regent, and the frustration of his hopes of becoming the First Minister of the Crown.

If any man in France would help the Count of Horn to the vengeance for which his wrongs cried out to heaven, that man was surely Noailles, who out of his own rancour might not trouble to look too closely into Horn's grounds of quarrel with the financier.

Chapter 10

THE PLOTTERS

The Duke of Noailles' lean, dark face was flushed with interest, his normal forbidding haughtiness relaxed as he listened to the Count of Horn. The tale was none too clear in detail, but in general it ran that the scoundrelly Scot had tricked the Count by deliberate falsehood into the investment of a million, and that of this he had cold-bloodedly swindled him, so that the Count was now facing ruin.

There were several things that a man less passionately prejudiced than Noailles might have required to know. As it happened, the Duke's eagerness to believe in Mr Law's turpitude left him without even the curiosity to learn how a man so notoriously in everybody's debt as Horn had come to be possessed of so much money.

Having told his muddled tale, the Count raved on. "This foreign adventurer, this cursed thief has become a danger to us all. The Regent is so bewitched and bedevilled by him that he dances to any tune the scoundrel pipes. Your Grace knows how from the wings he directs the Council of Finance, until dignity would no longer permit a noble of your rank to continue as its president.

"It was the intriguing of this spawn of Satan that sent d'Aguesseau into exile. It was at his rascally prompting that d'Argenson was made chancellor. And every day he wins some fresh concession from the

118

infatuated Duke of Orléans. The town is full of rumours of what he is about to do, as if he were already Comptroller-General."

Noailles exploded. "Ah, that no, my God !" He had listened with swelling anger to each of Horn's denunciations, each of which confirmed his own convictions. The assumption on which Horn ended provided so natural a climax to them that the Duke's feelings amounted to panic. "That never, by God!"

"It should not be," Horn agreed. "But... How to prevent it? What law in France could be invoked against him? What court?"

"Court?" Noailles echoed, and stared at him with dull eyes. Suddenly the light of inspiration flashed from them. "There is the Parliament. It has always resented him, ever since Argenson the Damned was made Chancellor by his offices. It would ask nothing better than to bring him down."

For a moment Horn was uplifted. Then he shrugged. "To bring him down! I dare say. But what can the Parliament do against the Regent. This is France, not England."

"Do you say so?" The tone rebuked him. "As for what it can do, that is to be studied. Certainly it is far from impotent.

"You'll remember that no royal edict – that is, no edict of the Regent's – is good until the Parliament has registered it. You'll remember also that the Parliament is the supreme court of justice in France, with power to move directly against any malefactor. Let us take counsel with the President de Mesmes. Something will be decided."

De Mesmes proved but too willing to consider what might be done. Not only was he, too, filled with rancour of Mr Law, but, a vain man, he had been drawn by his gallantry into participation in the Duchess of Maine's plots for the overthrow of the Regent.

If he welcomed the chance to strike at Law, he welcomed it the more joyously in that it enabled him to strike through him at the Duke of Orléans. He did not hesitate to reveal to Noailles that there were no lengths in reason, or even out of reason, to which he was not prepared to go. Of course for the good of France.

He took some days to consider and to consult a few of his colleagues, all of whom were in sympathy with his views, and then came bearing the considerable fruits of it, to a little gathering at the Hôtel de Noailles. To meet him the Duke had summoned his coadjutor Rouillé du Coudray, whilst the Count of Horn was present as the interested originator of the movement.

De Mesmes, a large, portly, pock-marked man, rather priestly of manner, soft-voiced and with a slight lisp, expounded at length the rascally plan with which rancour and treason inspired him. It was elaborate and yet simple.

"Against the Banque Générale as originally constituted no complaint is possible, no case could be made. For we are agreed, of course, that we must proceed strictly within the framework, not necessarily of existing laws, but at least of incontestable legality.

"Having carefully examined all the transactions by Monsieur Lass, I am of the opinion that the surest ground upon which to assail him would be that of probity."

Horn struck the table vehemently. "I'll pledge my honour for his dishonesty."

"Your honour!" sneered Coudray, with his usual sourness. "We want evidence, not pledges; and Lass is not the fool to leave evidence strewn about."

"We may dig some up," said the President with an oily smile, "however carefully he may have buried it. For instance, we may reasonably require to know what has become of the State bonds the bank received against shares in the Mississippi Company. Parliament will appoint a commission to investigate. The slightest irregularity there, would be a criminal matter, and Lass would be lost."

"Don't build on it," growled Coudray. "Lass is a gamester who boasts that he wins because he understands why men lose. He has the type of mind any chess player might envy. He can see a dozen moves ahead in every direction. Not the sort of man to leave traces of any malversations."

Noailles shrugged impatiently. "*Non semper arcus…*" He murmured, and left the quotation there.

"Precisely, Your Grace," lisped de Mesmes. "And, anyway, we need not depend upon that alone. If no irregularity should be discovered, we pass on to examine one by one the transactions between Monsieur Lass and His Highness, and we discover that the last money edict is illegal because the Bank usurps some of the functions of the royal accountants in the administration of national finances."

"Illegal, is it?" wondered du Coudray with scepticism.

De Mesmes became prim. "It represents a startling departure from all that is by law established. If there is no actual law against it, there is certainly no law to sanction it."

"There are no laws to sanction anything," growled du Coudray. "Laws are made only to prohibit. As a lawyer, Monsieur le President, you should know that. I'll observe only that if you make your laws as you proceed, you'll have no difficulty in convicting Lass of anything you choose. But you may have considerable difficulty in persuading the Attorney-General to take the responsibility of being your mouthpiece in this *ad hoc* legislation to serve your ends."

De Mesmes' ready answer showed how well considered was the plan. "The Attorney-General will not be concerned or necessary. His place will be taken by the commissioners. It will be their business to recommend a decree rescinding the offending edict. They will declare it illegal, and – another thing which has just occurred to me – on the authority of His late Majesty, they will declare it illicit and illegal for any foreigner or huguenot to concern himself directly or indirectly in the administration of the national finances, and discover crime where this has occurred. The Regent being inviolate, it becomes necessary to provide a deputy."

The President displayed his teeth in a grin at this conceit. "For that office we have under our hand this man Lass, guilty, if not of malversation, as may well be, at least of having seduced the Regent into taking these illegal courses."

Noailles shook his head. "You don't conceive that His Highness will permit any measures against Lass."

"Of course not," grumbled Horn.

Again that oily smile overspread the President's big face, and he showed how completely the plan had shaped itself from their talk. "Knowledge of our measures will reach His Highness too late. The commission will act in secret, and in secret the Parliament will issue a writ of *prise-de-corps*. Once Lass is brought to the Palace, he need never leave it again. He can be tried, sentenced and even hanged within its precincts."

Horn was breathless, Noailles aghast, and Coudray sardonically amused. It was the Duke who spoke, his tone irritably dubious. "These are extreme measures."

"But effective," chuckled Horn, now flushed with evil satisfaction. "Nothing less will serve than to present His Highness with an accomplished fact."

"But not necessarily with a corpse. Surely, Monsieur le President, it should suffice to banish him."

De Mesmes shook his head. "You are reckoning without His Highness."

"So are you," du Coudray mocked him. "He'll certainly require an account of you. He may even require your head."

"There are a hundred and thirty of us." The President was scornful. "What satisfaction can he demand?"

Coudray laughed. "It certainly may be difficult to hang the lot of you, as you'll deserve."

"Therefore he can't hang a single one of us, for if there's guilt we shall all be equally guilty. You may safely leave it in my hands, Monsieur le Duc. All I ask of you is the utmost secrecy. This foreign adventurer has too long been a thorn in our flesh. It is time to make an end."

But Noailles was sombre. "I don't like it," he said. "Much as I detest Monsieur Lass and his ways, I'll have no part in this."

"It is not necessary that you should, Monsieur le Duc. The Parliament will bear the burden lightly in the service of France. As I have said, it will possess the authority of Louis XIV, who expelled this same Monsieur Lass from the Kingdom."

Chapter 11

THE COUNTESS OF HORN

With no suspicion of the plot that menaced his very life, Mr Law was quietly pursuing the even tenor of those studies by which his system was to achieve its ultimate all-embracing scope.

To keep pace with his expanding fortunes and consequence, Mr Law had by now removed himself to the Hôtel de Nevers, that handsome palace built by Mazarin in the Rue Vivienne.

The great success of the Banque Générale, the high credit of the paper it emitted, and the facilities which this provided for commerce both at home and abroad were by now abundantly reflected in that increased prosperity which Mr Law had affirmed would follow upon the free and ample circulation of currency. Not only in trade, but in agriculture, too, both of which had been dangerously languishing, there was every sign of healthy activity as a result of the Bank's judicious loans.

At Mr Law's magical touch the Mississippi Company, worthless under Crozat, and although not likely for some time to show returns, was already proving by the gradual appreciation of its shares, those theories on credit which Mr Law had so lucidly and so vainly expounded to the sealed minds of the Council of Finance.

All this was predisposing the Regent naturally enough to allow the Scot to undertake the control of France's other languishing overseas monopolies: the East India Company, the China Company, the Sénégal Company, and the like.

And whilst completing arrangements for this, Mr Law's conceptions were opening out still wider horizons to the Regent's dazzled view.

He propounded a revolution in taxation. He would suppress all those internal customs' barriers, which were mere stumbling blocks to trade; he would abolish altogether the arbitrary taxes: the *taille*, the *gabelle*, the *corveés*, and the rest of those ancient, unpopular, complicated, vexatious imposts which paralysed commerce and required for their collection an army of parasites who fed upon the substance of the State whilst themselves producing nothing.

He would replace all this by a single uniform tax of one per centum on every man's revenue, a tax which could hurt no one; for, as he argued, the wealthy would have no reason to conceal his wealth, and the poor man would dare to become wealthy without the dread of being arbitrarily preyed upon.

There would be an end of barriers, of inquisitions, of collectors, of tax farmers, and with them of all those vexatious conflicts constantly resulting from the necessity under which men found themselves so as to guard their rights from predatory servants of the State.

Then, just as salt and tobacco became State monopolies, there no longer appeared to be any reason why trade in general should not be treated in the same way and brought under State control, to the profit of the nation as against the profit of the individual. The valid objections to this which had been urged by d'Aguesseau were not permitted to obscure the grandiose dream.

The Regent, listening to Law, questioning him, pressing for details and impressed by the glittering pageantry of wealth and universal prosperity which the Scot evoked, found himself regretting that he should lately have allowed d'Argenson to purchase the general farming of the revenue.

The Chancellor had actually found his inspiration in Law's flotation of the Mississippi Company. He had acquired the rights for an annual payment of forty-eight millions, and he had associated with himself a group of able financiers – the four brothers Paris – Duverney – launching a company which he called the Anti-System. For this he had found the necessary capital the more readily since he was able to assure the investors of a definite fixed return.

For Mr Law this was a minor obstacle to that complete control at which he aimed, and he dismissed it for the present as of no immediate importance. His projected activities in the realm of taxation must follow, and not precede, the expansion of the Mississippi Company by amalgamation with it of the other colonial trading companies. Of this it was at last decided that he should prepare a complete scheme for the Regent's consideration.

He was at work upon this one afternoon, in the room which he had made peculiarly his own in the Hôtel de Nevers and to which he had transplanted the rich furnishings of his own personal office in the Rue Quincampoix: the rosewood and ormolu writing table, the Aubusson carpet, the Van Dycks, the Watteaus, the Consoles, the Venetian mirrors and the rest. Saving that between the pilasters with gilded capitals the walls were panelled in embossed Cordovan leather, you might suppose yourself still in the Rue Quincampoix.

There was, it is true, less hubbub from the street, which lay beyond the spacious courtyard, and it was of a different character. Through the tall, open windows, subdued by distance, came intermittently the cry of a bellows mender, a water carrier, a rat-catcher, or the shriller note of a fishwife, but there were none of the unceasing deafening vociferations of the Rue Quincampoix.

Absorbed in his calculations, Mr Law heard not so much as the beat of hooves on the kidney stones and the creaking of a coach. Not until it rumbled and clattered to a standstill in his spacious courtyard did it disturb him into momentarily raising his head.

Laguyon, soft-footed and soft-voiced, came in, with the quiet announcement: "Pardon, monsieur. Madame la Comtesse de Horn begs urgently to see you."

125

"The Comtesse de Horn!" It certainly surprised him. He was only vaguely aware of the existence of such a person. "But I do not know the lady."

"Madame la Comtesse desires particularly to be received, sir. She begs me to assure you that her errand is of the gravest. Short of that, sir, I should not have ventured to disturb you."

"Of the gravest? Pish! The language of exaggeration. However, you may bring her in."

The lady whom Laguyon introduced was of slender build and more than middle height, cloaked in grey from neck to heel, her head covered by what in England would have been called a Nithsdale hood.

Mr Law rose and bowed. "Madame la Comtesse!"

Over her shoulder she watched the departure of the servant, and not until the door had closed did she fully confront her host. She thrust back her hood, her cloak rippled open, and she stood revealed.

Mr Law fell back a pace, and for a long moment, this man, so imperturbable in all circumstances, stared at her with dilating eyes and parted lips, the natural pallor of his dark face slowly deepening to the colour of lead.

Yet here was no Gorgon so to petrify him. No man who has written of her, and many have done so, has failed to describe her as of an uncommon beauty. It dwelt in no particular conformance with accepted canons, but was of a more elusive, spiritual kind, a radiance that glowed in her dark brilliant eyes, in the smile that seemed ever about to break on her generous mouth.

Her russet hair, defying fashion, was dressed low, and a heavy ringlet hung upon the white neck and shoulders that surged from a rose-coloured bodice. Pallor was her norm, but not so deep as at this moment when it made her eyes seem black. The rise and fall of her breast betrayed a quickened breathing, and the faint quiver perceptible on her lips told of an agitation that seemed poised between laughter and weeping.

Mr Law's startled eyes were without lustre as, frowning, he considered her.

"The Comtesse de Horn I was told..."

"I am the Countess of Horn," she said, in English.

"You!"

"Improbable, of course. Nevertheless the fact."

He took a step forward, his head craned. She made a gesture of opening her arms, a gesture as of drawing a curtain apart so as to make a fuller revelation of herself.

He passed a trembling hand across his eyes. His voice was husky. "Fact, do you say? But you are Margaret; the Lady Margaret Ogilvy."

"I was...in another life, when you were known as Jessamy John." Then her voice assumed an edge of irony as she added "I am glad that you have not quite forgotten me, although I am sure that you will have tried."

The sting of it restored to him his self-possession. He stiffened into his normal self. If irony was to her taste he knew how to supply it in abundance.

"You were?" he said. "Ah, true! King William made you... Countess of Orkney, was it? No, no. That was his other paramour, Elizabeth Villiers. You... Of what did he make you a countess? Or was it a duchess?"

The quiver of her lips was quickened. For a fleeting moment they bore a grin of rigor, those lips to which he had known laughter to come so readily and so irresistibly, from a nature wholly joyous. She let her arms fall to her sides, as if nerveless and gazed at him piteously through a blur of unshed tears. "Does it matter, what I was or may have been? Let it suffice that it is as the Countess of Horn that I am here."

"It will not surprise you if I understand less than ever why you should have come."

"If you did, your welcome might be different. I have no purpose but to save your life."

"My life! I seem to remember... No matter, I am not aware that it is in any danger."

"That is why I have come. To make you aware of it." And, bitter in her turn, she added, "Nothing less would have brought me."

Upon that, abruptly, in the baldest terms, she gave him her message. The Parliament was to issue a writ for his arrest that very day. It was to be executed at once. It was proposed to take him secretly before the tribunal of La Tournelle, to try him, sentence him and put him to death out of hand, before the news of his case could get abroad, so as to make sure of no rescuing intervention.

It was a moment before scornful laughter succeeded his surprise.

"What wild, fantastic tale is this? And if so secret, madam, how does it come within your knowledge?"

"The Count of Horn is in the plot. Sometimes he is indiscreet. You may have noticed that, for I understand that you have been intimate with him, though – God knows – you make odd bedfellows. Also he drinks too much, and in his cups he boasts imprudently." It did not escape Mr Law that there was a fierce contempt in her voice. "Last night he boasted to me that with the Duke of Noailles' assistance he is using the Parliament so as to destroy you. The President de Mesmes, he declares, is a puppet whose strings are pulled by him and the Duke."

Mr Law, on the edge of a sneer at this conception of wifely duty, was stricken silent by an instant's consideration of a tale that hung faultlessly together. Horn's vindictiveness working upon the rancour of Noailles, and the Duke's employment of his influence with a Parliament resentful of Mr Law's vast and increasing influence, were facts that could not be dismissed. Whilst it might seem incredible that the court of Parliament should dare to proceed to such extremes, yet, when Mr Law came to think of it, he discovered that he was utterly ignorant of the powers possessed by that body or of the extent to which they might be exercised.

"But, in God's name, madam," he cried at last, his mind still resisting conviction, "this cannot be done without some charge against me. In what is it pretended that I have offended?"

"By unduly influencing the Regent in financial matters and the danger that you, a foreign adventurer, should obtain control of the

State finances. That is to be the indictment, with perhaps something more that I did not understand, something about malversation of State bonds."

There was an end to his doubts. His prompt mind was swinging to consider the action to be taken, when her next words showed that it had already been considered for him.

"You have not an hour to lose. They may arrive at any moment now to arrest you. They must not find you."

"Not find me? Am I to run away?"

"You'll lose less breath by that than by what they intend."

Almost was he more taken by her turn of phrase, that trick of illuminating expression which he so well remembered, which had so delighted him of old, than by what she actually told him.

"Don't you understand?" she said. "They are resolved to hang you. The rest – trial and sentence – will be so much comedy."

"Myself, I hardly find it comic. But… Oh, they would never dare. Why, it would be murder."

"Of course. But murder clothed in the robes of the judiciary, wearing the mask of lawfulness. Will you wait for it?" She came a step nearer in her impatience. "Don't you perceive what they fear that they should act secretly? The Regent's intervention. Your only safety lies in the Palais Royal until the Regent can handle them. Come, John. I've told you there is no time to lose."

He took a moment yet to consider, then turned to cross to the bell-pull. ' 'I'll order my carriage."

"You'll be safer in mine," she told him. "It is at the door. Your liveries might even cause you to be seized upon the way."

He realized, of course, the prudence of this, and yielded out for fear for his life; yet reluctant to accept a gift at her hands, he faltered a little as he said: "You are very good."

Delivered of her scarcely veiled suspense, she laughed in relief, and it was in this laughter, displaying her strong, white teeth, lighting a face to which her colour was returning, that her full beauty and allurement were revealed. "I came to rescue you, and it is not my way to do things by halves." But even as she spoke that radiant laughter perished on her lips, and observing this, he wondered. She drew her hood over her head again, and her tone became peremptory. "Come, John. We had best make haste."

He was moving to hold the door for her when from below came the rumble of another coach entering the courtyard, and, as he checked to listen, the tramp of feet brought to a halt by a word of command.

They looked at each other wide-eyed.

"My God!" she exclaimed in distress. "Am I too late?"

He stepped swiftly to the window, and looked down. "Archers,' he said as he turned again to face her. Whatever he may have felt, he displayed no alarm. He even smiled. "It certainly makes your information appear correct."

She wrung her hands. "John! John! You are caught."

"No, no. Not yet. Wait."

He was standing in thought when Laguyon came in quickly, his lean face reflecting alarm. "Monsieur, there is an officer below, asking for you, with a detachment of archers and a carriage."

"So I've seen." He was quite calm. "Desire him to give himself the trouble of waiting a few moments. Say that I shall not keep him long. Then bring me my hat and cane and wait for me in the gallery."

As Laguyon departed, Mr Law turned to the Countess, who stood dismayed and trembling. "You are going?" she gasped.

"Of course. But not as you suppose. There is fortunately a service entrance in the Rue Colbert. Since they have no reason to believe me alarmed, they are not likely to be guarding it. My steward will conduct you to your carriage. You will add to my debt if you will drive away in it and round to that back entrance. I shall be waiting for you there. Come."

He crossed again to the door that led to the anteroom.

"You are sure, John? You are sure?" she asked.

"There is no cause to doubt. Come."

He was to remember afterwards that in opening the door, his ears had caught the quick, silken rustle of a gown. In the preoccupation of the moment he paid no heed to it.

They crossed the anteroom and emerged upon the balustraded gallery to find Laguyon already at the head of the marble stairs with Mr Law's hat and cane.

"The officer is waiting, monsieur."

"Very well. Ask him to be patient for yet a moment longer. Meanwhile you will reconduct Madame la Comtesse to her carriage."

He remained at the stairhead until the rumble of wheels below announced her departure. Then he went briskly on, and quitted the gallery by a narrow doorway on his right.

When her coach drew up at the entrance in the Rue Colbert, he was waiting. The vehicle rolled away at speed as soon as he had jumped in, turned into the Rue des Bons Enfants and so gained the Rue Saint Honoré.

With the danger now behind him, Mr Law became increasingly conscious of the oddness of his situation and of the presence of this lady who sat so stiffly erect beside him, the lady whom he had met with insult and to whom it might well be that he now owed his life. In all this there was much that he did not understand, much that he required to know, yet knew not how to ask.

"You have placed me deeply in your debt," he murmured.

"Which is detestable to you, of course."

"I could not be so ungracious as to agree."

"Could you not? Lord! Must we be formal, John?"

Whilst he observed how free she was with his name, he could not bring himself to make use of hers. "Is it formal to acknowledge what we owe? Let me hope that at least it will have no...no unpleasant consequences for you."

"Why should there be consequences?"

"From what you have told me, it is...your husband who is the instigator of the action against me."

"And from that you'll be inferring that my regard for you is greater than my regard for the Count of Horn."

"I should not permit myself the liberty of drawing inferences concerning you."

"You have never done so, have you?" There was a hardening of her tone.

He took a moment's thought before answering firmly: "Never."

"Really! Never? Well, you should know."

"Nor am I vain enough, I hope, to draw the inference that you suggest."

"You may save your tears. The disloyalty I practise in helping you sits lightly on my conscience. And not for the first time. I served you as well as I could at Sceaux by guarding your wife. It is fortunate that Margaret Ogilvy was only a name to her, that she had never met me face to face, or my task might not have proved so easy."

She broke off on a sudden subdued cry of alarm.

She had drawn aside the leather curtain, and put her head out of the coach, to withdraw it instantly.

They were approaching the open space before the Palais Royal, and by the tall iron gates she had caught sight again of the blue coats and red facings of a group of archers. She supposed them posted there by the Parliament for just such an eventuality, and said so.

Mr Law, however, was not perturbed. "It is not likely," he said. "But set me down at the side door in the Rue de Richelieu."

She pulled the cord, and to the footman, who came to the window as the coach was checked, she gave the order. They swung to the right, and halted presently at the door by which Dubois, in the days when he was content with the role of pandar, was in the habit of introducing the little ladies brought there to beguile the leisure of the young Duke.

A footman let down the step, but Mr Law was not pressed to descend.

"Make haste," she urged him, "before you are seen."

"I am without words..." he was beginning.

"All the better. There is no time for them."

"They must keep then until I see you again."

"Will that be necessary?"

He was jolted. "There is so much I should wish to know."

"But nothing you would be the happier for knowing." She touched his hand lightly. "Goodbye, John. Believe that I am glad to have served you. Go now."

He swung round so as to face her squarely, and in the wistfulness of her eyes he found encouragement to insist. He was deeply moved. "Let me see you again."

She shook her head. "It is not even likely that there will be the occasion. I am but a bird of passage. Lately come, I shall shortly go again. Give thanks as I do for my brief passage. I was sent to play Providence. That is all." She held out her hand. "Let us part friends, John – for old times' sake." Her voice broke on the words.

"Friends!" he echoed, with a touch of bitterness. Then, at last, he used her name. "Margaret!" He bore her gloved fingers to his lips, sprang from the coach and vanished through the little doorway into the palace.

The footman put up the step and swung to his place behind. The coach rolled away. Behind its leather curtains the woman sat rigidly erect, staring straight before her with eyes that the tears were blinding.

Chapter 12

THE BED OF JUSTICE

Mr Law sought in the first instance the Abbé Dubois and put him in a rage as much by the news he brought as by the fact that the Abbé's own spies should have left him in ignorance of what was being plotted. Having exhausted profanity, his reverence applied his wits. "By whom were you warned?" he asked.

"Does it matter?"

"It matters that we should know if the thing is true."

"If I were not persuaded of that I should not be using back doors, and I should not be here now."

The ferrety little eyes peered sharply. The Abbé stroked his hollow cheeks. "No. I suppose not. No. And here, you are safe. But you can't remain indefinitely. Of course you don't wish to. No. But before you go again we must see that the Parliament is brought to order once for all. There's more in this, I tell you, than just your own case. Let me consider."

Not until a couple of hours later did Dubois send the Regent a prayer for audience, and conduct to him not only Mr Law, but also the Duke of Saint-Simon and the Chancellor d'Argenson, both of whom he had summoned to the Palais Royal by making free with the Regent's name.

His Highness had just dined, that is to say, he had just consumed the cup of chocolate that constituted his noontide meal, to be taken only when the main labours of the day had been performed. It happened that this afternoon Madame de Parabère kept him company in his study, whilst he sought relaxation in painting. Monsieur de Parabère had lately died, which Saint-Simon, in his charitable way, regarded as the most considerate thing he had ever done. His magnificent lady bore her widowhood with manifest resignation.

Three oranges on a green dish and a jug of blue Delft ware supplied the elements of the still-life composition that engaged His Highness. Perhaps because he was encountering difficulties he turned the less reluctantly from his easel to face his visitors.

"What is this, Abbé?" he grumbled. "Am I never to rest?"

Madame de Parabère stirred in her armchair.

"Perhaps," she suggested, "one of these gentlemen can tell you whether I am right about that shadow."

"It is not likely. Still, take a look, Messieurs." He waved his mahlstick towards the model. "Can any of you tell me what is the colour of the shadow cast by that vase?"

Mr Law took it upon himself to furnish another question by way of answer. "But is a shadow ever anything but black?"

The Regent shrugged and flung upwards a glance of hopeless invocation. "The ignorance of the clever!" he sighed.

"Just so," said Dubois. "The clever are clever because of their ignorance of things which it is not worth while to know. Monsieur Lass at the moment is concerned with shadows far deeper than any that your Highness can paint."

The Regent set his mahlstick across the pegs of his easel, thrust his brushes into a vase, laid down his palette, and slewed round to face them.

"So be it. Let us, then, talk of something that you understand. It is evident that you come with news; experience suggests that it is probably disagreeable. Ah me!"

It fell naturally to the lot of Mr Law, as the person chiefly concerned, to enlighten His Highness. It had the effect of darkening with weary disgust that florid countenance.

"Incredible," he said. "Outrageous! I should not believe it but for what happened two days ago. A messenger from de Mesmes waited upon me with a request for the suspension of the money edict, warning me that the Parliament would not disperse until it had my answer. I replied that nothing would please me better than that its members should sit until they rotted.

"Of course, Baron, Monsieur de Noailles has never forgiven you for losing him the presidency of the Council of Finance, whilst Monsieur de Horn brought me a complaint that you had robbed him of a fortune, and the Parliament dislikes you because it fears in our financial plans a threat to its authority. Even so, what you tell me lends them an incredible temerity. You'll have some evidence that they actually seek your life?"

"I have it from a trustworthy source, which I am not able to disclose."

"And they would really set my will at naught, would they, rescind my edicts and present me with a *fait accompli* of that magnitude?" Elbow on knee and chin in hand, the Regent sat forward, frowning. "Incredible !" he said again.

Madame de Parabère laughed. "Haven't you discovered that it is always the incredible that happens? Yet here it is not so incredible as you suppose. Your excessive good nature, Philippe, is the encouragement of those gentlemen."

"Ah!" He looked at her with crooked smile. "Little raven, you've been listening to Saint-Simon."

"No, no," the Duke protested. "Madame merely sees what is obvious to everyone but Your Highness." With the familiarity he had ever employed with the Regent since the days when they had been playmates, he now continued: "Your easy-going ways have robbed you of all authority with those mutineers, and where a frown of yours should suffice to quell them, you may now have to employ artillery."

"They're drunk with vanity and presumption," boomed d'Argenson. "They keep encroaching, and they grow by what they feed on."

Saint-Simon took up the tale. "They're conceiving themselves not a Parliament in our sense, but a Parliament in the English manner, which is a legislative assembly representing the entire nation."

"With powers," Mr Law reminded the Regent, "to bring even the King to account, as happened in the case of Charles the First."

"*Peste*! I don't think that is quite in the best taste," the Regent reproved him.

But the words were almost smothered by Saint-Simon in his haste to add: "They will justify themselves by representing what they do as done in the interests of France. Governing bodies are never more suspect than when they plausibly urge the interest of the people and act under the mask of public benefaction."

"It will need great firmness, monseigneur," said Dubois.

The Parabère laughed. "You'll have to supply him with it, Monsieur l'Abbé."

But His Highness was less amiable than usual. "Chut! Quiet!" he growled at her. "Jests are out of season." His face displayed weariness and irritation. "In God's name, what can I do? Summon the States-General?"

D'Argenson was prepared with advice. "A bed of justice will suffice, Highness." And he went on to remind them that the last one held to recall the Parliament to a sense of its duty had been attended by the late King, who came to it unceremoniously in a grey riding-suit, so as to mark his lack of respect for the assembly, and brandishing a riding-switch with which he had all the air of threatening its members. It was high time, thought d'Argenson, to renew a salutary impression which by now had worn off.

From this they came to a discussion of the details of that bed of justice which is a matter of history. You will remember the craftiness with which it was planned, so as to take the members entirely by surprise, even to the extent of not holding it at Versailles, but of bringing the King to the Tuileries.

By this expedient the Regent avoided giving the members notice until they were already in session in their own palace, leaving them no more than the time necessary to reach the royal presence. This last-moment summons constrained them – one hundred and fifty-three red-robed magistrates – to come on foot by streets that were lined with troops as an intimidating display of royal power.

There, in the Tuileries, two days after it had been planned in the Regent's study, in the presence of the enthroned royal child, mantled in ermine, sceptre in hand, supported by the princes of the blood, the bastards and the peers, d'Argenson, as Chancellor and mouthpiece of the King, scarcely concealed the satisfaction with which, in his own phrase, he set about washing the heads of those too-daring gentlemen of the robe.

His voice resonant, his tone harshly denunciatory, he began by reminding them that they were a judicial and not a legislative body, and that to assume the functions of the latter amounted to a usurpation involving the severest penalties. He based his definition upon citations by Kings Francis I and Charles IX, unequivocally confirmed by the late King Louis XIV whom they would remember as having come before them without any sort of ceremony, and with an unpleasant grin he let fall a reminder of the existence of the Bastille.

Next he announced to them that the decree by which they had presumed to repeal the royal edict for the banking of revenue had been quashed by the Council of Regency, and that any attempt to publish their decree would amount to a breach of the law and be attended by condign punishment.

The King, he thundered, required them to cease from abusing the right of remonstrance graciously restored to them by the Regent. Unless they preferred to be again deprived of it, let them keep within the limits of that which concerned their functions; let them confine themselves to processes of law between His Majesty's subjects, and not again intrude, as they had lately presumed to do, upon affairs of State.

He ended on the minatory assurance that lack of compliance would be attended by the severest pains and penalties to each one of them, and that in the event of any repetition of their offence they could not hope to be treated with the leniency which His Majesty graciously and clemently showed them on this occasion.

They might scowl and writhe under the fierce contemptuous rasp of d'Argenson's tongue, under his covert threat of the Bastille for some of them, under the undisguised and sneering smiles of the peers, but their courage broke and withered, and they bowed their heads in sullen obedience.

The Chancellor had entered into no details of the offence contemplated against Mr Law, nor had the Scot's name been so much as mentioned. Nevertheless, the gentlemen of the Parliament perfectly understood that it was their sinister project concerning him which had brought upon them the humiliation of that bed of justice.

If, understanding, they hated Law the more, yet at the same time they came to fear him as they had never feared him until now. They assumed that in some way, forewarned of what was plotting, he had exercised upon the Regent an influence great enough to have produced their shameful discomfiture.

Apprehensive of yet worse to follow, they sent their Vice-President Blamont to offer Mr Law their excuses that, misguided by prejudiced counsellors, they should have contemplated a course the error of which they now perceived with profound regret.

To Monsieur de Blamont they joined the old Maréchal de Villeroy, who had been in the plot because he resented the government of French finances by any foreigner, and the Duke of Aumont, who had been working in the interest of the Maines. In addition to offering the Parliament's apologies, they came to beg Mr Law to employ his good offices so as to bring about their reconciliation with the Regent.

Mr Law, who had now tranquilly returned to the Hôtel de Nevers after two nights spent in Dubois' quarters at the Palais Royal, chilled that deputation by his frosty urbanity. In tones that expressed the very opposite he professed to value their representations and assured them that he would do their errand to the Regent. Thus he dismissed them, without, however, quite removing from them the haunting fear of the Bastille.

Actually the moment chosen to approach him could hardly have been less favourable. He had returned home a few hours earlier to be confronted with an indignant Catherine, who desired peremptorily to know where he had spent the last two nights. His answer had been short and simple: "At the Palais Royal."

Her lip had curled in sarcastic unbelief. "And the Countess of Horn? Was she there, too?"

Of the resentment provoked by her constant and groundless suspicions his cold exterior had never given sign; nor did he give it now, when the resentment she aroused was deeper and more bitter than it had ever been.

"If I thought that you ask for information I should supply it. But for questions that are mere ill-natured rhetoric I have no answers."

"Indeed! And her ladyship's visit to you here? What sort of rhetoric was that?"

"She brought me information of the first importance."

"A woman you pretended not to know?"

"It was no pretence."

"Indeed, a shorter word describes it better. It was just a lie."

He sighed. "I wonder if the delight of others in your womanhood has ever equalled my frequent regrets that you are not a man."

"Delight in my womanhood! What do you mean?" Indignation crimsoned her from neck to brow. "Whom do you mean? Whom have you in mind?"

"I seem to remember that there has already been mention between us of the Count of Horn."

"The Count of Horn? You know that the Count has had of me no more than my fingertips." The lovely, delicately featured face was mottled and disfigured by anger. She stamped her foot. "You are creating a diversion, to draw me away from your…your wickedness, your falsity, your relations with this woman, whom you say you did not know, yet who called you John and carried you off in her coach,

140

slyly, when you slunk out to join her at the back entrance. Perhaps you thought I didn't know. Whither did she carry you? Dare you tell me? Or would you prefer to tell the Count of Horn?"

"I have already told you. To the Palais Royal."

"You laugh! God a' mercy! You want to serve me tit-for-tat. I think I begin to understand you."

"If only I could return the compliment."

"Or perhaps," she raged on, without heeding him, "you actually find that carroty-headed woman to your taste. Go your ways, then. I shall know what to do. I claim a like liberty."

For a moment he was tempted to tell her what, owing to a laudable reticence in the Countess of Horn, she had not yet discovered, that this lady was that Margaret Ogilvy for whose sake he had killed Beau Wilson.

But he realized in time that the knowledge, far from producing a surcease of her jealous frenzy, would supply it with additional fuel, and might drive her to incalculable lengths. So he held his tongue and left her to the wild surmisings of his infidelity, which his icy demeanour made her ever, and, as Will would have told him, not unnaturally, prone.

It may have been fortunate for him that in those days there was much else to engage his mind and so provide not only relief from his unhappy domestic circumstances, but a balm for old wounds, an anodyne to the pain aroused in him by that renewed if fleeting contact with Margaret Ogilvy.

Chapter 13

TREASONABLE PRACTICES

A small group of disgruntled gentlemen, brought together to condole with one another were exchanging heated words in the library of Monsieur de Noailles' mansion at Vincennes. They were the men chiefly concerned in the Parliament plot: the President de Mesmes and the Vice-President Blamont, shaken to the soul of them and still in fear of arrest, the old Maréchal de Villeroy, persuaded that he was in like case, the young Duc d'Aumont, that lackey of the Maines, representing their interests, and the Count of Horn, the bitterest of them all in his disappointment.

They were almost lachrymose until Noailles, provoked by a sneer from Horn, made the assertion that their failure could have resulted only from betrayal.

"My God, here's shrewdness!" mocked the Count. "Where we lacked it was in not foreseeing that with such a multitude ours would be a secret of Polichinelle."

"A multitude?" said de Mesmes. "There were not ten men with knowledge of what was actually intended. Besides ourselves, the Vice-President Blamont, and the Councillor Beaumanoir, the only others who knew our full intent were the Duke and Duchess of Maine, and they would certainly not betray it."

"It's not so much a matter of betrayal as of indiscretion," said d'Aumont.

"That," quavered the old Maréchal, "is the least that can be said."

"It's the most," d'Aumont insisted.

"I ask myself," said Horn, "who can have talked."

"Do you ask yourself or do you ask us?" Noailles demanded.

The Count's hackles went up. "After all, you are right. Why should I ask myself?"

"Because you may know the answer."

"Is that an innuendo?"

"Oh, I'll be quite plain. If anyone has talked it's likeliest to be you. You drink too much, Count, and men who drink too much commonly talk too much."

"Ah, but this is more than I'll endure. It amounts to an accusation, and that without a grain of evidence."

D'Aumont struck in to avert a quarrel. "Gentlemen, are we to wrangle over something which, if done at all, will have been done by inadvertence and cannot now be undone? I am sure that the sensible course is to stand together so as to repair matters, and find other ways to achieve our aim."

"A timely reminder, Monsieur le Duc," de Mesmes approved, whilst Villeroy was asking, "What have you in mind?"

"Why, this is how I see it. Lass' crazy schemes will be the ruin of France."

"We discovered that some time ago," sneered Noailles. "In fact, before we planned to have the Parliament deal with him."

"The difficulty," grumbled Villeroy, "lies in bringing it home to the dog. The least that one can say is that his gambling ventures prosper."

"For the moment," said d'Aumont. "It's commonly the case for a while with gamesters. The danger is that even if they didn't prosper, the Regent would still support him."

"By God, Duke, you never said anything truer," was Horn's bitter comment, remembering his own case.

Noailles was not conciliated. "If we are to content ourselves with stating the obvious we shall make no progress."

"We shall make no progress in any case as long as the Regent shields him," said d'Aumont. "That's obvious, too. But it's as well to state it. It perhaps points the way."

"In God's name," quavered Villeroy, "the way to what?"

The others were staring round-eyed at d'Aumont. He nodded, tight-lipped. "I see that you understand. Well, there it is, and we may as well face it. As long as the Regent is where he is, Monsieur Lass will keep his heel on our necks."

Noailles grew stern. "As long as the Regent is where he is? Let us understand you. Are you proposing that the Regent be removed?"

D'Aumont affected a laugh. "I am proposing nothing. I am plainly stating a situation."

This was too much for Noailles. He came to his feet. "A plain statement that is an invitation to treason."

Again d'Aumont laughed. "An invitation to nothing. It is not for me to be inviting. Yet since treason is mentioned, it might be well to consider whether the greater treason, the treason to this France, which we all agree a foreign adventurer is ruining, should not forbid us to remain inert. But, I repeat, I merely indicate. I do not advocate."

Noailles' quick answer forestalled any other. "It is well for you, Monsieur le Duc, that you circumscribe that treasonable opinion. You make it plain that to talk further at present is at best a waste of time. I trust that no one else could even bear to look along the road of which Monsieur d'Aumont says that he merely indicates the existence."

D'Aumont became voluble in protesting his repugnance to any measures against the Regent. Actually, all his aim was to bring home to them how idle it was at present to talk of concerting measures for dealing with Monsieur Lass. It convinced none of them; but at least it enabled them to dine together in harmony and amity at Noailles' table.

Least of all did it convince Horn. He had been at Sceaux, and in that atmosphere so openly and poisonously hostile to the Regent, he had seen how close was d'Aumont in the councils of the Duchess. It was clear enough to him that d'Aumont sought to exploit the present situation in her service, and being actuated by none of Noailles' high-principled loyalty, the Count knew no reason why he should scruple, in the pursuit of his vindictiveness against Law, to hurt a Regent who had so brutally dismissed his plaint.

Therefore, having contrived to return to Paris in the Duc d'Aumont's coach, he went straight to the heart of the matter, applauding the Duke's clearsightedness and agreeing that the Regent's protection of Lass was in the present circumstances an outrage to be resented by every true Frenchman.

Of course, d'Aumont agreed with warmth. "In fact, when all is weighed, we discover that it is not really Lass who is ruining France, but the Duke of Orléans."

"The shrewd old King foresaw it," Horn agreed, "when he provided otherwise for the Regency."

"You are not alone in perceiving it. There are those with no interest at heart but that of France, whose proper aim is to right this wrong."

"I rejoice to hear it. More, I should always be ready to bear a part in so laudable an undertaking. It would be an honour and a duty."

Now, however much Horn might be regarded as a debauched fribble, it remained that by virtue of his lofty connections his name was of weight in Europe, and would be of particular weight in Spain, to which the Maines were looking for redress of their wrongs. Hence, when he expressed himself so frankly, d'Aumont perceived no reason not to be equally frank.

"The Parliament, overborne by the Duke of Orléans, has removed the Duke of Maine from the Regency. Against that there is now no appeal. He could be restored only by the King of Spain, who stands nearest to the throne of France, and as the late King's grandson, is actually the real heir presumptive, and therefore the natural Regent. He should be invited to take the office and then govern by deputy."

"And that deputy," said Horn, to whom much was now clear, "would, of course, be the Duke of Maine."

"Of course. There would then be an end to these abuses, to this dissolute governing by harlots, rakes, and money-changers."

"Not before it is needed, by God," said Horn, with virtuous fervour. "Count upon me for one."

"I rejoice to do so. You not only perceive the right, you wish to uphold it. That, my dear Count, is the true nobility."

It remained for d'Aumont only to persuade Horn to pay another visit to Sceaux and offer himself to the Duchess, who would give him a glad welcome and enrol him in the growing army that under her direction was working to this noble end.

Having pledged himself, Monsieur de Horn went home to request his Countess to prepare for this jaunt into the country on the morrow. He found her deep in Montesquieu's *Lettres Persanes*, which had lately appeared, wearing a gown of shimmering silk of palest green without panniers, so that her admirable shape and lovely length of limb were not dissembled.

Under its crown of lustrous russet hair her face and neck and breast were of a creamy pallor. All this and the brilliant eyes and vivid lips that seemed ever laughter-laden, which once had disturbed the senses of a king by no means ardent, and once had driven the Count of Horn to such distraction as almost to have changed his nature, made him deplore the lack of affection in the gaze with which she returned his own.

"To Sceaux," she said. "I wonder what attraction you find there that you should wish to return so soon. Or is the Baroness Lass again to be of the company?"

"The Baroness Lass!" His tone and grimace were convincing denial. "Reassure yourself, madame. It will not be the sort of attraction you will be suspecting."

"Suspecting!" She smiled, with a flash of perfect teeth. "I am not suspecting. I was asking. But it is of no importance."

He was goaded by her calm into a full and boastful disclosure of the part he hoped to play in pulling down the Regent, so that he might afterwards square the account with that thieving dog of a compatriot of hers who had robbed him of a fortune.

"Perhaps," she suggested, "it was his way of forestalling your attempt to rob him of a wife."

His annoyance was the sharper, because of the truth he discerned in this, a truth he was not even concerned to dissemble. "I would to God I had never seen the sickly creature."

Her laugh was not in the least wifely. "You thought to grasp a wanton, and found a prude. A thorny prude. My dear, I commiserate you. These vexations are occasionally inevitable in such a career as yours. As for this revenge you contemplate, it is no affair of mine. And, of course, my opinion will not weigh with you. Yet I am impelled to say that you would be better advised to keep away from the Maines and their plots, or you may end by suffering more than mere banishment from Court."

He stood over her, tall, handsome, and sneering. "You are right," he said.

She raised her brows. "Surprising admission!"

"I mean you are right that your opinion will not weigh with me."

"Forgive me. I was stupid. I am stupid sometimes."

"Often. But it is no matter. This is Monday. We shall go to Sceaux on Thursday."

"You mean that you will go."

"And that you will accompany me. Her Grace will be glad to welcome us again."

"Maybe. But I don't think I care to be welcomed by her Grace. I lack your interest in her honey flies. And in any case, I shall be leaving in the morning with Lady Stair for Saint Germain, and we shall not return until Saturday."

"You refuse, then, to come with me."

"I have been endeavouring to say so – politely."

He clenched his hands. "You are resolved to infuriate me."

"Must we exaggerate? It is only that I do not care for the posturing company at Sceaux, and that I am pledged to Lady Stair."

Her mocking air, even more than her words, made him bid her go to the devil and stalk out in fury.

It was intolerable that a man of his birth and station should be unable to constrain a mutinous wife, or even be in a position to threaten that he would close the Paris house and dismiss the servants. Such a threat in his straitened circumstances would be a *brutum fulmen*; for of the house, which was hired, it was she who bore all the costs of maintenance.

If on their first meeting in London two years ago her provocative beauty had enthralled him just as his own good looks and lofty birth had made him acceptable to her, yet but for the great wealth of which she disposed and the great estate of Harpington, of which she bore the title, it would never have occurred to him to seek her in wedlock.

Perhaps he had been less than prudent in neglecting to make sure of the exact tenure of that wealth. Because he was entirely mercenary he must be at more than ordinary pains to avoid revealing the fact; and as a result it was not until after marriage that money came to be discussed between them. Trusting in a husband's rights over a wife's property he had known no misgivings. The greater, therefore, was the shock that awaited him.

In the rich Harpington estates he discovered that she possessed no more than a life interest, with trustees who had it in their power to exercise a measure of control over the considerable revenue she derived from it; so that even this could not be accounted free, and certainly not free enough to permit him to control more of it than she chose to allow.

In the cruel light of that discovery, it seemed to the Count that he had overrated both her beauty and her charm. Disillusioned, he cast aside the mask of amativeness, cursed the fates which had tricked him into marriage, and resumed his normal ways of life rather sooner and more flagrantly than he might otherwise have done.

As for her, equally disillusioned, she regretted that she had not given heed to her brother, Stephen Ogilvy, who had been under no misapprehension concerning either his sister or her very ardent wooer. He knew the bruised condition of her heart, and how vulnerable it left her to an approach that came arrayed in deferential tenderness. He justly appraised the appeal to her senses of Horn's external graces and the claim upon her vanity of the wooing of a man of his almostly princely station. And he judged it a fire that would be soon burnt out.

An attempt of his to dissuade her from the marriage had almost led to a rupture between them. But when things fell out as he had foreseen and much sooner than he had foreseen, it was he who had shown her the weapons she possessed in her revenues and exactly how to wield them for her self-protection.

Thus she had remained mistress of the situation. The establishment in the Rue d'Argenteuil was maintained because she chose to maintain it. For the rest, she practised no petty meanness with her husband. From time to time she even supplied him with sums of money for his needs, most of which he had gamed or else spent on other women. In this he had been quite flagrant, and had she reproached him, she would have stirred in him no emotion but surprise.

He would amusedly have reproved an outlook more proper to the wife of a tradesman in viewing the world of fashion. But she did not reproach him. She amazed herself when, the mask being off, after so brief an experience of marriage, she found herself contemplating his true countenance with utter indifference; more, almost, it seemed, with relief, as if the revelation severed a bond that had secretly been irking her, and gave her back her freedom. Understanding followed, and with it a measure of shame.

Stephen had been right. Horn had never touched more than her senses. That bruised heart of hers, as Stephen knew, was quite incapable of love, although to a man of worth she would have given that duty and loyalty which the Count of Horn could certainly not command.

So that his raging departure from her presence left her supremely indifferent, whilst the prospect of his departure from Paris was vaguely uplifting.

Chapter 14

ADVENTURES OF CATHERINE

On the following morning, of a sultry day of August, the Count of Horn went riding on the Cours la Reine, where the world of fashion was wont to parade on horseback and in coaches, seeking the cool by the river and the shade of the chestnuts.

He was without purpose beyond the need for action and movement that assails so many when out of humour. He came to suppose, however, that he must have been inspired by fate to take horse that morning, for ahead of him, on a beautiful white mare that was by now as well known as her rider, he beheld the slim, elegant, upright figure of Catherine Law.

She rode attended by a groom, who followed a couple of lengths behind her. That she should ride there was no matter for surprise, for it was the frequency with which he had trotted down the Cours la Reine beside her which had first supplied food for scandal.

But that she should presently greet him with a smile of alluring welcome was matter for surprise, indeed, considering the fierce terms on which at Sceaux, for his excessive enterprise, she had last dismissed him.

In his amazement he drew rein so violently as almost to bring his horse upon its haunches. Then, finding that she, too, had halted and that she maintained the invitation of her smile, he ranged alongside of her, hat in hand, his head humbly bowed.

"This is gracious, madame. Exalting. It permits me to hope that I am forgiven a rashness into which I was betrayed by worship?"

"I have forgotten it," she said, and added: "I have something to say to you. You may ride with me if it be your pleasure."

"My pleasure! Oh, madame, the poor word to express my emotion."

She laughed lightly, and touched her mare with her whip. As they moved forward side by side, she glanced over her shoulder to make sure that her groom remained out of earshot.

"Let me confess at once," she said, "that I have ridden here daily for a week in the hope of meeting you."

This was to carry him from amazement to amazement. "Madame…"

"That is not to be misunderstood. Circumstances have arisen to suggest that we should become allies."

"Ah, that with all my heart, madame."

"There is the need," she gravely assured him. "Great need. For our own protection." And she added the reason without waiting to be asked. "Your Countess, Monsieur le Comte, is on terms that are too intimate with my husband."

He was so taken aback as to forget his manners. "Ah, bah! To what gossip have you been listening? She does not so much as know him."

"Does she not? Yet she comes to visit him at the Hôtel de Nevers, and she calls him by his Christian name. I tell you what I have discovered. If she tells you that she does not know him, that is further evidence of the guilty nature of their relations."

The oath with which he received the news merely an expression of his surprise. "Pray when was this?" he asked, his tone still incredulous.

"A fortnight since. On Monday of the week before last."

Reflecting that that was the day on which the agents of the Parliament had gone to the Hôtel de Nevers to arrest Law, only to find that their bird had flown, he asked himself was it possible that he now held, at last, the explanation of that flight.

If what Catherine told him were true, it must be that he had to thank his Countess for warning Law. But how, he asked himself further, could she have known what was intended? At once he found the answer. He remembered how he had boasted to her what, by his contriving, would be done to the Scot. Noailles, it seemed, after all, had not been without grounds on which to suspect him of indiscretion.

He drew rein in his sudden agitation. "Ah! The traitress," he exclaimed. "She betrays me, then!"

He appalled his companion by a fury of which she entirely misconceived the source. "No, no. That is not what I say. It is impossible to believe that it is already so."

"Not for me. God! What a fool I've been not to have guessed it."

But in a measure as she conveyed conviction to him she found it slipping from herself.

"I will not... I do not wish to believe it," she protested. "All my hope is that there is yet time to prevent this thing. That is why I appeal to you. Between us we could... Surely we could frustrate their wicked hopes."

"Their wicked hopes?" He perceived at last how they were at cross-purposes. "Shall we ride on?" he invited, and after they had set their horses in motion again he remained silent, taking thought.

"You see," she said presently, "what I mean when I say that we should be allies?"

"Of course I see." He was in no haste to clear up her misapprehension. In fact he was beginning to wonder what profit he might find in it. Meanwhile he drew a bow at a venture. "And there's something else I see: that the jade has all but ruined me by her jealousy. By all time devils, madame, between your husband and my wife it is likely to go hard with me, as with you. We are both abused. You may well speak of an alliance. What else is left us if we are to prevail against those betrayers?"

152

He checked, perceiving that his vehemence was drawing upon them the inquisitive, questioning eyes of some of those they passed. He drew still nearer and dropped his voice. "This is not a matter that we can discuss in public here in the Cours la Reine. It is too grave. Tell me, when can I come to you?"

This scared her. "Not to the Hôtel de Nevers. John would know."

"For that I care nothing. But I cannot enter his house considering what lies between us, nor can I ask you to come to mine. What then?" He considered for a moment. "I have a sure friend, one Colonel de Mille, a Piedmontese, who has a lodging he would lend me in the Place du Roule. It is opposite the Church of St Philippe, over a glover's shop, at the sign of a red hand." Without waiting for her assent he added the question: "When will you come?"

She changed colour; her breathing quickened. "But I could not. You must see that I could not. It is impossible."

"Ah, madame, what is it that you fear? Detection? Take your precautions. Come at dusk in a hackney coach."

"But if it were to become known? What would be thought? Oh, you should not propose it."

"Nor should I if I knew of a safe alternative. But if we are to resolve this ugly thing, if we are to study how to fight this infamy, a meeting there must be. Perhaps you have a friend whom you can trust."

She had not, she confessed, almost in tears, and so, yielding to a little more persuasion, driven by jealousy, stifling misgivings, she consented to come that evening to the Place du Roule.

She took the precaution of going veiled and closely hooded and in a hackney coach, as Horn had suggested, to that dingy house.

A slatternly old woman admitted her to the gloom of a narrow passage, where the air was fouled by a conjunction of evil smells. With a leering assurance that she was impatiently awaited by the Colonel's friend, the woman led the way up a creaking staircase. The mephitic atmosphere took Catherine in the throat, and with the dim illumination and the repellent guide, brought her a sense of being soiled and degraded by the adventure.

Her pulses quickened by a vague apprehension and in ever-growing reluctance, she came to the room above, where the Count awaited her. It was small and meanly furnished, but at least it was well lighted by a four-branched candlestick set on a shabby console under a flyblown mirror. The young Count, tall, handsome and very brave in blue velvet with thin gold lace, seemed in himself to supply an adornment that partly redeemed the sordid setting.

He moved eagerly to receive her, yet with a reassuring deference. He was voluble in gratitude to her for coming, conducted her to a settee of faded tapestry, and offered her wine from a flask which with a dish of cakes had been placed beside the candlebranch.

"No, no. Nothing, I thank you." She was definite in her rather breathless refusal. "You'll understand that I must not stay. My coach is waiting. You will have given thought to our case. You will have decided what measures we should take."

"Thought!" he echoed. "I have thought of nothing else since I left you this morning; but a decision is not so easy. My wife has gone to Saint Germain. She had left when I returned, so that I had no chance to speak to her. The only way I could find to serve you would be definitely to remove her to the country, to place the little fool beyond the reach of your abominable husband."

"Oh, yes. Yes." Her hands were joined, her eyes raised eagerly to his. "Yes. That might be the way."

"Ah!" He sighed, and sank to the settee beside her, yet leaving as much distance between them as the seat permitted. "But it is not certain. I could try persuasion, and I will. Unhappily I lack the means to compel obedience, especially since your husband, out of his cursed jealousy, has reduced me by his swindling tricks so that I have hardly a louis to call my own."

"Out of jealousy?" She was puzzled. "Because of your wife?"

"Oh, no. Because of you, madame."

"Because of me?"

"Is it possible that you did not even suspect that you are the innocent cause of my misfortunes? It should be plain. Monsieur Lass

does not want for perspicacity. He was quick to perceive how it was
– how it is – with me, how deeply I have come to worship you."

"And he resented it?"

There was a sudden note of eagerness in her voice which he could
not understand. It was as if this were news that she would welcome.
He shrugged. "Naturally. Whatever licence he may claim in the
pursuit of his own gallantries, however indifferent he may be,
madame, to your feelings, yet he will not suffer himself to be made
ridiculous. He regards you as his chattel, and he will brook no
damage to his property."

Her flush, her angry gasp told him how swift was the action of
this poison. So he continued to pour it: "That, in fact, is what he had
the effrontery to tell me. Yet when I offered him the satisfaction usual
between gentlemen, even waiving the question of my birth and
station, the poltroon refused it."

"You… You would have fought for me!" She was in consternation.
"You would have put your life in danger…"

"Could I employ it more nobly? If you do not know that it is the
least that I would do for you, then you do not know me at all, and it
is no wonder that you have misunderstood me." There was a
disquieting throb of passion in his voice. "In effect, however,
Monsieur Lass preferred the weapons of his loathly trade, and by
those he has accomplished my ruin. But although my worship of you
has cost me more than a million, you are not to suppose that I regret
a louis of it. For I swear to you, that having conceived this worship,
I would not be without it to recover twice what I have sacrificed,
which is, in fact, every louis I possessed."

Here, coming from a man of such noble parts, was matter to
quicken the pulses of any but the most level-headed woman; and in
some measure it quickened Catherine Law's. Her glance was
troubled. "You…you are not to speak so." If it was a protest, it was
also a prayer.

"Why not? Why are we ever required to repress the truth?" In his
warmth he drew a little nearer. "What is there to impose restraint
upon me, married to that cold, treacherous compatriot of yours, or

upon you whose husband has no sense of any duty to you?" She was raising a hand to check him, but he swept impetuously on. "We are fools, Catherine; fools to be troubling to prevent something that may not be prevented, that it may already be too late to prevent."

"No, no!" It was almost a wail. "I'll not believe that. And, fools or not, we must persevere. It is what I came here to consider with you."

"And I have considered it from every aspect, but can find no course of action."

"But you spoke of removing the Countess of Horn from Paris…"

"And I warned you that I cannot constrain her."

"Yet you will endeavour? Is there no inducement you could offer, no attraction elsewhere with which you could tempt her? Oh, give it thought, I beg you. Surely, surely you can discover a way to set a barrier between them."

"Because you ask me I must. Give me a little time yet. Perhaps Lady Stair would help me. She has become attached to Margot, and if I represent that it is a question of saving her from the designs of Lass…"

"You have it," she broke in. "That surely is the way."

"Let me consider further," he begged, and drew nearer still, so that he brought up against her.

As if the contact were frightening, she came instantly to her feet.

"I must go." Again she was a little breathless. "It is not safe to linger. I… I might be questioned."

With hands that trembled, she hastily lowered her veil and drew up the hood of her long cloak, whilst he stood deferentially before her. He could not but observe that he had scared her, and he was too skilled to increase her fears by any rash insistence. "We must confer soon again," he said. "As soon as I have found a way."

She looked round that abominable room, and inwardly shuddered at the thought of a return to it. "I pray that it may not be necessary. It is not safe. If it were known… If I were followed…"

"Yet it would be wise that you should know what I propose. It might well require your assistance. I'll send you word. Oh, but guardedly, have no fear." He took up the candlebranch. "I will light you down."

When he had watched her flutter like a frightened bird to her coach, he climbed the stairs again, never heeding the obscene cackle of the hag who kept the house, or her comment on the unusual brevity of beauty's visit. Back in de Mille's room, he held the candlebranch aloft to survey it. He realized that it could arouse only repugnance in a dainty, fastidious soul nurtured in the sybaritic luxury with which her husband surrounded her. But if he took no satisfaction in quarters that certainly made up no Temple of Venus, yet he thought he might rest content with the comedy he had played, with the richness of his invention, and with the restraints he had imposed upon it and upon himself.

No later than the morrow Fate played into his hands by furnishing him a sound pretext for asking her to come to him again. It happened that he visited the opera in a party organized by Madame de Sabran, and that the Regent also chanced to be present, accompanied in his box, as had sometimes happened of late, by Mr Law.

Espying the Count of Horn, and perhaps not merely offended to see him, but annoyed that he should be in the company of one of the Regent's own leading favourites, His Highness spoke to La Vrillière, who was in attendance.

"Is that man without the wit to take a hint, or is it out of effrontery that he lingers here? See that he receives an order in the morning to take himself into the country and not to come within fifty leagues of the Court unless he is bidden. You may add that if he is still reluctant to leave Paris we can find him a lodging here. In the Bastille."

Of this, word came to Catherine Law towards noon of the next day, in a note conveyed to her as she was stepping into her carriage, by a flower girl, in a bunch of carnations.

When a footman would have thrust her aside, the girl raised her voice in appeal, holding up her posy. "*Mes beaux oeillets, madame!* Fresh from the gardens of Horn. From the gardens of Horn, madame!"

To Catherine's servants this might be without significance; but not to Catherine. "Let her come," she ordered. Taking the posy, she bore it to her nostrils. "They are sweetly perfumed, child." She gave her a piece of silver, and left her calling down blessings upon the gracious lady's head.

Sitting well back in the coach, Catherine unwrapped the paper sheath from the stems of the flowers, and found within it the note she expected:

> Calamity has descended upon me, to thwart my endeavours. I am ordered into immediate exile, and must go not later than tomorrow. This no doubt at the prompting of JL, who desires my removal. It is important that we confer before I leave. I shall be waiting this evening.

It bore no signature, and none was needed. It filled her with dismay. Once the Count were removed, and assuming that his wife did not accompany him, there would be no one and nothing to stand between the Countess and Catherine's husband. The circumstance, conveyed in the note, that Horn's exile was of John Law's contriving, was only too credible and desperately alarming.

So, repellent though the notion might be of again visiting that horrible house in the Place du Roule, Catherine braced herself to it.

She was not to suspect that the rage of the gentleman she found awaiting her was purely histrionic. Nothing could have appeared more natural than that he should be distraught to find himself banished at the instances of a cunning rival who desired a clear field. She was not to suspect his secret certainty that the only betrayal of which his wife was guilty was the betrayal to Monsieur Lass of the Parliament's intrigue against him. True, he could discover no explanation of why she should have warned her fellow countryman, other than sheer malice towards himself; but with this he was satisfied, convinced, in spite of Catherine's details, that the Countess could have had no previous acquaintance with Law.

"Ah, madame," was his plaint, "this is monstrous, terrible. We are the victims of a wicked pair who enjoy the advantage of being well served by authority. As surely as I owe my banishment to your husband, just as surely has he been prompted to procure it by my wife. Not content with having ruined me utterly, with having robbed me of my last liard, that wicked man is now to rob me of my honour."

He stood over her, a tragic figure, whilst she once more occupied the faded settle, and reflected genuinely his spurious grief. From a velvet bag she drew a bundle of banknotes. "This banishment," she said, "from what you've told me is made worse by your financial distress. This may relieve it at least a little. It is only three thousand louis, all that I can bring you now without being detected."

"Madame!" There was horror in his voice. It was an outcry of protest or refusal.

"It belongs to you. It is a little part of all that of which you have been robbed, so you need not scruple to take it. Do not offend me by refusing."

"Madame!" he cried again, and it was almost a sob. He sank to the settle beside her, impulsively he caught her wrists and bore to his lips the hand that held the notes. "The money… What is the money to me? But the gesture… My God, Catherine, that is everything. It brings me to tears that you should have this thought for me."

"Take it. Take it," she insisted.

"In my need I am so mean as to allow myself to be persuaded. But I take it only as a loan…"

"No loan. It belongs to you, and you shall have more."

The promise was easy of fulfilment out of her husband's unstinting liberality.

"Yet from you, it must be no more than a loan. For what Monsieur Lass owes me I shall render my accounts to himself when the time comes." He took the bundle and tossed it carelessly on to the console behind them. Then he was again kissing the hands he had not relinquished, kissing them with a passionate fervour that began to disturb her. She sought to withdraw them; but his clasp was firm.

"Your goodness intoxicates me. That you should have had this lovely thought of me, of my necessities, moves me to the depths of my poor soul. How shall I prove my gratitude; my gratitude and my deep love?"

Again she strove to release her hands. "If we are to be allies…" she was beginning, and her tone was of intercession.

"Allies certainly. But more, far more than allies. Let me prove my devotion, my worship. What need those betrayers matter to us when we have each other?"

"You are not to speak so, monsieur."

"How else? And why not? Our loyalties should be only for each other? Ah, Catherine!" He loosed her hands at last, but only to embrace her and draw her, struggling, against him.

White and trembling, a piteous entreaty in her lovely eyes, her hands now straining against his breast, she implored him to be calm, to release her. "I should not have come," she said. "I should have known to what I exposed myself. Do not make me sorry that I trusted you."

Instantly he let her go. He drew back, and rose. "How can you be at once so kind and so cruel? You give thought for my trivial needs." He waved a contemptuous hand towards the money on the console. "Yet you deny my deeper ones." Abruptly he was on his knees beside her. "Ah, Catherine, have you no pity? You see me almost swooning at your feet, yet you repulse me. You give me money! Dear God, do you think I thank you for that when you deny me all else, when you withhold yourself? I was grateful only whilst I supposed that it was an earnest of your love, of your response to the passion that is burning me up."

"Hush, hush!" she murmured, as she might have urged a child. "This is not right…"

"Not right!" He was tempestuous. "Then all is wrong. Is it not right to listen to our hearts? Catherine, dear Catherine, in all the world there is nothing that is more right." Again his arms enlaced her, his head upon her breast, and whilst she stiffened, she no longer attempted to release herself. "Why need it vex our minds," he continued, "if those disloyal ones should have their way, when it is ours to avenge ourselves by repaying them in the same coin?"

He raised his head and leaned forward, boldly seeking her lips. But from this her hands again defended her. Troubled by his gusty passion, and panting in his clasp, she still protested. "If… If I knew that repayment was due – if I were certain."

"Can you still doubt it?"

"I must. We have no proof. After all, it is only what we suspect." Then on a firmer tone: "I am an honest woman," she declared, "and very loath to be other. Only…only proof of John's infidelity could change me. If I had that I should not care. But before I am an outraged wife who avenges herself, I must be certain of the outrage." She broke from him. It was as if she had found an argument that put an end to hesitancy. She thrust him violently away, moved aside and rose. "If your note brought me dismay, it also brought me hope that you had found a way to…to prevent the accomplishment of this betrayal. If that is not so, I must wonder why you should have brought me here again."

Horn realized at last that he was dealing with a woman who under all her levity still loved her husband enough to recoil from infidelity. But in spite of that, and whilst inwardly raging, he persisted. "I brought you so that I might warn you of what has happened to me."

"And nothing more?"

"There was my need, my overwhelming need, to see you again before I go."

To this she chose to pay no need. "Have I at least your promise that you will endeavour to take the Countess of Horn away?"

He looked down on her from his fine height, and his dark liquid eyes were sadly reproachful. "How you crucify me!" he complained. "How you are at pains to let me see that all your concern is for this worthless husband of yours."

"My concern is for myself, as I have shown you. And now you must let me go. Tell me only where you are to be found if I should need you."

RafaelSabatini

He sighed and passed a hand wearily across his brow before replying. "I shall go to Sceaux when I leave tomorrow."

"But that is not fifty leagues away."

"No. I must take the risk, so that for your sake I shall still be near you if you should need me, as I shall constantly pray that you may."

"But you will be in danger."

"Gladly if it earns me your sweet concern." He shrugged the notion away. "If I go from Sceaux before you send for me, you shall have word of it."

She bowed her head, murmuring her thanks. Her hands were drawing up her hood. "Now light me down the stairs."

He did not move. He was pondering her with glowing eyes. "Already! What an anxiety to be gone, to leave me. Ah, give me the sweetness of your presence for a few moments yet. I do not even know when I shall see you next. Do not be so avaricious of yourself."

Her uneasiness was mounting once more under this torrential pleading, apprehensive of worse to follow. His hand pulled down the hood which she had now adjusted. His arms were again about her.

"No, no!" she begged.

But his clasp held her so tightly against him that she could not even struggle. "Ah, Catherine, Catherine, don't deny me."

Paralysed in that firm embrace, which pinned her arms to her sides, half swooning in panic, she felt herself lifted bodily and borne helpless across the chamber.

"For pity's sake let me go," she feebly moaned. "Oh, this is base! Base!"

His only answer was a whisper fierce and urgent. "Hush! Hush!"

He reached the settle, and flung her down upon it. To do so, however, his hold slackened, and as if revived by that measure of release, once more she strove against him.

They fell to wrestling so furiously that the slamming of the street door went unheeded by them.

It was not until a fumbling, clattering step upon the stairs and a raucous snatch of song came to disturb his frenzy, that he suddenly checked and fell back a pace to listen. Whilst, as for her, those approaching sounds, which in that place at any other time must have filled her with panic, now actually brought relief.

Horn rapped out an ugly oath, and after a moment's breathless listening pause, turned and sped to the door, with intent to make it fast. But already he was too late. As he reached it, it was flung violently open, and a large, gaudy man of middle age stood blinking on the threshold.

At the spectacle that met him – the Count breathless and livid, and the lady frantically restoring order in her disarray, whilst panting and trembling she supported herself against the end of the settle from which she had risen – a slow grin took shape on Colonel de Mille's flushed face.

"Seems I intrude," he chuckled. He strove to be solemn, failed, and loosed a cackling laugh. He advanced a pace or two, reeled slightly aside on unsteady feet, swept off his hat, and bowed. "*Serviteur*, madame." He turned sheepishly to Horn. "Devil take me, Monsieur le Comte, I'd forgot you were here."

"Devil take you, indeed, you sot," snarled Horn.

"Eh, now that's damned uncivil. I don't care for it."

As they faced each other in truculence, Catherine perceived that her way to the door was clear. With shaking hands she dragged the hood over her head, pulled her cloak about her, and sped to the threshold. Instinctively Horn moved to intercept her, only to find the Colonel in his way.

"Stand aside, you drunken dog."

Far from obeying, annoyed by the epithet, de Mille leaned upon him, using his weight, which was considerable. "Sorry if I intrude. As I've said. Sorry. Curse me for a marplot if you will. That I can forgive. But don't be uncivil. Don't say I'm drunk. And don't call me a dog. I might bite you." Still stupidly barring Horn's way to the door, he chuckled again. "What's troubling you? Your poor little shy pullet?

Bah! Let her go if she wants to. Never hold a woman against her will. I never do. Not worth it. Poor sport. Let her go."

The sounds from below told Horn that, in fact, she was as good as gone already. For a moment he stood cursing de Mille.

Then abruptly he turned aside with a laugh that still held some anger. "You were damned inopportune, Mille. But perhaps it's no matter. She has yet to conquer her coyness. That will keep for another occasion."

But Catherine, huddled shuddering and panting in the depths of her hired coach, was crying aloud, "Oh, vile! Vile!" and vowing that no other occasion should there ever be.

Chapter 15

THE ROYAL BANK

Amazing as must ever be the public history of the Laird of Lauriston, it becomes yet more amazing when we acquaint ourselves with his secret history as it now develops.

By the winter of 1718 his operations had become of an incredible scope and complexity; yet he elaborated and directed them with a mind that must at times – as we have evidence – have been distracted by the thought of Margaret Ogilvy. It has been suggested, and no doubt with truth, that only by deep immersion in affairs could he find surcease of the tormenting longings resulting from his brief encounter with this woman who had been the lodestar of his early years. His awareness that the Count of Horn had gone into banishment and that his Countess remained alone in Paris, in itself presented him with temptations which only by sweat of soul could he subdue.

It also happened that the Regent's attachment to him – his infatuation, as some describe it, for the Scot and all his arts – should have been increased by the Parliament's intrigues and the peril which had overhung him. Then, too, the subjugation of the Parliament which had followed out of that affair had so immeasurably strengthened the Regent's own position that he need no longer hesitate to indulge the Scot in the prosecution of those wider financial schemes of whose soundness Mr Law had been labouring to persuade him. In order to make him quite safe by placing him above such dangers in the future, his Bank, to the profound disgust of Noailles and his friends, was by royal edict raised into a State institution. Its title was changed from Banque Générale to Banque Royale, and its notes were supported by the King's guarantee.

And now, at last, Mr Law was enabled to widen his vast horizons by a charter which joined to the Mississippi Company, and placed similarly under his absolute control, those other French colonial trading companies, the Compagnie des Indes Orientales, the Companie de Chine and the Compagnie du Sénégal. This amalgamation was given the title of the Compagnie des Indes, but was destined to continue to be popularly known as the Compagnie du Mississippi.

For the operations of this imposing concern, which was to hold the monopoly of the entire overseas trade of France, fresh and vast capital would be required, and for its acquisition Mr Law employed to the full those financial arts of which he had given such abundant proof and which none dared now, as formerly, to deride.

The upward move in value of the Mississippi stock was still only gradual, and it had not yet reached par, despite the marvels still related of the inexhaustible wealth of Louisiana.

If this state of things did not trouble Mr Law, who took long views, it certainly troubled his more cautious brother. William Law could foresee no early likelihood of improvement when he pondered the poor accounts that secretly reached them from overseas, so grimly in contrast with the glowing reports that were still being circulated. He pointed to the stagnation of the Mississippi stock when compared with the brisk movement of the stock of d'Argenson's anti-system, which was earning for its shareholders dividends of from twelve to fifteen per centum.

The elder Law derided his brother's timorousness. "Did you suppose that a land that has been so criminally neglected could be rendered immediately productive? The wealth is there. Perhaps not in the gold and precious stones which were just a glittering lure to dazzle dullards, but certainly in the actual land. You'll not expect mere soil to attract minds that are just mud. But, depend upon it, we'll soon be seeing it yield its riches. Overwhelmingly."

"Maybe," said William, without conviction. "Faith, it's what we'll be hoping. Meanwhile would it not have been better to wait at least until the Mississippi stock is at par before burdening ourselves with these other enterprises?"

"That stock will be at par when I so choose, which will be when we launch this Compagnie des Indes."

"I'd like fine to see it," said William, and wagged a dubious head.

"So you shall," his brother assured him, and went confidently to work to make good the assurance.

For his purposes he invented that expedient which has since come to be known as the option, and announced that before the end of the year the Royal Bank would take up the Mississippi stock at par. Two hundred shares at this level represented one hundred thousand livres, and this he undertook to pay for these two hundred, which at the moment might be purchased in the Rue Quincampoix for sixty thousand.

So as to render binding the engagement, he announced the deposit at once with the Bank of forty thousand livres, which he must forfeit if he failed to fulfil his pledge.

Since it was manifest that he could choose to do so only if there were less loss in sacrificing the deposit, it was concluded by a public gaping in astonishment that Monsieur Lass had the best of reasons for knowing that the value of the stock was about to rise. This alone sufficed to awaken a demand for it, which in itself sufficed to send the price upwards.

The real appreciation, however, was not to come until Law played his second and master card in this deep gamble. His issue in the new and all-embracing Compagnie des Indes was of fifty thousand shares with a par value of five hundred livres each, so as to make up a capital of twenty-five millions.

He placed, however, a premium on the shares, so that they were purchasable at five hundred and fifty livres in gold, thus producing a total of twenty-seven and a half millions. Of this only fifty livres were payable on application for each share, the balance of five hundred to follow in twenty equal monthly instalments, and the original fifty livres to be forfeited in the event of failure to complete.

In this manner Law, taking inspiration from the gaming table, attracted the gambler, who, by staking a comparatively trifling amount on the chance of a rise in value, became the potential owner of a block of securities representing a substantial sum.

Nor was this all. Having invented this allurement, he now imposed the further condition that shares in the new venture should be available only to shareholders in the original Mississippi Company, and that in order to acquire one of the new India Company's shares, known as *daughters* it was necessary to prove possession of four of the old, described as *mothers*.

It followed that those who wished to subscribe to the India Company were compelled first to procure themselves the necessary Mississippi stock. From his knowledge of human nature, he conceived that this obstacle would prove a whet, and he was justified by the immediate sequel. The price of the old stock took at last a vigorous upward movement, and soon the Rue Vivienne was blocked by carriages and the Hôtel de Nevers besieged by persons of quality, who came to beg of Mr Law the favour of allocation before the lists should close.

A story ran that the Regent, requiring a lady-in-waiting to accompany one of his daughters to the Court of Savoy, and mentioning that he did not know where to find a duchess for the purpose, was answered that he would find all the duchesses he could want in Mr Law's anteroom, and there might take his choice.

At the same time the Rue Quincampoix was resounding from dawn to dusk with the cries of less illustrious buyers and sellers.

Gathering momentum in its rise under this fierce demand, the price of the stock went soaring beyond par. The more it soared the more eager were the buyers, and soon the price stood at seven hundred and fifty livres, representing an appreciation of fifty-five per centum on the face value.

The effect was enormously to enhance the already solidly established credit of Mr Law. It was seen that he had made good all his assertions concerning the Mississippi Company, just as he had earlier triumphed over the mistrust and ridicule with which his Bank had been assailed.

William Law was robbed of breath as he contemplated the reckless ease with which his brother's genius extracted millions from nothing more than faith in what he might achieve with them. Again he would have had his brother rest content and apply himself exclusively to the development of the stupendous enterprise for which all these millions had been assembled.

But that supreme gamester aimed at the control of a far wider field, every stage in the conquest of which he was carefully plotting whilst waiting to be served by opportunity.

It was not long delayed. It came, as he counted that it would, when the spendthrift Regent stood again in need of money. Settlements were sought by his bastard, the Chevalier d'Orléans, there was an estate required by Madame de Parabère, and Jouflotte was clamouring for money to maintain her more than royal splendours. His amiable Highness, who had never aquired the art of refusing, turned to Monsieur Lass as the natural provider. Monsieur Lass was ready to oblige. His Highness might have fifty millions when he pleased. All that Mr Law would require in exchange would be an assignment to the Company of the administration of the mint, and the faculty of minting.

His Highness did not hesitate. He granted the assignment for a term of nine years, in ever-mounting esteem of this alchemist who conjured millions out of air. At least, that is what his brother now asked him was he prepared to do in order to pay for the concession. "For the Mississippi Company, let me tell you, John, cannot spare fifty millions for such a purpose."

As usual, Mr Law smiled upon his brother's qualms. "It was never in my reckoning that it should. The public will provide the money as readily as before."

And readily the infatuated public did provide it when for his purposes Mr Law made a fresh issue of shares in the India Company – this time to be styled the *granddaughters* – of the nominal value of five hundred livres but at a premium of no less than five hundred.

He was emboldened to this daring step by the rapid absorption of his previous issue, and this time in order to acquire the new shares he made it necessary to hold four *mothers* and one *daughter*, whilst the lists were open for only twenty days. The further attraction of a promise of a dividend of twelve per centum, caused the stock to be avidly subscribed.

The acquisition of the mint was no more than a subtle preliminary to the destruction of d'Argenson's anti-system and the absorption of its privileges. This, however, must wait until the public should have digested the heavy meal which Mr Law had just served up.

In the meantime he quietly added to his other undertakings the monopolies of salt and tobacco, and he obtained an edict forbidding remittances from one part of France to another to be made in specie, enforcing the use of banknotes for the purpose.

It was an edict that must have proved highly dangerous to any who enjoyed a credit less absolute than his had now become. Actually it was covered by the specious pretext of making for greater security, and so as to render this manifest Mr Law added to his other financial inventions that of the endorsement, by which a banknote could be made payable only to the person named on it.

It followed from this and similar measures that now, three years after the inception of his activities, virtually all the coin of the realm, amounting to some seven or eight hundred millions, had passed into the vaults of the Royal Bank, whilst its colossal paper issue carried the country's commerce.

At the turn of the year the Rue Quincampoix became a humming hive of activity, from dawn to dusk, and every little money-changer's office there functioned as a succursal of Mr Law's Temple of

Mammon, dealing with the overflow from the Royal Bank of the ever-increasing numbers who were eager to buy or sell.

Trade, which apprehension and lack of confidence in the financial policy of the government had rendered stagnant, was flowing freely once more, employment was being found for the idle hands of starvelings, and the wages of the poorest labour had already doubled.

If the dawn of prosperity was as yet no more than breaking, it already sufficed, after all the misery endured, to cause the nation to hail Monsieur Lass as its saviour and to pour blessings upon his name.

Chapter 16

RE-ENTER DON PABLO

Mr Law sat making calculations upon a large sheet that was already black with figures, besides three thumbnail sketches of a woman's head that might have been recognized by those who knew her well as that of the Countess of Horn.

To him thus absorbed was announced the Earl of Stair.

His lordship in sky-blue, with stockings rolled above the knee, may not have been easy on the eye but he certainly commanded it. He sauntered in swinging a cane, doffed his tricorne, made a leg, and professed himself Mr Law's obedient servant.

"I protest, sir, that if you continue to rise at your present rate you will soon be beyond the reach of us lesser mortals."

"Your lordship rallies me. Pray tell me how to serve you."

"I thank you. I should not dare. I find you housed like a prince."

"Say like a cardinal. This house was once Mazarin's."

"Is not a cardinal a sort of prince, and one who knows how to live and how to build? There is no such noble staircase as yours either at Kensington or St James's, and the tapestries with which you adorn it would be worth a king's ransom. But then a million to you is as a guinea to me. Permit me to envy you."

"Why not? It's a form of flattery. Were you seeking a million or so?"

The question, coldly asked, shattered the earl's air of banter. "Could you tell me where to find one?"

"At need, if that were the object of your visit, as it is in these days the object of most of my distinguished visitors: the *auri sacra fames*. However, it were to do your lordship injustice not to suppose that you will have a nobler purpose. Will you not sit?"

"In effect," said his lordship. He hung his cane on a button, drew forth his snuffbox, tapped it, proffered it, and thereafter found himself a chair and crossed his elegant legs. "In your wide fields of financial acquaintances do you number, I wonder, a Spaniard named Pablo Alvarez?"

"Pablo Alvarez?" Veiling his surprise, Mr Law paused a moment before answering. "I know him. Yes. I believe he is in London at present."

Stair shook his head. "For once you are at fault. He was, but he has decamped. He is bankrupt and charged with frauds in connection with the South Sea Company. London wants him."

"For what purpose?"

"Why, to hang him, I presume. He has been traced through Holland to France. No doubt he will be seeking to reach Spain, where he could account himself safe. But the present difficult relations between France and Spain, will prevent him from crossing the frontier without a passport. That is something with which he may not have reckoned. I have just seen the Regent, to beg that this man, if he presents himself, should not only be refused a passport, but be arrested and handed over to us. His Highness proved difficult. He would give me no undertaking." He sighed. "I fear that for all my efforts I have never succeeded in winning his affection. That is why I now come to you."

"To me! Your lordship jests. Can I do what the Regent won't?"

"You might guide the Regent's mind. You certainly possess the secret of it. It is common gossip that who would obtain anything from His Highness should ask it of Monsieur le Baron Lass. Which is as it should be." Stair smiled. "The man who holds the purse should call the piper's tune."

"All that's but blether," said the Laird of Lauriston.

"Ay. Maybe. The question is will you move His Highness to oblige us."

Mr Law, his face expressionless, again took a moment to consider. "As you please. I'll see what I can do. But understand that I promise no result. I shall use my own judgment entirely."

"With that I must be content, I suppose. My gratitude may not be much to you, but, such as it is, I hope you will condescend to earn it by this service." He rose to go.

"The million you were asking for would be more easily provided."

Lord Stair looked at him with narrowing eyes, hesitating. "And, for that matter, far more welcome, I can assure you." He paused before adding with a laugh that betrayed embarrassment: "I suppose you could not tell me where to find it."

"Why not?" Mr Law spoke carelessly, as one to whom the bestowal of millions was negligible. It amused him perhaps to beat down the arrogance of station with the arrogance of wealth. "Why not? Buy a thousand shares in the India Company."

"But they are a thousand livres apiece. My dear Law! That would cost me a million."

"It need cost you little more than a thousand louis. For all you need deposit is fifty livres for each share as a first instalment. Before the second instalment falls due the stock will at least have doubled in value. You can then sell enough to provide the second payment, and before the third is due you will have made your million or more. I'll waive in your case the qualifying shares, and instruct my man McWhirter accordingly. You'll find him at the Bank in Rue Quincampoix."

Stair's hooded eyes had become very prominent. "And if your prognostications do not come true?" he asked.

"You may lose your thousand louis. But you can depend upon my word."

"It's a gamble, of course."

"Hardly. A gamble implies a risk, and there's none here. But maybe you're over-virtuous to gamble even when there is no risk."

His impecunious lordship stroked his long chin, reflecting. Slowly he asked: "Where do you say I'll find this India Company stock?"

"At the office of the Bank, in the Rue Quincampoix. Ask for Angus McWhirter, a brother Scot, who's my man of confidence. I'll give you a note to him."

Lord Stair stepped down completely from the chilly heights of pride, on which he habitually dwelt. For once he was rendered almost effusive. When presently he took his leave, he did so warmly, professing himself Mr Law's profound debtor and with a last recommendation in the matter of the Spanish bankrupt.

Although he had betrayed no sign of it, it was distressing to Mr Law to learn of the troubles of his old friend Alvarez, and it was still on his mind when, two days later, and just as he was about to go to dinner, his brother surprised him by ushering into his room the very man who had supplied the motive for Lord Stair's visit.

Don Pablo Alvarez, a trifle more corpulent than when last seen, four years ago, in Turin, his sallow face more deeply lined, advanced upon Mr Law with open arms trumpeting his gladness to see him again, and swearing that as he was passing through Paris he could not forgo the joy of coming to embrace him.

It was not a joy that at the moment Mr Law could share. He suffered the embrace with fortitude. "I wish I could return the compliment," he said. "But then, my dear Pablo, I happen to know the trouble that accounts for your presence."

"Trouble! Ay, and what trouble! *Dios mio*, what trouble, my friend!" His black eyes were wistful as a hound's. "But will you tell me how the devil you come to know of it already?"

"From the British ambassador. He has asked me to persuade the Regent to have you arrested and sent back to London should you happen to be found in France."

The Spaniard stood a moment speechless in dismayed amazement. Then he exploded. "Mother of God! Will they go to such lengths as that?"

"Reassure yourself," said Mr Law. "I have no intention of obliging my Lord Stair."

Alvarez resumed a breathing momentarily suspended. "*Valgame Dios*! I should have known that. For an instant I felt the rope round my neck." He eased his cravat as he spoke.

Mr Law thrust him into a chair, soothed him with assurances of friendship and assistance, and asked for an account of his troubles. Volubly, the Spaniard related how he had been caught and ruined over South Sea stock. He had accounted it crazily overpriced, and had sold what he didn't possess, convinced that a fall was inevitable and must enable him to cover his transactions. But instead of falling, as any but a fool would have expected, the cursed worthless stock had risen further. He ended by swearing that if anything was certain in this world it was that the South Sea stock was a bubble that would very soon be pricked.

"But not soon enough for you," said William, "and meanwhile it's yourself is the bubble that's been burst."

"And so you bolted," said Mr Law. "Well, well, if we can't be honest we should at least be prudent."

"D'ye call me dishonest?" Don Pablo was almost lachrymose.

"Don't you? Or is it honest to sell what you don't possess, and then decamp with the money?"

"What money? I take God to witness I had none of their money. It is they who were clamouring for mine, since I couldn't deliver the stock. And now, it seems, they're yelling for my blood as if that will reimburse them."

"A preposterous world."

Don Pablo took him seriously. "It's not for you to find fault with it, you that had the wisdom to come to Paris. Would to Heaven I had come with you when you urged it. The greatest man in France today after the Regent, controlling its finances, dispensing millions, courted by princes, housed here like a king. Ay, ay! Who wouldn't envy you?"

"Let us rather talk of yourself, Pablo. You'll be on your way to Spain. But things are not easy between France and Spain at the moment. You'll need a passport if you're to cross the Pyrénées."

"Cellamare is providing."

"Who?"

"The Prince of Cellamare. Naturally it was to him I went for help on arrival here. He is arranging for me to travel as a valet to a young Spanish priest who is returning to Madrid."

"I see. And when does this priest of Cellamare's set out?"

"In a day or two as soon as he returns to Paris. He's away at Sceaux at present."

"At Sceaux!" Mr Law's expression became suddenly alert. "At Sceaux, eh? Do you happen to know what a Spanish priest should be doing in that carnival-haunt?"

Don Pablo shrugged. "How should I? Cellamare didn't mention it. All he told me was that this abbé – Porto-Carrero is his name – arrived from Madrid a couple of days ago and will be returning at once."

"So! He arrived from Madrid a couple of days ago and will be returning at once, and in the meanwhile he spends his time – his couple of days – at Sceaux." Don Pablo was puzzled by Mr Law's apparent amusement. "I thought it singular that your proud, almost unapproachable, grandee of Spain should be concerned to help an absconding bankrupt. But now things begin to open out. Your abbé begins to look like a messenger – a messenger between Spain and Sceaux. Is not that odd?"

"But the man's a priest."

"That is what is odd. If he were not a priest the case would be less curious. And this messenger is not only a priest but a man of birth. Porto-Carrero is no common name. Now, why should such a man be running messages? Don't you guess the answer?"

"Whatever do you mean? What answer is to be guessed?"

"That these are not messages to be entrusted to a common courier."

"Surely that's just an assumption," William interjected.

"To be sure it is. But there's no lack of ground for it when you know what goes on at Sceaux. They plot there; they dabble gaily in high-treason; the little Duchess has said that she wants to set the kingdom ablaze under the feet of the Duke of Orléans. In the intervals of their madrigals and serenades and play-acting and a deal of harlotry, they conspire to overthrow the Regent and bring in the King of Spain."

"My God!" Don Pablo gasped. "But if it's known…"

"Oh, it's known. But the Regent laughs at their plotting, accounts it so much *cabotinage*, shrugs his shoulders at the scurrilous verses her Grace's hireling poetasters write to defame him. He may have been right, so long as all the plotting was just so much buffoonery, but what you now tell me suggests that Spain is actually responsive. It becomes serious. Perhaps Alberoni sees his profit in advancing the plans of the Maines. I don't think the Regent would laugh at that."

"Man!" ejaculated William. "That's just what he'll be doing if you carry that tale to him. Its foundations are over-slight. Ye'll need some proof before ye bring so heavy a charge."

Upon reflection Mr Law was to agree with this. "We must provide it," he said. "Where are you lodged, Pablo?"

"At the Spanish embassy. The Prince of Cellamare has offered me the hospitality of his house until Porto-Carrero is ready to leave."

Mr Law looked at his brother. "That alone should convince you. Or do you think it natural in the haughty Cellamare to take absconding financiers to his bosom? As for you, Pablo, you shall go back to the embassy in my carriage, and my advice to you is to lie close until you leave. If you should come to see me again take your precautions. And now let us go to dinner."

Don Pablo did come again, in the dusk of the following evening. Obedient to Mr Law's injunction he came secretly in a closed sedan chair. His compelling purpose was that he needed money, although he wrapped this up in the desire to take his leave of his old friend.

He reported that the Abbé de Porto-Carrero had returned that morning to the embassy from Sceaux and would be setting out for Madrid early on the morrow together with a Spanish gentleman named Monteléon, who had arrived from the Hague.

Mr Law supplied his financial needs with that princely liberality and contempt for money in which it was his way to deal, and desired him a safe journey into Spain.

"You are assured, I hope," he said, "that you are safely covered by inclusion as a servant in your abbé's passport."

"Oh, entirely. As the Abbé de Porto-Carrero's valet I share his diplomatic immunity; for he will be carrying embassy dispatches."

To Mr Law this was the last link in his chain of assumptions. There was about him for a moment the stillness of deep thought following upon sudden revelation. "Embassy despatches, eh?" he said at last, his eyes intent. "Then I was hardly wrong in guessing him a messenger."

"And hardly right," laughed Don Pablo. "For he is certainly not the kind of messenger you imagined."

To this there was no reply. But after the Spaniard, effusively grateful, had departed, Mr Law called for his carriage, and went off to the Palais Royal and Dubois, demanding that he be procured an instant audience with the Regent.

The little Abbé laughed at him. "Not if Paris were blazing," said he. "His Highness has gone to supper, and the door is locked for the night."

"It must be unlocked," Mr Law insisted, and he went on briefly to tell Dubois what, according to his deductions, was afoot. "Let these men set out by all means," he ended. "But they should instantly be followed and arrested."

Dubois was now well on the way to the fulfilment of his ambition to become a second Richelieu. Therefore this matter should concern him closely. Nevertheless, he laughed more freely than ever. "Arrested! Arrest two gentlemen, both of them men of quality, upon no more than these vague suspicions of yours?"

"My suspicions may be suspicions, but they are not vague. Where is your common sense? You say they are persons of quality. Since when has an ambassador – even a Spanish ambassador – used persons of quality for his couriers?"

The Abbé shrugged. "Come, come, my friend. These gentlemen are going to Spain. It does not seem to me remarkable that they should oblige Cellamare by carrying his letters."

"But don't you see that they are letters which this Porto-Carrero appears to have come to France especially to fetch? Probably in answer to letters that he brought. Don't all the circumstances point to that? All the way from Madrid to spend four days in France and three of them at Sceaux, which is bubbling at present with treason. You have your spies, Abbé, and so have I. It happens that there is a vindictive young gentleman named Horn at Sceaux in whose movements I take an interest, and I know what I am saying of their occupation there in these days."

"Yes, yes." Dubois was becoming impatient. "I know all that and more. And so does the Regent. Let us say that all your assumptions are correct. What is certain is that the Regent would never sanction any action upon them; nor do I see what action we could take."

"I have told you. Seize the person of this young priest, and get his papers."

"My dear Baron!" Dubois was scandalized. "You can't realize what you are saying. Papers under the ambassadorial seal are inviolate – sacred. Wars have been fought for less than the offence you propose. And, anyway, why so hot? If His Highness chooses to laugh at these plots, why need you trouble about them."

Mr Law strove with his impatience. "My dear Abbé, you do less than justice to your repute for shrewdness. As long as the plotting is merely at Sceaux – the windy histrionics of a silly duchess – you and I could laugh with the Regent. But haven't we something more? A messenger has come from Madrid. The Spanish ambassador is in the business. Doesn't this mean that King Philip begins to take the matter seriously? And you want to know why I'm so hot. If whilst the Regent laughs they cut the ground from under his feet, what would happen to me? My friends of the Parliament nearly hanged me once. And, for that matter, what would happen to you, Abbé? Do the Maines and their friends love you so much that you would feel safe if the Regent were overthrown?"

"It's all a surmise," Dubois insisted, but more thoughtfully. "And I certainly dare not take such extreme and dangerous action on no better grounds. To seize embassy papers…"

"But if they contain evidence of treason?"

"We can't prove that until we possess them, and we dare not possess them until we have proved it. Amusing, perhaps. But it's a deadlock, and I certainly dare not break it."

"Is that your last word?"

"More, my friend. It's an epilogue."

"Then I must do as I can."

Dubois was alarmed. "What the devil's in your mind?"

"That I must do it for you."

"Are you quite mad?" Dubois had changed colour. "You may be a daring gamester, Baron. But this is a gamble that should daunt even you. You will be staking your head on it."

"Oh! My head!"

"At least your career. It would ruin you. For God's sake take thought, man. Leave matters that don't concern you."

"I've endeavoured to show you that they do concern me."

"But not to the extent of running into this danger. I beg you to be warned, my friend."

"Very well." Mr Law became abrupt. "We'll say no more. And now, another matter. Lord Stair called on me a few days ago…"

"About a defaulting bankrupt? I know. He told me that he had sought your aid. What is your interest in that?"

"The bankrupt is an old friend of mine, and I should like to oblige him. There is a document I require from you concerning him."

When he had stated it the Abbé was bewildered. "You become more mysterious than ever. Do you wish to assist Stair, or don't you? Devil take me if I understand you."

"You will eventually. Meanwhile oblige me as I ask. You see that it can do no harm. France has no interest in this man."

Because this, at least, was clear, the Abbé made no further difficulty. But he remained profoundly puzzled and even vaguely alarmed when Mr Law had left him.

Chapter 17

CELLAMARE'S SATCHEL

Don Pablo's journey was proving by no means a happy one.

As much the aristocratic young abbé as his companion, who was the son of the last Spanish ambassador to the Court of St James's, treated the banker with even less courtesy than they would have shown him had he, indeed, been the lackey he pretended to be. Thus the pretence became more than a reality. He rode outside the coach, beside the driver, as tight-wrapped as he could contrive against the cutting December winds, cursing the supercilious young men so snug inside a coach that was nearly of the size of a room.

His only comfort was in the thought that he was now well on his way to the Spanish frontier and safety. This, at least, until Poitiers was reached. Here, as the coach was lumbering over the bridge that crossed the Clain, he became aware that a small troop was coming briskly up behind them. In this there was nothing to disturb an ordinary man in ordinary circumstances. But Don Pablo's circumstances were made extraordinary by his unquiet conscience.

Kneeling on the box seat of the coach, he peered back over its roof at the approaching troop: a half-dozen, red-coated musketeers led by an officer and with a well-mounted, cloaked civilian riding in the rear.

Spurring forward, they swarmed about the coach as it came to the open ground beyond the bridge, and a command to halt in the King's name converted Don Pablo's mounting fears into grim certainty.

The vehicle rocked to a standstill, and the sharp-faced young priest thrust out his head to demand a reason for this interference, assuming it to be an error, and announcing himself as the Abbé de Porto-Carrero of the Spanish embassy, on his way to Spain.

The officer could not have been more courteous. If that were really the case he would beg Monsieur l'Abbé to forgive this momentary interruption of his journey. They were in pursuit, on behalf of the British authorities, of an absconding bankrupt named Pablo Alvarez, and their information led them to believe that he travelled in this coach.

The Abbé simulated indignation, and in his nervousness lost his wits to the extent of denying knowledge of any such person. He was accompanied only by Monsieur de Monteléon and a valet, as their papers showed.

The officer dismounted, and one of his troopers opened the door of the coach. Beyond the little ring of horsemen some idlers of the town, their numbers increasing, stood agape.

The Abbé proffered his papers. He was a short, dark complexioned young man of peremptory manner. His companion, lean and lanky by contrast, remained silent and of a disarming languor.

The officer scanned the two documents he had been handed. "All in order," he said, but he still retained them whilst speaking to the civilian rider, who had edged his horse forward, so that he was at the other's shoulder. "Take a look at them, monsieur. Do you recognize either as your man?"

The civilian leaned from the saddle to inspect each in turn. "No," he announced. "You may allow them to proceed, lieutenant."

"Thank you," said Porto-Carrero, and held out his hand for the papers.

"There is a servant mentioned here," said the lieutenant.

184

"Naturally." His reverence was supercilious. "I should not travel without one." A careless hand indicated him. "He is there, on the box."

"Permit me to take a closer look at him. Oblige me by climbing down, my good fellow."

Alvarez came to ground quaking to hear the civilian, speaking incredibly with the voice of Mr Law. "It is your man, lieutenant. This is Pablo Alvarez."

"*Voilà!*" The officer laughed. "The ruse had almost succeeded, Monsieur l'Abbé." With sarcasm he added: "I suppose he, too, will be a member of the embassy."

Porto-Carrero became violent. "I know nothing of him. I hired him in Paris a week ago."

"To be sure. To be sure. Get back to the box, my man. You'll all come along with us."

He slammed the door of the coach upon the still voluble and excited Abbé, and gave brisk orders. They went forward, and made for the Auberge Poitevin, Don Pablo accounting himself lost and understanding nothing of his monstrous betrayal by Mr Law.

In the inn yard, under the staring eyes of landlord and chamberlain, ostler and drawers, with maidservants hanging out of windows and idlers forming a background, the travellers were invited to alight and to consider themselves under arrest.

Porto-Carrero, now grown abusive, was threatening France with all but a Spanish war to avenge this outrage, whilst the tall civilian quietly ordered the luggage from the boot to be brought indoors where it might be examined.

"It will cost you dear, I warn you," screamed the Abbé, beside himself. "Our passports prove us of the embassy, and our persons and baggage are sacred."

But Mr Law's exasperating calm was not disturbed. "The only one of you known to us is a defaulting bankrupt escaping to Spain. You'll not find it odd that we must discredit your assertions notwithstanding your passports. Passports may be counterfeited. You will be so good as to let me have that satchel, Monsieur l'Abbé?" He held out his hand for the leather case which Porto-Carrero's arm was hugging to his side.

The ghastliness of the Abbé's face and the froth bubbling at the corners of his mouth as witnesses to his panic must have assured Mr Law that all his assumptions were justified. "This, sir, contains embassy despatches. It bears the arms of the Spanish embassy and the embassy's seals. Look for yourself, sir."

"That is my intention." Mr Law possessed himself of the satchel. "There could be no more convenient receptacle for a defaulter's plunder. In these days of banknotes a million could be carried between these covers."

Montéléon put off his languor to intervene. He was very haughty. "You are surely out of your senses, sir. Because a rascal has imposed himself upon us so as to travel with us, gives you no reason for this violence. I warn you, sir, that you interfere with these despatches at your peril. Your grave peril. We will return to Paris with you, and the Prince of Cellamare shall answer for us. That surely will satisfy you. You cannot be so ignorant as not to know that if you refuse and break those seals the consequences will be very serious for you."

All this oratory, however, seemed wasted upon that obtuse civilian.

"Whether we are to disturb the Spanish ambassador on your behalf, and whether you return to Paris with us will depend upon what I find in this satchel."

In his own room in the inn, with the two still protesting young men and their pretended servant in attendance under guard, Mr Law, with scant respect for the arms of Spain which they bore, broke both seals and lock and emptied the contents of the embassy satchel on the table at which he sat.

It was, he realized, the boldest gambling throw he had ever made, and if his deductions were wrong and these papers innocent of treason, the consequences would be as grave as Dubois had warned him.

But his deductions were not wrong, and the appalling evidence in his hands by far exceeded his every expectation. As he glanced through those documents and verified their nature, the two young men, the Abbé in black, Monteléon in mulberry velvet, no longer protested. They stood before him, stricken and silent as a couple of detected thieves.

At last he looked up, as stern of eye as of tone. "Lieutenant, you will remove these three men, and lock them up for the night in separate rooms, so that they remain, as they would say, *incommunicado*. I'll take order about them in the morning."

There was a word of command, and realizing that further protests would now be unavailing, the Abbé and his companion went out, hangdog, between their guards.

Alone, Mr Law gave closer attention to the material spread before him.

First there was a note from the Prince of Cellamare to Cardinal Alberoni, detailing the enclosures which His Eminence was requested to bring to the notice of King Philip. It began with the sentence, "*I have waited until the vines were ripe before attempting the vintage, and ripe I think Your Eminence will now account them.*" It went on to outline the plan of campaign to be conducted by King Philip's uncle, the Duke of Maine. The Regent would be abducted by sure men, an easy matter, considering his careless, unguarded habits. Of what should be done with him when abducted there was no mention. It was a detail to be left, no doubt, to the discretion of the King of Spain. Immediately thereafter His Majesty should enter France, and he would be assisted by the regiment of the Duke of Richelieu, which was in garrison at Bayonne. They could count upon the support of the Parliament of Paris and of the nobility of Brittany, the hereditary foes of England, a kingdom which it was the Regent's evil policy to ally with France. King Philip would then be proclaimed Regent, to which office, as the grandson of Louis XIV, he had the paramount right, and he would be represented by the Duke of Maine, who as King Philip's Lieutenant would discharge the functions of the regency.

If this had been all, it would have been enough. But there was much more. Incredibly there was the draft of a letter which

King Philip was invited to address to the infant Louis XV, in the following terms:

> MY BROTHER AND NEPHEW – Never since Providence placed me on the throne of Spain have I lost sight of the obligations of my birth. Louis XIV of eternal memory is always before my mind. I seem always to hear that great prince saying to me at the moment of our separation, 'The Pyrenees exist no longer'.
>
> Your Majesty is the only descendant of my elder brother. My dear Spaniards, who love me tenderly and are assured of the love I have for them, are not jealous of the sentiments I evince for you. I flatter myself that my personal interests are still dear to a nation at whose breast I was nourished. How, then, can your faithful subjects regard the treaty that is being signed against me, or, rather, against yourself? Ever since your exhausted finances have been unequal to bearing the current expenses of peace, it has been sought to ally Your Majesty with England, my most mortal enemy, so as to make war upon me. To those conditions I shall never subscribe. They are unbearable to me.

Mr Law was not impressed by the epistolary manner which the poetasters of Sceaux sought to impose upon His Majesty of Spain.

He turned to a list, in the same hand as that letter, of the influential nobles upon whose support King Philip might confidentially count. In addition, several others, not named in the list, among whom the Duke of Aumont, the Duke of Polignac, the Duke of Richelieu, the Marquis of Pompadour, and the Count of Horn, had each written in his own hand a letter offering loyalty and service to the King of Spain.

Here, thought Mr Law, was abundant matter to check the Regent's amusement at the conspiracies of Sceaux, matter that might well bring a dozen fine heads to the block, among which would be that of his own bitterest enemy. It was also matter that would make him safe from those dread consequences of violating the sacredness of ambassadorial seals which Dubois had so deeply feared.

Well content, he locked all away, and called for supper. Later, towards midnight, with a cloak over his arm, informed of where Don Pablo had been bestowed, he went to pay him a visit.

He dismissed the man on guard before the Spaniard's door. "Go take your ease. I may be some time with this prisoner. I will send for you again when I have done."

He unlocked the door, and went in. The room was lighted by two candles flanking the remains of a meal and a jug of wine. Don Pablo, seated dejectedly on the edge of the bed, his head in his hands, and possibly a vision of the gallows at Tyburn before his eyes, looked up out of a yellow face. Recognizing his tall visitor, he flung an angry oath at him, and started up.

"You amuse yourself with me, *por Dios!*"

"And I hope that I shall amuse you also," said Mr Law. "To begin with, here is a passport for you, and here a cloak with a hood, in which to wrap yourself. I've removed the sentry, so as to leave you free to remove yourself. If you go by the back staircase you are not likely to meet anyone, for the household is abed. It will not matter very much if you are seen; but it will save me trouble if you are not. The post house is in the next street. Knock up the postmaster, get yourself a horse, and ride for Spain as if the devil were after you. If you deal generously with the postmaster he'll not trouble you with questions. And I've brought you another thousand louis in good notes of the Royal Bank.

"Don't stay to thank me, for it is I who am obliged to you. Your default and bankruptcy have done me a great service.

"I said I hoped to amuse you, but you had better wait to laugh until you are over the frontier. Good night, a good journey, and better fortune, my dear Pablo. Go with God."

"Oh, my friend!" Don Pablo stood shaking before him. "And I thought, God forgive me, that you had betrayed me. Oh, my friend, my friend!" He choked on the words, and suddenly burst into tears.

"*Que verguenza!*" Mr Law reproved him. "Oh, shameful! Is this how you laugh? Steady, man! It's not a time for blubbering, or for lingering. Come, my friend. Blow your nose, and be off."

Don Pablo seized Mr Law's hand, wrung it, kissed it, and drenched it in tears. "God reward you! My saviour!"

Mr Law took him by the shoulders, and thrust him towards the door. "The tale will be that you escaped in the dead of night by the window. And so fare you well, my Pablo, until your next bankruptcy."

Chapter 18

THE LETTER

Three days later, Mr Law was back in Paris with his two captives, seeking the Abbé Dubois at the Palais Royal.

It was two o'clock on a cold, winter morning when he arrived there, and the Abbé was already abed. Mr Law, however, insisted upon his being awakened, and whilst rearing his night-capped head, and hissing and growling like an angry cat, yet Dubois consented to receive this untimely visitor.

"Devil take you, Baron, couldn't your business wait until morning?"

"You shall be the judge of that," was the cool reply by a man in whom the Abbé discerned a certain jauntiness oddly at variance with his habitual impassivity.

Mr Law set down his large sable muff, and from under his fur-lined pelisse produced a black leather satchel bearing a coat of arms in gold and two broken seals.

At the sight of this Dubois' face lengthened and his eyes dilated. In his excitement he tore off his nightcap. "My God, what have you done?" he croaked. "Have you dared, after all, and despite my warnings?"

"Here," said Mr Law, "is the answer." He poured the contents of the satchel on to the bed. "But for me all would have gone snugly to Madrid under the embassy seals. Instead, there you have the lot."

It was not quite true, for Mr Law had abstracted, for ends of his own, the Count of Horn's incriminating letter.

In an anxiety that left no breath for further questions, the Abbé pounced with trembling hands upon the papers. As he read the first of them he sucked in his hollow cheeks into which the colour came slowly creeping. When he had read the last he looked up. His pale eyes were glittering. He grinned. "*Pardieu*! You've been lucky," he cried. "For you might have had to pay with a broken neck for these broken seals."

"I am always charged with luck when I prevail by calculation. Bah, my dear Abbé, I never gambled on a greater certainty, because for once in my life I cogged the dice. You see, I did not go after Monsieur de Porto-Carrero, but after an absconding bankrupt. I overtook him at Poitiers, travelling as the servant of a Spanish abbé. Of course I arrested him as well as his companion, the Abbé, and another gentleman. And, of course, I went through their luggage, solely in the hope of recovering some of the plunder. Could I have done less? In such a case, dealing with detected criminals, I could not be restrained by an embassy seal which might have been counterfeited. And here you have what I providentially discovered."

"So that's the tale, is it?"

"Unless your reverence can think of a better."

"Not I, faith! It will serve. It will serve admirably. Where art your prisoners?"

"Monsieur de Porto-Carrero and his companion are in the cellar of the Hôtel de Nevers, at your orders. As for the bankrupt, he unfortunately escaped during the night."

"Ah! That would be the Spaniard for whom you had me supply a passport. How vexatious that he should have slipped through your fingers."

"Vexatious, of course. But he's no matter. He served his purpose. Without him all this would never have been discovered. So that we are in his debt. All we need remember is that he has proved the agent of Providence."

Dubois thrust a bony leg from the bed, swathed himself in a bed gown, and gathered up the papers. "Come to His Highness, Monsieur Providence," he said.

But Mr Law shook his head. "Not I. You may have all the credit, Abbé. I have no wish to appear in the role of policeman, and there's no need to mention my name. You will allude to me simply as your agent, which is what in effect I was. Monsieur l'Abbé!" He made a leg, and went out.

An hour later, the Regent, rolling from supper, unbuttoned, and with a deep flush on his face, discovered Dubois in his anteroom, shivering in a bed gown, by the fire.

The Abbé was annoyed by the mirth his appearance provoked. "I am not here to amuse Your Highness."

"It is on such occasions that you best achieve it." His Highness hiccoughed. "And why the devil are you here?"

Dubois flourished the satchel. "To bring you a packet of treason."

"At three o'clock in the morning? That's treason in itself. For shame! There will never be a cardinal's hat for you by these crude methods. Never. Go to bed."

"Will Your Highness be pleased to realize that I should not be here at this hour if the matter were not of fearful urgency?"

But the Regent, who seldom knew how to be grave, certainly carried too much wine for gravity now. "What is of fearfuller urgency, is that I should get to bed. To the devil with you and your treasons, Monsieur l'Abbé. Good night."

Laughing and bawling for his valet, the Duke staggered into his bedchamber, leaving the Abbé scandalized and fuming at having deprived himself of sleep merely to witness this levity.

His revenge came, however, on the following morning, when closeted with the Regent in the room known as the Winter Cabinet, at the end of the Little Gallery, he spread before him the ambassadorial papers.

His Highness, freshly shaved, perfumed and powdered, brisk and debonair, had turned from the fire by which he was standing to greet the Abbé flippantly. Had his reverence, he asked, really been so discourteous as to try to keep him from his bed last night or had he merely dreamed it. But his manner changed when he had glanced through Cellamare's letter. By the time the other exhibits had been examined he was more serious than Dubois had ever known him, a thundercloud darkened the fleshy, fresh-complexioned face.

The rest of this Cellamare affair, whose discovery was so signally to enhance Dubois' credit, both at home and abroad, is in the history books. King Philip's ambassador, coming suavely to request the return of his satchel, was placed under arrest that same day; his papers were seized and closely examined by Dubois, as Secretary of State for Foreign Affairs, and Le Blanc, the Secretary of State for War, after which the Prince was escorted under guard to the frontier. On the following morning a detachment of musketeers was sent down to Sceaux to arrest the Duke and Duchess of Maine, and a good deal of china was broken by the tempestuous Duchess, who stood on her toes to increase her child-like height, and screamed that she was a granddaughter of the great Condé, in the vain hope of intimidating the officer who demanded her surrender.

"You may arrest me," she declared, "but you will never subdue me."

She was packed off – like Eve, as one chronicler has it, expelled from her terrestrial Paradise – to Dijon, there to cool down and think things over, and thence, a few months later, subdued or not, to be pestering the Regent with letters in which, derisorily, she protested loyalty.

Her feeble Duke, inveighing passionately against his wife for having led him by the nose into this treasonable quagmire, was locked up in the fortress of Donkers in Picardy.

As for the others, those betrayed by Cellamare's list and those yet more signally betrayed by their own letters, they were, with the exception of some who contrived to escape, rounded up and lodged in the Bastille to await the Regent's pleasure.

The Count of Horn was not of these, because his letter to King Philip remained in Mr Law's possession. Equipped with it, very late at night, following upon the day that had seen the Regent unleash the hounds of his justice, the Scot had himself conveyed in a sedan chair borne by men in plain liveries and preceded by a lantern-bearer to the house in the Rue d'Argenteuil that was tenanted by the Countess of Horn. Perhaps in an excess of prudence he announced himself to the porter as Monsieur du Jasmin, begging to be received by the Countess despite the lateness of the hour.

As he conceived, the name did not mystify her for more than an instant. After all, it was an easy guess that "Monsieur du Jasmin" must stand for "Jessamy John". Less easy was it to guess why he should come seeking her. She was already abed, and there was a moment of tremor and hesitation before she consented to rise and receive him.

He was conducted by a footman, not to the salon, but to her boudoir, a graciously intimate room as seen in the subdued candlelight. Its rococo panels framed a brocade of a faded rose-colour and it was furnished with a deal of chinoiserie, of lacquered cabinets and choice porcelains. There was a clavichord in satinwood and a tall harp beside it. An Indian carpet covered most of the floor.

She came to him in a peignoir of white silk that clothed her from neck to heel and lent height to her slim stature. Her russet hair, piled high, was without cap or powder. There was surprise and something akin to alarm in the dark eyes that intently considered him as he made his bow. He was urbanely formal.

"You are gracious to receive me, madame. I trust that my errand will justify the intrusion and excuse the hour of it. Had I not been detained this evening by the Regent I would have come much earlier."

Her questioning eyes continued to regard him in silence, waiting, whilst he loosened his pelisse and let it hang open, disclosing the richness of his dress, of stone-coloured velvet with narrow gold lace.

She spoke at last, formal in her turn. "Put off your cloak. Come nearer to the fire. The night is cold."

He drew a paper from his muff, then left it with his pelisse and tricorne on a chair, and went forward as he was bidden, but ignored the hand that waved him to a kidney-shaped settee. "I have come to discharge a debt," he announced.

She smiled. "I am aware of none."

"I should be insensible, indeed, if I were not. Pray look at this."

Frowning, she took the paper, and the frown deepened as she read that letter in her husband's hand to the King of Spain. She raised bewildered eyes. "I do not understand."

Very briefly he told her of the plot which history knows as the Cellamare Conspiracy. "There are several such letters at this moment in the Regent's possession, for which those reckless penmen will be fortunate if they do not pay with their heads. That can happen only if His Highness should display a clemency rare in princes when dealing with such plots against them. Meanwhile, the writers of those letters, saving only de Nesle and Pompadour, who have fled and are being hunted, and Monsieur de Horn, whose letter I have been able to subtract from the package before it reached the Regent, are already in the Bastille."

"But…" She broke off, and it was a moment before she again found words. "You are singularly generous. Indeed, I do not understand why you should do this for the Count of Horn. I can hardly suppose that you love him."

"But I must suppose that you do."

"Is that your reason?"

"It should suffice. But I have said that I discharge a debt. You may have forgotten that I owe you my life. I am glad to be able to repay in kind."

"Your life?" Her eyes were round; her expression so startled as to puzzle him.

"When you warned me of what the Parliament intended."

"Oh, that!" She seemed to breathe more freely. It was as if she had supposed him to allude to something else.

196

"I do not exaggerate. Return that letter to your husband. Thus we are quits."

"To your great relief, no doubt."

"Naturally. I have always, I hope, been scrupulous to pay my debts." He paused a moment, and then added: "There is no reason to prolong this intrusion. If possible it will be best if you do not tell your husband how you have recovered the letter for him. You will suffer me to take my leave, madame."

He bowed and was already turning aside to recover cloak and hat when she checked him. "A moment, John. This letter… If it should be discovered that you abstracted it…would you not be compromised?"

"If it were discovered. But there is no fear of that so long as you do not tell the Count that you had it from me, and no need for concern."

"But there is. There must be. Is it not treason to conceal treason?" She was suddenly resolute. "I will not have you do it."

"Not do it? You have not understood that nothing less will save your husband?"

"My husband!" The curling lip, and the slow scorn with which she invested the ejaculation, took him by surprise. "You know my husband. You used to be a judge of men, John. Can you suppose that I would have you put perhaps your very life in peril for such a man?"

His amazement deepened and brought discomfort with it. He was reminded of something that Lady Stair had said, and words and tones that had vaguely mystified him on the day when Margaret had carried him in her coach to the Palais Royal. He answered lamely, "It is not for the Count of Horn that I do this. It is for you."

"Ah, yes. For me. Once before you put your life in danger for me, to deliver me from the vile designs of a worthless man. Let that suffice. It is not a sacrifice I could accept twice in a lifetime, and certainly not for the sake of the Count of Horn. Take back this letter."

"Madame, I beg you to reflect…"

"It needs no reflection. Oh, I see. I shock you by my lack of wifely duty, my sheer disloyalty. There are other loyalties in life. There is loyalty to one's own self, to one's own heart and soul and dignity. Other loyalties must be earned before these can be subdued."

His face had darkened. "I hear you with regret," he said. "Oh, and with reluctance…"

"Reluctance to have me unveil my life to you. I understand."

"No, no. It is just that I hoped you had found happiness."

"Happiness?" She uttered a little mirthless laugh. "I have come to wonder what it might be," she said, and reminded him of something he had said once to his brother in much the same words. "I caught a fleeting glimpse of it once; a mirage, a will-o'-the-wisp that flashed and vanished."

Because he thought that he understood the allusion his discomfort deepened.

"Oh, to be sure I have not been lucky in my husbands," she went on, "for which I have only my sorry wits to blame. I am paid as a fool should be. Once, John, you thought well of me."

Emotion caught him and betrayed him out of his aloofness. "Once I loved you," he amended, and saw the colour flood into her pallid face.

"How deceived you must have been in me. For I am just a poor creature to be so easily deceived by outward glitter." She sank to the chair, by which she had been standing, and leaning forward, her elbows on her knees, she continued reflectively, a quiet bitterness in her words.

"Ned Wilson should have sufficed to cure me. Yet when the Count of Horn wooed me I was so foolish as to hope that with him I might yet repair the wreckage of my life. My brother Stephen warned me. You remember Stephen. He was your friend. He warned me, but I preferred to trust my silly intuitions.

"Only when I was fast in wedlock did I come to know the Count of Horn to be what Stephen said and what you know he is: a profligate, a fortune-hunter, an animal, who wooed me because he believed me to be a wealthy woman. He was not wrong, for I am wealthy; very wealthy; and yet he was wrong because my wealth is beyond his reach, protected from him by an entail. You see, I have a son."

The announcement was as a sword through his flesh. She saw him wince and lose some colour. "Does that hurt?" she asked with a sudden plaintive tenderness, as if sorry for the wound she dealt. "You did not know?"

"I did not," he answered, and asked: "King William's son?"

The pain in her eyes showed him that he had stabbed her in his turn. The ghost of a smile fluttered on her lips. "Did you suppose that I had known other lovers? Yes. King William's son. The estates of Harpington are entailed upon him. I enjoy in them no more than a life interest."

He was master of himself again. "In that at least, then, I may congratulate you."

"And commiserate me in all the rest. Now that I've laid so much bare to you. But then I wanted you to know. I wanted you to understand why I will not have you take a risk for the Count of Horn. That you should have wished to do so for my sake is a thought that I shall treasure, John; perhaps the greatest treasure I shall ever have now. Do not deny it me by insisting that you merely sought to pay a debt. Confess that this was not altogether true."

The pleading note was more than he could resist. "Not altogether true, perhaps," he gently agreed.

"You thought to save me sorrow, supposing this man Horn to be dear to me." She stood up. "Instead..." She choked on the word. It became a sob, and for a moment afterwards she was silent, steadying herself. "Forgive me. Your action has stirred depths that I thought were stilled for ever. Was there ever, I wonder, so much irony in any woman's life. To have been the wife of two men and the mistress of a third, and yet in all my life to have loved but one man, to whom I have been neither."

Between longing and indignation he was sorely shaken. "I hear you say it, and yet how to believe it? When once it was in your hands to choose, you chose otherwise."

"It was never in my hands to choose. What help had I?" she demanded almost fiercely. "What help when...?"

There, abruptly, she broke off. She turned from him to stare into the fire, so that he could no longer see her eyes.

"When what?" he asked.

"When..." She seemed to grope. Then in a low voice she added: "When you had killed my husband."

"Was that why you did not follow me to Holland? Why you ignored my appeal, left even my letters unanswered?"

She took time to answer, as if she hesitated. "Was it not enough?" she asked at last. "What would the world have said?"

"The world! Need we have been concerned with the world? And what, after all, could it have said? That I had killed your husband because for his own foul profit he was complacently ready to procure you to the King and all but made a jest of it in his cups."

Still she did not meet his glance. "That...that would have been accounted a pretext," she faltered.

For a moment he stared at her in silent amazement. "Am I really to believe that such a thought prevailed? Yours was an intrepid, self-reliant soul. You were all courage, Margaret."

"Perhaps it needed courage to let you go." As abruptly as she had turned aside, she swung to face him again. "Oh, do not let us pursue it. It wounds too deeply. You must take back this letter, John, for I will not have you place yourself in danger."

' 'There is no danger."

"Do you think to deceive me? You may be a great man in France today, the close friend of the Regent, courted by the noblesse, dispenser of millions, invested with almost kingly power, but all that would not suffice to shield you from the consequences of treason."

He shrugged. "Let me take the risk of it. I am used to risks. I have lived by them, and prospered. Besides – reflect! – what can I do now? You'll see that I have burnt my boats. Can I go to the Regent and say 'here is a letter which I purloined from the packet'? That would be ruin, indeed, for he would be left wondering how many more I had purloined. If I were to take back that letter it could only be to destroy it."

"I see," she acknowledged gravely.

"And dismiss your fears; for the only risk I run is that you or the Count of Horn should denounce my theft; and that," he added with a smile, "of course you dare not."

"Had I not better burn it, then?"

"If you wish, but it would be wiser first to show it to the Count, so that he may have proof that it has not reached the Regent's hands."

She stood for a moment still hesitating; then she loosed the neck of her peignoir, folded the paper and slipped it into her bosom.

His eyes, intent upon her graceful movements, were hungry, and his face was drawn as if with pain.

Meeting his glance again she gave him a wistful smile. "What you have done, John, is magnanimous, all things considered. It is worthy of you."

"It might be magnanimous if it were done to serve the Count of Horn."

She shook her head. "I would not deny myself the consolation of knowing that it was done for me."

"Nor I the satisfaction of having done it. And now…if you will give me leave… It is very late."

He waited for her to offer him her hand. Instead she stood straight and stiff before him, her eyes dim, her lips tremulous. "It is not likely that you will come again. And I dare not ask it, unless you should ever need me. Nor is that likely. But if ever it should be…" She made a pathetic little gesture of arms and body that was fully expressive, and abruptly held out her hand. "There is nothing I would not do for you, John."

He was bearing her hand to his lips when it was suddenly snatched away. Startled, he straightened himself to find her gazing at him through tears.

"I wonder, John, would you bestow a crumb of comfort on a poor, lonely woman to whom you are very dear; leave her a memory to cherish, a heartbeat about which to weave her daydreams. Take me in your arms, John, and hold me close for just a little moment. Throw just an instant's bridge across the abyss between us. Could you?"

"Margaret!"

He strained her against him so that every line of her became impressed upon him. He bent his head and kissed her on quivering lips that were very readily surrendered.

"It will be fifteen years next month since you so held me," she murmured. ' "We were almost children then. Do you remember?"

"Do I remember!" He kissed her again before she gently put him from her.

' 'Now go," she said.

His obedience was instant. "Goodbye, Margaret. God have you in His keeping."

She watched him as he gathered up cloak and hat and muff and went quickly from the room, and it was for long thereafter that he was so to remember her, standing like a straight, white pillar, sad-eyed, where he had left her.

Chapter 19

THE HONOUR OF
THE COUNT OF HORN

Paris had been agog that same evening with the news of yesterday's arrest of the Prince of Cellamare and the hunt for the others in the conspiracy in which he had been engaged. When word of it reached the ears of Colonel de Mille, who was aware from Horn's indiscretions of the Count's part in those dangerous activities, he conceived it a friend's duty to get word of it to Horn so that betimes he might place himself in safety. Because uncertain of the Count's whereabouts, not knowing whether he was still at Sceaux, he decided to seek the Countess in order to inform himself. Although it was very late when he reached this decision he made up his mind to go to her at once, even if it should entail dragging her from her bed.

Coming down the Rue d'Argenteuil at about an hour after midnight, he beheld issuing from the Count's house and silhouetted against the light of a lantern, a tall figure, which he supposed to be Horn's. He lengthened his stride and raised his voice.

"Hi! Monsieur le Comte! Hi!"

But paying no heed, the tall figure stepped into a waiting sedan chair. The chairmen took up their burden, and with the lantern-bearer marching ahead, the chair moved off.

Still shouting and still unheeded, the Colonel reached the house. The porter, to whom he was known, paused in the act of closing the door to inform him that the Count of Horn was not in Paris and that the gentleman who had just left was a Monsieur du Jasmin.

"Monsieur du Jasmin!" the Colonel echoed. "An odd name. Was he seeking Monsieur le Comte?"

"No, my Colonel. He was visiting Madame la Comtesse."

"Parbleu !" said de Mille, and checked on a further exclamation of shocked surprise.

What next he did was in obedience to his instincts for never neglecting to gather information that might conceivably be turned to account. He went off at speed on the trail of that sedan chair, guided by the lantern that was swinging now in the distance. It might be profitable to know who, in effect, was this Monsieur du Jasmin, who visited Madame at midnight.

The porter closed and locked the door at last, for the night as he supposed. But within some ten minutes he was brought back to it by a loud knocking. This time he was confronted by a man heavily cloaked, who thrusting him aside stepped past him and let the cloak fall open as soon as he was within.

"Monsieur le Comte!" ejaculated the porter in surprise. "Why, only a moment ago Monsieur le Colonel de Mille was here and I told him that you were not in Paris."

Horn paid no heed. His manner was fevered, breathless. "Madame la Comtesse?" he asked sharply. "She is at home?"

"Madame will have retired for the night, I think."

That appeared to be enough, for the Count went leaping up the wide, dimly lighted staircase, two steps at a time.

His wife's maid stood before him in the antechamber with word that Madame la Comtesse was in bed. With a mumbled answer he took up a lighted candlebranch from a side table, and still cloaked and hatted entered the bedchamber unannounced.

The Countess was reclining, propped by pillows, her soul still quivering from the emotional storm through which she had passed. She raised herself and turned sharply to survey this rude intruder.

"You!" she said, and a subtler ear than his might have gathered from the monosyllable that none could have been less welcome at that moment. "Why are you here? What do you want? Why do you break in on me in this gross way?"

"You'll have to forgive me," he rasped. She saw that he was pale and that there was a wildness in his air. "It's not a time for madrigals. If I've ventured to break the ban and come to Paris, it should not be necessary to tell you that the matter is serious. It's a case of life and death in fact."

"Whose life, pray, and whose death?"

"Whose? *Mordieu*! Whose but mine? I am in mortal danger, madame. So let that excuse my brusqueness."

"Is it also the reason why you keep your hat on?"

"It's not my hat that matters, madame, but my head."

"Whilst you retain it you might at least uncover it. Still…"

"Oh, curse my hat!" He swept it off and cast it from him with an obedience that might have surprised her if she had not already guessed the source of his manifest panic and the reason for his presence. "I am a hunted man. I am entangled in that cursed plot of the Maines and that old fool Cellamare. You'll have heard that it has been discovered. Cellamare and the Maines and some others have already been arrested. The evidence is in the hands of the Regent, and amongst it there's a letter I was mad enough to be persuaded to write to the King of Spain. Unless I can place myself at once beyond the reach of the Lieutenant-General I am a dead man."

"Then why are you here? Why have you ventured into Paris?"

It was a moment before he could control the rage that surged in him at this cool indifference to the deadly peril he disclosed. At last he found his voice to answer her. "I… I had to come. I need your help. I am without money, and I must have money if I am to escape. For God's sake don't look at me like that, Margot. It's not the moment. I know my faults. I know I've a cursed nature. But

205

underneath it all I've loved you, Margot, and if you'll help me now, in this desperate pass, I swear to God you shall have no cause to complain of me hereafter. Our separation need be only temporary, and…"

"That is what I fear," she interrupted. An ineffable smile curled her lip. "The past exists. The future does not. And I know you too well by now to suppose that once this danger is behind you…"

"Don't say it, Margot. Don't say it!"

"Indeed, there is no need. Instead I might ask you for a better reason than you have given why I should help you."

"My God!" he cried, his temper rising again. "Do you realize what you are saying? What sort of a woman are you? Can you lie there unmoved on your bed when my very life is threatened? After all, madame, I am your husband."

"You remember it, do you?"

"I do," he roared, whipped to passion by this outrageous coldness. "And I have a husband's rights. The right to command what I have been weakly content to beg from you."

She smiled into that flushed, distorted face, those blazing eyes. "I said that I might ask you for a better reason than you have given. Not that I should ask it. Nor need you suppose that I am moved by the reason that you give me now, which is not so much a reason as a sort of threat. You shall have what you need. Not for your reasons, but for my own."

Before that promise he judged it wise to smother his wrath. His tone became conciliatory.

"They will be sound reasons, I am sure, Margot. I know the goodness of your heart."

She slipped from the bed to seek in the drawer of a little table a small bunch of keys. Whilst rummaging there, because standing between him and the candlebranch which he had set down, her night rail was rendered diaphanous by the light. At this vision of her, his expression changed. The sensualist awoke in him, subduing even his anxieties. He fetched a sigh. His voice was suddenly soft as a caress.

"How lovely you are, Margot!"

The words and the tone sent a shudder through her very soul. She moved swiftly aside so that a tall secretaire became interposed between them, screening her to the height of her breast. She bent to insert the key, leaving visible no more than her russet head.

He came nearer by a step. His voice continued subdued, on a pleading note. "After all, my dear, why so much rancour? There may have been differences between us; but they are only a ruffling of the surface. Underneath, God knows, we are made to understand each other. I could never tell you all that you inspire in me. I may have committed follies. I know I have. I admit it readily. But if you conceived the tenderness of my feelings for you, you would be more patient with me. For I love you so much, my dear. In the moment that I first beheld you I knew you for my woman."

He had been advancing as he spoke, until now there was only the secretaire between them, and a great fear of him such as she had never known, a fear and a sense of nausea arose in her. She strove to control the tumult of her breast, to dissemble the horror that shook her at the thought of being so utterly in his power, at the mercy of this untimely amorousness.

From a drawer of the secretaire she had taken a rouleau of gold pieces and a bundle of banknotes. In a secret recess under that same drawer lay Horn's letter to King Philip. Already her fingers were upon the spring that governed it, with intent to give him the letter, and so deliver him from his worst fear, when she checked on the sudden perception of the potent weapon she possessed against her needs.

She commanded herself, sternly to meet his glance and to keep her voice level. "Here you should find a thousand louis. It is all that I have under my hand. It should suffice you for the present." She placed the money on top of the secretaire. "Take it, and please go."

He stuffed the rouleau into one pocket, the notes into another. His eyes were intent upon her. "I open my heart, then, in vain to you. 'Take it and go,' eh? Dismissed like a dog. And what if I should not choose to go? I have some right here, I believe."

She steeled herself to answer coldly. "That is possible. But your danger is certain. This is the last place to which you should have come, certainly the last in which you should linger, for it is the first in which you will be sought since they have failed to find you at Sceaux."

"At Sceaux?"

"Were you not there? And have not all who were at Sceaux already been arrested? If they are hunting you, as you say, having failed to find you there, this is the next place where they will look for you."

For a moment he appeared daunted. Then, recovering, with an abrupt gesture of disdain, "Ah, bah!" he cried. "At this hour? Even the Lieutenant-Criminel must sleep sometimes."

"Do you deceive yourself with that?" She drew a bow at a venture. "The Baron de Nesle was of your party, was he not? He must have fled from Sceaux at the first rumour of discovery, and like you he made the mistake of coming to Paris. He was dragged from his bed by the Lieutenant's archers at three o'clock yesterday morning."

His change of countenance announced that the shaft had gone home. "Thousand devils! Is that true?"

It was not. But he had shown her that the falsehood might safely be maintained. "How else should I know that de Nesle was one of you? Ah! You begin to see that every moment is spent here at your peril. You'll go at once unless you want to put the rope round your neck with your own hands."

He shuddered at the image this evoked. And then, on an inspiration, to the lash of fear she added that of cupidity. "So lose no time. Let me have word of where you are, so that I may send you further supplies."

That made an end of his desire to linger, indeed, of all desire but the desire to be gone. She must be right, he admitted with a foul oath. And at last, with curt thanks, less for the favours received than for the hope of more to follow, he recovered his hat and departed, leaving her almost swooning in relief from the loathing he had inspired.

It had begun to snow when he reached the street, and close-wrapped in his cloak he made his way down to the Rue St Honoré. In that great artery, after a moment's hesitation, he turned westward, and followed the long length of it and so up the faubourg to St Philippe du Roule. It had occurred to him that he should be safe for the night with his friend de Mille.

Despite the hour he was not kept waiting at the Colonel's door. It was opened to him almost at once by de Mille in person, still fully dressed and carrying a candle, which his hand sheltered from the draught.

He expressed his surprise in an oath. "Is it you, Count? Come in, come in. A moment sooner and you'd not have found me. I am only just home. And it's your affairs have kept me abroad on this foul night."

In the vestibule the Count shook the snow from cloak and hat. "My affairs?"

"To be sure. I've news for you. But come up."

He went ahead, holding his candle high, to light his guest.

Above in the dingy room that brought memories to Horn of his last frustrated interview with Catherine Law, the Colonel poured him a glass of Burgundy and laced it with brandy. "This will warm you, and, faith, you'll need warming."

Horn took it gratefully enough, assuming that de Mille alluded to the chill of the place, for there were only cold ashes in the untidy grate. He drank the half of it and smacked his lips. "What is this news of yours?"

"You won't like it." The Colonel paused, then, brutally, announced: "You're a cuckold. That's the news."

Horn stared at the half-sneering grin on those thick lips.

"You're drunk, de Mille, of course. That's not the sort of jest I care for."

"Jest! Listen, my friend. You'll know that that business of the Maines has blown up?"

"Of course I know it. I slipped away from Sceaux only just in time to avoid being caught there. But what has that to do with it?"

"I'll tell you. I happened to go to the Rue d'Argenteuil to ask where I might find you, so as to warn you. It was long after midnight when I got there, just as a man whom I supposed at first to be yourself was slinking out of the house. From the porter I learnt that he had been with Madame la Comtesse – a fellow calling himself du Jasmin. As your friend, in your interest, I desired to know who might be the gentleman with so odd a name. I went after his chair. And where do you suppose it led me? To the Hôtel de Nevers! This man who was shut up with madame in the dead of night, and who gives a false name, is your dear friend Lass. I leave you to draw your own conclusions."

Horn stood very still, his white face set and inscrutable. It was natural that his first thought should be for Catherine Law's announcement that it was the Countess of Horn who had betrayed to Law the Parliament's intentions. Whilst this he had believed, her further assertion that there was an intimacy between Law and the Countess he had, for ends of his own, merely affected to believe. If, when de Mille's tale was added to that, still more were needed to convince him, he conceived that he had it in the utter indifference to his danger which his wife had just manifested and in the contemptuous manner of her response to his prayer for assistance. No wonder that the traitress, still throbbing from the embraces of her lover, should have used him with that insulting coldness.

Upon this conviction passionate speech burst from him at last. "As God lives I'll kill that scoundrel with my hands. He shall find that I am not the man to lie still under dishonour."

"That's right. Think of your honour." And the Count, moving savagely about the chamber, was too distraught to ask himself if he was mocked by this Colonel who knew so much about him. "A spry fellow your Scot, and a humorous. Whilst you're at pains to seduce his wife, he pays you in advance and in kind. If anyone but you were in question I could almost admire his impudence."

"I don't admire yours," growled Horn. "Devil take your foul tongue." He continued to pace the room in his simmer of rage. "I'll kill the loathly dog. Kill him. But first I'll have a word to say to

Madame la Comtesse, which that slut shall remember for as long as she lives."

Thus the outraged Count of Horn proposed. But after a raging sleepless night in de Mille's quarters, by an unhappy coincidence, he reached the Rue d'Argenteuil next morning at the same time as a detachment of military police that happened inopportunely to be seeking him there.

Denied the satisfaction of even seeing his Countess and delivering himself of all that he had rehearsed, he was thrust into a coach and driven off to the Bastille.

Naturally he feared the worst, and it was not until some days later that he learnt to his surprise that he was imprisoned, not as he had supposed for his share in the Cellamare conspiracy, but simply for rupture of ban. In the perquisitions made at Sceaux it was discovered that he had been present there, and it was only because he was within the fifty leagues to which he had been banished that his arrest had been ordered, that he had been sought and found in the Rue d'Argenteuil, and had been flung into prison without any sort of trial. He was mystified but far from relieved. Impatient to be revenged, he recalled that someone had said that vengeance is a dish best eaten cold, and he took what comfort he could from that.

Chapter 20

THE PUBLIC DEBT

Vast though they were beyond anything known in the realm of finance, the achievements hitherto of the Laird of Lauriston were dwarfed by the expansion he was to give them whilst the Count of Horn was languishing in gaol.

It may be that in the pursuit of ever more colossal undertakings he sought an anodyne for the heartache that he had brought away from his last interview with the Countess of Horn. It may even be that since she had avowed her feelings for him he was driven, despite the abyss between them which he could not hope to bridge, to rise to heights that should overpower imagination, and so render him an object of secret pride to her. Such aspirations have been known. Or, more simply, it may be that he was driven by a boundless ambition, which was not to be satisfied until he had brought the entire economy of France within his audacious grasp. More probably the source of his incredible activities is to be sought in a conjunction of these spurs, and it is as much beyond surmise as it is idle to determine the respective part of each.

Following upon the immuring of her husband in the Bastille, an imprisonment for which she had every reason to be thankful as for a deliverance, the Countess of Horn left Paris, the house in the Rue

212

d'Argenteuil was closed, and, as Mr Law was to learn from Lady Stair, she had retired to a château acquired by her in Dordogne. He guessed that this withdrawal might be not merely out of respect for the proprieties imposed by her husband's increased disgrace, but out of dictates of prudence as concerned Mr Law himself. He bowed to it in a resignation blent with approval, and flung himself passionately into work.

As a result, whilst the Count of Horn sat gnawed by vindictiveness within four walls, whilst the Duke of Noailles and his following and the Parliament of Paris were rancorously watchful for opportunity to destroy this foreign adventurer, whilst Catherine Law alternated between exalted gaieties and ill-natured suspicions of a husband from whom she derived her ever-mounting eminence in the *beau monde*, the splendid star of the Laird of Lauriston, ever more effulgent, climbed steadily towards its zenith.

By now the monopoly of the trade with all French possessions in America, Asia and Africa was firmly within his grasp. He was adding to his fleet, by building and purchase, until soon now it should number some seventy ships. He was developing the commerce in Canadian pelts, which was beginning to assume importance, and he was master of the monopolies of salt and tobacco.

Leaving all this precariously balanced upon his system of credit at a time when the conditions of credit were only imperfectly understood, he gave his attention to obtaining additional powers, with the ultimate aim of assuming the office of Comptroller-General of the Finances which was held by d'Argenson.

As a preliminary step, now that he had buttressed his position by the control of the mint, and in order to obtain the farming of the taxes, he intoxicated the Regent by a staggering proposal to take over the national debt, the colossal burden of which, still amounting to fifteen hundred millions and costing the Treasury an annual interest of eighty millions, he now judged his credit strong enough to bear. Only from a man who had already displayed Mr Law's financial wizardry could the Regent have taken such a proposal seriously.

When His Highness had recovered from his stupefaction, he consented at least to hear the details of the scheme, and summoned d'Argenson to attend that exposition.

Closeted with those two in the Palais Royal on a day of August, Mr Law juggled with figures, countered arguments and smothered objections until both the Prince and the Comptroller-General were dizzy.

His proposal when summarized was that on condition that he be granted the farming of the taxes and paid for the necessary loan an interest at the rate of three per centum, equal to only fifty millions yearly and therefore representing an annual saving to the State of thirty millions, he would issue notes for the necessary capital amount, and with these the State creditors would be paid off in a given order.

He would issue, he announced, as a commencement one hundred thousand shares nominally of five hundred livres, and when the Regent, thrusting out a dubious lip, wondered if he could count upon their being absorbed, Mr Law revealed the lure by which he proposed to attract the public. It was a lure that amounted, indeed, to nothing less than a constraint.

The monopolistic net into which he had swept up by now all the great trading concerns, grouping them under the aegis of the India Company, had left the national debt as virtually the only other available medium of investment. Once this was taken over by the Company, the investing members of the public, the *rentiers*, would have no choice but to place their money with it if they were to continue to enjoy an annual return. It was of an overwhelming simplicity.

Convinced, at last and the conviction growing to enthusiasm, the Regent was brought to consent.

It was in vain that d'Argenson, no longer of a booming eloquence, but almost spluttering in indignation, still opposed the measure. Before him lay the prospect of being deprived of his tax farm, and, as Comptroller-General of the Finances, of being left with no finances to control.

"Your Highness cannot fail to perceive that this is merely a substitution of the India Company for the State; no more, in effect, than a dangerous conversion of the bonds of the public debt into shares in the company of Monsieur Lass. Nor can Your Highness neglect the interest of the shareholders in the tax farms, to whom we have been paying a dividend of twelve per centum. Is it just that their annuities should be arbitrarily reduced to three per centum?"

"Not arbitrarily," said the Regent. "You assume that they will reinvest in the shares of the Company. They are under no compulsion to do so."

"I think Monsieur Lass has made it clear that they will have no alternative. If this project is carried into effect, the India Company will become the only subject of investment in France, and it is precisely upon this that Monsieur Lass is counting – that the enormous capital of a milliard and a half cast out of investment in the State can find no other refuge but in the shares of his Company. Can Your Highness imagine that these annuitants will rest content with a rate of interest that must of necessity be enormously reduced?"

The Regent looked questioningly at Mr Law, who had been listening with a smile, and left him to answer the objection.

"That is an assumption for which there is no real warrant, Marquis. The interest of three per centum which is to be paid by the State to the Company for a loan will produce forty-eight millions annually. The tax farms yield, as you should know, a profit of sixteen millions; the balance necessary to produce the eighty millions which the bond-holders have been receiving and will receive again, can well be spared from the profits of the Company."

"That," said the Marquis, violently "is to build on something that does not yet exist."

"Your pardon, Marquis. It exists and must exist increasingly as trade develops."

"Must! I perceive no such assurance." D'Argenson's dark countenance was flushed with indignation. "What your all-embracing company may do is still in the realm of speculation. And I tell you frankly, sir, and you, monseigneur, if you will permit me, that to place this tremendous monopoly of trade in the hands of the State is an experiment fraught with appalling dangers. The stimulus of competition among merchants, which is the real mainspring of a nation's wealth, is abolished; those experienced traders will be replaced by inexperienced officials of Monsieur Lass' appointing. Disorganization must follow, and extravagance will become unbridled once the consequences of it are imposed upon the nation as will be all those losses which independent merchants must avoid or perish."

"I seem to hear again," said Mr Law, "the late Chancellor d'Aguesseau. It will be in your memory, Marquis, that when he urged those very arguments, yours was the only voice that opposed them."

"Not so," d'Argenson contradicted him. "My support was for your banking system only. None envisaged such a monstrous all-encompassing grasp as this upon the nation's economy. I declare it a madness to expose the country to the dangers inherent in so sudden a disturbance of the generally accepted financial practice, and I can foresee only disaster."

"Yet the arguments against my banking system were similar. Their fallacy has been exposed by results, just as the fallacy of these will be exposed. And meanwhile the State's obligation to find an annual interest of eighty millions is a burden lightened almost by half at a stroke."

This last was the consideration that made an end of d'Argenson's dialectics, but by no means of his fierce resentment. On the contrary, it was immeasurably increased by the blow to his pocket as well as to his pride, for the anti-system was now irrevocably smashed and the great profits he had derived from the tax farms were lost to him.

Remembering how he had supported Law's banking proposals at a time when all opinion had been against him, d'Argenson looked malevolently upon the Scot as a snake that he had nourished in his bosom. Defeated both as a financier and a lawyer, he went from the Palais Royal that day as Mr Law's bitterest enemy.

Later, at the Hôtel de Nevers, when Mr Law announced this triumph to his brother, far from arousing in him an exultation comparable with his own, he was met by dismay framed in arguments akin to those of d'Argenson and advanced with far greater frankness.

The steady, prudent, younger Law was aghast at a project of such perilous magnitude. Aware that his brother had been contemplating this scheme, which he regarded as a terrifying gamble, he had put his trust in the Regent's fundamental acuteness and had been confident that His Highness would reject it. Even now he could scarcely believe that audacity and plausibility should so far have overborne prudence and carried the day.

He sat glumly in his chair, listening to a paean of victory, that brought sweat to his brow. Instead of the fanfare of trumpets which Mr Law believed that he deserved, a groan was all he got from William.

"It frightens me," said he.

"It must be that you don't yet understand. In simple terms, I am replacing a credit that is old and moribund by one that is new and vigorous."

"How long will it retain its vigour when supporting this terrific load – a couple of milliards added to what we already carry? It's a load that will crush us."

Mr Law derided him. "Cassandra foretelling the doom of Troy."

"But I'll hope, not like Cassandra, unheeded by the doomed."

"Doomed! Pray consider, Will, that once we have the edict and I complete the conversion we shall have raised an establishment that will unite in itself the banking, the commerce and the administration of all the finances of France. It will constitute the most formidable financial power that was ever wielded."

"That is what daunts me: this monopoly of powers such as are exercised only with difficulty even when normally distributed. Are you equal to it?"

"With your help, Will."

"Oh, as to that, my help is yours for the bidding; every ounce of it. But you'll need a deal more. Lord! Whither will it all lead us in the end? I'd feel better if I saw aught in the trend of things in Louisiana to encourage us. The Mississippi's proving no Pactolus. Will it ever? Aye, smile, John. You account me fearful, I know. The fact is I haven't your gambler's nerves."

"Confess at least that I've not fumbled the dice so far."

"I do, John. I'll say that you've the devil's own skill in reckoning the chances. But – God's sake," he groaned, "could you not be content with what we have? Is there no end to your greed?"

"Greed!" Mr Law was provoked into laughter. "What greed do I display? I can plunge my hands into millions, yet what do I take for myself? What possessions have I acquired beyond that little property of Guermande down in Brie, to humour Catherine, so that between whiles she may play the châtelaine? The train that I keep in Paris may be princely, but it is no more than I could maintain on the fortune I brought with me into France. Greed, forsooth! I've told you before, Will, that with me the game is all. And," he added, with a sudden grimness, "it is all I have. Why grudge it me?"

"It's not grudging it you I am. It's fearing it may break you in the end."

Mr Law shrugged. "A soldier knows that he risks his life. That does not prevent him from being a soldier. Each of us must dree his weird as his nature bids him." Airily he quoted Montrose: " 'He either fears his fate too much or his desserts are small, that dares not put it to the touch to gain or lose it all'."

"Ah, well. Ye ken what came of that."

"Maybe I'll build better than did he."

"If you think it canny to build on sand, which is what I doubt you're doing."

"The sand will turn to rock once the yield from overseas begins to flow."

"Ay, ay. But will it flow in time?"

"Why shouldn't it?"

Will sighed, and mopped his brow. His deliberate Scottish accents were gloomy. "I'm thinking ye'll need to work a miracle, like Moses when he struck water from his rock."

"With this difference, that whilst he merely brought forth water I shall bring forth gold. Meanwhile there's work to be done against the granting of the edict."

That edict was promulgated before the end of the month, and registered by Parliament in smothered anger. It cancelled the existing lease of the tax farms and conveyed them to the India Company. It ordered the reimbursement of capital to the shareholders in the farms as well as to all annuitants in the public debt. The holders of these securities were to present themselves at the Treasury, each to obtain a quittance for the amount of his holding, which he was immediately to take to the India Company to be discharged there either in gold or banknotes as he wished.

Considering the premium established by now upon the paper currency it was confidently reckoned that this would be preferred to specie, and the Regent had agreed that to meet the consequent requirements Law should print a sufficiency of notes. These were subsequently to be destroyed in a measure as they were paid in to the India Company for the purchase of the shares of the new issue.

Chapter 21

THE GOAD

At about the time of the publication of that edict which was to hoist John Law to the very pinnacle of achievement, rendering him the economic master of France and wielder of an intoxicating power, the Earl and Countess of Stair paid a visit to the Laird of Lauriston and his lady which was not without importance. On the part of his lordship the visit, under its social aspect, possessed an official significance.

Mr Law was by now too great a man to be overlooked by foreign powers. The vast dominion he had gathered into his hands, so that all the trade of France and her colonies must flow as he directed, made it desirable not only for individuals but even for nations to conciliate him.

There is abundant evidence that the Earl of Stair had received instructions from his government in this sense. He came, then, with proposals of commercial relations to be established between England and France, with offers of service to Mr Law in England, not merely general but also particular in the matter of lifting the ban against him.

Mr Law received these inspired advances with a perfect, non-committal suavity, inwardly unmoved.

With the angular Countess, however, it was a very different story. The news she gave him left him placid only on the surface. Her kinswoman, the Countess of Horn, had just arrived in Paris, brought back from the Dordogne by the need to concert with Lord Stair as British ambassador measures concerned with her English estates.

"She is not likely to remain here long, nor to show herself, considering the imprisonment of her disgraceful husband."

She paused as if awaiting Mr Law's comment, her close-set, shrewish eyes intent upon his discouraging impassivity. As he offered none beyond an acknowledging inclination of the head, she went on.

"Madame de Horn has confided to me that you are a very old friend – a friend of the days of that scapegrace Beau Wilson."

The sly smile and the unfortunate allusion were both detestable to him. His sternness induced her to offer him a sigh. "It was as I feared. The poor soul has no more fortune in her second husband than in her first. But there! I tell you this because it is my dearest wish that in her unhappy circumstances she should quit France and go home to England, and I have thought that you, as her friend and having her interests at heart, might add your persuasions to mine. I have a hope that your influence might bring about what all her friends desire for her."

"I fear that your ladyship flatters me by exaggerating that influence," he answered gravely.

"I can't believe it, Mr Law. I protest I can't. And, anyway, I hope that you will make the attempt – unless," she added, with a renewal of the smile he found so hateful, "unless, of course, you should prefer that she remain in France."

"It is beyond me to imagine why your ladyship conceives I might prefer it."

"Ah!" Her smile grew into a laugh. The shrill note of it drew Catherine's attention from his lordship, and Mr Law was almost startled by her pallor.

"What is amusing, Lady Stair?"

Her ladyship was arch. "That is a secret, my dear; and a wise wife should not pry too closely into her husband's secrets."

"Lady Stair confesses her lack of wisdom," his lordship jested. Catherine did not heed him. Her eyes were searching her husband's face. They found its stony composure suspicious. But she kept her questions until their visitors had left.

"Lord Stair tells me that the Countess of Horn is back in Paris." Her voice was strained and unsteady. "Does that happen to be Lady Stair's amusing secret?"

"That is how she was so foolish as to describe it."

She considered him with a crooked smile. "I marvel at the effrontery of that woman to show herself here when her husband is in disgrace in the Bastille."

"Did not Dalrymple tell you that she came especially to seek his good offices in the matter of her English property?"

"He told me that. Yes. And something else that I have been far from suspecting: that her property in England is the estate of Harpington. Isn't that the title of the woman who was your mistress until she became King William's?"

Mentally he reeled under the blow. Outwardly he miraculously preserved his self-control. "That I would have married her had the chance been mine you have always known. That she was ever my mistress is a lie. You have never ceased to attribute mistresses to me, Catherine, and I have never wasted breath to deny your suspicions, however fatuous. But where Margaret Ogilvy is concerned I tell you again that it is blackest falsehood."

"That will be why you are so sharp-set to defend her whilst so indifferent in the case of others."

"To be sure suspicion must feed upon itself and swell by what it feeds on."

"Suspicion! If it's a suspicion it feeds upon what you supply. Why did you never tell me that this woman is Margaret Ogilvy? Why conceal it if you had nothing else to conceal? And she had the effrontery to seek you here – here in my house! Suspicion, you say!" She laughed bitterly. "You had better know that it is a suspicion shared by the Count of Horn. Indeed, not a suspicion – a conviction for which he will yet call you to account. You'll tell me perhaps that it is only suspicion that for the sake of that abominable woman you murdered Edward Wilson?"

"Murdered!" He shrugged despairingly, shaken from his calm. "It was, then, to a murderer and a seducer that you came in Amsterdam? Believing so much evil of me yet you did not hesitate to seek me."

"Because I loved you – God help me for a fool. I followed you to comfort you in your need. To my undoing."

"You came to comfort me?" His lip curled. "To comfort me with the tale that the woman I loved was the King's mistress?"

"To cure you of your infatuation for a strumpet, as it should have done if you had any proper pride. To care for you in your loneliness and exile, as God knows I have cared for you, only to be so ill-requited that I have wished myself dead these years." Then in a sudden increase of passion she railed at him. "Go to your woman. Go! She is here in Paris, waiting for you. Why else has she come? Do you think I don't realize that the need to consult Lord Stair is no more than a pretext? Go to her then! Go!"

She flung out of the room on that, and he made no attempt to stay her, realizing how far beyond the reach of argument she was placed by the violence that possessed her spirit.

He was left in an emotional disturbance as deep as any that he had known in a dozen years and more. It rested upon the anger he had repressed and perhaps a little upon the knowledge that Margaret was again within his reach. The temptation to seek her must in any case have assailed him, but it could never have been as overmastering as it was rendered by the cruel terms in which Catherine had loosened such tenuous bonds of duty to her as he still retained.

It was in this distracted state of mind that he came to his work-room, where he found his brother and Angus McWhirter waiting.

"We're here to see you, John, about opening the lists for the new issue. I've drawn up the notice we discussed, for your approval. Make sure that the terms are correct, then settle the amount to be issued, so that Angus may take it to the Bank."

Mr Law, at his writing table, bent over the sheet his brother placed before him. The figures swam under his blood-injected eyes. He passed a hand wearily across his brow, as if to brush away the emotions that were clouding thought. He read the document twice.

"It should serve, I think," he said at last, as he handed it back.

His brother stared at him. "God's sake, John! Are you ailing?"

"Ailing? No."

"But the figures, man. You've not settled them."

"Ah, yes. The figures." He thought a moment, only to discover that he was in no case to think. He recalled that he had decided and agreed with the Regent that, in order not to deluge the market, the issue should be a gradual one. "Say we make it a half-milliard. That should suffice for a commencement. A third of the total, isn't it?"

He wrote the figure at the foot of the document, and again proffered it.

"And the terms?" asked William. "Are you settled in your mind that they are to be as before; that is, with faculty to acquire them by instalments? Yesterday you mentioned a doubt."

"Did I?" He raised a dull glance. He sought to recall what the doubt could have been, failed, and shook his head, his manner incomprehensibly vague. "No. I think it will serve. As before. Why not? You can publish it in the morning, Angus, and make ready for a siege."

"Ay, ay, I'll be ready, never fear, Mr Law."

They left him, and he sat back to think, but not of the gigantic operation he was launching. Had his mind been on that, and his brain of its normal clarity, he could not have failed to perceive that he had made his first miscalculation, and one that carried in itself the seeds of disaster.

But his mind was swinging like a pendulum between Catherine and Margaret, between resentment and longing, each emotion serving as fuel for the other. Catherine charged Margaret with being his mistress, and by the malevolent intensity of her persuasion almost begot in him the desire to make it true.

There was yet another poison Catherine had distilled for him, that now served to quicken this desire. The need to consult Stair, she had said, had been no more than a pretext to bring Margaret back to Paris, within his reach. It might be so. He did not quite believe that it was, not even when he recalled the leers of Lady Stair. But he certainly desired to believe it.

According to Catherine that rascal Horn was of the same mind as herself. So that his wife and Margaret's husband shared the foul conviction. If he were to yield to the temptation that assailed him now at the thought of Margaret's accessibility, he would be doing no more than justify those two in their persuasion...

That was the goad that drove him, soon after dark, alone and on foot to the Rue d'Argenteuil.

Chapter 22

REVELATION

It did not occur to Mr Law on this occasion to employ a *nom de guerre*. Boldly he had himself announced by his own name, and the footman who bore the announcement returned almost at once to conduct him to that same boudoir of rose damask panels and black and gold chinoiserie in which she had last received him.

She stood before him in the informal sacque in which ladies of fashion took their ease at home. It was cut low at the neck and of the colour of *feuille morte*, which, save for its lack of lustre, almost matched her russet hair.

She smiled as she greeted him. "How did you learn that I am in Paris?"

"I wish that I could say that some subtle sense brought me the knowledge. But, in effect, it was nothing subtler than my Lady Stair."

"Why have you come?" was her next question.

"For this," he said, and gathered her into his arms and kissed her lips.

She did not deny him. But she cut short the embrace and put him from her, with a half-reproof. "This is not wise."

"Nor wisely intended."

"Ah!" Her glance was keen. A feverishness in his manner made her suddenly solemn. "Will you not sit?" she invited, and herself sank to a chair, spreading her gown. "You will have some deeper reason."

He remained standing over her. "Reason is not concerned. I merely obey the instinct to come to you as soon as I learn that you are within reach."

She disregarded this. It was plain that her casualness was forced, she was ill at ease.

"Had you delayed until tomorrow you would no longer have found me. The business with Lord Stair that brought me is done, and there is no reason for me to stay."

"That is utterly to crush the wild hope I fostered."

Again she scrutinized him, and her lip quivered. "It cannot be that you are making love to me, John," she said between question and assertion.

"Is it odd that I should? Is there good reason why I should not?"

"It is you now who talk of reason. But I, too, have my instincts, and they rebel. Come, John, let us be sane. I know that I am to blame for this. I was wanting in discretion when last you were here. I suffered my feelings to master me for a moment. But I trusted you, and trusting you I believe it could have no sequel. Do not spoil that. Please, John. Do not diminish my esteem for you."

"Esteem!" He was aggrieved. "You had another word for it when last I was here."

"I have said that I lacked discretion. And now you are proving it." Her tone was sad. "Be generous, my dear. You found me in an hour of weakness, a poor distraught woman with a fresh, raw wound to add to the many life has dealt me. At such times we are apt to leave a slack rein to our feelings."

"What has changed since then?" he demanded. "Has Horn become more worthy, or Catherine less of a shrew? Is either of us less lonely or alone?"

"That is nothing to the matter. It draws us no nearer to each other."

"Not if we are fools," he cried, and sank to one knee beside her, grasping the hands that lay limp in her lap. "Margaret my dear, must we be fools, indeed? Are we never to draw strength and comfort from each other in the loneliness in which each of us is wasting?"

Her agitation deepened. Her eyes looked almost black in the whiteness of her face. "What do you know of loneliness who hold an empire in your strong hands? Does not that suffice you, without seeking a poor woman for your toy?"

"That is a cruel thing to say to me."

"Cruel! If you cannot understand that the cruelty is yours, you do not know what cruelty means. Did I lay bare my heart in an unguarded hour so that you should come and tear fresh wounds in it?"

"Nay, Margaret. To heal the old ones, and to heal my own at the same time. Why will you deny me?"

"God knows I would deny you nothing, John. I am yours if you want me, but... Oh, God !" she wrenched her hands from his and covered her face, sinking back into her chair. "I have prayed that you never would. Not this way." There was anguish in her voice. "I suppose that I have given you cause to think me a woman whom you can ask to be your mistress. That is what wounds: that you should so regard me."

Mortification and frustrated longings wrung from him unpardonable words. "To be sure I am not a king. You shudder as if in horror. But you had no horror of the Dutchman after I, like a fool, had removed the husband who for his profit would have yielded you to him."

She uncovered her face again, to look at him, and he beheld it charged with pain and anger. "And now you insult me! You dare to reproach me with that. You dare because you never understood. You had neither the wit nor the faith that would have made you understand.

"Did you never ask yourself why you were not hanged as sentenced, nor yet why Mr Bentinck should have opened for you the prison door and provided for your escape, on the sole condition that you left England at once and never returned in King William's lifetime? Did you not? Then I will tell you.

"When you lay under sentence in Newgate I went to the King to beg your life. He questioned me on my relations with you. But that is no matter. He was kind, with a kindness that frightened me. He would consider, he said, and I should hear from him. I did. He sent his lackey Bentinck to offer me your life and liberty…on terms."

"Oh, my God!" cried the man at her feet, overcome by sudden revelation, moved now in his turn to hide his face in his hands.

Her lips twitched in a crooked smile that was like a grin of pain.

"You begin to understand. The bargain I was offered revolted me. I cursed that smug Dutch gentleman, and called upon God to punish him and his master. Then I thought of you, and took fright. I reflected that my life was ruined in either case, and that yours, at least, might be saved. And your life was the price I accepted for my harlotry."

So far she had spoken in a low voice that was charged with sorrow. And now its pathos deepened. "I was not born to be a harlot, John, as you should know. I was a woman of a high pride and of the dignity that comes of virtue fiercely guarded. Yet a harlot I became for your sake, so that for years you might loathe me, and in the end reproach me with it as you have done tonight."

"Margaret!" The name broke from him in a sob. He bowed his head almost to the ground. He took the hem of her gown and bore it to his lips. "I am not worthy even of so much. As God hears me I would rather that I had hanged. How could I guess? How could I guess?"

At the agony in his voice, the humility of his act, all passion fell from her. Her hand moved over his head in a caress. Very sadly and quietly she spoke. "Had your faith been stout enough there would have been no need to guess."

"Do me justice," he cried, starting to his feet. "When Bentinck came to me in Newgate there was no mention of you."

"And you never asked yourself why he should come at all, and offer you so much."

"Indeed, I did. And I supposed it common justice; that they recognized the sentence as excessive, yet did not wish to admit it openly. I killed Wilson in a fair encounter, as any court of honour must have adjudged, and gentlemen are not to be hanged for that, whatever the edicts."

"Yes," she admitted slowly. "There is that. It is what I have thought."

"If I had known, if he had dared to tell me, I must have cast my life back in his teeth."

"Which is why he did not tell you. Afterwards...why should I have given you knowledge of something that was past mending? It could serve only to torment you, as it torments you now when a gust of anger left me without the generosity or good sense to continue to hide it."

"Never think that." At last he looked at her again, and found her in tears. "The only present shame is mine for...for having provoked the avowal. Yet, however this thing may haunt me, in my soul I must be glad of the knowledge. For there you are enshrined again, wholly pure as you were in the days when I had no thought of you that was not of worship. Of your charity, Margaret, forgive me for this hour."

"I do, in thankfulness."

He stood straight and squarely before her. "And now, Margaret?"

"Now?" She contrived to smile up at him through her tears. "It is time, I think, to say good night." She stood up. "Good night and goodbye, my dear. It will be best for both of us that it should be goodbye. Finally goodbye."

"If I believed that, life would have little purpose left."

"You say that in the weakness of the moment. There is abundant purpose in your life, John, and I doubt not that I shall find some in mine."

Tenderly she brought him to take his leave. "It shall be my constant prayer," he said, "that the life you have preserved for me may be worthy of the dreadful sacrifice you made."

"I thank you for that. They are healing words." She took his head between her hands, drew it down and kissed him on the lips. "God have you ever in His keeping, my dear."

It was a prayer that was not immediately to be answered, for he departed in torment, and in torment abode in the days that followed. Only the knowledge that she had quitted Paris kept him from yielding to the overpowering need to see her again, and left him moving like a sleep walker whilst the greatest hazard of his gambler's life was being played.

Chapter 23

THE ZENITH

It required a shock to snatch him out of his somnambulism, and it was McWhirter who supplied it a week later.

This henchman of his came to the Hôtel de Nevers one morning of mid-September in a fever of jocund excitement.

"Man," he declared, "ye bade me be ready for a siege, and the devil's own siege it is. D'ye not know what's toward in the Rue Quincampoix? The issue of shares is going fast. There was never such a garboil. It's just Bedlam yonder, so it is. The street is agog with *agioteurs*, and the price this morning stands at three thousand livres. Six times the original value, no less. It's fair cluttered out of my senses I am, with all the world clamouring to buy."

"All the world?" echoed Mr Law, his quick instinct, suddenly aroused, already scenting in McWhirter's exultation something that was amiss.

"Ay. All the world. I'm thinking we'll scarce need the extra printing of notes. Though, to be sure, there's an awkward side to it. A mob of annuitants who've cashed their receipts at the bank are bleating and protesting for shares at the price of issue as their right, and at this rate we shall soon have none to sell them."

"God's death!" thundered Mr Law, now thoroughly awake. "When were the lists opened?"

"A week since, of course."

"Upon whose authority?"

McWhirter stared open-mouthed, amazed at so much vehemence in a man whose imperturbability had passed into a byword. "Why, upon whose authority but your own?"

"Mine!" Mr Law looked at him in horror. "When did I give it?"

"Wasn't it in the note of terms Mr William and I laid before you?"

Elbow on the table, Mr Law took his head in his hands.

"And where's the great harm, after all?" wondered the crestfallen subordinate.

"The harm! And the shares stand already at three thousand livres. If this rage of speculation continues where is it going to land us? Damn the *agioteurs!*"

McWhirter, accounting the explosion merely rhetorical, stood silent, wondering and waiting.

Mr Law groaned. He struck the table with his fist. "However did I come to overlook it?"

He perceived, of course, that what he had foreseen – the factor, indeed, upon which he had built – that the State creditors for the fifteen hundred millions must avail themselves of the only available channel of reinvestment in the India Company – had been equally foreseen by every speculator of ordinary astuteness. Foreseeing it, they had made haste to buy the shares in order to make the State creditors pay dearly for them when they came to reinvest. And the operation was made easy for them by the fact that a comparatively small cash deposit sufficed to give them possession of a share. It was not that he had overlooked the inevitability of this. He had seen it as clearly as the mischief that might follow out of it, and he had intended to provide before the lists were opened. The omission was due to the obfuscation of his mind, coming from his scene with Catherine, at the moment of considering the note of terms.

He commanded himself now, so that he might grapple with this complication. "Measures must be taken at once, Angus. The State creditors have every reason to complain. It is a scandal that they should be mulcted in this fashion so as to make fortunes for men who are gambling on a certainty. In one way or another the mischief must be checked before it goes further. Meanwhile, let the Bank hold what shares remain. Announce that the subscriptions are complete. Ask Mr William to come to me this afternoon."

The decision he took was to open at once a new subscription list for the second half-milliard, which he had not intended to offer for some months to come, whilst establishing by edict now, as he should have done earlier, that these shares could be acquired only against Treasury receipts for bonds surrendered. In this way, by eliminating the intermediary stage of converting the receipts into currency, he ensured that the bond-holders must have the first call.

As a remedial measure it was sound enough, but it was belated. The harm had been done and an impetus given to unbridled speculation the end of which it was impossible to foresee.

In the meantime the price of the India Company shares continued upwards, and even the State bonds, which had been at a depreciation of sixty per centum, were now above par and virtually unprocurable in view of the further impending conversion.

Considering what had happened to the first issue and the sharp rise that had taken place, the announcement of the second lists resulted in a no less feverish activity in the Rue Quincampoix. The price racing upwards from the three thousand livres which had startled Law, was soon standing at six thousand.

The neighbouring streets of Saint Denis and Saint Martin were encumbered with waiting coaches, and in the Rue Quincampoix itself pandemonium reigned about the Bank, not only by day but throughout the night, so that in the end the dwellers in the neighbourhood complained of it. Barricades had to be set up at both ends of the street, guarded by troops when closed, which was from nine o'clock at night until nine o'clock on the following morning, and opening and closing to the sound of a bell.

At the Treasury Offices from morning to night there were long queues of bond-holders, in a frenzied scrimmage to surrender their bonds and obtain their receipts, so as to convert them into the soaring shares at the earliest moment.

Outside the Hôtel de Nevers the Street was blocked by the carriages of persons of quality, who, taking advantage of their social rank or personal relations with Mr Law came directly to him to procure the part of this Golconda to which their holdings of State bonds entitled them.

Because into the edict constituting the Company Mr Law had astutely prevailed upon the Regent to introduce an article providing that no derogation should attend the possession of its shares, a nobility, impoverished like the King by the prodigality and wars of Louis XIV, besieged the mansion of this worker of financial miracles. All that was proudest in France made antechamber to him, suing for admission to his august presence, so that it might court his favour.

At his hands the Duke of Bourbon exchanged his Treasury receipts for a block of shares of a value already so enhanced that he was enabled to pay his debts and begin to rebuild his magnificent Château of Chantilly. He was sought by the hump-backed, irascible, young Prince de Conti, fiercely complaining that having obtained at the time of the first issue his receipts for an exceptionally heavy holding of depreciated bonds, he had been too late to convert them into shares even at treble their original value. He had fortunately abstained – fortunately, that is, if Monsieur Lass would now do him right and grant him out of the second issue those shares at their face value.

His was, of course, the case of many an annuitant, lacking, however, the Prince's exalted rank to embolden him to carry his case into the holy of holies of that Temple of Mammon.

Mr Law obliged him, and de Conti departed from the Hôtel de Nevers vowing himself for ever Mr Law's devoted servant and bearing away shares which he could already sell in the Rue Quincampoix for eight times their value, and thus realize at once a fortune.

Similarly, and with greater willingness, Mr Law favoured his friend the Duke of Antin, who had also been left by the first issue with his receipts unconverted, and there were many others of the best and proudest blood of France, such as the Prince of Rohan, the Prince of Guémenée, the Duke of La Force, and the Duke of La Vrillière, who left the Hôtel de Nevers pledged by gratitude eternally to his service.

Whilst these noble clients besieged him in his Sybaritic study, their ladies crowded Catherine's salon, bearing gifts and invitations whereby to swell the adulatory court that was being paid the House of Law.

As an expression of the great social consequence she had now attained Catherine was presently moved to give a white ball for their daughter, then in her thirteenth year. It was eagerly attended by the most brilliant gathering the Court could furnish, actually graced by the Duchess of Berri, the foreign embassies, and even the Papal Nuncio, who publicly embraced the winsome little heroine of the fête.

The child's hand was being sought in marriage for the sons of some of the noblest houses in France, whilst her little brother, of the same age as the King, was commanded to Versailles to become His Majesty's playmate.

These intoxicating triumphs, through which Catherine moved with splendours almost royal, attended ever by a turbaned black boy from Sénégal – a gift from the Duke of Antin – to carry her purse or fan, were not without their effect upon her and even aroused in her a sense of gratitude for the husband whose greatness had procured her them. Her attitude towards him became more conciliatory than it had been for years, and this came the more readily to her since learning that the Countess of Horn's visit to Paris had been of the briefest.

Knowing that the Countess had left almost as soon as she had arrived, Catherine had reached the conclusion that there might, after all, be no grounds for at least some of the charges she had flung at her husband in such unmeasured and offensive terms. Penitent, she sought by submissiveness to offer amends.

He did not make it easy. Sardonic of lip and eye, he observed her timid advances, and once, when she pressed them to the point of wearying him, he let her know that he was not deceived, that he attached no false value to them. In his impatience he became almost brutally bitter.

"Do not you, too, dear Catherine, be at the trouble of wooing the mighty Baron Lass, the patron of princes, the hierophant of Mammon, the director of empire, who tomorrow may be His Majesty's Comptroller-General. Do not be dazzled, my dear, by the greatness of which you share the effulgence. To you I am just John Law of Lauriston, Jessamy John, as they used to call me."

Her eyes were piteously reproachful. "I would to God you were. Why will you be so unkind? Why hold such mean suspicions of my motives?"

"Is the right to harbour mean suspicions yours alone?"

This was a home thrust. It gave her pause. She even went so far – and it was far to go for a woman of her pride – as to confess some fault and to sue frankly for his forgiveness.

Aware of how much this must cost her, and at the same time uneasy in his conscience, the end of it was that he was so far moved as to comfort her with an assurance which in other circumstances he would have disdained to offer.

"It is a suspicion," he said, "with which you need not again torment yourself. Whatever Margaret Ogilvy may have been to me in the past, before I became your husband, let me tell you again that she was never my mistress. Since I am under no necessity to say what is not true and seek no profit from it, you need not hesitate to believe me. And I can add, if it will make an end of all this, that I am never likely to see Margaret Ogilvy again."

The flush that mounted to her cheek, the sudden quickening of her glance and its wistful gentleness went through him like a sword.

"There was no greatness about you, John," she plaintively reminded him, "when I came to you in Amsterdam. You were a broken man in those days. You should remember that. It will teach you how false are your reproaches now."

But although he humbled himself by admitting that he remembered it, the persuasion abode with him that the departure from her habitual frowardness was due to satisfaction in the social eminence to which he had raised her with himself.

It was an eminence that had not yet reached its zenith, though fast approaching it.

The absorption of the India Company's second issue of shares was so rapid and left so many still unsatisfied that he could perceive no reason to delay opening the third and final list. Accordingly he did so in October, and witnessed the same avidity to subscribe.

Once more there was a clamant mob of nobles in his antechambers, and amongst them came again the Prince de Conti. The little hunchback proved of those to whom appetite comes with eating. Not content with having amassed a fortune by the favour Law had shown him at the time of the second issue he came now demanding participation in the third on the same terms.

Urbanely Mr Law denied him. "On the last occasion, monseigneur, there was reason why I should oblige you. Today I must first think of all those who have not yet realized their conversions. You will see that I should be blameworthy if I neglected their just claims."

The grasping Prince, however, cared nothing about that. No plea of justice was likely to put him off. He urged his rank, spoke forcibly of the value of his favour, as a gross hint of the harm that might be wrought by his disfavour.

Mr Law remained unmoved, unless it be by a contempt which he scarcely dissembled. "It was my hope that I had won that favour on the last occasion. Do me right, monseigneur."

Baffled, the Prince took at last a sullen leave, forgetting on this occasion to profess himself Mr Law's servant.

With that third issue, the operation which Mr Law had originally intended to spread over a year was completed in little more than two months, and the national debt of fifteen hundred millions was liquidated, to the inexpressible and marvelling satisfaction of the Regent.

More than ever enthralled by Law's genius, His Highness now at last invited him to assume the exalted office of His Majesty's Comptroller-General, and since it was not permissible for any man who was not a Catholic to hold an office of State, Mr Law duly qualified by changing his religion and going to Mass, to the great scandal of McWhirter as well as of Catherine. Thus he became *de jure* what already he had been *de facto*, and d'Argenson was further incensed and embittered by removal from that office and the need to content himself with the retention of the Seals as Chancellor.

The Laird of Lauriston perceived clearly enough, and not without uneasiness, that for this swift achievement of his aims following out of the liquidation of the national debt, he had to thank his initial false step, which alone had permitted the *agioteurs* to take advantage of the situation and steal a march upon the legitimate State creditors.

Meanwhile the avalanche of speculation which they had started rolled on so irresistibly that by Christmas the shares of the India Company were changing hands at the staggering figure of fifteen thousand livres, which was thirty times their face value. A frenzy of gambling ensued, the like of which had never been witnessed, and this was by no means confined to the stock of the Company. From the remotest provinces of France, and even from abroad, there was so steady an invasion of Paris by fortune-seekers, that soon the city with a quarter of a million more than its ordinary inhabitants could scarcely house them. Here were further chances for the speculators. They snatched up all available lodgings in anticipation of the vast demand for them, which must raise the rents to fantastic heights. They bought up the necessities of life, perceiving that the cost of living must inevitably increase for the same reason. The Dukes of La Force, d'Antin and d'Estrées, forgetting the obligations of their birth, embarked through nominees in the wholesale purchase of cloth, candles, chocolate, coffee and sugar, whence a scandal followed. Similarly, seats on the coaches from the country were bought up in advance by speculators, and legitimate travellers were compelled to wait weeks before they could be accommodated.

In the Rue Quincampoix grotesquely exaggerated rents were paid for any booths wherein business might be transacted; a cobbler who owned a stall there, found himself growing rich by letting it to *agioteurs*; the hunchback Bombario, trading upon the superstition that accounted it lucky to rub against his hump, hired out his misshapen body and the hump itself as a writing pulpit upon which transactions might be recorded in the street, and was reputed by this means to have earned a hundred and fifty thousand livres in a few days.

Trade flourished as never before. Reckless expenditure followed inevitably upon the easy amassing of fortunes, and the merchants of Paris, especially those who dealt in precious wares, in gold and silver plate, in jewels which were being extensively imported from England, and in costly fabrics, were enriching themselves by dealings on a scale and at fabulous prices that had never existed even in their dreams.

Coachbuilders and horse dealers could scarcely meet the demand that assailed them, often from men who yesterday would have been glad enough of shoe leather with which to go on foot.

Those with land to sell could obtain three and four times the prices in which six months earlier they would have rejoiced. Routs and balls, fêtes and junketings, fireworks and gaming engrossed this jubilant and suddenly enriched people, noble and simple alike.

Theatres, dance halls, restaurants and gaming houses were thronged by folk with money to burn. The Opera was packed every night from floor to ceiling and never had displayed such brilliance of costumes and such glitter of jewels, whilst the enormous increase of carriages in the streets rendered life perilous for those who still went on foot.

The demand for labour had grown with this surge of affluence, and because of the great influx from the provinces and from abroad, which had increased by one-third the population of Paris, with a consequent insufficiency of essentials to meet the swollen demand, a rise in wages had followed.

The artisan who had been content with fifteen sous a day was now earning sixty, and was, therefore, a jubilant supporter of Mr Law, slow to perceive that since bread which had cost a sou for two pounds was costing now four sous a pound, with other commodities similarly augmented, his increased prosperity was no better than an illusion.

For the purveyor of all this phenomenal opulence, the magician whose genius had, by an avalanche of paper currency, lifted France out of the slough of bankruptcy and want into this unprecedented prosperity, there was almost deification. Whenever he rolled through Paris in his superb coach, with its magnificent bays in silver harness and a couple of footmen behind in his livery of claret and silver, if men stopped short of genuflecting to him, at least hats were swept off and cheers for him resounded such as had seldom resounded for anyone under the rank of a king. If he showed himself in the Rue Quincampoix a guard was necessary to hold off the mob that might have crushed him to death out of sheer worship.

Yet whilst outwardly imperturbable, urbane and splendidly liberal to all, in his mind he was not quite easy. Himself a gamester by careful calculation, he looked askance upon all these inexpert gamesters who, without reckoning the odds or possessing the ability to do so, plunged blindly and recklessly into speculations for which that momentary inattention on his part had supplied the impulse.

When presently the labouring classes came to understand that their swollen wages no longer kept pace with the price of necessities, swollen in their turn by the increase in wages, they clamoured for still higher pay, which, being granted, was followed again by still higher prices.

Observing this, the Laird of Lauriston realized the elusive natural law – unperceived or else ignored by those who for their own ends have sought the favour of the masses by inspiring claims to higher pay – that the value of an individual in any community is a relative value which no power on earth can change, and that attempts to change it violently must be attended by direst consequences.

He understood that to pay the individual more than that subtly determined relative worth was merely to lower the purchasing power of money, for it led inevitably to a readjustment of all other values, so as to conform with the one that had been altered.

Realizing this, Mr Law perceived that he was now confronted with a new and disquieting phenomenon, the phenomenon of inflation, for which there was as yet no name. He perceived here the first sweeps of a vicious spiral which he possessed no means of checking, and the end of which was not to be foreseen in the artificial circumstances which his system had created.

Then, too, the news from Louisiana, upon which his main hopes were founded, continued to be anything but good, and so far but little of its potential wealth had crossed the ocean. It was a subject upon which the steady, sober William Law was being brought to despair.

"Will you tell me, John, how and where we are to find a dividend that will bear any relation to the price at which the stock is standing?" His tone was irritable. "What will be happening when the holders realize it?"

Mr Law preserved a wooden countenance. "You start at shadows."

"Shadows is the very word, and devil a substance to cast them."

"The men who buy at these inflated prices are expressing their faith in the future. They perceive what you overlook: that whilst the wealth of the Mississippi may be inexhaustible, time must be allowed for the development of this young colony. Time must be allowed between sowing and reaping. Let that be our motto. It should enhearten the sober and perhaps restrain the reckless."

"You speak glibly of the reaping. Have you seen the last reports from Duchamp?"

"I have. They were best put in the fire before others see them. They're not for general consumption. We don't want a panic."

"You hope to postpone it?"

"I count upon averting it. All I need is time. Let me have that, and the harvest will follow."

"Time!" William was moved to impatience. "Time! That is the cry of every bankrupt, always praying desperately for the unexpected to come to his rescue."

"Damn you for a pessimist," said Mr Law, but he smiled indulgently. "Come, Will. Courage! A little faith!"

But William Law was out of faith that morning. "I seem to hear King Philip II crying, 'Time and I are one.' But if you put your trust in time, at least contrive that it be better employed by the colonists than is now the case."

"Ay, there's something in that," Mr Law agreed. "I'll take thought."

Chapter 24

MURDER

Early in the following year the easy-going Regent proclaimed an amnesty for the Cellamare plotters, and whether touched or merely amused by the letters of the Duchess of Maine, with their professions of devotion and loyalty so oddly at variance with her conduct, he restored her Grace to liberty and allowed her to make her peace with him. This she found easier than making it with her husband, who continued to blame her plotting for his tribulations.

The Bastille opened its ponderous gates for the conspirators of Sceaux, and with them came also the Count of Horn, released from that duress, but still under the ban requiring him to keep himself not less than fifty leagues from Court.

He re-entered the world practically without means, for he had lived at his own charges in prison, and by denying himself no luxuries had exhausted the moneys he had received from the Countess before his arrest.

In the Rue d'Argenteuil he found her house closed, and he learnt in the neighbourhood that Madame la Comtesse was in the Dordogne. This by rendering still more desperately urgent his necessities, deepened his hatred of Mr Law in whom he beheld the author of all his woes.

As a result it happened that in the course of that chilly March morning Colonel de Mille, whilst frugally breaking his fast on bread and olives, a marinade of artichokes and a jug of *petit vin*, was surprised by the advent of a rather dilapidated Count of Horn. Not only was the young nobleman pallid and puffy from long imprisonment, but his once elegant suit of biscuit-coloured satin was crumpled and stained, his stockings soiled and his wig out of curl.

Recovering from his astonishment the Colonel embraced him, felicitated him upon his release, gave him a chair and the freedom of his breakfast.

"I keep Lent, you see, like the good Christian that I am not."

The Count eyed the olives and the artichokes, sniffed the wine disdainfully, and professed himself without appetite.

"Money is my need," he announced. "I am going down to the Dordogne to square accounts with Madame la Comtesse as soon as I've squared them here with that rascally lover of hers. A settlement is overdue. But as I've a soul to lose I'll see that they pay with interest."

"That's laudable," said the Colonel, "provided you don't expect me to finance the enterprise. No moment could be less propitious. I may perhaps command ten louis, and you're welcome to the half of it. But I doubt if that will take you as far as the Dordogne."

"You're laughing at me, I suppose," growled Horn.

"My child, I weep over you. And over myself. I'm a dried-up source. Though, if I can't supply money, I can supply advice. Begin with Lass by all means; but go about it in the proper manner. Put your sword to his throat, and demand the return of your million. He'll account his life cheap at the price. For what's a million to that usurer? In these days he flings millions from the window for all the world to catch."

"Damn your jests."

"It's a jest with the germ of earnest in it." The Colonel took a pull at his wine, grimaced over its sourness, and wiped his coarse lips. "On my honour it is what I should do in your place. It's the only way to deal with a thief who enjoys that fellow's power. His Majesty's

Comptroller-General. That's where he's climbed whilst you've been in gaol. You talk easily of squaring accounts with him. Do you suppose you can call out a man of that eminence? Faith, my way is the only way, and may God damn me but I'm so hard-driven myself these days that if you take it I'll lend a hand for a share in the plunder."

"Can you be mad enough to propose it seriously?"

"Sane enough. Though I confess it's nearer to purse cutting than I've come yet in my evil days. It's perhaps not to be done just as I suggested. That is merely the scheme in the raw. It needs shaping. Let us consider."

They considered so effectively that on the following morning Mr Law's secretary, Lacroix, placed before his master a letter which occasioned him some thought.

McWhirter was with him at the time, having come from the Rue Quincampoix for his daily orders. He had to announce the safe arrival of a cargo of spices from the Indies which should prove highly profitable, and a small parcel from China of bohea which might be transhipped for sale in England where a beverage prepared from that curious roasted herb was beginning to find favour with the quality.

When all this was settled, Mr Law handed over the letter Lacroix had brought him.

Signed "Duchatel," it announced that the writer was a holder of five hundred shares in the India Company which circumstances were compelling him to liquidate at once. For so large a parcel he could not expect to command the full value of the day, and to cast it upon the market must almost inevitably produce a fall in the price. Also he had the best of personal reasons for not wishing it to be known that he was the seller, for which reason also he confessed that the name he gave did not disclose his real identity. Therefore he offered these shares privately to Mr Law for an immediate payment at the reduced price of seven million livres. If, as he hoped, Mr Law was interested, and, in view of the secrecy desired by the seller, would attend in person to make the purchase at noon on Friday next at the Cerf Volant in the Rue Quincampoix, he would be placing one of the noblest families in France under a profound obligation.

"Ay, ay!" said McWhirter when he had read. He went over the letter a second time, more carefully. "Ay, ay!" he said again, and looked up. "Will the shares be forgeries now?"

Mr Law shook his head. "In that case he would not wish to deal with me personally. A broker would be more easily deceived."

"Ay. True enough. And what for would he wish to deal with you in person?"

"He gives a reason: secrecy."

"To be sure. Ah well, then, there's a good half-million profit for you."

"It's too much."

"I'm thinking the same. But there's no lack of fools in the world."

"Nor of knaves," said Mr Law. "Still, we'll not cast away a half-million on suspicion. You shall attend for me at the Flying Stag, Angus. I'll give you a note to say that you're my man of confidence, and that this gentleman may trust you in every way as he would myself."

What de Mille had left out of his calculations was that in no circumstances would a man of the Comptroller-General's present consequence attend in person to transact an operation of this nature.

Never doubting that the bait must bring Mr Law to the appointment, the Colonel waited confidently in a room above-stairs, accompanied by a rascal named Lestaing, who stood to him much as he, himself, stood to the Count. Horn was not with them, since his presence must at once have put Law upon his guard. He waited in the adjoining room, to intervene only if it should become necessary.

McWhirter presented himself punctually.

"Monsieur Duchatel?" he inquired.

"Your servant, Monsieur le Baron." The Colonel bowed; but when he had straightened himself, he stared. This man was almost as tall as Law and affected the same type of black periwig. But that was all the resemblance. "You are not Monsieur Lass," he exclaimed.

"His deputy. This will explain." McWhirter proffered his note.

The Colonel glanced over it. "I see." He considered for a moment, and concluded that whilst this might not be Law, the money was Law's, which was all that mattered. "Have you brought the money?" he asked.

"I have it here." The Scot tapped his bosom where it bulged.

In the next heartbeat the Colonel was upon him.

He had whipped a small but serviceable bludgeon from his pocket, and as he stepped forward he aimed at McWhirter's head a blow that must have stunned him had the Scot's reflexes been less prompt. McWhirter swerved his head out of the line of the descending weapon, which fell, instead, upon his shoulder, partly numbing it.

Before de Mille could repeat the blow he found himself grappled in so tight a hug that he was unable to use the bludgeon again. Close-locked they swayed across the room, hurtling against a table, which went over with such a thud and crash of the crockery standing on it that it must have resounded through the house.

The Colonel tripped over one of the legs of it and went down upon his back, with McWhirter on top of him, whilst in that interlocked fall the bludgeon slipped from his fingers and rolled beyond his reach. He now found a knee on his chest, pinning him to the floor, and sinewy hands reaching for his throat.

"Lend a hand, Lestaing," he roared. "Lend a hand, damn you!"

But Lestaing had taken fright at the noise. He had pushed open the lattice and was already astride the sill. Without heeding de Mille's urgent cry, he lowered himself, hung a moment by his hands, and then let himself drop to the yard and made off, to be seen no more.

McWhirter's hands had found the Colonel's throat, whilst he glared at him with one eye through the curls of a periwig that had become displaced, and was covering half his face.

"Lie still, you thieving bandit, till the archers come for you," he growled, and to ensure obedience bumped the Colonel's head upon the floor. "Lie still."

So much noise warned Horn that things were not going smoothly, and brought him in a rush from the adjoining room. He beheld the

Colonel in distress under the knees of his opponent, whom he supposed to be Law, for the displaced wig was acting as a mask.

At sight of the enemy whom he was there to despoil, apparently in the act of strangling de Mille, all the Count's rancour boiled up to rob him of his wits. As much to bring help to the Colonel as to gratify his passion of hatred he acted upon blind instinct, whipped out his sword and passed it from side to side through the man's body.

The Scot went limp, and as the Colonel heaved him aside and rose gasping for air and drenched in blood, McWhirter writhed and coughed dreadfully for a moment before sinking to lie still and prone upon the floor.

Standing over him, Horn snarled: "So, you dog, you are paid at last." Then across the length of the body Horn and de Mille looked at each other, their faces ghastly.

"You fool!" gasped the Colonel, with a hand on his heaving chest. "You cursed fool! What have you done?"

Horn was grinning horribly. "I've saved your life," said he, to whom the question seemed ungrateful.

"And you're waiting for me to thank you, I suppose. By God, let us get out of this whilst we can and if we can, or we'll hang for it."

He stooped to recover his hat from the floor, then lurched across the room to depart. But a thunder of steps rumbling up the stairs made him check and turn. "The window," he panted, and started for it. Horn who was nearer to it was the first to throw a leg over the sill. But not soon enough. The door was flung open, and the landlord followed by three of his lads swept in.

One glance at the body prone in a puddle of blood upon the floor was enough. Whilst two of them sprang across the room to seize the Count before he could drop from the window, the other two laid hands on de Mille, who was now too limp even to struggle.

In grasping the sill, Horn had lost his hold of the sword, with which he might have offered a murderous resistance. Disarmed, panting, distraught, he suffered himself tamely to be captured.

It was not until the archers were marching the pair away to the prison of La Tournelle that Horn was to realize the full extent of the catastrophe that had overtaken him. If he had left the Flying Stag under arrest for murder, he had borne with him at least the satisfaction of having made an end of the scoundrel who had robbed him of his money and seduced his wife.

Upon that he would base his defence when he came to take his trial; and considering the powerful enemies created for his Majesty's Comptroller-General by his rise to power, the Count of Horn should not want for friends to support him, to plead his righteous cause, and to justify him. He could count upon such great nobles as the Duke of Noailles, the Duke d'Aumont, the Marquis d'Argenson and the whole body of the Parliament, and in the end of it all he could already see himself hailed as the deliverer of France from the evil thrall of a foreign adventurer, a Scottish Jew.

It all became so clear and inevitable to him, that as he trudged alongside of the hangdog de Mille, through the Rue de Venise into the broader thoroughfare, he was in danger of exulting.

It was only when they were halfway down the Rue Saint-Martin that this heroic dream was suddenly shattered. They had been thrust aside by their guards to make way for a magnificent coach, drawn by a pair of superb bays, and with footmen behind in claret and silver. As it passed them the leather curtain was drawn aside, and a long, stern, handsome face framed in a black periwig looked out of the window.

It was the face of Mr Law – of Mr Law, whom the Count of Horn had left dead in a pool of blood on the floor of a room above-stairs in the Flying Stag – on his way to pay one of his occasional visits to the Banque Royale in the Rue Quincampoix.

As the Comptroller-General's brilliant eyes, frowning inquiry, rested for a moment on the prisoners under guard, the Count of Horn felt his stomach turn over within him.

Chapter 25

THE WHEEL

It was not as the saviour of a nation that the Count of Horn took his trial with Colonel de Mille. The indictment pronounced them just a couple of common thieves and murderers, and as thieves and murderers both were sentenced to be broken alive upon the wheel.

In counting upon dukes and peers to stand by him, at least, Horn was not disappointed. And not only dukes and peers, but princes, too, beginning with his own brother the Prince of Horn, came pleading to the Regent. But all the plea the circumstances of his conviction permitted was that he might be hanged or beheaded. Thus it was sought to spare him the infamy of the wheel, an infamy that must besmirch members of all his family, and so deeply in Germany, where he had great connections, that for three generations none of them might be admitted to any noble chapter or hold any office under the State.

The Regent, deeply shocked by the outrage, displayed unusual sternness and rigour, accounting it his duty to stand firm and allow the law to take its course.

He quoted Corneille to the pleaders. "It is the crime that makes the infamy," he answered them, "and not the scaffold."

He was reminded that Horn had once been in the circle of his own intimates and that, in fact, he was actually a remote kinsman of the Regent's.

"Very well," he answered. "I must bear my share of the ignominy."

The Abbé Dubois and the Duke of Saint-Simon were exhorted to employ on the condemned man's behalf their great influence with His Highness. Dubois was too busy at the time preparing himself to be received into holy orders, so that he might be installed Archbishop of Cambrai, as a preliminary to receiving at last the coveted red hat.

Saint-Simon, however, who was about to go into the country, to spend Easter on his lands, tells us in his memoirs that he did intercede, using every argument he knew, and that he actually wrung a promise from the Regent that Horn should be spared the wheel, and be beheaded instead.

But as after the Duke's departure there was no announcement of any modification in the sentence, it was widely concluded that other influences were at work against the doomed man.

It was recalled that Angus McWhirter was one of Law's chief lieutenants, and also that there had been a long and bitter feud between Law and Horn. Hence, and considering that Law's influence with the Regent was paramount, it was not unnaturally concluded – and there was no lack of those to encourage the conclusion – that it was the Comptroller-General's counsel that sustained an inflexibility so unusual in the easy-going Regent.

Appeals for intervention had been addressed to Law from every quarter. Amongst the many who had sought him were the Prince de Conti, who had last parted from him in anger and with injurious terms, because of unsatisfied greed, the old Duc de Villeroy, who had always been his enemy, and even d'Argenson, to whom he had become detestable since the ruin of the anti-system and the Marquis' loss of the Comptrollership.

To all of them, without entering into details, Mr Law replied that finance and not justice was his department and that he would account it an unpardonable presumption in himself to submit their pleas to His Highness.

Villeroy, turning pale with anger under his rouge, had begged that if Monsieur le Baron would not intervene in Horn's favour, at least, he should abstain from intervening against him, whereupon Mr Law had pulled the bell cord and requested a footman to escort Monsieur le Maréchal-Duc to his coach.

D'Argenson, hectoring as was his nature, had stormed that Monsieur le Baron was treading a dangerous path.

"I have endeavoured to make it clear," said Mr Law, always urbane, "that in this matter I tread no path at all."

"That is precisely what is dangerous," shouted the Marquis, and stamped out.

Monsieur de Conti had similarly prophesied that Monsieur le Baron would ruin himself if he did nothing to arrest the doom of the Count of Horn.

"That should be a matter for regret to you, mon prince," said Mr Law, thus by implication reminding the malicious little hunchback of how richly he had profited by Mr Law's prosperity.

"Nay, sir – for rejoicing, if you persist in your aloofness."

In this manner those three who detested him, and now detested him the more for having been under the necessity of appealing to him, departed in a still deeper rancour because of what they accounted the arrogance of a refusal that had lacerated their overweening pride.

The last to seek him in this matter were Lord and Lady Stair. Horn had been a close friend of theirs. It was they, in fact, who had introduced him to Law's household. To strengthen themselves they sought to enlist the aid of Catherine, and induced her to lend it. She recalled her tender passages with the Count and was disposed to condone his attempts upon her virtue, charitably and femininely attributing them to the excessive ardours she had aroused in him and had even encouraged until they became too ardent.

Together the three sought Mr Law in his study, and when they found him coldly unresponsive to their prayers, Lord Stair had recourse to a crowning argument.

"My dear Law, it is being widely said that you have intervened already, in a contrary sense; that Monsieur de Saint-Simon had obtained a promise that Horn should be spared the wheel, but that you have since persuaded His Highness to disregard it. That, my friend, is not an imputation under which you can comfortably lie."

"Why not?"

"Why not! You admit, then, that it is true."

"I do not. But if it were, who could blame me? The murdered man was a valued friend and loyal servant. I should be doing poor justice to his memory if I raised so much as a finger for the least mitigation of the punishment of his assassin."

"That I can understand. But you do yourself no good service if you permit the general belief to be confirmed by the execution."

"A mere argument of expediency, my lord."

And then her ladyship made an unfortunate contribution to the discussion. "Have you never killed a man, Mr Law?"

Mr Law's grey eyes were stern in a face whose natural pallor was deepened by indignation. But his voice, if charged with bitter irony, was level. "Is it possible that your ladyship insults me by comparing an act of mine in the way of honour with a brutal murder committed by a thief?"

Stair accounted it necessary to hasten to his wife's aid. "No, no," he cried. "But when you charge Horn with being a thief you are forgetting that he believed he was recovering his own, of which he was under the impression – of course the mistaken impression – that you had defrauded him?"

"Is that also to be laid to my charge?"

"You should not ignore that it might be. Horn was talkative. He complained bitterly and widely."

"And because he was a liar and defamer as well as a thief and a murderer, I am now to plead for him. Let me tell you something which is not generally known, in which you may discover yet another reason for my intervention. Horn believed that it was I, myself, who had gone to the Flying Stag, whither he sought to lure me by a letter in a false name. He came into the room only when McWhirter and de Mille were struggling on the floor. He could not see McWhirter's face because his wig had fallen across it. So that when Horn passed his sword through McWhirter he believed that he was passing it through me."

"Oh!" It was an outcry of horror from Catherine, who sprang to her feet, her face suddenly white.

Mr Law turned to her. "You said?"

"Oh, John!" She was fiercely vehement. "You'll believe that if I had known this I should never have joined Lord and Lady Stair to plead with you. I should never even have brought them to you. Why didn't you tell me?"

Mr Law stared at her for a moment, surprised by her vehemence. Then he shrugged. "It is not important. I should not trouble to mention it now but that his lordship constrains me."

Catherine sank to her chair again, a limp figure of distress, whilst Lord Stair gravely inclined his head. "Of course, there is no more to be said."

Lady Stair, however, would not yet accept defeat. Her pale, mean eyes had glowed in contempt upon Catherine. Malice deepened her ladyship's resemblance to a hen. "There is one fact you would be wise to consider, Mr Law, for your own sake. The Count of Horn was talkative, you say. So he was. And he told the world not only that you had defrauded him, but that you had seduced his wife."

There was a low moan of horror from Catherine, whilst his lordship threw up his hands in despair. But Lady Stair went ruthlessly on: "When you say that he killed your agent, believing him to be you, you say something which, if known, must be held to extenuate the deed. It must be held a crime of passion, a thing done, not in the course of a theft, as has been supposed, but to vindicate his honour." On a queer note of triumph she flung out the question: "Now will you think it worth while to use all your influence with His Highness?"

There were beads of sweat on Mr Law's brow, along the line of his wig. He drew a handkerchief from the pocket of his coat of heavy, purple Indian satin, and passed it across his forehead. Yet his voice still preserved its quiet level. "Your ladyship will perceive that what I have just told you – of the mistake that Horn made – is known to no one else. Your ladyship will hardly be threatening to publish it unless I do as I am bidden?"

"Good God, no!" cried Stair. "How could my wife have such a thought? You would insult her by supposing it. She only points out to you what will be concluded if it transpires."

"It cannot transpire save from one or the other of you. And if it should," he added, his eyes glittering upon Lord Stair, "I should require a severe account of it."

The ambassador's face flushed scarlet. It was a moment before, bowing stiffly, he answered. "Always and in all things at your service, Mr Law."

He turned to his wife, now breathless in panic of the mischief she had wrought. "Come, madam, we take our leave." He bowed again coldly to Law and then to Catherine. "Madam, your humble obedient."

When in frosty dignity they had departed, Catherine looked at her husband through a blur of tears. He stood by his writing table, deep in thought, a frown darkening his brow.

"John, was it true what that woman said?"

"What did she say? She merely repeated a falsehood put about by that shameless man Horn."

"A falsehood?"

Because he scorned to lie to her, he answered: "As it happens. Yet it might have been true and would have been true but that Margaret would not have it so."

"Oh, John!" she cried.

He looked at her with his bitter smile. "What's to surprise you? Yourself you believed it true. You taunted me with it when suspicion was your only evidence. And why this wail of outraged virtue? Have you nothing on your side with which to reproach yourself? Or is it possible that you still do not realize how much? Trace all this mischief to its source. Or don't you know where to find it? Then I will tell you.

"Knowing Horn's evil repute you encouraged his gallantries. Against my wishes you went to Sceaux in order to afford him opportunities, and but that his Countess watched over you, it is likely that you would have succumbed."

Fiercely she broke in. "Did Margaret Ogilvy say so? Did she tell you that?"

"Where was the need? Yourself you told me, when on your return from Sceaux you said that you never wished to see the Count of Horn again. Whether you have seen him since or not you will know better than I. I have not spied upon you."

Again she interrupted fiercely. "Because you did not care. Do you make a virtue of it?"

He paid no heed, but went relentlessly on, "Your laudable resolve not to see Horn again was taken too late, the harm was already done. It happened earlier, when the flagrancy of his pursuit of you and your encouragement of it were giving rise to scandal.

"With the innuendoes of Lady Stair in my ears I thought it time to take steps to protect my honour. I requested him to cease attentions to you which were becoming too assiduous. You will recall that he attempted to strike me, and taking the will for the deed I demanded the ordinary satisfaction that obtains between gentlemen. He refused it with fresh insult. But I happened to have other weapons for this needy gallant, this *canaille*, whom I had put in the way of fortune; and whilst he was making love to you at Sceaux I broke him.

"After that he was driven by vindictiveness upon his doom. First he allied himself with my enemies, then, when that failed him, he set a trap for me into which poor Angus went to be murdered. And now I am warned that unless on Tuesday he is spared the wheel, I shall be charged with basest motives for having urged the Regent to show no mercy."

His bitter laugh cut her like a whip. "Do you begin to see, Catherine, the havoc your easy smiles have wrought?"

She was rocking herself in anguish, her hands locked between her knees. "I thought you did not care," she wailed. "That is what drove me, goaded me. If you had cared, John, do you suppose any other man would have had those smiles? Those smiles that you call easy?"

"You are my wife. You bear my name. You are the mother of my children."

"Have you always remembered that, John?" She asked the question plaintively.

"Always, though never given credit for it. Always, though constantly charged with imagined infidelities. Always until lately, when temptation snapped the bond of duty your levity had worn thin. However, as I've said, to that temptation it was denied me to succumb."

"For that, at least, I suppose I may thank God," she cried.

"And Margaret Ogilvy," said he, as he sat down at his writing table. "It was the virtue of this woman you miscall that made the barrier."

She sat for a moment miserably considering, then spoke very quietly. "At least you have been honest with me, John, and I owe it to you to be honest in my turn. When I suspected – when you gave me cause to suspect your relations with the Countess of Horn, I sought the Count again. I deliberately used his…his interest in me, in the hope of forming an alliance with him, so that he might place his wife beyond your reach. I was desperate…desperate to save us both, John. Can you understand?" Without waiting for his answer, she went miserably on to make a full avowal of her aborted association with Horn.

Whilst his countenance remained impassive, yet, despite himself, his heart was touched by a confession which but for his preconceptions might well have vouchsafed him more than a glimpse of the true state of her feelings for him beneath their habitually shrewish surface. For a spell when the tale was told there was silence between them, save for the quiet weeping of the woman huddled miserably in her chair.

When at last he spoke again it was very gently. "Dry your tears, Catherine. What is done is done, and it shall never again be mentioned by me. I accept my part of the blame. Do not imagine that I don't perceive it, and how much we are both of us the sport of destiny."

She roused herself to look at him. He sat erect, staring sternly before him, his hands gripping the arms of his chair. She was all humility. "You can be generous, John. More generous perhaps than I deserve. But what now?"

"Now?"

"What are you going to do?"

"Do? Why, nothing."

"But you must. You know that woman Lady Stair. You know her malice. Do you think it will allow her to keep silent, that she'll not tell the world that McWhirter was killed in your place? Hasn't she warned you of what would then be believed? Oh, why, why did you tell them?"

"It was a folly, I confess. I perceived my error as soon as the words were out. But I was hard driven, as you saw."

"If it were put about that the Count of Horn thought he was killing his wife's lover, that would partly rehabilitate him as she said."

"Does it matter? He is naught."

"My God, don't I know it? Am I thinking of him? I am thinking of you, John. His rehabilitation will be at your expense. Don't you see?"

"I see," he said. But what he suddenly saw was that it would also be at the expense of Margaret's good name.

"Then you will go to the Regent?"

"It will be better," he said, his tone flat and dull. "Yes. I will go." He rose. "I will tell Laguyon to order my carriage."

In passing, he paused, looking down upon her, touched by an anxiety for him, of which he had long since ceased to believe her capable. Meeting her raised, piteous glance, he smiled wistfully, and his fingers lightly touched her dark brown head. "Poor Catherine," he said, and sighed. "Fate has had great sport with us both."

She swung round in eagerness to answer him; but he was gone before she could find words, and it was late when he returned, to discover her waiting in a fever of impatience. His dark look proclaimed his failure before he spoke.

"A wasted effort," he announced. "I have never known His Highness so hard. There is no obstinacy like the obstinacy of a weak man. He would scarcely listen to me. For once he was in a mood of nobility. 'It is being said already,' he told me, 'that in this realm there is one law for the noble and another for the simple.'

" 'It shall not be said in the case of a brutal murder by a vulgar thief.'

"I did not leave it there. I told him that I begged leniency for my own sake. I told him that it was being bruited that out of vindictiveness it was I who was urging His Highness to this severity. He was angrily ironical. 'We shall bear the blame together, then. You should be happy in the association.' And that was his last word."

On the following Tuesday – the Tuesday of Easter Week – in the Place de Grève, the high-born Count of Horn and Colonel de Mille suffered the dreadful, brutal punishment of being broken alive upon the wheel.

On the day after that, as the Regent drove through the streets of Paris, he was greeted by acclamations of a fervour he had never yet known.

For his stern undiscriminating justice the populace hailed him as its protector. It was being said – according to the Regent's German mother – that however lenient His Highness might be towards offenders against himself, he forgave nothing that was done against a subject.

Mr Law sneered when it was reported to him. "He will now account himself justified of his severity."

But when later in the day Mr Law himself drove forth, he was shocked to find himself the object of similar demonstrations of respect and affection, and he took shame in the thought that it sprang from the belief that the Regent's severity was largely due to his advocacy.

Again he sneered as he spoke to his brother who rode with him, "He said that we should share the blame. Meanwhile we share the plaudits. And, faith, one is as distasteful as the other."

Chapter 26

FAREWELL

Arising out of all this, a queer mood of disgust with all things was still upon John Law when, a week or so later, he learnt that Margaret was again in Paris.

He was perhaps justified in accounting it no less than a duty to present himself at the house in the Rue d'Argenteuil; but it is not to be pretended that inclination had no part in it.

On this occasion there was neither porter nor footman to admit him. He was conducted by the Countess of Horn's maitre d'hotel through a house enshrouded as if it were untenanted. Only the boudoir, where he was again received, had been cleared of its mantlings and was gay as of old with its damask and its lacquers.

There Margaret came to him, straight and lissom in her black, a mourning assumed out of regard for the circumstances rather than for the actual dead.

"I thought that you might come," she said, with a wan smile, and put forth her hand.

He bowed over it and bore it to his lips. "Did you hope it?" he asked.

She gave him a slow, searching look before replying. "I scarcely know. All this has distracted me so much that my senses are a little numbed."

They sat down, with half the room between them. "I am merely passing through Paris," she informed him. "Pausing only to set affairs in order. Naturally I shall not now stay in France. The name of Horn has been made too infamous." She paused before adding: "In all this miserable affair the only ray of light for me is your escape from the fate that man intended for you."

The words took him by surprise. His long face became grim. "I see that Lady Stair has lost no time."

"She came this morning to condole with me."

"And to bring you matter calling for still deeper condolence."

"She told me that it is widely known that you persuaded the Regent to show the Count no mercy."

"That was kind of her. Did you believe it?"

"That you so persuaded the Regent?" She smiled with tight lips. "No. I happen to know you, John."

"Thank you, Margaret. It is as well that you should learn the actual truth. I all but embroiled myself with His Highness by pleading with him to be lenient."

She opened wide her lovely eyes. "That, in all the circumstances, is more, far more than was to be expected."

"No," he said. "It was proper that I should think of you and of the danger of this thing which Lady Stair has told you is widely known. I feared that if I sat still, your name might come to be smirched together with mine. As it is, unless her ladyship's tongue is bridled it may yet happen."

"You mean that men will say you were my lover, and that the Count of Horn's real purpose was to kill you so as to avenge his honour. It is a half-truth and might so easily have been a whole one. But for me it is no matter." Her tone was listless. "I am going out of it all, away, home to England."

"Is the decision irrevocable?"

"Do you know a better?"

He had thought he did; a nebulous thought that had brought him to her. But now her steady questioning glance served to clear his mind and spread reality before him. He had known that she could not remain in France; he had dimly considered that she was now free and, as he conceived, alone and defenceless, whilst, himself, in his present revulsion and for her sake, ready to abandon all that he had so laboriously built.

It had been vaguely in his mind that they might go together, to Italy or Spain or Holland, and together at last attempt to re-fashion their lives. But her eloquent almost challenging eyes told him all that had been obscured from his distorted perceptions, reminded him that he had nothing to offer save that which she had already firmly rejected, made him understand that their circumstances were nowise altered by Horn's death, as at a superficial glance it had seemed, or, if altered, were altered only by the erection of a fresh barrier.

As if she read his mind, this is what she told him when presently she spoke.

"I wonder, John, if the world has known a story more ironical than ours. 'The very events that have removed the obstacles between us have replaced them by chasms that may not be crossed."

"If it were not for Catherine," he said, "I could build a bridge."

"A bridge across two graves." Sadly smiling, she shook her head. "Do not deceive yourself. To do so merely sharpens torment, denies you peace. One of my husbands died by your hand, the other for his association with you. Even if you were now free to marry, how should we dare? We should be constrained to live in hiding, shunned, aware of the contempt that would everywhere be ours, and living thus we might come in the end to hate each other. Take the thought of that, if not as a balm, at least as a cautery for your wounds. I should be on my knees to you, John, for pardon, for having come again into your life to unsettle it, if I had not the excuse that I came to rescue you when you were in danger."

"That you came I shall never regret," he cried, "whatever the present pain. It brought me to knowledge of your great sacrifice, it restored to me the reverence in which once I held you, and the loss of which left me without reverence for anything. For that, at least, I am thankful."

"Then keep the thought of it to sweeten your memory of me, as my memory of you will be sweetened by that assurance. Seek happiness in Catherine, John, for I know that Catherine loves you and for me that knowledge would be a barrier if there were no other. For, believe me, there is no happiness to be built upon another's sorrow."

"Catherine!" he cried, in repudiation. "Should I have come to you as I did a year ago if I believed it? Catherine loves herself too well to have any love to spare. Of me she loves no more than the splendours I provide her. I cannot think that if misfortune overtook me I should find Catherine at my side."

"I wonder if you are not mistaken. In my heart and from what I saw at Sceaux I believe you are. But even if I should be wrong, you have still your children. Find your happiness in them, as I hope to find mine in my son. He will always remind me of you, for it was for your sake I got him. And now, dear love, it must be farewell between us. You were born to be fortunate, as I was born to be gay. Do not be false to your nature as fate has made me false to mine."

He realized that this was the irrevocable end. There was no more to say.

For the last time, and for a moment only, he held her in his arms. Then he went forth to meet the storm of which the first unsuspected clouds were gathering.

Chapter 27

MUTTERINGS OF THE STORM

Whilst the people who had acclaimed Mr Law for his princely liberality and for the prosperity which he had brought to their humble ranks, were acclaiming him more loudly still for what they believed to have been his part in the justice done upon the Count of Horn, the quality began to look askance upon him for the same reason.

Whilst artisans and others, whose daily earnings had by now been quintupled by the grace of John Law, were doffing their hats when he passed and shouting "Long live Monsieur Lass," the nobles, many of them enriched by him, were beginning to mutter his name with execration.

However much Horn, in their eyes, may have merited death, yet they began to tell one another that it was time to look to their privileges when a foreign adventurer usurped a power that could insist upon the infamy which had attended Horn's execution. For this was the tale, sedulously disseminated by the vindictive d'Argenson, and soon to take the still uglier shape that Horn had been wrongly convicted; that he was not the thieving murderer he had been represented, but an avenging husband whose misfortune it had been to mistake his man.

It was his friend the Duke of Antin who brought Mr Law the warning that this tale was spreading.

"Of course I know it for a foul lie," said his Grace. "But how to prove it? The world loves a foul lie, and the fouler it is, the better it loves it."

D'Antin had the rare experience of beholding the imperturbable Mr Law livid with anger. "The truth was proved at the trial. And here is the evidence." He sought and produced from amongst his papers the Duchatel letter.

"Conclusive enough, in all faith," the Duke agreed. "What can be done to make it known, I'll do. But slander is of rank and hardy growth."

"I am aware of the source of it," said Mr Law. "But, of course, it is too late to seal it up."

Nevertheless, he went off to the British Embassy, demanded to see Lord Stair, and made his plaint in uncompromising terms.

"This abominable tale, my lord, is a mean return for the profit you have had from me so as to repair your down-at-heel circumstances. I warned your lordship that if this thing were put about I should require a strict account of you."

They faced each other across Stair's writing table, the tall Scot and the short one. The ambassador strove with his dignity. His face was white, his prominent eyes bulging with wrath. He spoke stiltedly. "I resent your terms, sir. Yet I'll condescend to assure you that the rumour is not of my circulating."

"Will you condescend to assure me that it is not of your wife's? Or do you take shelter behind her ladyship's petticoats? If you deny that between you you are responsible for the slander, I shall give you the lie. For by my own indiscretion, it was known only to you that McWhirter was mistaken for me."

Stair's livid face, attempting a lofty smile, achieved a death's-head grin. "You will have the decency, sir, to remember my office here, and that it precludes me from asking satisfaction."

"The Count of Horn took some such tone with me when I required him to cease his attentions to my wife. I broke him for it, as I shall break you, my lord."

"Break me!" gasped his lordship, and laughed in derisive anger.

But Mr Law had already turned on his heel and was striding from the room.

He went straight to the Palais Royal and Dubois. He urged his demands peremptorily. "Monsieur l'Abbé, that man Stair is circulating a lie that hurts my honour."

The Abbé looked up at him, startled by the absence from his tone of its normal urbanity. "And what, pray, can I do about it?"

"If nothing suggests itself, I'll tell you. He denies me satisfaction, sheltering himself behind his office. Strip him of it."

"Strip him of it? In God's name, how can I do that?"

"How? Are you not Secretary of State for Foreign Affairs? Require Lord Stanhope to recall him."

"God save us!" Dubois was appalled. "What are you asking? You know there are limits…"

"There are none. You are slow to understand. These slanders may endanger me, and I am not to be endangered. I carry on my back the whole burden of the finances of France, like Atlas shouldering the world. If through the malice of that man I am made to stumble, there will be chaos. Do you understand?"

The Abbé scratched his fulvid head, sucked in his hollow cheeks. "But you are asking for extreme measures, Monsieur Atlas."

"No less. You'll take them, or you may never get to Cambrai, and there'll be no red hat for you."

"And now, God forgive you, I believe you are threatening me."

"No. I'm warning you. Or shall I ask His Highness to do it?"

"But no, but no," the Abbé soothed him. "You'll understand, at least, that I could not take such a step without the Regent's authority."

"For that all you need do is to explain the gravity of the case. His Highness doesn't want to see the finances in confusion, as they will be if I am overthrown by a campaign of slander. So make it clear to him. If necessary let him know that either Stair goes or I resign the Comptrollership. But you'll find that so much will not be necessary. Good day to you, Monsieur l'Abbé."

He stalked out, and Dubois went quavering to the Regent.

"I should never have believed that Monsieur Lass could be so violent," he lamented, in delivering his message.

It took effect the more readily because His Highness had no affection for the ambassador, and a courier set out that very day to inform Lord Stanhope that the Earl of Stair was no longer *persona grata* at the Court of France. Privately, Lord Stanhope was acquainted by Dubois with the fact that Stair had become obnoxious to Mr Law. It was enough. For such by then was Europe's view of the financial preponderance acquired by France and such the respect for its architect that no foreign government accounted it prudent to incur the Comptroller-General's displeasure.

Within the week the Earl of Stair had the mortification of being recalled and the further mortification of knowing whence the blow descended. He made what mischief he could whilst packing his bags, and let it be widely known by whose agency he was being sent home in disgrace.

Although there was little love for him, and, as the Regent's mother wrote, the Regent was glad to be rid of him, yet his recall served, as he reckoned, to deepen in Court circles the growing resentment of the pride and power of a Scotsman, so swollen that he could break ambassadors at his will. Law became the more detested, because it was now perceived how much he was to be feared, and this detestation began to study ways to sap the ground under his feet.

The Regent, aware of that wave of weighty hostility against his Comptroller, threw all his prestige into the scales against it, honouring Law in public on every occasion, and showing himself frequently with him in his box at the Opera. If, as a consequence, none dared to display open incivility, yet the campaign against him was preparing underground, led by his whilom friend and now bitterest enemy, the dispossessed d'Argenson.

The Marquis' shrewdness perceived that vast and imposing though the financial edifice of Mr Law's construction might be, the frenzy of speculation had rendered it top heavy. This frenzy continuing, the shares of the India Company had reached by now the monstrous price of twenty thousand livres, which was forty times their issued value.

Just as this nourished the hostile hopes of d'Argenson and his associates, so it renewed the fears of the prudent William Law. Armed with a sheet of figures, he sought his brother on a day of spring, a little while after Stair's recall, the day on which the shares had reached that phenomenal level.

"I've brought you a statement for the year, John, which you should study. It shows a profit on overseas trading of seventeen millions, with another seven millions from benefits on tobacco, salt and minting. Add to this sixty-three millions between interest on the national debt and profit on the tax farms, and you have a total revenue of some eighty millions. This might provide a dividend of five per centum on the capital for which the shares in the India Company were originally issued. Will you tell me what is the imperceptible fraction of that available for the ten milliards which is the present capital value of the stock?"

Mr Law studied the sheet cursorily, and tossed it back. "You are telling me that for a reasonable interest on that capital we require four or five hundred millions, whereas at present we possess but eighty. That is merely to renew the old arguments."

"Do you know of any fresh ones?"

"As I've told you before, those who buy at these prices must understand what are the present resources. They are easily computed. It follows, then, that they buy for the sake of future profits from the colonies when developed."

"Ay, ay, when developed. But when will they be developed to the extent of offering an adequate return on a capital value such as this? You promised to take order about the colonists of Louisiana. But nothing's done. Every report shows that native labour is proving useless without proper direction, whilst the white population is composed of wastrels who will not work. The riches on which you count remain locked in the soil."

"I've not overlooked it. In fact, I've prepared a plan, and have waited only until I could persuade the Regent to let me adopt it."

He disclosed it. It was a plan clearly inspired by the system of press gangs that obtained in England for the navy. Now that he possessed the Regent's authority he would apply it in France, so as to populate the colonies.

He would see Le Blanc, the present Lieutenant-General of Police, and decree a round-up of all useless idlers, gaol birds, thieves, able-bodied beggars, vagabonds, prostitutes and the like, and ship them out to find an honest outlet for their activities on the Mississippi plantations. Thus he would give those wretches the chance of a fresh start in life, whilst cleansing France of their undesirable presence and enriching her by the fruits of their labours in the New World.

It dissipated some of William's gloom. "I like it fine. I'll allow it's a canny notion." Then with a return of his misgivings, "I would you had thought of it earlier," he grumbled. "If you had had the notion two years ago, we might be garnering the fruits by now. As it is… what if overblown faith should turn to panic? Have you thought of that?"

"It has never been out of my reckonings since those crazy speculators got to work to drive the price to these wild levels."

"Can you provide for it?"

Mr Law shrugged irritably. "They say I work miracles. But, after all, I am not God. I can only hope that they will possess themselves in patience until shipments from Louisiana bring us that abundance. Meanwhile, we'll do as we can. A little judicious manipulation of the market, by making gambling easier, may keep them entertained."

"Do you sleep o' nights, John?"

"Peacefully."

"Ay, ye've the gamester's temperament. Would God I shared it. I might sleep easier myself."

"Perhaps my handling of the stock will help you."

Craftily he went about it. He brought down prices by apparently forced liquidations which compelled weak holders to sell, and then allowed them to rebound, only to drive them down once more. These fluctuations rendered speculation wilder than ever, but, thus deliberately encouraged, they achieved the immediate object of distracting attention from the lack of dividends by supplying quick gains for the fortunate operators.

But whilst Law gave his attention to this pumping so as to keep the ship afloat until harbour should be reached, d'Argenson went about intensifying the storm by which he hoped to wreck it.

He decided to open his campaign with an attack upon Law's paper money. He computed that the banknotes in circulation represented some two thousand five hundred millions, which was three times the value of France's minted gold. This grossly excessive paper currency, which rendered Law's position extremely vulnerable, resulted from the original omission to provide that only bondholders of the national debt should have the right to subscribe for the respective issue of the India Company stock.

As a consequence, by the time a great many of them had been paid off in notes, they were unable to acquire shares unless prepared to pay the inflated prices demanded by the speculators who had snatched them up. Out of reluctance to do this they had clung to their banknotes, so that these had not come to the India Company to be cancelled as was projected, but remained to swell to a dangerous extent the circulation.

Quietly at first, but sedulously, d'Argenson's agents spread the tale that Law was depositing for himself abroad large quantities of the French gold he had obtained in exchange for worthless paper. Alarm spread quickly and a run on the bank for specie was led by the Prince de Conti, who by the favour of Mr Law had amassed an enormous fortune.

In order to turn his paper into coin the Prince came to the Rue Quincampoix ostentatiously with three wagons, upon which he loaded the gold and the silver which he drew from the Bank. The effect of this spectacular action was to spread the general alarm upon which de Conti reckoned. The share market was suddenly paralysed, and the operators fell into queues to besiege the Bank with their demands for specie.

For a moment it looked as if this avalanche must sweep away Mr Law and his system. But the public had to deal with absolute power which could be yielded with unscrupulous skill, and Mr Law was prompt to wield it. By an immediate edict he officially depreciated specie in contrast with paper, by one tenth, and he was prepared, if necessary, to depreciate it further.

It was not necessary. In counter-panic the run ceased abruptly. Those who had queued to withdraw their gold, now queued as impetuously to return it.

At Mr Law's instances the Prince de Conti was severely reprimanded by the Regent and all but threatened with impeachment for his part in a conspiracy which might seriously have imperilled the finances of the State. Peremptorily he was ordered to return at least two-thirds of this specie to the Bank.

The position being restored, and in order to prevent a repetition, a further edict was promulgated delimiting the amount of specie to be possessed by any private person, completely forbidding its exportation, and restricting its use in trade to small payments only. At the same time an injunction was placed upon the manufacture of plate and articles of gold and silver beyond a certain weight.

It was one of those desperate measures of compulsion which governments in difficulties have occasionally adopted, and which, of whatever immediate result have never ended otherwise than in disaster. Its effect now was to sow disquiet in the public mind. Of this, d'Argenson, foiled in his first assault, took advantage to attack in another quarter. This time it was against the India Company that he unmasked his batteries.

Operations happened to be favoured for him by a spreading scandal resulting from the activities of Mr Law's press gangs, which by now were operating throughout France. The measure, wise and provident in itself, if belatedly adopted, was being grossly ill-conducted.

The men charged with the impressments, and commonly known by now as the Bandoleers of the Mississippi, were executing them with a brutality that shocked the country. The fundamental dishonesty so commonly displayed by underlings in the exercise of government authority, especially in the case of coercive measures, was actively at work.

By the peculation of those responsible, hordes of unfortunates of both sexes, carted to Bordeaux for shipment, were left on the way without proper nourishment or shelter, so that many of them perished miserably.

The survivors were embarked in overcrowded floating hells to be further decimated by disease and death, whilst those hardy enough to reach Louisiana alive, instead of labouring, were soon pursuing in the New World the activities which had made them infamous in the Old. And even this inhumanity was not the worst of it.

The Bandoleers of the Mississippi were not slow to perceive in their functions the opportunity for further and still more remunerative corrupt practices. They no longer confined their impressments to rogues and vagabonds. Many a respectable citizen found himself caught up in that infamous net to the end that he might ransom himself by payment.

The knowledge of these abominations spread rapidly, and the blame for them was assigned to Law at the prompting of his enemies. The mutterings of a storm of execration swelled up and at last broke upon him. Instead of the acclamations to which he had become accustomed on his public appearances, he was greeted now by obloquy, and more than once his carriage was pelted with filth and stones.

As indomitable in the face of this as he had been imperturbable in the face of plaudits, he took immediate steps to put an end to the abuses. The press gangs were abolished, and agents were dispatched to Germany, Italy and Switzerland, to recruit industrious labour of experience on the land with the offer of two hundred and eighty acres in Louisiana free of all rent and imposts for three years.

Even the gloomy William admitted the excellence of this measure, if not one that could ease the battle against time which must be more strenuously joined than ever now that the activities of d'Argenson were becoming apparent.

The Marquis was rendering the public conscious of the ludicrously inflated value of the India Company stock, with the assertion, which it was now impossible to contradict, that it would be many years before any return might be expected, if indeed ever, considering the scandalous failure of the colonizing experiments.

He reminded the world of the high rate of interest he had paid on the stock of the anti-system, which Mr Law had crushed and replaced by a stock that bore no fruit at all. He and his friends eloquently advocated those who held these fictitious values should convert them into stable ones: houses, land, jewels and the like.

The eloquence did its work. The confidence already shaken by the enforced measures, was shaken further by that insidious advocacy, and holders of the stock began to realize. Gathering momentum, the realization came to sweep the Rue Quincampoix like a wind of catastrophe, bringing about a rapid fall in the price of the shares.

When they had dropped from twenty to twelve thousand livres, William Law beheld in this the beginning of the verification of those fears which had been his ever since his brother had extended his operations from banking to the monopoly and direction of the nation's commerce. He adjured his brother, at least, to save the Bank by sacrificing the Company.

"The Bank," he contended, "is built on solid foundations, and can withstand these seas tossed by speculation. Let the gamblers of the India Company take their chance. If they lose, they can blame only their own rashness."

The advice was sound; but Law faced with these malign influences was no longer the cool gamester of former days. Anger and anxiety robbed him of his clarity of vision, dulled his gift of unerring calculation.

The man who had thriven by studying why others lose and by his accurate estimation of the odds, was made as reckless as the commonest punter, and, like the commonest punter, practised a desperate tenacity in the face of this adverse fall of the cards. So it was with something of defiance that he rejected his brother's advice and chose, instead, to have recourse to expedients.

Greatly daring, he made an ostentatious appearance on foot in the Rue Quincampoix, arrayed in the robes of his office of Comptroller-General and attended by a brilliant retinue of nobles, which included the Duke of Antin and the young Duke of Bourbon.

The odium visited upon him as a result of the operations of the press gangs had faded by now from the public memory, so notoriously short, and his appearance in the panoply of his high estate, handsome, serene and masterful, became the occasion of a demonstration above all his expectations. D'Argenson, who had hoped that he would be beaten to death for his daring, might gnash his teeth in disappointment.

He paused in an almost royal progress to greet some of the more prominent *agioteurs* and hold them in talk. Airily he announced that very soon the Regent would be promulgating fresh edicts of great advantage to the Company. Further profitable properties, he assured them, were shortly to be added to its already vast possessions, whilst the new colonists setting out for Louisiana were industrious men chosen for their expertness in cultivation. Although an immediate yield was naturally not to be expected, the India Company's foundations were too sound to leave in the discerning any doubts of its ultimate success. The fall in values could, therefore, be no more than a passing phase, and those deluded men whose timidity had produced it would soon have reason for regrets.

Remembering that his every forecast, even when most derided, had never failed to be fulfilled, his words were attended by a revival of confidence and a recovery began at once.

Chapter 28

CATASTROPHE

Coming home from that triumph in the Rue Quincampoix, Mr Law found Catherine awaiting him in a fever. At sight of him, serene, if faintly flushed, she ran to meet him with something between a laugh and a sob.

William was with her, and no whit less anxious. Both spoke at once.

"Thank God you are safe, John."

"Safe?" He smiled, a little quizzically, upon this breathless solicitude. "Why, what was to be feared? Of course I am safe, and so, too, I think," he added, with a glance at William, "is the India Company. Before I left the Rue Quincampoix to the old cry of *Vive Monsieur Lass*, the stock was already rising again."

"You'll want to talk to Will," said Catherine. "I'll leave you now that I know that all is well with you. But I'll come back when he has gone."

He watched her from the room, his smile enigmatic.

The anxiety for him which she betrayed supplied a climax to a change that had been apparent in her ever since that talk of theirs following upon the last visit of Lord and Lady Stair. Penitence for her unwitting part in the events which had aroused the hostility against him and perhaps the assurances he had given her, had served to soften her. Her shrewishness had melted into a humility by which she sought to make amends.

"We grow considerate," he said, as the door closed upon her.

William's manner was a reproof in itself. "All morning the poor soul has been in hell for you, John. She was like a wild thing when she learnt where you had gone and the risk to which you might be exposed. She was bitter with me for having let you go, as if I or anyone under God could ever hold you back."

"Fearing, I suppose, what d'Argenson was praying for: that I should be torn in pieces."

The kindly William was reproachful. "Are you sure that you don't want for kindness towards her? A little tenderness and there's nothing you couldn't do with her. If I hadn't always known it, I'd have learnt it from her distress this morning."

Mr Law sighed. "A little tenderness and the termagant would reappear. There would be a renewal of her eternal groundless suspicions to fire her jealousies again. She's suffering from conscience at the moment. A passing ailment." He was pacing the room as he talked, and talking as if he thought aloud. "I think I know my Catherine by now."

William shook his head dolefully. "You constantly convince me that you don't. Will you never perceive how you fail to do her justice? Jealousy, after all, has its roots in affection."

"In affection for one's self. I know."

"Sometimes perhaps, and sometimes for another. It may not always be easy to distinguish, especially if you come to it with notions preconceived that distort your vision. Have you ever thought that jealousy is a torment, dear, to some women?"

"What then? Am I to be patient with that?"

"If you contribute to it."

"Is it possible that I have now become an *homme à femmes* in your eyes, too, Will? I thank you."

"There is your past," William reminded him. "That overgay youth of yours."

"That! Bah! The past is done with."

"The past is never done with. It is always and in all things there, to explain the present. Only by infinite patience could you have brought her to forget it."

"Patience! Faith, Will, I've always been accounted a patient man. But no patience is without limits. I bore with her groundless jealousies until they distracted me; then in self-protection I made myself impervious and insensible to them."

"And thereby sharpened them the more. She would explain your indifference in only one way. That made her resentful, and out of resentment she became shrewish; because she was shrewish you armoured yourself in yet stouter indifference. And so, each reacting upon the other, the gulf between you has steadily widened."

Mr Law stood still and looked at his brother, the quizzical smile once more on his thin lips. "You seem to be describing the inflation of values that is exercising us. But what is this, Will? Has Catherine made you more than ever her advocate?"

"By her conduct this morning," William agreed emphatically. "If you had seen her distress as I did, her very anguish at the thought of your peril, you could never doubt her affection for you. I was with her, John, and I tell you again as I've told you before that under all the seeming levity of her nature, under all her frowardness, that woman loves you. I'll never believe but that by gentle handling you could shape her to your will."

Still looking at him, with a lift of the brows, Mr Law took thought a moment; then slowly shook his head. "If I could believe that..." he began, and there broke off with a laugh. "No, no, Will. You overlook the alternative: that her distress was rooted in fear that if I were destroyed, the social eminence so dear to her would be destroyed with me. There would be an end to her salon, with its throng of nobles and its sprinkling of abbés and chevaliers, to pay their court to her; an end to playing the châtelaine at Guermande; an end to her lackeys, her equipages, her black boy, and the rest. Matter enough in all that to alarm Catherine."

William's eyes were sadly reproachful. "I'm wondering what proof of your error would satisfy you."

"I wonder with you," said the elder Law. He laughed again, without mirth, and upon that the discussion closed, for they were interrupted by the entrance of Laguyon to announce that dinner was served.

William stayed to dine with them, and the talk at table was of the morning's events in the Rue Quincampoix, with Catherine listening in alternating dread and satisfaction and an occasional interjection.

The stout and even gay confidence Mr Law derived from those events put heart anew into his doubting brother, so that when William departed it was in the conviction that he had been unduly mistrustful of the future, and that under the stimulus John had applied to the market and under his astute guidance a recovery might yet follow to give them the time they needed.

It did follow, and in the ensuing weeks the shares rose gradually once more from the point to which they had fallen. By the time, in the late summer when they had recovered to fifteen thousand livres, the belief was general that the slump had been no more than the manifestation of a transient and groundless panic.

At this level of fifteen thousand, however, a halt was called by the insidious underground campaign which d'Argenson had never relaxed. His strength lay in the fact that he fought with weapons of reality against a system built upon illusion.

Again both the timorous and the astute gave heed to the Chancellor's skilfully disseminated argument that in realization lay the only safe escape from an edifice that must inevitably crash. The recovery d'Argenson described as the mere up-leap of an expiring flame, and he went to work to prove it so.

When eventually the stock began once more to sag, and in a measure as it sagged, the price of commodities underwent a fresh increase, raising the level of wages with it, and these again driving the price of commodities still higher. And now the falling stock began ominously to drag down with it the value of the banknotes.

The beginning of a general loss of confidence set in.

Despite the edicts putting the paper currency at a premium over specie, it was being secretly exchanged at an ever increasing discount for gold and silver, which were being hoarded for the sake of their inalienable intrinsic value.

Fresh edicts, imposing fines and even imprisonment upon anyone holding more than five hundred livres in gold, were being secretly ignored. For no people will allow itself to be shamelessly plundered of its own without resisting. Rewards offered for delations and the domiciliary perquisitions that were being made aroused hot indignation, both against the Comptroller-General and against the Regent by whom he was supported.

Mr Law could no longer close his eyes to the mounting dangers of the situation. Considering that there were no real values to be set against that half-milliard in banknotes that remained uninvested in the hands of the creditors of the State, coercion was his only remaining weapon with which to combat the growing depression.

In despair he had further recourse to it. He subjected specie to a fresh devaluation, made the use of paper currency obligatory, imposed still harsher restrictions upon the manufacture of gold and silver articles of every kind, and forbade the use of jewels into which the paper currency was now being rapidly converted.

The result was that the government became entangled in and hobbled by the endless regulations which a government must impose when it attempts to interfere with the free and natural flow of values.

He was too astute not to be aware of the perils such measures must invoke; but he continued to take a gamester's chance, and rather than leave the India Company to its fate, as William pleaded, refused to divorce it from the Bank, which, once delivered of that incubus, might well have weathered the storm.

He still trusted desperately to time for his salvation in despite of those who were cogging the dice against him. But when in its slump, the price of the shares had come down to ten thousand livres, his enemies came out into the open. The general confusion which was ensuing and the increasing reluctance to accept the paper currency compelled the summoning of a Council of State to deal with the situation.

It met under the presidency of the perturbed Regent, in that same tapestried chamber of the Palais Royal, in which four years ago Mr Law had first expounded the system by which he proposed to rescue France from financial embarrassment. Its members were almost the same, including even the Duke of Noailles, who, whilst no longer of the Council of Finance, was still a member of the Council of State.

The Marquis d'Argenson, covering his malice with a mask of concern, and condoling with Monsieur Lass upon these adverse winds of fortune which were threatening destruction to a system that once had seemed of such fair promise, came with a plan worked out to the last detail calculated to accelerate its ruin.

He expounded that a situation which he described as ominous resulted at once from the inflated value of the India Company's stock and from the greatly excessive amount of paper money in circulation.

Whilst censuring in veiled terms the forced measures which were aggravating the ruinous course, he proposed that it should be arrested by pinning at five thousand livres the price of the shares and reducing gradually, month by month, the value of the banknotes, so that by the end of the year they should have reached a definite reduction of one-half their face value, at which it might be hoped to stabilize them.

Aghast at such a proposal, still more aghast at the manifest favour with which it was received, and perceiving the malice by which it was dictated, Mr Law controlled his indignation only with difficulty as he started up to protest against it.

"The Chancellor blames my forced measures for a state of things which he proposes to amend by forced measures infinitely more outrageous. I warn Your Highness and all you gentlemen that the decree for which the Chancellor now asks will precipitate a catastrophe. It will create a panic whose repercussions may be appalling. And since his intelligence is too acute not to perceive it, I make bold to ask is that what Monsieur d'Argenson desires?"

"A shameful question," Noailles reproved him.

"Indecent," mumbled old Villeroy. "Indecent is the least that one can say of it."

It required the intervention of the Regent to subdue the storm of outcries that beat about the Comptroller-General's head.

"Messieurs! Messieurs!" The Regent waved plump white hands to repress them. Then, gently, he remonstrated with Law. "My dear Baron, you must not, in the heat of the moment, impute to Monsieur le Marquis base motives which I know him to be incapable of harbouring."

Mr Law bowed his head. "I will withdraw a question which Your Highness assures me I was wrong to ask." He had recovered from his gust of anger. "As for the value of the India Company's stock, if it is definitely fixed, as Monsieur le Marquis proposes the least that can follow will be a further loss of confidence in it. Left to itself, the stock should ultimately find its real value, and this value in time – and before long, once the new colonists have shown their worth – may easily be as high as speculation has set it."

Someone laughed. Mr Law, however, paid no heed.

"When we come to the paper currency, however, it is easy to demonstrate the disastrous error of the Chancellor's proposal. Do not be deluded into believing that any decree will succeed in gradually reducing its value. Once the intention is known, the notes will depreciate immediately, amid not merely by the one-half that is ultimately intended. Consider now, I beg, that there are in circulation some two milliards in round figures.

"Of this, for one and a half milliards the Bank holds real value, in specie, in trade credits and in fiscal revenues. That leaves only a half-milliard – one quarter of the total – for which there is not cover, a half-milliard that would have been destroyed had it returned to the Bank through the India Company, as it must have returned had not the swift rise brought about by speculation prevented State creditors from buying the stock save at prices they were unwilling to pay."

"By whose fault?" growled d'Argenson.

"Oh, I will admit the fault," said Mr Law. "It was my one miscalculation in all this."

"Your one established miscalculation," Noailles amended.

"As you please, Monsieur le Duc." Mr Law was disdainful. "I am not to quibble. Permit me keep to the point. For the sake of this excessive one-quarter in the issue of notes it is proposed to depreciate the value of the total in circulation by one-half. Whom will that profit? Does it even make sense?"

"Not to me, messieurs," said His troubled Highness, and he looked round the board for support, but found only Saint-Simon's.

The little Duke, who is often prim but rarely coarse, tells us of the terms in which he denounced the proposal. "It amounts," he said, "to what in matters of finance and bankruptcy is known as *montrer le cul*. By the proposed decree we should exhibit it so uncovered that all would be accounted lost far beyond the reality."

But d'Argenson thundered that even this was better, in the face of the facts, than that the State should continue to support a falsehood which was fast becoming evident to all the world.

"And therefore," said Law, with biting sarcasm, "it is proposed to represent the falsehood as greater than it actually is. As a means of combating falsehood that possesses at least the virtue of originality."

D'Argenson's retort was violent. "Sneers, sir, are not argument," he cried, his heavy jowl thrust forward. "There are facts to be faced. They are not to be swept aside by sarcasm. We are confronted with the natural, the inevitable reaction from a transient prosperity – transient because false – induced by your system. The situation is desperate. Perhaps you do not yet choose to realize how desperate. It can be met only by desperate measures."

The Council's support was hot and unanimous, with the single exception of Saint-Simon; and even Saint-Simon did not further press the objection he had raised. Having expressed it, he conceived that he had done all that could be expected of him or that was permitted him by his resentment of Law's intervention, as he believed, in the case of the Count of Horn.

The end of it was that, however reluctant – for his faith in his Comptroller-General had as yet been only slightly impaired by the events – the Regent felt himself compelled to bow to the fierce unanimity of his council, and Mr Law went home in angry despair.

He was justified of this by what followed as soon as it became known that the edict had gone to the Parliament to be registered and what were the measures it decreed.

Whilst the profiteers – the "realizers", as they were called – who had converted into real estate and tangible values the fortunes they had made were more or less secure, the great mass of the people raised a storm of protest at this menace of arbitrarily cutting in half the value of the paper money of which their hands were full. Rich and poor alike, believing themselves ruined, assumed that Law was the real author of the edict. Uproar against him, and against the Regent for abetting him, were immediate and of a violence that swelled rapidly to formidable proportions.

A mob, made up from every class of society, in which the most clamant and virulent were the market women, blocked the approaches to the Hôtel de Nevers, not, as before, to acclaim Monsieur Lass and hold out its hands for the wealth of which he had been the dispenser, but to heap curses upon his name and to deafen him with its howl of threats and denunciations. It was held in check only by the stout gates of the courtyard until a detachment of musketeers, dispatched by the Regent, cleared the street and remained on guard there.

Meanwhile another mob was clamouring about the Palais Royal, swarming the iron railings to express in similar fashion its anger with the Regent.

Such was the general fury in the days that followed, so alarming were the street scenes, so hostile the siege of the Bank's premises, also guarded now by troops, and so scurrilous the lampoons and pamphlets inciting the people to fresh violence that d'Argenson himself began to be appalled by the storm he had raised.

When after five days of this turbulence, it still showed no signs of abating, he took his courage in both hands, and went off to wait again upon the Regent.

He had learnt that the Parliament in its latest session, in order to gratify its abiding rancour of Law, by whose influence it had been humbled, and at the same time to present itself in the cherished role of the people's buckler, had decided to refuse to register the offending edict.

The Regent received the Chancellor in his private cabinet, attended only by the elegant La Vrillière. His manner was unusually stern.

"I hope that having let hell loose upon us, you are now persuaded of your lack of wisdom, Monsieur le Marquis."

The big man bowed himself double. Agitation had mottled his rugged, swarthy face. "A desperate disease, monseigneur, demands a desperate cure."

"So you said before the Council. I fear you lack originality. Do you think to soothe me with stale apophthegms out of Montaigne?"

"If that were all, I should be less distressed, monseigneur." And at once he related what the Parliament was preparing.

His Highness received the news with a gust of angry laughter. "So! My old friends of the robe have discovered a way to win the popularity of the mob."

"Your Highness expresses it exactly. May I respectfully submit that you should deprive them of that satisfaction by anticipating them: cut the ground from under their feet by, yourself, revoking the edict."

"You submit that respectfully, do you?" His Highness shook with anger. "If you had been half as respectful in submitting your demand for the decree, we might have been spared this disgraceful uproar. You will permit me to tell you, Marquis, that I find your submission impudent?"

D'Argenson was now shaking in his turn. "Your Highness will do me the justice to remember that to a man the Council shared my view."

"But you were the advocate, Monsieur d'Argenson, and not even to be restrained by the arguments of Monsieur Lass, who precisely foresaw what must follow. A panic of appalling repercussions was what he foretold. And we have it. A wise man would have remembered the overwhelming proofs of prescience we have had from the Baron in the past. If I had been the king I should have insisted that he be heeded. Unfortunately I am only the Regent. However, it is idle to look back. This vicious edict shall be revoked, and we'll hope that it may do something towards arresting the evil. La Vrillière, you will give yourself the trouble of conveying that at once to the President de Mesmes."

At the same time, in the kindly hope of reassuring Law, whose distress he conceived, the Regent sent word of what he had done on his own responsibility: that the edict was cancelled and that the banknotes and the shares in the India Company were to be left at their current values.

Upon Law's mind the messages produced an effect the very opposite of that which was intended. Infuriated, he rang for Laguyon, and ordered his carriage.

Hearing of this, Catherine stood suddenly before him. Pale and worn and red-eyed from weeping, her delicate winsomeness had been sorely ravaged by the terror of these last days. "Where are you going, John?"

"To the Regent."

She remonstrated fearfully. She implored him not to leave the house. "The people's mood is horrible. They are like wild beasts. I am frightened, John. Only this morning, and in spite of the guards, I heard them shouting 'Death to Lass'!"

"Death to Lass!" he echoed, and laughed. "A month ago it was 'Long live Monsieur Lass'. Why heed the voice of the rabble with its 'Hosanna' today and 'Crucify' tomorrow'?"

"I will not let you go," she cried.

"Not let me?" He was suddenly stern. He seemed to grow taller under her pleading eyes. "That is mere folly, Catherine. Unless I act, unless I check the capers of those lunatics about the Regent, it will be the death of Lass, indeed.

He went past her to the door. But as he reached it, he turned. She was looking after him wild-eyed, huddled in the chair to which she had sunk, and her lips moved quiveringly, as if she were praying.

The spectacle touched him, and he may well have asked himself in that grim moment, when whilom adulatory friends were all falling away, leaving him to stand lonely and alone to face the seething hatred of thwarted greed, whether his brother might not be right, whether there was not here, as William protested, a faithful heart, under the levity and shrewishness which perhaps his indifference had provoked.

To reassure her he put on a confident smile, and his tone was suddenly gentle. "Courage, Catherine. Have no fear for me. I assure you there is not the need. I shall not be long away."

The grounds for her fears were soon to become apparent. Outside the Hôtel de Nevers the street was made safe enough by the guards. But in the space before the gates of the Palais Royal a small crowd of demonstrators was noisy, and execrations rained upon Mr Law when his liveries were recognized. To enter the palace by the ordinary way it would be necessary to drive through that mob, and since this might be provocative, he ordered his coachman to go on and set him down at the side entrance in the Rue de Richelieu.

He was obeyed, but the crowd came rolling in the wake of the carriage, swollen as it went by word that the detested Monsieur Lass was now within reach of its vengeance.

A half-hour later, to the Parliament then in session, the President de Mesmes was able to announce the glad tidings that the carriage of Monsieur Lass had been smashed to fragments in the street. Jubilation, however, was presently tempered by disappointment when further word was brought that unfortunately the Comptroller-General had no longer been in the vehicle when it was wrecked.

In fact, when the ugly incident took place, Mr Law was closeted with Dubois, demanding to be taken to the Regent, and inveighing against a revocation that could only serve, in his view, to pile confusion upon confusion.

To Dubois, no longer a merely titular abbé, but by now an ordained priest and Archbishop of Cambrai, to the see of which he had lately been raised, the reason for Mr Law's indignation was anything but plain. On the contrary, if there was poison in a given measure, a contrary measure should supply the antidote. The Regent was distressed enough already. Monsieur d'Argenson was with him at that moment, having been commanded, and Dubois displayed what he termed reluctance to trouble His Highness further on so vain an issue.

Mr Law's mood became savage. "You call it vain? My dear Archbishop, don't scruple to quarrel with me if it's to your profit. You will merely be in step with all those I have enriched. The gold with which I have gorged them has nauseated them, and they are now vomiting their spite over me."

"My God, my God! What are you saying? How you wrong me!" The weasel face was puckered in real distress. He looked more than ever like Monsieur de Voltaire. He had made great profit out of the system, and whether grateful or not had no wish to quarrel with one who if goaded might make revelations that would be awkward for any man, but doubly awkward for an archbishop. "Come to the Regent, then, if you insist. But upon your own head the consequences."

As it happened, engaged in a fresh discussion of the situation with the Chancellor the disquieted Regent actually welcomed Mr Law's arrival. His reception was of an affability seasoned with condolence.

"Ah, Baron, Monsieur d'Argenson is telling me that things continue to take an ugly shape."

Mr Law was blunt. "They'll take a still uglier one as a result of this revocation."

Behind him Dubois clucked deprecation. Monsieur d'Argenson breathed hard, whilst the Regent became haughty.

"Will you tell me what alternative remained considering the public clamour? Here!" He picked up a sheet from his writing table "Read this filth."

It was a lampoon of more than ordinary scurrility, telling the Regent what to do with his paper money. Mr Law ignored it.

"There never was an alternative to the edict, monseigneur, once it had done its mischief. All that remained was to ride out the storm it raised. Storms after all have a way of spending their fury. But now…" He spread his hands in a gesture of protest and hopelessness. "We cannot even count upon that. The hope is shipwrecked on this admission of dishonesty."

"Dishonesty!" Both Regent and Chancellor uttered the indignant exclamation together.

"Dishonesty," Mr Law insisted. "What else? To revoke an edict that halved the value of the currency is to confess that the edict was unnecessary. If unnecessary, if the banknotes may retain their face value, how is the attempted reduction to be regarded but as a dishonest means of profiting the Treasury?"

The Regent sat down suddenly, blank dismay on his face. He looked at d'Argenson and his voice shook. "Here is something that you left out of your calculations, Marquis."

"But…in the face of the public clamour…" d'Argenson was faltering when Mr Law broke in without ceremony.

"It is something that escaped the Council also. I foretold what must follow, that the people would not be content to accept the course of a gradual reduction, but would at once account the notes discredited, and that, faced with the dread of ruin, the public indignation would be terrible. Was anything else to be expected?"

D'Argenson reared his great head to meet the attack. Eyes blazing in a livid face, he confronted Law. "For the author of that ruin, sir, you permit yourself a singularly bold tone."

"It is yourself is the author of the ruin. When machinations to discredit the paper currency by a run on the bank for specie had been foiled, you had recourse to this still more disastrous expedient, dissembled by linking the notes with the depreciation of the India Company's stock."

The Chancellor turned angrily to the Regent. "I beg Your Highness to protect me from these imputations."

"How?" The Regent, already half-won by Law's forcefulness, looked coldly at the Marquis. "Are you no longer able to protect yourself? You have but to answer Monsieur Lass."

"Then I answer without fear of contradiction that if I advised the edict it was because the ruin had already overtaken us. Your Highness knows that we must go much further back to discover the source of this disaster. It springs from a crazy attempt to convert France into a single colossal stock company. The effect of such a system has been to enrich rascals of every class; to ruin the middle class, which is the most honest, industrious and useful class of all; to confuse the conditions of life, corrupt the public morals, and pervert the national character. That is what has been achieved by assuming control of commerce and removing it from the hands of the experienced merchants who had formerly conducted it on their own responsibility and at their own risk."

"Even if all that were true, which I am not prepared to admit," said Mr Law, "it still applies only to the India Company; and even then the ruin, which involved only the speculators, was by no means irreparable. But so far as the Bank is concerned, these allegations are utterly false. As I showed the Council, the Bank is fundamentally sound."

"With an issue of paper of a half-milliard beyond its resources!" roared the Chancellor, beside himself.

The Regent smacked the table, to call him to order. "Monsieur le Marquis, I do not like raised voices."

The Chancellor, in confusion, bowed his apologies. Mr Law became still more incisive. "Let me remind you again that that is only a quarter of the total issue, and that for the remainder, as I demonstrated, the Bank holds solid value. In no case was a cut of one half to be justified by a shortage of less than one quarter. As for this quarter, given time and prudence it could gradually be absorbed."

"Do you say so?" d'Argenson sneered. "Then you may easily prove it by taking time and prudence. By the revocation of the edict the situation is restored."

"Restored? Is it possible that you still believe it? Have you already forgotten my contention that by this revocation we shall be branded with dishonesty?"

"We have only your word for that, Monsieur Lass."

"And when has my word not been verified by the ensuing facts?"

"By God! Your modesty!" ejaculated the Marquis.

But Mr Law never heeded him. His tone, invested with a slow forcefulness, preserved its quiet level. "At the meeting of the council I forecast that the edict would raise a storm. That storm may have exceeded your expectations. It has not exceeded mine. It reduced the paper currency at a stroke to half its value. My present forecast is that the revocation will render it quite worthless."

"*Peste*! I hope not," cried the Regent.

D'Argenson could still assert himself "Your Highness need fear no such consequences."

The Regent's glance sought Dubois, who had remained a silent witness. "In God's name, Archbishop, why don't you say something? Have you no views?"

The fact was that for some moments the Archbishop's attention had been elsewhere. He had been intently listening to a swelling murmur outside which had escaped the other three, engrossed as they were. He raised a forefinger, his eyes wide with apprehension. "Harken!" he enjoined.

Even as he spoke there was a resounding crash, and the murmur, swelling suddenly, announced itself clearly as the roar of an angry multitude.

"I am afraid," said d'Argenson, "that the courtyard has been invaded."

The Regent rose. "Come with me," he commanded, and passed from his cabinet to the gallery that overlooked the court.

From one of its windows they beheld the place packed by a violently clamant mob. In the foreground, three stretchers were displayed, and on each there was a human body.

La Vrillière out of breath came hastening along the gallery. In gasps he brought out his ugly news. In the storming of the Bank that morning by a crowd that demanded specie for its paper, three men had been crushed to death. The mob had brought the bodies to the Palais Royal, as if to justify by them their angry demonstration. He also brought word that Mr Law's carriage had been reduced to fragments, but that coachman and footmen, at least, were safe within the palace.

"God help us!" said the Regent, but without any sign of fear. For all his softness, he was not without personal courage. "Find Le Blanc. Tell him to clear the courtyard. Let it be done without unnecessary violence. Come, messieurs."

Followed by the three he returned to his cabinet and flung himself ill-humouredly into the chair at his writing table.

"Well, Chancellor?" His voice rasped harshly. "Do you still insist that we need not fear the consequences foretold by Monsieur Lass?"

Within the frame of his black periwig the Chancellor's rugged swarthy countenance was almost green. For once his booming eloquence failed him. He stuttered before he brought out the answer: "Do me right, Highness! After all, the edict was your own."

"I see. So now you place the responsibility upon me. But I am not the King, as I told the Council. I am only the Regent, and I govern by a Council, whose unanimity I am not to withstand. In this disastrous affair the Council was swayed by you, by reliance upon your foresight, by faith in your calculations." He paused, his glance sternly upon the Chancellor, who for once in his life stood mute, confounded. Then he went on: "I will not ask, monsieur, how far those calculations were inspired by prejudice, to use no harsher word. But I must require of you that you bring me the seals of your office this afternoon."

"Your Highness!" gasped the broken Chancellor.

His Highness waved a hand. "You have my leave to withdraw."

After a moment's palsied hesitation d'Argenson bowed low, bowed as if under a crushing weight. Then drawing himself up, and without so much as a glance at the others, he marched heavily out of the room.

If his vindictiveness had opened an abyss for Mr Law, he was, himself, the first to hurtle into it in disgrace, his career shattered, his great ambitions wrecked.

There was a silence after he had gone. Then the Regent, dismissing the dark thoughts that absorbed him, looked at Dubois. "Monsieur de Cambrai, you will send today to Fresne, to require d'Aguesseau to return. In this pass we need a man of known integrity in the Chancellorship. I pray that it may serve to restore some confidence. That is all that I can do." His glance shifted to Law. "And now, Baron?" he asked.

Mr Law was again miraculously calm. "Your Highness will, of course, require me to resign the Comptrollership."

"If it is your wish to relinquish the helm at such a moment."

"Not if Your Highness thinks I can still be of service."

"I know of no one else whose knowledge of finance I would more surely trust."

Mr Law bowed. "Your Highness is very generous. Very magnanimous. My system, as your Highness perceives, has been laid in ruins. Still, if you command me, monseigneur, I will study means to make what repairs may yet be possible."

"May God guide and prosper you in that," was the lugubrious prayer, on which the Regent dismissed him.

Chapter 29

THE NADIR

Unobtrusively and unrecognized, Mr Law made his way back to the Hôtel de Nevers, and the waiting, distracted Catherine.

He greeted her with an ease that belied his feelings, "You see how idle were your alarms."

"Idle!" Her voice was shrill with reproach. "Do you think I do not know that your carriage was smashed to matchwood, and that it is only by the mercy of God that you were not in it at the time?"

"You haven't realized yet that I work miracles."

She seized his arms as if she would shake him. "How can you laugh, John, at such a time? How can you?"

"Calm, my dear. Be calm. The masses are fickle, mere emotional animals, never long of the same mind. This mood will pass, and all will again be well. Before long you'll hear them shouting 'Vive Monsieur Lass,' as before. Meanwhile, I've taken thought for you. You will leave tonight for Guermande with the children, and remain there until this storm blows itself out."

"Go to Guermande? I?" She spoke as if scandalized. "And leave you here to face these dangers alone?"

"Dangers! Faugh! Do not let us exaggerate."

"You would have me believe that there are none. Then why do you wish me to go?"

"Because I shall have a more tranquil mind for what is to do if I know that you and the children are safely away from these disturbances."

"And I? Should I be tranquil if I went? Should I know a single moment's peace, wondering whether you are alive or dead? I remain here, John. Understand that. Of the two evils it is the less."

This unusual resoluteness took him by surprise. He still sought to persuade her to leave Paris for a while; but in the end, finding all insistence vain, he yielded reluctantly to her determination to remain. Deeply touched by it in that hour of trouble and by its renewed implication of an affection in which he had long since ceased to believe, he recalled his brother's last representations to him, and for a moment wondered again whether it was possible that William's sight was clearer than his own. He might have given it deeper thought had his mind not been commanded and obsessed by the need to consider means of arresting the cataclysm that was overtaking them.

To this he applied himself at once, and what could be done he did, so that the Regent, with revived hope had reason presently to praise the prodigies by which his Comptroller-General still sought in these unutterably difficult circumstances to direct the finances of the Kingdom.

His plan for absorbing the excessive banknotes lay in the re-creation of a public debt for those four or five hundred millions, offering it to the State creditors who had failed to purchase India Company stock, and whose hands remained full of paper currency for which they could find no investment. Meanwhile, in order to gain time, he delimited by edict the use of specie by restricting the amount to be withdrawn from the Bank on any given day. At the same time he shortened the banking hours, and enjoined leisureliness upon the cashiers in exchanging the paper offered. Where formerly he had arbitrarily depreciated specie in order to enhance the value of paper, he now took the opposite arbitrary course of raising the value of specie by one-third, so that less should be required to meet the daily tender of banknotes.

He laid other plans calculated to restore credit once the situation had been stabilized. His hopes of winning out were strengthened by the cessation of the fury of the fickle populace, which had so far spent itself that he could once more show himself in public without danger of being stoned. He was even seen once or twice at the opera in the Regent's box.

A few weeks, however, served to show that all hope of recovery was vain illusion.

In those last throws of the gamester to retrieve what was lost, he was to find that d'Argenson and his party had cogged the dice too heavily against him before being reduced to impotence. The Chancellor's edict and its revocation had so ruined the credit of the paper currency that no conceivable measures could restore it. Merchants were refusing to accept it, or if they accepted it at all they did so at their own valuation, and this fell so low that within a month of d'Argenson's edict the louis d'or was selling for a hundred and twenty livres. Those who retained specie in contravention of the edict employed it secretly for the purchase of their requirements. The prices of commodities which had soared under prosperity, continued still to soar in adversity because of money's loss of purchasing power. Bread was selling at five sous a pound, which was ten times its normal cost, with meat, butter, eggs and wine in proportion. For cloth previously purchasable at fifteen livres the ell, one hundred and twenty-five livres was being paid.

This catastrophic alteration of values bore most heavily upon the industrious bourgeois, the backbone of the State's prosperity in every age, and upon the labouring classes, which were no longer able to find employment. As all this became swiftly aggravated, producing chaos in the national life, the tide of execration against Law and the Regent, which for a moment had receded, rolled up again, storm-tossed once more when that universal misery had fully succeeded the universal false prosperity of a year ago.

Obscene lampoons against the Regent became of daily publication, and once again neither he nor Law could drive through the streets without being exposed to insult and to the danger of violence.

At last there came a day of early autumn when after a peculiarly hostile demonstration against the Regent during a performance of *Phaeton* at the opera, Mr Law confessed himself defeated and the game lost, and made admission of it to his brother.

"Not only must I own defeat, but by owning it I may do a last service to the Regent. I owe it to him for the loyalty with which he has supported me through all."

William Law was too fully and dolefully in agreement with him to argue, nor did he wish it, for in the pass to which things were come he almost found relief in this decision.

So once more and for the last time the Laird of Lauriston sought the Regent, and found him in gloomy consultation with Dubois.

"Ah, Baron," His Highness greeted him, "I was about to send for you. You will have heard what happened to me last night at the opera. Not the rabble this time, but men of good condition, people of quality, the last support remaining me in this crisis."

"That is what brings me, monseigneur." Mr Law was becomingly and sincerely solemn. "Your Highness needs a whipping boy. That is the only office I can now fill with advantage to you."

"Eh?" His Highness was startled.

"I am here, may it please Your Highness, to resign the Comptrollership."

"You have taken fright, then, have you?"

The Scot's long, noble countenance wore a melancholy smile. "No, monseigneur, not fright. I have become poignantly aware that it will be in Your Highness' best interests. Your Highness will announce that you have dismissed me."

"I see. I am to fling you to the lions, eh?"

"The measure will be so generally approved that the lightnings of public wrath will be deflected from Your Highness' head."

"To strike yours instead, Baron. I do not happen to be made of that kind of wood. I do not accept your resignation."

"Permit me to observe, monseigneur, with the utmost submission, that it is as much Your Highness' duty to accept it as it is mine to offer it."

"And you will permit me to observe, Monsieur le Baron, that I am not to be instructed in my duty."

Mr Law, nevertheless, went on instructing him. "Your Highness stands for France. I stand only for myself, and do not matter. Once you have dismissed me – who am regarded as the cause of all this evil – some calm will be restored; then a reaction will follow, and make it possible to carry out the plan I have outlined, and others which your Council will be able to devise, for restoring order."

The Regent pondered gloomily. "Devil take it, I am to play the coward, then; cast all the blame upon you, and shelter myself behind you. That is the sum of your advice. *Eh bien*, my dear Baron, it is not how I conceive it. The responsibility is equally mine."

"Not equally, monseigneur. The application of the system devolved solely upon me, and I am guilty of two miscalculations. The first was not to have provided against the speculative buying of the India Company's stock before the State creditors had been given the opportunity to acquire it. The second was not to have foreseen how frenziedly the greed of profit would drive up that stock once speculation in it had begun. The ill will that has precipitated this ruin was beyond my control. But had I avoided those two errors and perhaps others, it is possible that ill will would have been denied opportunity. In time the exploitation of Louisiana might have become, as I still confidently believe that it will, a source of inexhaustible wealth to France."

The Regent looked at Dubois, dull-eyed. "Can I possibly do this, my friend, and preserve my self-respect."

The Archbishop's lean face twitched. "Since Your Highness asks me, I do not hesitate to say that you can do nothing else. Monsieur Lass has supplied – nobly supplied, if I may say so – the sword that cuts this Gordian knot. As he points out, monseigneur's duty to France asks no less."

"No less than that I acquire some rehabilitation at the Baron's expense! *Parbleu*, it's a noble thing to be a prince. And the Baron, Archbishop? What is to become of him? Not even his life may be left him once it is assumed that he is in disgrace and that the full force of public hatred may be loosed upon him."

"Do not be concerned, monseigneur. I shall not be here to meet it. My brother, who, I am relieved to think, shares none of this execration in which I am now held, will remain for as long as Your Highness considers necessary in winding up the Bank." He paused a moment, whilst the Regent, with rumpled brow, sat staring gloomily before him. Then he resumed. "Because of slanders that may spring up when I am gone, Your Highness will bear with me if I add that whilst I have made the fortunes of many I have taken no thought for my own. With opportunities to enrich myself such as probably have never been afforded to any man, I will ask Your Highness to believe that I have not placed a single louis out of France. The Bank's reserve of gold will prove it. Such wealth as I have acquired here, which, apart from my lands of Guermande, may amount to some ten millions, I leave behind."

"Ah, that, no!" the Regent impulsively protested. "So much is not necessary, my dear Lass."

"Most necessary, Highness, for my honour. It will remain in order to shield me from defamation."

Sadly the Regent bowed his head, and for a moment there was silence. "If I let you go," he said at last, "it is in the hope that I may recall you once all this has died down, once order is restored, once the yield of Louisiana, due to your enterprise, shall, as I hope, have repaired our finances. You see, my friend," he ended on a sad smile, "I still have faith in you."

He stood up, and held out his hand. Mr Law accepted it and bore it to his lips. "My heart is full of gratitude for those words, monseigneur." Then, erect once more, placid as ever, elegant and commanding, he added: "Whenever Your Highness thinks that I may serve you, a word will bring me."

But his smile as he spoke was sardonic, for he was too fully assured that his repute could never survive the full discredit which he now invited in payment of his debt to a prince who had so fully trusted him.

Chapter 30

THE PASSPORT

He sat once more, at dusk, in that spacious, lofty, handsome room of his, panelled in dark Cordovan leather, between pilasters with gilded capitals, enriched by its choice pictures and sumptuous furnishings, whilst a mob, athirst for his blood, now that he was stripped of all his greatness, howled bestially under his windows, held at bay only by the Regent's musketeers. For word had gone forth that he was dismissed with ignominy – flung to the lions, in the Regent's own words – and the leonine rabble, regarding him as a legitimate prey, was avid to avenge upon him the ruin and misery of France.

With him, pale and uneasy, were William Law, his secretary Lacroix, a confidential clerk from the bank named Normand, who had taken McWhirter's place, and the directors of the two principal amalgamated companies. They were receiving his final instructions, which he delivered pacing the long chamber, his shoulders bowed, his hands behind his back.

When the last word on the subject of finance was spoken, Lacroix, Norman and the others took a distressed, affectionate leave of him, and the brothers were left alone together.

"And so, Will, we reach the end. An ignoble end. By way of the Capital we come to the Tarpeian Rock. It may be that I should have given heed to the geese when they cackled their warnings. It may be that I sought to grasp more than a man may hold: that I should have remained content, as you begged me, with the Bank, and not sought the manipulation of a country's commerce. It is even possible that d'Argenson said no more than is true when he borrowed the more honest opinion of d'Aguesseau that the business of government is to govern and not to trade. Yet if the matter had been fairly tested perhaps the result might have been different. I do not know. But I must think so for my credit's sake."

William, watching him, listening in distress, was too generous to say that the end was no more than he had foreseen. "Conjecture will be idle now, John," was all he said. "For the rest, you may leave it to me to clear things up for the best."

His brother paused in his pacing to lay an affectionate hand upon his shoulder. "God knows, Will, I am sorry to leave you the burden of this last task."

"You have no choice, and you need take no thought for me. What, after all, is my task when compared with yours? Our concern now is how to get you away. You hear those infernal wolves. How they've changed their howl since a year ago, when they packed the street to shout 'Long live Monsieur Lass!' Given the chance they'll eat you alive."

"Faith, it might be best."

"And Catherine?"

Mr Law turned away with a gesture of helplessness. "Best for her, too, poor soul. Prosperous, the master of fortune, I was of little account to her. Perhaps of no more account than I deserved to be. Broken, I shall be of none."

"You make too sure, John."

He shrugged. "We judge the future from the past."

"So we do. But how much may you not have contributed to that past? I have urged you more than once to ask yourself."

"And I have been asking myself just that. Making an examination of conscience, as they say in the faith which I embraced for worldly advantage. But I haven't found the answer. And now there are more urgent matters to engage us. We haven't much time. Let us come to the essentials."

He had spoken impatiently. When he resumed again he was more deliberate.

"Once it is known that I have gone, this siege will cease and Catherine's way will be clear. For the rest…she has her jewels. Their value is considerable. There is this palace." Wistfully he looked round at the room's opulent appointments which he had assembled with such appreciative care, to render it a mirror of his own fastidious mind. "Then there is the property of Guermande. It is all that I am asking the Regent to allow me to retain, so that I may make some provision for her. When sold the proceeds should not be negligible. There are the children, too. God knows I am no more of a success as a father than as a husband or a financier."

"And you, John? What provision have you made for yourself?"

Mr Law shrugged. "I take with me eight hundred louis in gold. More than enough for immediate needs."

"And after that?" William spoke in dismay.

"Perhaps Madame Fortune will provide, unless she has now jilted me for good and all. Anyway, it is all that I take away of the two millions that I brought to France. I still have my wits, though, from what has happened, you may doubt it."

William's glance was sorrowful. "Are you to go back to your gamester's trade?"

"When did I relinquish it?"

"But to live by the turn of a card, the fall of the dice!"

"Always provided that I get away with my life. If I don't I shall be spared the trouble. And there is one thing I forgot. I am without a passport. Obtain me one tomorrow from His Highness, and send it after me to Guermande. I'll stay there till it comes."

He slipped away late that night, after the mob, grown tired of its bloodthirsty clamour, had gone home to bed.

Despite William's earnest pleading, he took no leave of Catherine, fearing emotional remonstrances, judging it best for both of them in all the circumstances. She did not even know that he had gone until

the following morning, when William handed her the letter her
husband had left for her, in which he sued her pardon for his past
shortcomings and for all the distress with which, by the malignity of
fortune, he was now visiting her.

She wept as she read, and wild and stormy were her upbraidings
of William for not having warned her of his brother's intentions.

By then Mr Law was well on his way to Brie and the Château de
Guermande, which he scarcely regarded any longer as his own. With
Grandval and his wife, the couple who were its caretakers, for only
servants, he waited there three days impatiently for the passport that
should enable him to leave France and go once more upon his
travels. He remembered how Catherine in the past had so frequently
taunted him with the complaint that she was married to the
Wandering Jew. This time, at least, he would spare her the grievance
that he dragged her with him from land to land.

He thought of her and the children with some wistfulness in that
time of brooding, pondering how different life might have been had
she been more patient with him and he with her. He almost surprised
himself by the sense of loneliness the absence of wife and children
brought him. A failure in all things, he told himself, it was as a
husband and a father that he had failed most abjectly. His boy, he
reflected, had been the playmate of the little king; his girl, scarcely
in her teens, had been sought in marriage by some of the best blood
in France. Hereafter, with obscurity for only prospect, they might
come to curse him for having raised them to those dizzy heights
merely to cast them down again into obscurity.

If in his present loneliness and in his groping for a future the day-
dream of seeking Margaret in England crossed his troubled mind, it
scarcely now presented itself in the guise of a temptation. Pride alone
would have forbidden him to go empty-handed to one to whom
even when his hands were full he had not dared at the last to offer
himself. But there was more than pride to forbid it. There was the
memory of those words of hers, that happiness is not to be built
upon another's sorrow. And he now believed that happiness with

Margaret, even if attainable, would bring Catherine a grief that was not merely, as once he might have supposed, of lacerated vanity.

On the dull evening of his third day of waiting at Guermande he was moodily pacing the terrace when a great travelling carriage drawn by four splendid horses, came swaying through the now leafless park.

He stood still in the chill air, puzzled, to watch its approach.

As it swept to a halt at the foot of the terrace steps, he made out on its panels the arms of the Duke of Bourbon, and his wonder was increased. The postilions drew rein, the single footman swung himself to the ground to open the door and let down the step, and then his amazement reached its climax as he watched Catherine alight, followed by the two children.

For a moment he stood as if petrified. Then, when light and lissom as a young girl she sprang up the steps, he roused himself, and hurried halfway down to meet her. He caught her by the shoulders and whilst she was between laughter and tears he showed her a face that was drawn with pain.

"Catherine! Why are you here?"

"To bring you your passport," she answered lightly, as if it were a jest.

"Was that necessary? Would not a courier have served?" His tone was gently reproachful. "It was to spare us this – to spare both of us – that I left without farewells. Now... Oh, but come in, come in. It is cold and you will be tired. I will call Grandval."

Confused, bewildered, he moved towards the house, the children, two well-grown striplings, clinging to him, one on each side, and Catherine keeping pace with them. The footman followed with valises.

She was telling him that the Duke of Bourbon, like a true friend, of which few remained them, had sent his travelling carriage as a parting gift to John Law. But to this, his mind in travail, he scarcely gave heed.

The elderly Grandval and his buxom wife came hastening to meet them and to take his orders.

At last, in the rather sombre hall of the château, with its ponderous Louis XIII furnishings, the children having been carried off in the care of Grandval's wife, he and Catherine faced each other, and with a hand that shook she proffered him a parchment. "The passport," she said, and her quivering voice broke on the word, her eyes watched him anxiously.

He took it, and put her in a high-backed chair beside the massive oak table. Infected by her malaise, he was at a loss for words. "I think," he said at last, because he must say something, "that you always loved Guermande. It is dull now. But in spring and summer you know how beautiful it can be. I hope that you will be happy here. If not, you can sell it. It is yours. It...it is all that remained me in France, or anywhere. Not much after what has been, what might have been. But..."

"Far more than I need. More than I want," she answered him. "It is not only at this time of year that I should find it dull. Dull and lonely. Very lonely." She rested her head against the back of the chair, and closed her eyes as if in weariness of body and of soul. She was very white, her travelling cloak had fallen open, and under the muslin fichu her bosom rose and fell in deepening agitation.

He considered her with wistful concern. "You are tired," he said. "A glass of wine will revive you. Grandval will be bringing it."

He unfolded the parchment, and to scan it in the fading daylight he turned his back to a high window. An exclamation broke from him. "Why, what is this? You are included here."

She spoke as if suffocating. "Is it not my right?"

"Your right!" He laughed. "But is it a right that you would wish to claim at such a time?"

She sat up, and gathered strength. "The time above all entitled me to claim it. That is why I have, myself, brought you the passport. I do not choose to be left behind."

He stared at her, and saw the tears roll down a face that for all its pallor preserved an odd composure. A strange gift hers, he thought, to weep without grimacing.

"You told Will once," she went on, "that all that I loved in you were the splendours you provided. It was the cruellest of many cruel things you have thought of me, and the most unjust. I am here to prove it." Then in a quickening tone, she asked him, as she had asked him once before: "What splendours were yours when I came to you in Amsterdam so many years ago? You were then a broken proscribed fugitive, John, as you are now. I came to you then because I thought that you must need a woman's breast to weep on. And that is why I come to you now. But for your distress at this ruin of your ambitions, I could thank God that it has overtaken us. For it gives me this opportunity to prove your error." Very softly, she ended: "If you want me, John, we will go on our travels together again. If not…"

He sank to his knees beside her and put his head in her lap. He, too, was weeping.

RAFAEL SABATINI

CAPTAIN BLOOD

Captain Blood is the much-loved story of a physician and gentleman turned pirate.

Peter Blood, wrongfully accused and sentenced to death, narrowly escapes his fate and finds himself in the company of buccaneers. Embarking on his new life with remarkable skill and bravery, Blood becomes the 'Robin Hood' of the Spanish seas. This is swashbuckling adventure at its best.

THE GATES OF DOOM

'Depend above all on Pauncefort', announced King James; 'his loyalty is dependable as steel. He is with us body and soul and to the last penny of his fortune.' So when Pauncefort does indeed face bankruptcy after the collapse of the South Sea Company, the king's supreme confidence now seems rather foolish. And as Pauncefort's thoughts turn to gambling, moneylenders and even marriage to recover his debts, will he be able to remain true to the end? And what part will his friend and confidante, Captain Gaynor, play in his destiny?

'A clever story, well and amusingly told' – *The Times*

Rafael Sabatini

The Lost King

The Lost King tells the story of Louis XVII – the French royal who officially died at the age of ten but, as legend has it, escaped to foreign lands where he lived to an old age. Sabatini breathes life into these age-old myths, creating a story of passion, revenge and betrayal. He tells of how the young child escaped to Switzerland from where he plotted his triumphant return to claim the throne of France.

'...the hypnotic spell of a novel which for sheer suspense, deserves to be ranked with Sabatini's best' – *New York Times*

Scaramouche

When a young cleric is wrongfully killed, his friend, André-Louis, vows to avenge his death. André's mission takes him to the very heart of the French Revolution where he finds the only way to survive is to assume a new identity. And so is born Scaramouche – a brave and remarkable hero of the finest order and a classic and much-loved tale in the greatest swashbuckling tradition.

'Mr Sabatini's novel of the French Revolution has all the colour and lively incident which we expect in his work' – *Observer*

Rafael Sabatini

The Sea Hawk

Sir Oliver, a typical English gentleman, is accused of murder, kidnapped off the Cornish coast, and dragged into life as a Barbary corsair. However Sir Oliver rises to the challenge and proves a worthy hero for this much-admired novel. Religious conflict, melodrama, romance and intrigue combine to create a masterly and highly successful story, perhaps best-known for its many film adaptations.

The Shame of Motley

The Court of Pesaro has a certain fool – one Lazzaro Biancomonte of Biancomonte. *The Shame of Motley* is Lazzaro's story, presented with all the vivid colour and dramatic characterisation that has become Sabatini's hallmark.

'Mr Sabatini could not be conventional or commonplace if he tried'
– *Standard*

Printed in Great Britain
by Amazon